Every Chance You Get

Book Cover by Sloan Spencer

Illustrations by Vera Osipchik

First edition 2026

Contents

American Rugby Terminology

- **A-side** — Players who generally start games, often the team's best players.

- **B-side** — Players who do not start games, but wait for their turn. Often referred to as the team's reserve players. Sometimes they are players who need more practice.

- **Backline** — The backs (players #10 – #14).

- **Boot** — Cleat.

- **Boot up** — Get ready to warm up.

- **Conversion** — A two-point kick attempt taken after scoring a try, where the kicker tries to send the ball between the opponent's goalposts.

- **Fifteens** — A full eighty-minute rugby game with fifteen players against fifteen players. Typically played in the fall and spring.

- **Full eighty** — Playing a full eighty-minute game.

- **Kit** — Usually a duffle bag full of boots, uniform, and a change of clothes. Can also refer to just a uniform.

- **Line out** — A means of restarting play after the

ball has gone out of bounds (into touch). Typically two players will lift another player into the air to catch the ball as it is being thrown back into play. The opposing team will do the same to try and gain possession of the ball.

- **Offsides** — A player is in an offside position if that player is further forward (nearer to the opponents' goal-line) than the teammate who is carrying the ball.

- **Pitch** — Field.

- **Quick hands** — Passing and catching the ball quickly and efficiently, often in a fluid one-pass motion, to maintain momentum.

- **Rookie** — A first-year player.

- **Ruck** — A formation when players from opposing teams are on their feet, bound together over a ball on the ground. The goal is to get the ball to emerge from the back of the formation for the scrum-half to play.

- **Scrum** — An ordered formation of players, used to restart play, in which the forwards of a team form up, with arms interlocked and heads down, and push forward against a similar group from the opposing side. The ball is rolled into the scrum and the players try to gain possession of it by kicking it backward toward their own side.

- **Sevens** — A shortened version of the game, typically played in the summer tournament style. Seven players against seven players, played for seven-minute halves.

- **Sir** — The referee, regardless of gender.

- **Social** — A little party right after the game with both teams. There's food, beer, and sometimes drinking songs. Everyone is dirty and tired. General comradery.

- **Subbed out** — Player is replaced by another.

- **Try** — Touchdown. Five points.

- **Vet** — A seasoned player.

THE POSITIONS

Forwards (very strong, tackle the most, members of the scrum) :
- #1 & #3 — Prop (Loosehead & Tighthead)

- #2 — Hooker

- #4 & #5 — Second Row (Number 4 Lock & Number 5 Lock)

- #6 & #7 — Flanker (Blindside & Openside)

- #8 — Eight man (Number 8)

Backs (fast and agile runners, score most of the game points) :
- #9 — Scrum Half

- #10 — Fly Half

- #11 — Left Wing

- #12 — Inside Center

- #13 — Outside Center

- #14 — Right Wing

- #15 — Fullback

To Zoloft—Thank you for helping me finish this
book. You're a real one.

Content Warnings

Just because this is a romantic comedy, doesn't mean the spice is lacking. There is a lot. I always try to make the spicy scenes hot, sweet, and a little humorous. If you've read my other work, you'll know what to expect. For a full list of content warnings, please click or scan the QR code and it will take you to my website.

Playlist

Every Chance You Get — Spotify

SOS by Rihanna
Give It To Me by Timbaland, Justin Timberlake, Nelly Furtado
Get Down On It by Kool & The Gang
Blackbird by Delta Rae
Bad Things by Cailin Russo
If You Go Down (I'm Goin' Down Too) by Kelsea Ballerini
Top of the World by The Chicks
Know It All by Billy Strings
Dirty Thoughts by Chloe Adams
Wildflowers by Miley Cyrus
Toxic Pony by ALTÉGO, Britney Spears, and Ginuwine
YES MOM by Tessa Violet
Landslide by The Chicks
Put Your Money On Me by The Struts

Chapter 1
Collision

Jonah

I thwack the bottle against my palm to get every drop of lotion, before I give up and ask the dressing room, "Does anyone have extra body glitter? I ran out."

Dylan tosses me his stash and gives me a funny look. "We're supposed to be firemen for our next set. Why do you want glitter?"

"The older ladies tip better when I wear it."

He snorts. "That's because they're still holding on to their *Twilight* fantasies."

"What's that?"

"*Twilight*? The teen romance fantasy book-turned-blockbuster hit? It's got like werewolves and vampires. Do you really not know that movie?"

I hate it when this happens. Yet another movie reference I don't get. I chronically disappoint people when they realize I'm serious. Often I pretend to know what they're talking about and give them a friendly smile and nod. It's amazing how people like you so much more when you're in on a joke or reference.

Before Dylan can ask any more questions, Robbie bursts through the door with the subtlety of an elephant. "Who's feeling lucky?" He waves around a small stack of papers and dances his way to me. "Jonah," he croons, and dangles a Mega Millions lottery ticket while seductively sliding down the zipper of his hoodie. "You know you wanna."

Robbie and I went out briefly a few months ago. After

realizing a good portion of my family is queer, I thought I'd try my hand at dating men. So, I downloaded Grindr and had a surprising amount of interest! Who knew so many men were interested in a blond, six-foot-three rugby player stripper?

When I saw Robbie on the app, I got so excited I almost swiped the wrong way. He's always been super nice, and, like, obviously hot. A total catch.

He understood I was dipping my toes into the gay pool and took things slow. So after three dinner dates, he leaned me against my front door and I ducked down in a fit of giggles, with an alarming sense of NONONO. We called it off with no hard feelings.

Turns out I'm not queer, but not for a lack of trying.

Things may not have worked out with Robbie, but I am a lucky guy. In my twenty-five years on this earth, I have won two brand new cars, charmed—and stripped—my way through college, I have the ear to play almost any instrument, I can find a four-leaf clover in almost any field, and I have the best family ever. Sure, it sucks that my mom died when I was a little kid, but I'm fortunate to have a big family: my dad, my two brothers, and two sisters.

Good looks and a captivating smile have taken me far—even with law enforcement. I've skirted almost every traffic ticket. Heck, I should have had my license taken away by the state of Pennsylvania by now, but the joke's on them—I don't even know where it is.

There was also this one time I called Pabst Blue Ribbon's customer service hoping they would sponsor our rugby team. They ended up not only sponsoring us, but sending me and three friends on an all-expenses-paid trip to Las Vegas. I got a free shirt too! I lost all my money in the casinos, but on the taxi ride to the airport, I found a bag of casino chips worth ten thousand dollars on the floor of the cab.

Pretty sweet trip if you ask me.

"The jackpot is $540 million," Robbie says, and the next thing I know, I'm handing him a fiver from my stash and slipping the ticket in my wallet.

"Alright, boys," Kim, our manager, says as she walks into the room. She hands each of us a firefighter helmet for our routine. "We have a full house tonight, no thanks to my marketing skills. Ian and Robbie, I want you to take the bachelorette party on stage right. Dylan and Anthony, you're stage left. Jonah, smackdab in the middle."

These are our positions after we perform our group dance and we disperse throughout the crowd. Hearing them go wild when we step off stage and seek willing victims is my favorite part of any shift. The energy is sky-high, and the excitement pulsing through the room is unmatched.

I love my job. Who wouldn't want to work at Strip Tease, America's only strip club slash hair salon?

No one in my personal life knows I'm a stripper. I've always been vague about what I do because my family already thinks I'm a screwup that flits through life banking on good looks.

They're not entirely wrong, but that's beside the point.

Stripping is how I've paid my bills since college. It's how I afford to play rugby. Right now is the off-season, but spring is almost here, and with it, new dues, money for travel... it all adds up. Thankfully I can still swing shifts around rugby and it doesn't mess with my sleep schedule too much.

The sport I love definitely keeps me in shape for my job, though. Honestly it's a win-win.

I'm pleasantly surprised when I look out from the stage to find Kim wasn't lying—the club is at capacity. Her voice comes back to me, reminding me I'll be front and center once the first part of our group dance is over.

When familiar music plays, my body takes over. Dancing

has always come easy for me, the same way playing rugby and making music do. Once my body grabs the rhythm, the choreographed moves feel like an answer. What I lack in book smarts I make up for in musical prowess.

After a couple of sets, I head back to the changing room while Donovan and Jax do some solo work. As they're wrapping up and collecting their cash, the rest of us get in position on stage.

The lights go out and sirens scream.[1]

Holding my helmet with one hand and my crotch with the other, I body roll in tandem with the guys and slide my fireman's suspenders over my shoulders. I get lost in the cadence and sweat beads across my body. I've never been in better physical shape than I am now, but it's impossible to get through just one dance without sweat pouring off my body.

A hush falls over the crowd when the music dies off and the lights dim for dramatic effect, but it doesn't last long. There are only a few seconds of silence before high-pitched squeals and whistles break through. Music blares once again, and the five of us rip off our tight white T-shirts, sending on-lookers into riot mode.

With seconds left in our dance before I have to bring someone on stage, I scan the crowd. Kim always says to pick the bride or groom from stage right so we don't have to spend time dilly-dallying over who comes up. She always talks with the group ahead of time to make sure they're game, but we always get consent in the moment, too.

I expect to find a bride in the bachelorette party that Ian, Robbie, and I are making our way to. What I don't expect is for the bride in question to be Robyn.

Professional rugby player and social media icon, Robyn

---

1. SOS by Rihanna

Cassidy.

My future sister-in-law.

OH NO.

Standing three feet away, I'm frozen in place as the bachelorette party around us screams and pats her back. But my line of sight catches on my sister Angie sitting right next to her with the same shocked expression.

"Jonah, what the fuck?" Angie screams. "You're a stripper?"

My skin prickles, and my chest tightens as a wave of heat engulfs me. I catch Kim, not too far away, give me the *Hurry, you're wasting time* flick of her wrist. There's panic coursing through me as I process being caught in my deceit and the fear of disappointing my boss. I turn off my thoughts, hoist Robyn over my shoulder, and carry her to the stage.

I just need to do as I'm told.

A stagehand has already placed a chair front and center under the spotlight, and the crowd's screams have met an all-time high when I set her down. She's wearing a white cocktail dress, and she's done up to the nines, but it does nothing to hide the blush creeping over her face and down her chest.

"This is not happening," she gasps, her eyes blown in disbelief.

Unable to stop myself for fear of reality setting in, I continue my routine and stalk around her chair. "Should I stop?" I ask in all seriousness.

"No." She places her hands against her flaming cheeks and shakes her head. "This is the funniest and the most awkward thing that has ever happened to me. Proceed."

I'm glad she finds it funny. Robyn can find humor in almost anything. She's perfect for my grumpy brother Isaiah and their paramour Dell. I just learned what that means. It's like another partner, not a punk rock band.

It is pretty funny, isn't it? Stripping for my future sister-in-law. Isaiah is going to lose his marbles when he finds out. Before he was with her, he not-so-secretly pined for her and routinely made death threats toward me for casually mentioning that she was the love of my life. It was never that serious, but it's fun to rile up my older brother.

If she's game, I'm game.

I walk behind her chair, trailing my hand from her elbow, up her bare shoulder and across her back before swiftly coming around and hiking my leg over her lap and sitting. Like most women who come to the stage, she can barely keep it together. Her giggling only spurs me on and turns my fear into excitement and pride. I'll deal with the rest of my family finding out later. Right now, I want to make my friend Robyn have the most memorable bachelorette party ever.

Taking her hands, I place them against my bare skin and force her to touch my chest and abdomen. She screams with a mix of nervousness and laughter but allows me to continue. When I move her hands to my unbuttoned pants, she turns her focus on me and tenses.

I lean forward and whisper in her ear, "Don't worry. I won't make you touch that. Zay might actually kill me if I did."

Also, it's completely against the club's rules for a patron to touch my dick.

I give her my all and get lost in the high for the next four minutes. Normally, I see dancing and stripping as nothing more than work. I understand people come for a show, and many of them are squirming in their seats. That's the purpose of this whole setup. What many people don't understand is the feeling almost never goes both ways. I'm thinking about my next step and positioning the person in the right way—there's no time for attraction. There's no time to maintain a boner while you're doing the worm on top of your stage partner and then hoisting them up in the air up-side-down so their face is level with your crotch.

There's just no time!

When the song fades and Robyn's stage time ends, I'm in nothing but my gold G-string and sweat. Because of me, Robyn's body is covered in glitter, her hair mussed up from me gently grabbing fistfuls of it earlier. She hugs me on stage, beaming from ear to ear. I hoist her up one more time and carry her down the stairs to her waiting party. When I set her down next to my sister, I'm incredibly aware that my ass is hanging out.

Oh well. Angie's seen me in less.

"I may be scarred for life," my sister says. "How long have you been doing this?"

I clear my throat and pull at the back of my neck. "Since sophomore year of college."

"Jonah!" I'm about to shrivel under my oldest sister's gaze, but she surprises me when she punches my arm and adds, "Look at you sticking to something!"

"Uh, yeah."

"That's great!"

"It is?"

"Yes. As long as you like doing it."

"You're not going to make fun of me?"

"Oh, I'm definitely going to make fun of you at family dinner tomorrow."

"That's fair." Nothing is off-limits in our family. Once your laundry is out, everyone's grabbing at it and making it their business.

Robyn grabs my other arm and squeezes it. "Thanks for the best bachelorette party I could have asked for, dude."

"Jonah," Kim says as she comes up to us. "I need to steal him away. I'm sorry, ladies."

"Oh, sure." Robyn grins. "We'll see you tomorrow for dinner."

I give them both a glittery sweat hug and follow Kim backstage.

"Do they know you?" she asks.

"Yeah, they're my sisters."

"Oh," she replies, her tone unsure. "That's... different." She leads me to the dressing room and tosses me a fresh tank top and gray sweatpants. "You have a private request."

Chapter 2
Private Show

Jonah

I love private shows. As extroverted as I am, I love the change in energy going from the big stage to an intimate setting. Sometimes they don't even want me to dance; they just want to talk. I think there's something about my energy that's comforting to people.

I'm lounging on the leather tufted couch, when a red-headed woman stumbles into the room as if pushed, and stands there in a pose that is the opposite of comfortable. She's wearing a sleeveless black turtleneck dress that goes to her knees and a pair of heels. I'm five feet away, but even in the low light I can make out a waterfall of freckles down her bare shoulders to her hands. Her back and shapely bottom are facing me as she takes a deep breath.

"Are you okay?" I ask.

"I hate my sister," she says to the closed door.

"You don't have to be here if you don't want to be."

"No, I do."

She still seems tense. "Do you wanna talk about it?"

She doesn't answer or move right away as the low beat of sexy club music passes between us. "I'm going to turn around, and you will not say anything. Got it?"

"Yes, ma'am."

With a shuddering breath, she carefully turns on the ball of her foot, and my mind races when her stunning freckled face and piercing green eyes light up my memory.

"Professor Wilde!" I beam.

She lurches forward with a warning glare and finger pointed at me. "Shh! Don't say another word."

Oh my God—it's my former biology professor, who I've had locked up in my spank bank since my first senior year. I took her nature study class as a required cultural enrichment course and failed it, but man, she's the only reason I kept going back to class. Or signed up at all.

She's a bombshell.

Wait, isn't she married?

"But—"

She slaps her hand over my mouth. "No. You're going to dance for me, and you will not say a word. I'm going to leave here, and we're both going to act like this never happened. Nod if you agree to these terms."

I nod, and my dick swells. There's something so sexy about her taking charge like this. In all my fantasies about her, I was always the one taking control, bending her over her desk or pushing her up against a bookshelf. At school she was always soft-spoken and mild-mannered, unless she was actively denying my advances. What started out as flirtatious remarks to gain favor and better grades, turned into frequent takeovers of my mind while rubbing one out.

But that mild-mannered woman is nowhere to be found. There's a dominating powerhouse standing above me with her fingers ever so slightly digging into my jawline, and I'm confused but certainly turned on by this change in pace.

There's definitely a wet spot on my sweatpants now.

I'm not going to question this. I *want this.*

I stand slowly and keep my eyes trained on her. She's a petite woman, and I tower over her, but the fire in her gaze tells me she's in total control. She takes my spot on the couch and reaches into her dress to pull out a stack of cash from her bra.

As hot as that is, I hold up a hand. "No charge."

She furrows her brow. "Why not?"

Kim said I had twenty minutes, and I intend to make every second count. There's a bouncer stationed just outside the room for the safety of the dancers and patrons. If Professor Wilde had wanted to, she would have stepped out the second she recognized me—but she didn't.

"Did you request me specifically?" I ask.

Her throat works, and I'd bet anything if it wasn't so dark in here I could see blush spread across her face. But her face is locked tight. "Yes."

She knew who she was getting. She requested *me*, her former student.

The corner of my mouth quirks. "I'm not charging you for something I want, too."

Her only reply is a sharp inhale[1].

My cock strains against my G-string as I tap the remote mounted on the wall for a new song to start. With a salacious smile I couldn't wipe away if I tried, I saunter back and relish the way she drinks in my body—landing on the tent I've created in my pants.

Normally, I have a fairly standard routine for these private shows, but I can't remember how it goes now. Her full attention is all I want.

When I'm close enough, I prop a knee on the cushion next to her thigh and grab the back of the couch. I've never been close enough to smell her, because surely I would have remembered this lavender and vanilla scent.

I roll my hips against her chest and then duck down to run my face against the side of hers. Even with the music pumping, I can hear her heavy breathing. I grab her hands, place them on my ass, and grind against her. Normally it costs extra for people to touch me, but even without accepting a dime from her, I feel rich being under her touch.

---

1. Give It To Me by Timbaland, Justin Timberlake, Nelly Furtado

Firm, curious hands slide down my thighs and squeeze. They glide up my back and over my shoulders before I stand up and carefully peel away my white tank. I sway my hips—rolling in time with the music—and drop my arms down. In a second, I am straddling her again and trying to wrap her wrists with my shirt. But all too quick, she's retracting her hands and discarding the shirt on the floor in a huff.

"Don't tie me."

"Okay," I whisper, thankful she let me say even that.

"But you can touch me," she says, guiding my hands until they're a centimeter from her chest. "Would you like that?"

My dick throbs before I can answer. "Of course, ma'am."

With her change request, I redirect her hands to the back of my head. My hands glide down her chest and, holy smokes, I'm touching Professor Wilde's tits. I'm rubbing my very hard dick against her and *she's letting me.* I know this is my job and I probably shouldn't take it personally, but a woman of this caliber is allowing it, so I'll shut up.

"Fuck, you're pretty," she rasps, and a delightful melody of praise hums through my body.

I stand up and flash her a grin before turning around and sitting in her lap. I lean against her, and her hands travel from my hips to the juncture between my thighs and groin. It's then that I notice it—the absence of her wedding ring. It's like finding an unexpected gap in a defensive line, and I'm booking it for the breakaway. If I'm honest with myself, I wouldn't stop at this point even if she wore a ring.

I really want to speak. I want to tell her to touch me and play with me and get me fired. I want her to whisper in my ear and tell me I'm pretty again.

Before I move her hands where I want them, she's dipping them under the waistband of my gray sweats, and her nails scratch along my thighs. I swallow hard and watch as she slides down my sweatpants, but they get caught on my unmistakable erection. But she doesn't pull them down any further. Not yet, at least.

"Do you like that?" she whispers into my ear. She snuggles in and I internally combust. "Do you like when I touch you?"

I nod and let out a super manly whimper.

One of her hands leaves my thigh briefly to grab a few bills, and she slides them under my G-string. "I'm so glad you're finally listening to me, Jonah." She holds the stack of cash in front of our faces and asks, "How far will this get me? You may speak."

"Anything you want," I whisper way too fast. Again, I don't give a shit if I make any money from this encounter, so I don't bother counting it. I don't even bother taking it. I should pay her for this!

"Will you get in trouble if you give me exactly what I want?"

"Yes."

"Do you want to get in trouble?"

"Yes, Professor."

"That's what I like to hear," she purrs. "Now pull your slutty gray sweatpants down and show me how bad you want it." In two seconds I'm fully naked as Professor Wilde's tiny, *beautiful*, freckled hands touch my chest and toy with my nipples. "Stroke yourself."

In a flash, I give a rough tug to my aching head. Boy, if you had told me three years ago that Professor Renée Wilde would watch me stroke my cock and bite my earlobe, I would have paid better attention in her class. I would have been a teacher's pet. Front row, hand raised, and assignments on time. I would have been begging her for extra credit during office hours.

Her body behind mine is soft and warm. Her chest and butt were the primary focus of my time in class. I desperately wanted her to show some cleavage, but she always wore sweaters, which only made me want to unwrap her. I wanted to strip her bare, kiss up her thick thighs, and lay my head on her soft stomach while she pet my hair.

But this—with her tweaking my nipple while the other hand massages my abs—it's better than any fantasy I've ever had of her.

I stroke myself and wait with bated breath for her to say anything. Is she going to comment on the size of my dick? I think it's a good size. Commendable. Admirable, even. I keep everything bare down there. Does she like that? Does she not? Fuck, what does she like? I want to be what she likes.

"Can I touch—" she whispers.

"Yes," I huff, the eagerness in my voice painfully obvious.

Warm breath ghosts over my ear, and she trails fingertips from the base of my shaft to the pre-cum dripping over my crown, sending me hurtling toward an early grave.

"Do... do you like it?" I ask nervously.

She grips the head, and my lower half tightens. "I told you not to speak."

A sound of soft frustration falls out of me because for the first time in one of these private shows, I *want* to be the one who talks.

"You want my praise, don't you?"

I nod far too many times, and her grip intensifies.

"You haven't earned it yet. But you can prove yourself to me. You always talked too much in my class... Maybe you should put that mouth to better use."

AM I DREAMING RIGHT NOW? There's no way this is real life.

"Yes!" I jump off the couch and turn around, pulling her legs apart and dragging her closer in two seconds. I shove her dress up past her waist, and my nose runs along the fabric of her satin panties like a magnet.

Oh God, it's so warm and wonderful here.

She lifts her bottom to help me pull off her panties, and they're discarded somewhere. I don't know; I'm too busy staring at the gorgeous red curls between her legs.

"We don't have much time," she warns.

I shake myself from my brain freeze, spread her open with both thumbs, and dive in tongue-first. She's not very wet, but within a few moments, I lick every inch of her plush center and she's glistening. Her moans send shivers down my spine, and my cock begs me to bring him out to play.

"Yes," she breathes and grabs a fistful of my long hair. "Your fingers now. Fuck me with your fingers, too."

I do, in fact, die when I insert two fingers, and she gasps when I locate her sweet spot. Knowing I bring her this kind of bliss makes her pleased expression even more beautiful.

Please tell me I'm doing a good job.

Renée—Professor Wilde—rides me, smothers me, the evidence of her arousal coating my face. "Don't stop," she commands. "I'm almost there."

I want to say *I wouldn't dream of it*, but the last thing I'll do is remove my mouth from her. I reply with strong suction to her clit as I thrust my hand in and out, the sound of wet slapping flesh more captivating than the music playing in the background.

Every muscle in her body constricts. "I'm coming! Keep going but stroke yourself."

In five pumps flat, I'm coming too, shooting my load somewhere on the floor or the base of the couch, I don't know. Mind blank, I'm blissfully lapping up her cum as our bodies sag.

The descent of our mutual climax is short-lived when there's a familiar knock at the door. "Time's up," the bouncer says from the other side. "You have ten seconds."

Renée is up in a flash, stumbling over my kneeling form and pulling her dress down. "Thank you," she huffs. "This never happened."

She's almost at the door when the words fall out of my mouth without permission. "Was I good?"

As her hand rests on the doorknob, she turns back and a genuine smile lights up her flushed, freckled face. "You were a very good boy." She shuts the door behind her, and I'm left feeling proud, a little confused, and kneeling in a puddle of my own cum.

It's nearly closing time, and Renée is nowhere to be found when I get back into the club. Neither is Angie, Robyn, nor her whole bachelorette party. I guess we'll have a lot to talk about at family dinner tomorrow.

Back in the dressing room, I collect all my tips for the night, but I don't bother counting them. I can't hear the surrounding conversations, and I barely register my drive home or walking my giant dogs down the janky sidewalk. All I can think about is Professor Wilde coming undone for me, her calling me a good boy, and the insatiable urge to do it again.

That's all I think about when I take my shower and jerk off to the same dream. It *must* have been a dream.

When two wet noses nudge me, my eyes peel open, the early afternoon sun warring with the blackout curtains. "Morning, boys," I grumble. I sit up in bed and plant my feet on the hardwood floor and rub my eyes.

I share a rowhouse in North Philly with three roommates, but my one-hundred-eighty-pound Great Pyrenees dogs prefer to sleep in my room in the bunk beds I made them. It's a tight fit, but I don't mind. They're a lot of work though, especially in the city.

Dry food clinks around in the bottom of their metal dishes, and they dive in. I give them a good scrubby pat behind their fluffy white ears. "Good boys."

I don't think I'll ever be able to hear that phrase again in the same context.

How hard would it be to find Renée Wilde?

Chapter 3
A Fortunate Family Dinner

Jonah

Only fifty-five minutes late, I enter my childhood house with dogs in tow and Renée on my mind. I can't shake it. Never in a million years did I think something like last night would happen between us. I always wished and fantasized about her, though I never thought it would become a reality. And after failing her class, I was sure I'd never see her again. I was certain I dreamt the whole interaction last night at work, but before my post-work shower, I caught the scent she left on my fingers—an intoxicating reminder of just how real it was.

This never happened. She clarified that what we did would not be repeated. I guess that's fair. It's usually how things go for me. Women want Good Time Jonah, and I'm not saying that as a stripper. They don't keep me around for long because I'm easy and fun—I'm not serious boyfriend material. I'm their stepping stone before they find the right person, or I'm their rebound, and I'm fine with that. I'm almost twenty-five; I'm too young to settle down anyway.

Striding through the front door, I'm lost in thoughts of Renée's freckles when I'm suddenly assaulted by my family whooping and hollering. My brother-in-law Rafael pushes play on a speaker, and "Pony" by Ginuwine fills the house. Then everyone's up and pulling singles from their pockets to fling them at me.

I groan but can't fight the smile. "Yeah, yeah..."

"Give us a show!" my baby sister Ivy yells.

"Wait," I chuckle, pointing to my toddler twin niece and nephew. "I'm not allowed to swear in front of them, but I can strip?"

"No one's stripping," Isaiah grumbles, and he gets up from the table with three empty plates. Before he walks past me, he leans in close enough I can feel his thick beard against my ear. "You ever do that again, and I'll dig the grave myself."

I turn to Robyn. "You told him?"

"Oh, don't listen to him," she laughs. "Of course I told him. But let's agree that will never happen again."

My jacked soon-to-be brother-in-law, Dell, raises his hand. "Wait, I want a turn. My gran has been looking for a new class to teach at the senior center, and this might be perfect!"

Dell's a personal trainer and has a physique like a body-builder. The man can bench 405. *Maybe I can trade him lessons in stripping for personal training sessions...*

Before I can ask, I'm being pulled into the galley kitchen by Dad and Angie. My newest nephew, Mateo is completely zonked out, strapped to her chest in a baby sling. I'm loading up my plate with the leftovers when I sense a disturbing silence.

"Why didn't you tell us?" Angie asks in that famous oldest sister tone. She's always digging into our brains, trying to figure us out, but sometimes it's just not that deep. Being a children's therapist suits her. She's spent the better part of her life raising all of us siblings, but she doesn't need to worry about me anymore, despite what everyone else thinks.

I should give her something to chew on, though. She has a look in her eyes that tells me she's going to root around until she uncovers something.

"You guys gave me so much crap for barely graduating college. I don't know. I didn't want to disappoint you even more."

Dad crosses his arms and sighs. "Bud, we're very proud of you for graduating college. We'd be even prouder if you'd use your degree in music, but if this is what you want to do, then do it."

His encouraging words are an unexpected downpour, and I'm caught without an umbrella.

As familiar as Angie's probing is, it's the opposite for my dad. Him showing this level of care and concern is foreign. He grieved the loss of our mom for most of my life, so I've never really connected with him. I was only three when my mom died, and while my dad was physically around, he wasn't mentally. But he's been going to therapy—go Dad—and turned a new leaf in the last couple years. He's really come out of his shell, and I'm totally here for it.

"I mean," I shrug, "dancing is fun."

"As long as you enjoy it." Angie smiles and hugs me from the side so as not to disturb the tiny sleeping infant. I sneak a solid whiff from the top of his head covered in wispy black strands.

Mmm... that's nice.

My sister joins Robyn and Dell in the living room while I scarf down braised pork.

"You know," Dad says, "utensils are available."

I shrug. "No sense in dirtying extra dishes."

My brother Dane joins us in the kitchen with Isaiah behind him. Dane is three years older than me and smack dab in the middle of the five Johanssen siblings. He's built more like me than anyone else in the family.

Growing up, Dane and I stuck together most of the time, along with our buddy Joaquín, whose older brother is married to my sister, Angie. We're all very layered in each other's lives like that. Ivy was always trying to wiggle her way into hanging out with us, but in typical older sibling fashion, we ignored her a lot. But she's a fighter, that one. Now she's training to be a midwife.

"So what's going on with the team?" Dad asks. We all currently or formerly play for Philadelphia Men's Rugby Team. Isaiah medically retired a little while ago, but Dane, myself, and Rafael still play.

Dane takes a sip of his beer. "We're trying to level up from Division 1 to the Premier League," he says.

I nearly choke. "We are?"

"Do you ever pay attention?" he asks. "There have been dozens of emails and team meetings about this."

"I'm just joking," I say, lying. "I know."

Dad grins. "That's great. Sounds like it's gonna be a lot more work."

"We definitely need to level up if we're gonna make it happen," Dane says. "The team tried a few times in the last decade or so, but could never make it. This next season is gonna be crucial." He pins me with the same blue eyes everyone in this family has, and his imaginary team captain hat in place. "We're gonna have to trim some fat and focus," he says.

I flex my biceps. "I'm in great shape."

Isaiah rolls his eyes. "He means the team will need to buckle down and get serious about winning."

"Oh."

"Actually show up to practice on time," Dane says, blunt as ever.

A ruckus of laughter flows from the living room, catching my attention. I give my dad and brothers a salute as I make my way to see what's so funny. "You can count on me!"

• • • • • • • • •

Later, everyone moves to the backyard, sitting on patio furniture while people coo over kids and dogs. Zo and Nico are climbing over one dog as Dane plucks hair clumps from another. There's a quick buzz from my phone and I peek to find the group chat with my coworkers.

> Robbie: Anyone's life change forever last night?

Huh?

> Dylan: Nope. Looks like we keep buying animal print G-strings and shaking our asses.

Oh, the Mega Millions. Duh.

"Does anyone know if the jackpot was hit last night?" I ask everyone, but no one's paying attention. Grabbing my wallet from my back pocket, I lazily riffle through it until I find the folded paper and look up the winning numbers online.

03, 17, 32... I check my ticket and see the same first three numbers in the top grid, followed by the same numbers, 58 and 63.

No way...

I blink rapidly at the last number in the bottom grid, the single Mega Ball number. 10. *Cool, that's my rugby position.*

I switch my focus back to my screen and zoom in on the bottom grid for the Mega Ball number.

10.

"Uh..." I mumble. Just a tiny blinking light is active in my brain right now. This can't be real.

Rafael comes up to me and pats me on the back. "You okay, man? I haven't seen you concentrate that hard... ever."

I pass him the ticket and my phone. "Are you seeing what I'm seeing? This has to be fake, right?"

His brow furrows, but he scrutinizes each number. Raf is the smartest person I know. He's a freaking chief financial officer. An officer of money! He'll be able to—

"Ay, dios mío, Jonah," he whispers. His eyes bug out when he faces me, the ticket pinched between his fingers. "Is this yours?"

"I bought it from my coworker last night."

I've never seen Raf's eyes wider than they are now when he hisses, "Jonah, you just won $540 million dollars."

The next few minutes pass in a fog, all sound and mental wherewithal fading away, leaving me barely able to process what just happened. Rough hands shake my shoulders, and when I come to, I'm sitting on a patio chair with my entire family surrounding me.

"Did you hear what I said, Jonah?" Raf asks, kneeling in front of me so his eyes are level with mine.

I shake my head.

"I said, you cannot tell anyone outside of the family about this."

"Why not? I just won the freaking lottery."

"Because that's how you'll lose it all. While you were off in La-La Land just now, I did some cursory research, and everyone online says you should remain as anonymous as possible. Previous winners say once family and friends find out, they come for your winnings, and you can lose relationships quickly if you ever turn off their cash flow."

"But I don't need all of this. I can totally give everyone money."

Angie stands. "He's right, Jonah. It's bad enough that all of us were here to find out." She turns to everyone and pins each with a stern expression. "Absolutely no one here is *ever* going to ask Jonah for money. It's not worth damaging our family."

"Well, if I can't give money to everyone, what am I supposed to do?" Just then, the best idea comes to mind. "I'm gonna buy a yacht!"

"No," everyone says at various levels of frustration.

"First things first," Raf sighs. "I'm setting you up with a financial advisor and a lawyer or two."

"Why can't you do it? You're a money guy."

"Because I'm your family, I'm already a CFO, and I'm not a lawyer. You need pros managing your assets."

"What's an asset?"

"Jesus Christ," Dane mutters.

Dell takes a step forward, his insanely large arms crossed. "Dude, as someone who comes from a lot of money, Rafael is right. You need to protect yourself." Dell's family owns Castle Whiskey, a huge, five-generation family brand based out of Kentucky. I remember the day Isaiah told us his new boyfriend was not only loaded but came with a seemingly endless supply of great whiskey.

Now we've both hit the jackpot.

Dell turns to Raf. "I can give you the name of our lawyers and financial advisors. They've been with us forever."

They chat, and everyone else joins in the conversation, making plans for me and discussing what this will mean, and what the best course of action is. There's talk of non-disclosure agreements, and like always, I'm left out of the important conversations.

My hand itches to text my coworkers and tell them the news, but I stop myself. *Maybe I could tell just one more person... They're basically family anyway.*

I dial Joaquín, who answers the phone on the second ring. "Joner Boner, what's going on?"

Panic settles in all at once, and my face heats. The urge to spill everything threatens to escape. He would have found out if he had been here at family dinner anyway. And he's here like half the time, so...

Dane clocks me as I hold the phone to my ear, his jaw tense. "Jonah, who are you talking to?"

He launches himself at me, but I'm quicker. I escape his grasp and run deeper into the backyard. The dogs bolt from their spots on the grass and chase me along with my brothers.

"Joaquín, I won the lottery," I squeal, before I'm tackled to the ground by Isaiah. My dogs playfully attack my enormous brother, who's trying to take the phone away from me.

"You what?" Joaquín exclaims.

Isaiah rips the phone from my hand and hurls it to Rafael. "Deal with that," he snaps, then turns to me and smacks me hard in the chest. "We gave you one rule, dumbass—don't tell anybody!"

He grunts as Yogi and Rugger lunge at him, trying to yank him back by his shirt. The sound of ripping cotton has him springing to his feet, but not before he lands one last hit on me.

Yogi and Rugger don't let up their good-natured assault until Isaiah is five feet away and his T-shirt hangs in tatters. Dane steps in, redirecting them with that calming, veterinarian touch of his.

"But it was Joaquín," I protest. "He's family, and he's my best friend. Do you honestly think we could've kept this from him?"

Dane sighs once the dogs settle. "He's right," he says to Isaiah. "You know how nosy he is. He would have figured it out."

Isaiah's answering harrumph is aggressive. "No one else, Jonah."

I throw my hands up in surrender. "Okay." I get up and dust myself off. "Can I still be a stripper?"

Chapter 4

Move In Day

Jonah

Three months after my windfall and my life forever changed, I step out on a concrete driveway next to overflowing greenery. Yogi and Rugger shove past me as they barrel out of the door of my brand new, fully-loaded Yukon. "Home sweet home, boys! Go explore!" The pair of them take off like a bolt of lightning to sniff every square inch of their new home.

Did I buy a one-hundred-acre plot of land in West Chester with an eight-thousand square foot stone house built in 1920 just because it came with a barn and plenty of space so my boys could run and live the life they should live? Absolutely. But it wasn't just the barn that sold me. This "magnificent estate" (as the real estate dude put it) also came with two goats named Thelma and Louise and a flock of ducks that I've named The Quack Pack.

My siblings kept harping on me to get these dogs out of the city. They kept saying, "*These dogs are for guarding animals, not tussling with your roommates in North Philly.*" Well, here we are in the literal country, where we can stretch out and live like the wild men we are.

I moved everything yesterday by myself. It was pointless to hire movers when my entire life could fit inside one vehicle. I was going to ask my roommates to help, but my family kept badgering me not to tell anyone. Then the lawyer and tax attorney I hired repeated the same thing. Just like Rafael said, this is a common mistake most winners face. Their friends and family will ask for handouts repeatedly, and it'll never stop. Relationships will become strained because of it. Feelings will get hurt. It totally sucks because I want to shout from the rooftops that I won half a billion dollars!

But Rafael and my lawyers are right, I guess. I don't want anyone to resent me, so I'm keeping my mouth shut.

I left my roommates and simply said I was moving out. Then, I gave my old Jeep to Shirly, the homeless lady in my neighborhood. I stuck twenty grand with a note in the glove compartment for her. I hope she's doing all right. She was always so nice.

Since my family was there when I found out, I couldn't keep the secret from them, thank goodness. So with the help of my lawyers, I set them each up with two million dollars and a trust for two million more when everyone turns forty-five. Dad got the full four million right out the gate and officially retired from his corporate engineering job last week.

After begging and pleading, Rafael and Joaquín let me tell their moms about my windfall. Christina and Ana basically raised me. When I tried to set them up with money, they flat-out refused. I kept trying, but Joaquín said his mamá is too proud.

I'm gonna keep trying though. What else am I supposed to do with all this money? My lawyers told me I couldn't just have a lump sum sitting in a bank account. It's all like, invested now. I only get a certain amount each month, and I have to ask my finance guy before taking out anything over twenty grand. And no one liked my idea about getting a yacht! Where's everyone's sense of fun and adventure?

On the other hand, I've been thinking about that ten grand in casino chips I found in a Vegas cab a few years ago—the ten grand I blew in less than six months. I didn't spend it on bills or tuition or anything meaningful. The sad reality is, I don't even know what I spent it on. I don't want to make that same mistake again, so I'm listening to those smarter than me. Trying to at least. It's a struggle to find the balance between having fun with my money and not living up to my reputation as a fuckup.

I quit my job at Strip Tease, not because I wanted to, but because I had to. It was too hard to keep my winnings a secret. I almost spilled the beans about a dozen times. Returning to work was different; not only did I have a massive secret, but every time I entered that private room or even walked past it, I remembered Professor Wilde.

I still have her panties—and they look so good wrapped around my hand when I stroke myself to the thought of her.

For the past few months I've been inundated with legal jargon and real estate stuff that I still don't understand—all of it making me feel like I'm in over my head. I've been so busy with meetings that I haven't been able to find her. She said to pretend what we did never happened, but I can't.

"This is incredible, Jonah," Joaquín says as he exits his own car and parks next to all the others. The warm summer breeze dances through his long, dark curls, he takes a deep breath of the invigorating, fresh country air.

Joaquín lives in DC and splits his time between there and Philly. He's a project manager for the company he runs with Rafael. They own, renovate, and lease apartments and homes. He's always busy, but he's never too busy for me.

We're both free spirits, he and I. He's a lot more calculated and was always the one helping me pass my classes, but he's always down for an adventure and can shift gears on a dime. Even with hundreds of miles between us, we're still in sync with each other. Ang is the same way with Raf. It must be a Johanssen/Jimenez thing. We were inseparable growing up, and nothing changed after Joaquín came out as trans—we still went together like peanut butter and jelly.

My whole family is already inside my new house helping set things up. My sisters are going from room to room talking about paint colors. Dad is poking around in the utility room and inspecting the hot water heater. But no one has entered my secret room yet, and I'm itching to show it off.

I gather everyone and take them to the finished basement with a smile a mile wide. With my hand on the door handle, I turn around to speak as everyone waits. "I know you all said I had to be smart with my money and not spend it all willy-nilly, but..."

"Jonah," Raf says. "What did you do?"

"You wouldn't let me get a yacht, so what else am I supposed to do out here all by myself?" I fling open the frosted glass door to reveal a soundproof room filled with instruments: my old drums with some fresh additions, a keyboard, bass, violin, and trumpet, electric and acoustic guitars, microphones, amps, the works.

With a surprised "Whoa," Joaquín jumps past everyone, eager to get to the keyboard. "This is awesome!"

I scramble for my stool behind the drums and throw my hands out. "C'mon, Raf. You can't be mad. I already owned half of this. I just filled in the missing pieces." Even Dane and Isaiah are cracking smiles when they each find their respective instruments.

Raf stares at me. "You did *not* have an entire recording studio, and this house was *not* listed with one."

Joaquín plays the opening from "Get Down On It" by Kool & The Gang, and my brothers and I follow suit.

"See it as an investment in my happiness," I beam. I get lost in the music and silence Rafael with the funkiest beat. Nico squirms in his arms, and Raf just shakes his head before—there it is—a dimple forms in his cheek when his lips curl. Got him! He sets his son down, and his daughter's already clapping along—terribly, I might add. I'll have to work on that with her.

Rafael takes a deep breath and glances at Angie, who's

already in the groove. Ivy dances with our baby nephew in her arms.

"Fine," Raf chuckles between verses. "This was a good idea."

Damn right it was. Music's in my blood. All of us Johanssen kids inherited some kind of musical gift from our mom, God rest her soul. Angie played the violin in the school orchestra with Rafael. Ivy's singing voice can bring me to tears. And Zay, Dane, Joaquín, and I started our family band, Agony Nectar, before I even hit junior high. We played mostly rock and punk, but I've always been a sucker for anything with a good beat. I can hear a song once or twice and match it note for note. It's a gift—what can I say?

We play a few more songs, including an Agony Nectar original called "Stab Me," where Dane lays out some of his best emo lyrics. Joaquín and I take the rest of the family on a walk around the grounds while the dogs explore. It doesn't take them long to find the ducks and goats, and Dane, being the vet that he is, starts training the dogs as we go. I guess everyone was right; they really were meant for a country life like this.

When we get back to the house, I notice a woman walking across the street with two young kids, each holding something. When they get closer and step onto my driveway, I walk toward them as the rest of my family heads into the house.

The woman is wearing jeans and a T-shirt, her hair pulled back in a ponytail except for the long curtain-like bangs framing her face. All at once I register her striking red mane and the curves of the woman I've been spanking it to since college.

Professor Wilde is standing in my driveway.

When she realizes who I am, she stops in her tracks and forces the two young girls on either side of her to stop as well.

"What are you doing here?" she asks.

"I live here. I just bought this house."

"No, you didn't."

"Yes, I did."

"How? You're a—" she peers down at the girls quickly before flinging a stern *you-know-what-I'm-trying-to-say* look.

I can't tell her the real reason I can afford this place. I shrug and hope she doesn't ask for more of an explanation. "What are you doing here?"

She sighs, but before she can answer, the taller of the two little girls hands me a plastic container.

"We're your neighbors! My name is Delta. We live across the street."

My mind flashes back to all the times Professor Wilde mentioned her daughters in class. God, they're the spitting image of her—the same freckles, the same nose, the same eyes. And that hair... same vibrant shade, but the smaller one, maybe six-ish, has curls. Delta, maybe nine, looks like she cut her own bangs, and they're now awkwardly growing out.

She points to the little blue house with white shutters and a detached garage next door, maybe a rugby field's length away. All the houses after hers are clustered together, and none of them has a yard bigger than a quarter acre.

My property dominates this end of the road. I can't even see my nearest neighbors on the other side of my corner lot, their house hidden by hills and thick trees.

"Hi Delta. My name is Jonah." I tip the container and examine it. "Did you make me cookies?"

"They're no-bakes. That means you don't put them in the oven. You scoop them onto the counter, but you can't eat them right away because they're too hot. We ate four from your batch, but we can make more—"

"That's enough, sweetie," Renée says, gently gripping her

daughter's shoulder.

"I love no-bakes. Thank you. And what's your name?" I ask the smaller girl. "Did you help make these?"

She hides behind her mother in response.

"This is Lo. Short for Loretta," Renée says in an uneven, borderline reluctant way.

"Well, I'm gonna eat every single one of these."

"Do you wanna come over and see my new bike?" Delta asks.

"Heck yeah."

"No," Renée cuts in harshly. "We're not gonna—he's—no," she stutters, as if she has too many thoughts and can't decide which one to say, if at all. Which, same?

I can't believe she's standing right here—that she's my new neighbor. The idea of a hot and heavy second round between us clicks into place like a slot machine hitting triple sevens.

Oh yeah. That's happening.

If this isn't the universe practically screaming that my former professor and I should roll around in the sheets, then I don't know what is.

"You know," I say with a smirk, "we should probably exchange numbers. Since we're neighbors and all." So *I can text you dirty little things that'll make you squirm,* I think to myself.

"I don't think so."

Classic Renée Wilde. Denying my advances and making me hornier because of it. But the dial to my sexy professor craving has been turned up since our spicy private room in the club. I *know* what we're capable of together.

And I will be having seconds.

"Who's this?" Joaquín asks, walking up to join us.

"My new neighbors. Look, cookies!"

"Hi, I'm Joaquín."

"Hi. We were just leaving," Renée says, turning her girls

away before heading toward the street. "It was nice meeting you both."

Dumbfounded, I stand there watching the three of them walk down my driveway.

"You okay, Joner?"

I snap out of it. "Yeah. No. I don't know." We start back toward the house. "Remember that former professor I told you I hooked up with at Strip Tease? That's her."

Joaquín whips around to steal another look. "Really? Dude, you are punching up—and I don't just mean in the age bracket. Ella es bonitaaaa."

"Yo sé."

"Think you'll hook up again?"

Side by side we climb the stone porch stairs, and I clap him on the shoulder, grinning like a man with fate on his side. "That's a sure bet."

Chapter 5
A Controlled Life

Renée

I usher the girls into our backyard, out of sight of the last person I expected to be our new neighbor, and the last person I wanted to run into.

"Mom, can we play restaurant?"

All I can do is nod in response, too in shock by what just happened. My girls leave for their tiny outdoor kitchen—a child's size table with a bucket sink next to the smallest garden bed ever, but it's the only one I could fit in this yard.

I busy myself with dishes inside and listen to the girls play in the backyard.

I should have listened to the blaring voice of reason that warned me hooking up with my former student, no matter how attractive he is, was a supremely stupid idea. Curiosity and desire spiked as I watched him dance that night. I had no intention of hooking up with him, but once my plans fell through, and my sister, Amber, discovered who he was, there was no stopping our inevitable end. As much as I would like to deny it, I had an incredible time. I wanted more of him, but I needed a clean break, and nothing was going to prevent that.

As the girls prepare their "restaurant," Delta patiently shows her younger sister how to pick just the weeds from the garden. Lo listens and follows along. Not for the first time, I imagine what Lo might say back to her older sister. Delta is nine, and Lo is seven, but for the past two years—ever since their father died—Lo hasn't spoken a word.

Not a day goes by that I don't ache to hear her voice.

Her father—my late husband—is another story. Missing him isn't something I struggle with. Not in the least.

The back slider opens, and Delta's bubbly voice fills the kitchen. "—and his name is Jonah, and he's going to come over and see my new bike!"

"Is he?" Amber says with a smile. She's still in her country club uniform, and judging by the polo and khaki shorts, I'd guess she worked the drink cart on the golf course today.

A few loose strands of her strawberry-blonde hair fall down her freckled neck from her high bun. I had a similar build before kids—short, slimmer, cute as a button, if I say so myself. Now, at thirty-eight, with two kids, a job, and bills piling up, staying in shape isn't a high priority, or even doable anymore. And that's fine. My body has served me well, and she's beautiful, stretch marks and all.

Amber has been living with us ever since Greg died, and I don't think I could survive without her. Flighty as she is, she's the most loyal person I know. She will cancel plans at the drop of a hat, but if it involves me or my daughters, she's locked in and confirmed. If it's anyone else, she doesn't care if she bails; it's no sweat off her back.

When Amber came back into my life, it was at a time we both needed each other. She had been in and out of drug rehab and was financially cut off from our parents. The day I called and asked for her help, after nearly a decade of not speaking, she made a plan—a commitment—to get clean for herself and for us.

I'm so thankful, and so proud of her.

My sister grins at me. "You met the new neighbor? What's he look like? He must be loaded to buy that place. I wonder if he's a member of the country club."

Before I can warn her in some adult-coded way, Delta's chirping. "He's a man, and he has long hair like yours, Aunt

Amber. And he said he likes cookies, so Lo and I are gonna make him more. Do you wanna help us bake cookies in our restaurant?"

"I do. You know I'm always offering my help in the kitchen at work, but our pastry chef, Pierre, is still mad at me for losing my Band-Aid in the big mixer of chocolate mousse. Can you believe that? One stupid Band-Aid. My finger wasn't even bleeding anymore. I don't know what he's so upset about. It's like the kiss we shared after the staff wine tasting last year means nothing to him. But can I be honest with you? If he wanted to kiss me again, I'd let him. I like his little mustache."

"You kissed a boy?"

"No, a very temperamental man who plays with chocolate all day. Now go outside and get your kitchen in order. I'm gonna change and talk to your mom for a minute, and then I'll join you."

"Okay!" The girls leave us without another thought and race to their restaurant.

She turns to me, eyes narrow. "Alright, this new neighbor," she says. "What kind of rich is he? Old rich? Foreign rich? Some developer who'd tear down a gorgeous eight-million-dollar estate just to throw up a cheap subdivision?"

I grip her arms and lock eyes with her, mostly to shut her up. "Amber." I pause. "Do you remember when we went to Strip Tease for your birthday?"

Her eyes light up. "Yes. Can we go back? We almost never get to do anything fun together."

I cock my head back, affronted. "We have fun."

"If you have to say that with your eyebrows touching, we don't have enough fun."

Ugh, she's not wrong. We really don't go out together much. *She* does—she goes out with her new friends and coworkers. Amber actually has a social life. If I'm not working at the university, I'm at home. Amber lives with us, so she'll babysit anytime I ask, but I try not to ask often. She uprooted her whole life in Nashville and moved here on a whim just to support me, so I don't ask for anything extra.

Amber's the fun-loving aunt, the extroverted sister. I'm the stick-in-the-mud and the voice of reason. I'm the one organizing the chaos into some kind of predictable structure so I can give my girls the best shot at a bright future. Their abusive father dying? That was the first real, terrifying step in that direction.

She runs her thumb over the crease in my brow. "There you go," she says. "So... are we going back to Strip Tease? I could go for a hair blowout and a lap dance right about now."

I shake my head. "Our neighbor. It's Jonah."

The words hang between us as she tries to connect the dots.

"Jonah Arc?"

"What?"

"No, wait. It's Joan of Arc."

"What are you talking about?"

"The guy in the Bible who built the ark."

"Noah?"

"I'm pretty sure his name was Joan... or Jonah. I don't know; I didn't pay attention in Sunday school, okay? You got me."

"Amber, listen to me. When we were at Strip Tease, you made that ridiculous bet with me when you found out that one stripper was my former student."

The "bet" in question was really more of a birthday gift for her.

Amber's always saying I do nothing impulsive. Nothing just for me. Even the tiny garden in our backyard isn't mine in any indulgent way. It's practical—only vegetables, just enough to supplement our groceries.

Believe it or not, being a biology professor doesn't make it easy to make ends meet as a single parent. Amber contributes what she can with her tip-based server salary and from her... extracurricular activities, but things are tight.

She still manages to get out and have fun. And I know she's right... I don't do anything for myself. Impulsivity used to be a cornerstone of who I was. Sure, some of that fades with age—especially when you're a parent—but the more she brought it up, the more I realized how far I'd drifted from that version of myself.

I am no longer the kind of person people would call reckless. But that night—finding Jonah on stage—something shifted.

When I told Amber who he was, she insisted, practically shoved cash into my bra and pushed me into that back room. Said it was the best birthday present she could ever ask for. I couldn't deny her—not when I knew she was right, and not when she deserved whatever she wanted for always showing up for me.

Hooking up with him wasn't on my radar—nor was riding his pretty face and staring at his incomprehensibly long eyelashes until I came in a way I hadn't in years. I thought he'd give me a private little dance and maybe he'd let me touch his arms and get a better look at his tattoos. I imagined nothing beyond that.

But once the door closed behind me, it felt as if the widow and the mother of two were left in the dimly lit hallway just outside. Inside, it was just me... and him. A young, starry-eyed man, glitter-dusted and watching me like I was some kind of fantastical fairy who came to make his dreams come true.

Logic snapped like a dry twig underfoot. It was like I stepped into a capsule where time, consequence, and responsibility didn't exist.

Only desire.

Eyes wide, Amber gasps, "Yes. Your former student, that's right!"

"That's him," I say gravely. "He's our new neighbor."

She rears back. "How is that possible? He's a stripper. How can he afford that property?"

"I don't know."

"Maybe he has a rich family. Though, why would he strip if he's wealthy?"

"Again, I don't know. What I know is that we are staying far away from him."

"Oh, come on," she drawls, her tone teasing. I just know she's about to coax something out of me. "You go out once a month to fuck submissives, and the end-all-be-all of subby men, who was so baby girl you couldn't stop daydreaming for weeks afterwards, plops himself next door and you're gonna tell me you're never going to see him again?"

Dammit. I should have kept my mouth shut.

But this, gossiping about our sexual exploits, is something foundational in our sisterhood—it's not how all sibling relationships work, but it is for us. We spent so long without each other that once she was finally back in my life, I clung to her like a lifeline. She brought back all that essential, in-between stuff that's never really explained about girlhood, but feels so right when it's presented to you. Girlhood had been missing from my life, even though I fight tirelessly to foster it between my daughters.

Fresh out of undergrad, I married Greg Matherson, a music producer from Nashville who swept me off my feet and promised me everything. He was fifteen years my senior and worked alongside my parents for most of that time.

I grew up as the child of bluegrass legends, David and Ophelia Wilde. Both musicians, both singer-songwriters, they traveled all over the United States with me in tow, eventually spotlighting me on their stage. Me, a brave little girl with a mandolin and mighty voice, who sang alongside country music's greatest. We were on *Austin City Limits* and we even played at The Grand Ole Opry. I've been to holiday parties at Dolly Parton's house, and watched Shania Twain's television while she folded laundry next to me.

After I married and moved away, my parents continued to work and tour with artists like Billy Strings and Ed Sheeran.

At eighteen, I left my family on the road and attended college in California. Greg consistently checked in on me, inquiring about my studies and urging me to stay focused and avoid distractions from boys (or girls, in my closeted mind).

I obviously saw it much too late that he was grooming me. To the untrained eye, he was always a safe, appropriate distance away. But I always had butterflies for him, and he knew it. He played into them and teased me for having a crush on him. In my naivete, my infatuation with him never felt wrong, but inevitable.

Somehow, Greg's charm and promises still swayed me, despite my rich childhood filled with music and tour buses. He knew exactly the things I wanted at the time—to rest from travel and touch grass, literally in this case. He saw my love of nature and encouraged a teenage Renée to find her passion in biology. My parents, equally encouraging, supported this too.

We married the week after I graduated college. And sure, he kept his promise and moved us into a beautiful home right there in Nashville. He paid for both my master's degree and my doctoral degree so that I could teach the very thing I loved.

But as time went on, he wove lies into my head about my parents. He insisted they were manipulative and abusive for parading me around like some prize horse, profiting off my talent. It didn't matter that my parents set aside all the money I earned. It didn't matter that I once loved playing the mandolin and singing my heart out. He convinced me the only way to get back at them was to cut them out of our lives.

Then, without telling me, and seemingly out of nowhere, he bought a house in West Chester, Pennsylvania. We didn't know anyone, and I left my brand new job because he made this decision for us. When I questioned how he was going to do his job, he said his clientele would come to him.

But when I saw our new house, a fraction of the size of our last one, I knew something was wrong. There was no studio, no grand foyer. There was a single-lane driveway off a main road and a kitchen so small we had to hang pots from the ceiling.

There were nights of endless, unanswered questions, and demands as proof of love. "If you really loved me, you'd give me babies," he would say. "If you really loved me, you'd support me through this career transition and work full time."

Over time his demands became less and less loving. Disdain and anger reigned supreme and I didn't know how to handle that. I had never grown up around such aggression and violent words.

The day he found out I had an IUD implanted in secret, things became exponentially worse.

"EARTH TO RENÉE," Amber exclaims, throwing me back into the present.

I shake my head. "Sorry."

"You okay?"

"Just went down a rabbit hole."

She watches me carefully, knowing where my mind wanders. I wish I could erase everything about Greg and restart. She wishes that too.

"Do you wanna talk about it?" she asks.

"No. What were you saying before?"

"Jonah, our new neighbor. You can't seriously tell me you're going to ignore him when he's so clearly your type."

"I don't have a type."

"Tell that to the all the submissives you've painstakingly selected and fucked over the last year and a half."

I sigh, because she's not wrong. Amber is a server at Maple Ridge Golf & Country Club, and she makes enough money to get by. But her side hustle as a Dominatrix is really where she thrives. Let's just say, some of her rich and powerful patrons at the country club are some of her best customers as a Dominatrix.

It's because of her I discovered my inner Dominant.

I knew nothing of kink or BDSM or a Dom/sub dynamic before her. But when she explained it all to me on one of our first girls-only evenings after Greg was gone and my daughters were fast asleep, I couldn't turn off my curiosity.

She spoke, and I hung on every word. I researched, asked questions, and joined forums. I had spent my life married to someone who stripped everything away from me. So the idea that I could finally be in control—that I could call the shots—felt like just as much of a victory as living free from Greg's suffocating rules and the life we had together.

Then, for a few uncharacteristically indulgent nights, I called up my former coworker Tracy, a newly retired chemistry professor, and asked her to babysit.

Amber took me to a few different play parties set up through a kink club just outside of Philly. She set me up with a training partner, someone who taught me what submission feels like before ever teaching me how to dominate.

It was through those parties and that kink club that I found a handful of submissives that I could trust—ones who also weren't looking for anything more than our scenes. Ones who didn't mind that I only did this once a month.

Once a month.

That's all I ever allow myself. Anything more than that, and I feel like I'm abandoning my children, and I feel selfish.

That night at Strip Tease, with the raucous laughter of

bachelorette parties, and the smell of sweet cocktails and hairspray, I found something unexpected.

The plan that night was twofold: one, celebrate Amber's birthday; and two, meet up with one of my subs to roleplay a scene where I catch him cheating on his nonexistent wife. A little public fun—nothing that could get us arrested—followed by a night at the hotel down the road.

But when he bailed at the last minute, sending a flood of apologies, I set my sights on Jonah. And nothing, and no one, has ever been as satisfying as fucking Jonah Johanssen's mouth.

"You're really not gonna hit that again?" Amber asks, taking a bottle of white wine out of our fridge and pouring each of us a glass.

"It was wrong of me to do it."

"It's not like he's your student anymore," she shrugs.

Memories of his time in my class all come back at once, and I roll my eyes. "He's young, and dumb, and he has hotter, younger, dumber people to hook up with. He does not need or want my attention."

"Wanna bet?"

Chapter 6
Serious Players Only

Jonah

"**F**inish strong," Coach Batsakis yells, right as our hooker throws in the ball for a lineout. It's our last phase of practice, and we've been run ragged tonight.

I'm lined up in the backline, playing fly-half. I've played all over the field—I'm what they call a utility player, which just means I can play any position, and I also say yes to everything. But since all my brothers are forwards, they constantly roast me for being a back. The forwards versus backs rivalry is as old as the game itself.

Forwards are the big, rough-and-tumble dudes who do all the hitting and lifting and grunting. They love smashing into people and rolling around in the mud. Total chaos. Backs like me are the fast ones who *allegedly* care too much about our hair and keeping our kits free of grass stains. Whatever. Someone has to swoop in and score all the points.

There's always beef. Forwards think we're lazy and pretty. Backs think forwards are slow and dramatic. But hey, someone's gotta hang out wide, wait for the ball, and make the magic happen. That's me. Just out here, doing my thing, looking hot, and running fast.

You'd think as a utility player I wouldn't fall victim to the rivalry, but no—whatever position I'm playing, I adopt the mockery. I like to fit in, okay?

Our jumper tips the ball and tosses it to Small Fry, who immediately passes it to Jimmy (a.k.a. my brother-in-law,

Raf), who runs it several yards before offloading it to me to get out wide. By the time the ball makes it down to Wheels at winger, he finds a gap in the D line and scores.

Coach blows the whistle, and everyone joins him at midfield to stretch out. "Alright, boys. Good practice today. While you stretch out, I want to fill you in on where we are with the Premier League. As you know, we've been trying to level up to the eastern Premiership for a decade now."

We have?

"We've always been close, but it's never been enough. Going premier will not look the same as Division 1. The team needs players who live, breathe, and sleep rugby. Players who want to win and to see the team grow. We need big donors and sponsorships, but most importantly, we need commitment from you all. If you want to play for funsies, go join a different team in this city—there are several.

"Thanks to a certain Johanssen brother's fiancé, we have secured the largest sponsorship to date with Castle Whiskey."

Applause breaks loose and someone whistles. Isaiah isn't even part of the team anymore since he medically retired last year, but everyone knows who he is, and most remember when he was captain of this team.

"Yes," Coach chuckles. "That was a tremendous relief, but it won't be enough."

A lightbulb goes off in my mind, because *hey... I have lots of money!*

I turn to Dane, who's stretching his hammies, and slap his shoulder. Wordlessly, I shoot him a super subtle, brother-only communication through our minds.

"Ow," he hisses. "What was that for?"

I'm about to whisper in his ear, but Coach cuts me off. "JoJo, save the side convos for after."

I wince. "Sorry, Coach."

He sighs before continuing his speech, but I zone out,

thinking about how I have the easiest solution to our problem. Why didn't I think of this sooner? I chuckle to myself because it's just like a back to swoop in and save the day, isn't it?

As everyone packs up their bags to head home, I pull Raf and Dane to the side. "Guys, why don't I just give the team the money we need?"

Raf gives Dane a look I can't decipher as a long pause settles between the three of us.

"You haven't talked to him yet?" Raf asks Dane.

"Talk to me about what?"

"Listen, bro." Dane pulls at the back of his neck. "We know you have the money to do this for the team, but we don't think it's a good idea."

"Why not?"

"Coach and I discussed current players and who should realistically move up to the Premiership, and who should remain and only play for our tourney team."

The Philadelphia Men's Rugby Team is large. It's composed of three teams: Division 1, Division 3, and a wheelchair rugby team. But during the summer, after regular season play is over, we turn into the Philly Fathers (a.k.a. the Daddies)—a social, sevens, tournament-only team. We wear ridiculous jerseys and drink on the sidelines. Think of people partying on a pontoon boat that's blasting yacht rock. That's kind of the vibe we bring to the table—er, pitch.

"Only the tourney team? Wait, what happens to the D1 and 3 teams?"

Raf shrugs. "They're being dissolved, dude. Didn't you listen to Coach?"

Oops.

"If you want to keep playing Division 1," Dane says, "you'll need to join another club."

"Why would I join another club? I'm going to play with you guys in the Premiership."

Dane sighs, "No, you're not. That's what I was trying to say. Coach and I don't think you're serious enough for that level."

"But I'm one of the fastest players on the team! I can play any position!"

"But you're not committed, dude. You're always late to practice, you don't listen, and you fall back on the plays you have the muscle memory for."

Raf places his hand on my shoulder. "Being in great shape isn't gonna cut it."

I study him. "How are you even going to make Premiership work? You're a CFO for two companies and a father."

"And yet," he drawls, "I make it to practice on time."

I groan.

"Truth is," he continues, "I'm probably going to quit one job."

I turn back to Dane. "Come on..."

"This is why we didn't approach you about donating to the team," Dane says. "We knew you'd be salty about it, and we don't blame you. But we need serious players, Jonah—"

"I can be serious," I blurt. I don't care how desperate I sound because I am. It's not enough to play rugby for just any team. I want to play with my brothers. This has always been a thing that has united us as a family. Playing in a pre-teen rock band was the first thing that brought us together. But rugby, playing on the same fields with a common goal, was something I wanted more than anything with my older brothers, including Raf. I looked up to them all. What started as me, their annoying little brother tagging along for everything, turned into a mutual respect on the pitch.

At least, I thought it was mutual respect.

"Let me prove myself," I vow.

Dane gives me a disbelieving look. "I have been trying to get you to commit ever since I became captain, Jo. Isaiah tried to do the same thing when he was captain. Why should I trust that this time is different?"

Because the threat of losing this connection with you guys really freakin' hurts, I think to myself. But I don't say that because that's way too vulnerable.

"I... I don't know, okay? I don't know how I'm gonna do it, but I'm going to. Please don't kick me off the team. And I want to fund everything else."

"But we can't be beholden to your money," Raf says.

Huh? "What does beholden mean?"

"It means we would feel like we have our hands tied to keep you on the team if you were a major donor."

"Oh. Um... okay. But I still wanna give the team money even if that means I don't make the Premiership team. Can we like, make a contract or something?"

Raf looks pleasantly surprised. "Look at you. Learning a thing or two from all those lawyers." He turns to gauge Dane's reaction. "What are you thinking?"

Dane narrows his eyes at me for a long time, and I don't dare interrupt his assessment. I just hope my puppy-dog pout is doing the trick. "Fine."

"Yes!" Relief washes over me before I wrap my brothers in a hug.

"You have this summer and fall season to prove yourself. And I don't want to just see you arriving on time. No excuses. I want to see you improving yourself and others."

"I can do that!"

"We have a lot of games to win, and every point counts toward leveling up. I need you to be dedicated to your position."

"And," Raf adds. "You'll have to donate to the team anonymously. No one can know, remember?"

"I'll talk to my lawyer first thing in the morning!"

"Put a plan together, JoJo," Dane says.

Planning has never really been my strong suit, but if this

is what I have to do to stay on the team with my brothers, then a plan is what I'll make.

By the time we finish our conversation and grab our bags, the rest of the team has left. As we walk to the parking lot, I take inventory of our surroundings. We play outside in a public park, but the field isn't exactly well-kept. I know the team sinks money into covering what the public parks and recreation department can't. On more than one occasion, we've found used needles on the field.

The team has always dreamed of having its own indoor training facility. A pipe dream, really. But if someone is already secretly donating money...

"Hey Raf?" I smile.

He stops. "Yeah?"

"What if an anonymous donor, *me*," I stage-whisper the last word, "donated funds specifically for a dedicated training facility?"

The second that thought sinks in, excitement bursts over his features, and he's looking at Dane.

"How much would something like that cost?" he asks Raf. Of the three of us, Raf would know more about real estate prices.

He looks to the night sky, tossing his head back and forth, crunching the numbers. "If we renovated, probably something just outside the city, I'd say at least a couple million."

The three of us exchange looks of varying giddiness.

But the warning words of my lawyers and siblings bring me down. "Oh wait, I'm not supposed to spend my money all willy-nilly."

Dane puts up his hand. "Hold on." He flicks his gaze to Raf. "You said 'renovated?' We'd buy something that needs work..." he says, as if he's trying to convince himself. "Something that could build the community."

Raf smirks. "The city offers tax breaks for beautification

projects."

"So, we can do this?" I beam.

"I think it's worth exploring," Raf says.

"Yes," Dane and I say in unison.

"Can I hire your company?" I ask Raf.

"I think Jimenez Brothers Properties may have room for something like that. But you'll need to get other quotes. Everything stays above board and is as transparent as possible. Except for who's donating the cash."

"Of course!"

"I'll talk to the rugby board at our meeting this week," Dane says. "Jonah, confirm with your lawyers what you can donate and we'll go from there."

"This is gonna be so cool!" I squeal.

Raf throws his arm around me for a hug before sliding into his Range and giving us a wave.

When Dane and I get to our vehicles, I glance over and notice he's resting his head on his steering wheel. I'm flying high with possibilities, but his shoulders are too close to his ears, and worry nips at me. He looks especially grouchy for someone who has a shot at premiership rugby and a dedicated club training facility.

Is he still worried I won't see my commitments through?

I tap on his window, and he rolls it down. "You okay, bro? I swear I'm gonna try."

"It's not that," he mutters. "I just checked my voicemail. One of my farmer clients wants me to put down a perfectly good horse this week."

"Why?"

He sighs. "Because she's old and blind, therefore no use to him."

"Oh." I frown.

Poor Dane. This has to be the hardest part of being a veterinarian.

"Do you do that kind of thing a lot? I know you do it for

dogs and cats when it's their time. But farm animals?"

"Yeah," he says, shrugging. "I try to re-home those animals to the best of my ability, especially when there's nothing really wrong with them. But sometimes nothing works out."

"I can take the horse."

He furrows his brow. "Did you put any thought into that before speaking?"

"Um... Honestly, no." Dane opens his mouth to say something, but I cut him off, spilling my thoughts in real-time. "But it would be perfect! I have space, a barn with stables, and two dogs who need more livestock to guard. They're getting possessive over the ducks. They need more to take care of."

When Dane stares at me, I can see the wheels turning behind his eyes. "I don't know..." he says.

Shoot. How do I convince him more? Dane is a total softy on the inside, so I play into that.

"Come on. Are you really gonna euthanize a sweet granny horse just because she's blind, when I have the space and protection she needs?"

His eyes narrow. "She needs love, too."

"I can love her!"

Dane crosses his arms. "She could live another eight to ten years."

I cross mine back. "I'm not going anywhere."

"She'll need regular veterinary care."

"Good thing my brother is a vet. C'mon. I need to take responsibility, right? A horse is a big deal, I get it. But I can do it."

Silence lingers as we face off under the parking lot lamplight. He bites his lip the way he always does when he's about to make a hard decision.

"Fine. I'll talk to the farmer and arrange the transport."

"Yeah!"

"But I'm serious, Jonah. There's a lot to know about taking care of a horse."

"Well, I don't have a job anymore, so I have the time to learn."

The corner of his mouth quirks up the smallest bit, and I savor the satisfaction. "Okay," he concedes. "I'll call you tomorrow." He swallows. "Thanks, Jonah. This is really nice of you."

Dane isn't one to serve up appreciation like this, so I find myself pleased as punch to be the one receiving it. I just hope I can show him I can be responsible, and that I'm worthy of his trust and appreciation again.

Chapter 7

Making Plans

After meeting with one of my lawyers about the plans for funding the training facility, I got the approval to proceed. He agreed with Rafael that framing it as community beautification would be a smart idea, and now he's chasing that lead and getting all the boring paperwork in line while I get to focus on the fun stuff.

That's why I'm holding a case of Yuengling in one hand while I open the door to Raf and Angie's house. Tonight we're going over plans for the training facility. Plus, any time I can hang out with my amigos, I'm down.

I spot Joaquín's car in the driveway and smile. I knew he was driving up from DC for this, but excitement prickles under my skin at the possibility of working together with my best friend on a dream project.

I punch in the door code and inhale the smell of garlic. "Hola carnales. Huele rico." I announce before taking off my shoes. I learned Spanish from Joaquín and his family since we practically grew up together. They always make fun of me because I have a really hard time getting the accent right, so I just gave up. Now our families refer to what I speak as "frat bro Spanish."

Joaquín hushes me before wrapping me up in a hug. "Kids just went down," he whispers in Spanish.

"Oh, sorry," I say, hoping I didn't wake the kids. "Smells good."

A couple of hot pizza boxes and garlic knots sit on the

kitchen island. Ang and Raf have lived here for a couple of years now. He bought the historic Philly house in hopes of flipping it, but he fell in love with it—while falling in love with my sister—and they moved in right before the twins were born. The house is gorgeous and massive, but each room is like you're walking into a different story. The living room is gothic, the bathrooms are straight out of Barbie's Dream House, and their library/sunroom looks like it belongs east of the Shire.

Their kitchen? Completely yellow. Cabinetry, walls, countertops, refrigerator, stools—all of it looks like it came from some 1970s home decor magazine. Does it match anything else in the house? No, but my sister loves it, and Raf loves anything his wife loves.

"Come find me if you need a live demonstration," Raf says to Angie over his shoulder before striding into the kitchen. A grin splits his face, and he grabs a plate.

Joaquín laughs. "Ang reading something good?"

"A bear-shifter romance."

The two brothers chuckle, and then their meaning catches up to me. *Ew.* But also, I kind of want that.

My thoughts drift to Renée, and I wonder what it would be like if she let me in like that—if there was some kind of ease between us. Lately, she's all I can think about. Every time I drive by her house or look out of my living room window, I try to spot her, but no luck. She can't possibly be avoiding me, is she? I know she told me that night at Strip Tease that what we did (as glorious and life-changing as it was) could never happen again, and I was supposed to forget it ever happened. But surely those rules are not still in place now that we're neighbors.

I need to figure out a way to get her number.

"Alright Jonah," Raf says, pulling me from my head and back to reality. "Tell us where you are with your lawyer."

I swallow my pizza and set my plate down. "Right. He

approved the funds for our training facility and will write up the contract once we want to buy a place."

"That's awesome," he replies. "The rugby board gave me approval to make our real estate purchase if we got the funds, which... looks like we do."

"I actually found a few places I think will work for your team," Joaquín says, opening his laptop. He clicks and scrolls before settling on what he's looking for. With Raf and me on either shoulder, we watch on as he explains each property and what it offers. One of them is an old inner-city high school, which may be too big for what we need. Another is an old YMCA, and the last one is essentially a big blank canvas—not much more than cinder block walls and an expansive outdoor space where we could easily hold outdoor training sessions.

The Jimenez brothers riff back and forth with shop talk terms I'm not familiar with. Taxes this, building codes that. Interest rates and estimations. I'm happy with any of these choices, but I'll leave the decision to these two. With their combined experience, they're going to make the right choice. I'm just happy to see my friends so excited. The team is going to go nuts when they find out about this too.

"Alright," Raf says after a long discussion. "Our first choice is the Y, then the blank canvas, then school."

Joaquín bobs his head. "I'll reach out tomorrow to the brokers and arrange the tours." He turns his smile on me. "This is major. If we win this, it'll be our biggest project so far."

"What do you mean, *if*? You guys have it."

"C'mon Jonah." Raf sighs. "We talked about this. The team will need to get at least two other quotes and make the best choice based on finances, quality, and timing."

"But you guys are the best." I shrug. "And what do you mean by timing? We'll buy the building and start working on it."

"Um, no," Joaquín chuffs. "If we won this project, it would be at least four months before we could start renovating."

My jaw drops. "Four months? That's forever," I whine.

I've never been a patient person. I suppose it may be a symptom of the ADHD I let run wild and unmedicated. It's not that I'm against medication, I just forget about it. That's how I end up elbows-deep in a project, only to give up on it when the next best thing comes around to distract me.

Four months before renovation could even begin on this facility? Yeah, I don't like that.

"If I paid more," I say, "could you move some things around and start sooner?"

Raf levels me with a stare in that older brother way he has, even though he's not blood. "A state-of-the-art facility will not guarantee we make the Premiership. You know that, right Jonah?"

I nod.

"It will help for sure, and it will entice better players, but this will take time. That's if we are chosen to build," Raf says, then stares at his brother for a silent answer. He shrugs. "I guess we could hire a larger crew to start work on this."

Joaquín thinks about that. "The apartments in DC just finished up." He pauses a moment longer before asking, "What if I moved back here?"

"Really?" Raf and I ask together.

"Yeah," he says, his lips turning up at the corners. "I've been thinking about it, and I miss our family. Especially now that you have the kids... I want to be here to see them grow up."

Joy bursts in my heart at the thought of my best friend moving back. The drive from DC to Philly is about three hours without bad traffic, so he's always made the drive whenever he could for work and family events, but to have him back would be incredible!

My brain floods with childhood memories—riding bikes

to and from our homes, countless sleepovers and band practices, video games, and the general ruckus kids get into.

And I want that again.

Raf clearly loves this idea too, but he stares off into nothing, like he's running calculations in his brain. "What are we gonna do about our projects in DC?"

"Well, we were going to hire another project manager here in Philly, right? Why not hire one for DC instead, and I'll work here?"

Raf takes a sip of beer and thinks about it before nodding. "That works."

Content, Joaquín crosses his arms and leans back in his stool. "Mom and Mamá are going to freak out."

"I'm freaking out," I beam. "We're gettin' Agony Nectar back together!"

On my drive back home, the city slowly giving way to the country, I think about what the team's future holds, of all the possibilities in front of us. I think about my best friend moving back. But when I drive past Renée's house, I notice a single light filtering through the curtains on a second story window, and my thoughts drift.

I have a big, beautiful home waiting for me not two hundred feet away, but I want to be where she is. I want to know why her light is on. Is she grading papers about wildlife? Is she reading a bear-shifter romance?

Thoughts of her swim around me as I let my dogs outside one last time before bed. And when I lay in bed, I imagine her waiting for me, every inch of pale, freckled skin on display and her long red hair splayed out.

My hand will have to make do for tonight, but come tomorrow, I'm going to get what I want.

I always do.

Chapter 8

Good Lord, He Got a Horse

Renée

The heat coming off my laptop is no match for the little fan built into it. Even so, I've been grading assignments all morning, so I take the little inferno as my sign for a break. I dislike online summer classes—I feel disconnected from my students, and there's no way they're learning as much as they could if we were in person.

From my seat on the couch, I take off my reading glasses and rub the corners of my eyes before fixing my gaze outside. I stand for a closer look through the window, only to find a large trailer unloading a horse onto Jonah's property.

Good Lord, he got a horse.

I shake my head. Caring for a horse is the last thing I think Jonah Johanssen could handle. It's only been two years since he was my student, so I can't imagine he's changed all that much. Responsible is not a word I would use to describe him.

Infuriating, yes. That is partly my fault, though. Every semester a new group of students sits before me, and my hopes are high. I should have learned by now that most students are not there for their love of biology—they're there for the credit, and I am but a stepping stone on the way to their future.

He never took my class seriously; he never showed interest in the material. He was there to interrupt me and flash that megawatt smile.

Distracted, he was also. I don't know how many times I looked up from my presentation to find him texting, or whispering to the person next to him, or flirting with girls the second class was over.

My phone buzzes on the ottoman. My eyebrows raise when I see the name of the man who stood me up at Strip Tease. The man I was supposed to dominate and degrade for cheating on his fake wife.

> Matt: Please give me another chance, Mistress. I'll do anything. I'm so sorry. I'll never do it again.

It's the tenth time he's messaged me asking for forgiveness or providing an excuse for his absence. After his first reply, I simply told him I would punish him, but I never gave him a definite answer about whether I would ever forgive him. I enjoy holding this kind of power over him. Truthfully, I don't know if I will see him again.

The first time we were together, he showed up twenty minutes late, but he clearly enjoyed my punishment too much because then he didn't show up at all. I have exactly one night a month to free myself, wither a submissive into a boneless mess, and get my rocks off in the process—I'm not wasting it on no-shows, and Matt is learning that.

The urge to respond is tempting, though. Right as I'm about to type my first letter, I realize it's quiet in the house—too quiet. Amber's working at the country club, but where are the girls?

"Loretta? Delta?" I call, but hear nothing in response. I bust through the back door to scan our backyard, but they're not out here either. A cold sweat breaks over my skin. I run toward the side of the house, yelling for the girls, my voice cracking. From the corner of my eye, I catch two little redheads over at Jonah's petting the new horse.

I curse under my breath and storm towards them. There's two other men standing nearby, and my hackles rise even higher. My children's safety is my number one priority, and even though I've spotted them and *know* where they are, the panic doesn't lessen. They are still standing next to men I don't know.

When I'm close enough, I grab my oldest daughter's hand. "Delta," I bark, my voice harsh, and I hope no one can sense my raging fear. "You do not leave our yard without my permission. You know that."

"But Jonah got a horse, and her name is Ginger—"

"I don't care if Jonah got a Ferris wheel. You don't leave the yard without asking."

Hand wrapped around Lo's, I start back to our house, but Jonah stops me.

"It's okay, Professor Wi—I mean, Renée."

I whip around and bore lasers into him. "It is *not* okay, Mr. Johanssen. It is not okay for children to go on the property of a stranger."

Delta tugs on me. "But we—"

"I don't care that we've met him already. There are other people here I don't know, and..."

The other young man standing next to Jonah steps over, his expression curious and knowing. "Hi, Professor Wilde." He stares at me as if we know...

"Oh my goodness." I breathe, and an ease settles over me. "Dane Johanssen, what are—" Reality cuts through the fog of my panic like a lighthouse when I remember I had two Johanssen brothers in my biology classes.

Dane was a perfect student, a dream for someone like me. In his senior year, he transferred to Keystone State University to concentrate in veterinary sciences. Since biology was his major, I had him in five different courses through his master's and doctorate years. He came to class with a mission to learn everything. Hand in the air more often than not, his curiosity had no limits. He sought me after class during office hours to discuss his assignments. I set him up with an internship, for Christ's sake.

My grip loosens on the little hands in mine, and I shake my head. "I can't believe I forgot you're related to Jonah."

I really can believe it though, because Jonah and Dane are nothing alike, apart from their very obvious familial features. I expected another star student when I found out Jonah was related to Dane, but I was wrong. My hopes fell dramatically when I realized Jonah was not, in fact, taking my classes to study the magic that is natural science.

Dane leans in for a hug and, though surprised, I release my daughters' hands and accept. "It's good to see you again," he says and steps back. He smells of dog hair and barn, but there's a whisper of body wash under it all. "You live next door?" he asks.

I shrug. "Looks like it."

Dane hooks his thumb over his shoulder. "This is our dad, Neal."

The older man steps forward to shake my hand. It's firm, but gentle, and his little smile tucks a dimple under his salt and pepper beard. God, do these three look alike. "It's nice to meet you," he says. "Sorry it was under duress."

"Okay, what the heck," Jonah harrumphs. He settles his palms on his narrow hips. "They get hugs and a handshake and I don't?"

"We gave you cookies," I say flatly.

"Did you like them?" Delta asks.

His eyes become saucers. "Did I like them? Do sheep wear sweaters?"

To my horror, both of the girls giggle, Lo's volume barely registering, and I find myself disarmed at his answer. His—dare I say it—cute answer?

I dare not.

"No," Delta laughs. "They don't wear sweaters. They have

wool."

"That's what I'm saying." He gestures wildly. "They wear wool sweaters."

Delta's about to respond, but hesitates, and hauls me down to her level to whisper in my ear, "Can we make him more cookies?"

My heart cinches at her request because I want to give this to her, the experience of welcoming new people into a community, but it's Jonah we're talking about. I'm trying to wipe the man away from my mind, but the damn wiper blades are frozen to the windshield.

I will not do another relationship again—not one with feelings at least. I cannot afford to lose myself and safety. And I'm certainly not about to start something sexual with him. I don't allow myself feeling for the submissives I fuck, and I make sure they don't have them for me. Why would I risk adding a sexual component with my new neighbor? That's a recipe for disaster if either of us caught feelings.

I don't have an answer for my daughter because I don't have an answer for myself. So I simply whisper back, "We'll talk about it."

Before I'm even standing all the way up, Jonah hands over the horse reins to his dad, then crowds me. His face has lost all its levity, and the only time I've ever seen it look so serious was when he was between my—no. I'm not going there.

"I promise this won't happen again," he says, his voice a little lower, a little softer. "With the girls, that is."

"You can't exactly prevent them from coming over."

"No," he says, and pulls at the back of his neck. "But, I'll send them back. I don't want to make you uncomfortable."

A flicker of warmth ignites in my chest, but I keep my expression neutral.

"Girls, why don't you ask Dane over there what horses like to do for fun?" I ask, because I need them to clear out for a second so I can address Jonah.

They scamper five feet away, on the other side of the mare, before I nod to him swiftly. "I would appreciate that."

His serious expression evaporates when the moment stretches, and a deep smile forms on his face. "You know... you could give me your number."

"Um, no."

"Why not? What if the girls are over here playing with the ducks and I want to warn you? Or what if you forgot to close your garage door and need me to run over and close it while you're out?"

He makes infuriatingly good points. I really don't want to give him my number because that is a dangerous hill to fall down. The temptation to text him or read his would be too great, too toe-curling.

Yet, for some unspeakable reason, I find myself nodding. "Fine."

He pulls out his phone and hands it to me. He bites his full bottom lip like he's suppressing a grin, but it's not working. Even when he tries to hide it, his untamable sunshine shoots out.

I unceremoniously enter my information in the most transactional way possible and hand it back to him. "There."

"I'll text you later."

"Don't."

"Why not?"

"Is it regarding the safety of my daughters or home?"

He shrugs. "Could be."

"Those are the only two topics you may contact me about."

"What if I have a biology-related question?"

"You never had them when you were in my class, so why would you have them now?"

His hand flies to his chest as if someone shot him, but his teasing tone says otherwise. "Ouch. Let me make it up to you. Why don't you come over for drinks tonight?"

"Give me your phone. I've changed my mind. I'm deleting my number."

He shuffles out of my reach. "No," he chuckles.

I sigh and cross my arms. "My number is for emergencies only."

Jonah watches me for a beat too long, his blue eyes bright, but they darken the lower they travel. A devilish smirk creeps over his face, and for a moment, I wonder if he even knows he's smiling, or if his default expression is one meant to put people at ease (or turn them on).

He winks. "Emergencies only."

I peek once again to make sure the girls are far enough away, but still I lower my voice as far as I can. "What are you doing here?" I ask, gesturing between us. "What's your endgame?"

"Can a man not make a drink for a woman?"

"Not this woman," I deadpan, and turn away. "C'mon, girls. We're leaving. Goodbye Dane. It was nice to meet you, Neal." I say nothing to Jonah.

Delta and Lo give the mare one more pat each, then run back toward the house the only way little children can, without a care in the world and floating on a breeze.

I walk back, but before I'm out of earshot, Jonah calls out, "I'll text you."

The girls are almost to the house and can't see me, so I flip him the bird without turning around.

"Mom, can we go visit Ginger again?" Delta asks once we're back in our yard. "Did you know she's blind? Can we take her carrots?"

Loretta glues herself to my side and tugs on my shirt, her eyes the size of twin moons, and her smile vibrant. It's her way of saying please, and what I wouldn't give to hear her actually say it.

I can't deny them this. My daughters deserve their own

horses, and if I could, I'd give them stables full. So with a reluctant nod, I agree they can visit Ginger another day *with* my permission and supervision.

Squeals curl around the yard and find their way into my heart as the girls cartwheel and somersault away.

I can do this for them, I think to myself. I can resist Jonah's misguided charm for the sake of the children's happiness.

I've done far harder things.

·· • • • • • • · ·

Jonah

I can't stop the smile plastered to my face as I watch Renée walk back to her home while giving me the middle finger. She's feisty. I didn't know she could be. In class, she was always so mild-mannered and even-tempered, even when I was getting under her skin. Her voice was always calm, cool, and collected. But this side of her—and I'm not just talking about her pronounced butt I want to sink my teeth into—this firecracker side, is lighting me up.

"What was that about?" my father asks as the three of us cross the backyard, leading Ginger to her new home in my fully stocked stable.

"That would be my lady friend."

Dane rears his head back, and his eyebrows furrow. "What?"

Dad is almost as confused.

"She was my professor for a nature study class I took a couple of years ago."

"That you failed," my brother adds, unnecessarily.

I shrug and guide Ginger into the stable. "And we hooked up."

Dad looks like he's about to choke, but Dane rolls his eyes.

"No you didn't. And she's married."

"You hooked up with your professor, son?"

I run my hands along Ginger's face and scrub behind her ears. "Not when I was a student. It was right before I won the lottery... the night before, actually. And she's not married anymore."

My brother is too stunned to speak. He just looks at me, fumbling for even one word, but nothing concrete forms.

"Does she know about your winnings?" Dad asks.

"No."

"Good."

"Why can't I tell her though? She wouldn't tell anyone."

Dad shakes his head before plucking the new horse brush off the shelf and running it through Ginger's tufts. "It's not just about her telling anyone. It's about her asking for money because she knows how deep your pockets are."

"But she's seen where I live."

"It's different, Jonah. Just stick to what the attorneys said."

"That's no fun. And she's so hot, I just wanna... I don't know..." I trail off because I really don't know how to finish that sentence.

"Give her everything she's ever wanted?" Dad offers.

My brain bulb clicks on. "Yeah!"

Dad sighs. "Son, I don't think Renée is your speed."

"Oh, that's okay. Not a lot of people can run as fast as me. I wouldn't hold it against her."

"No, bud—"

Dane cuts him off. "He means she's way out of your league, much older than you, and in a different part of her life than you."

"I just wanna hook up with her. She can't be that much older than me," I say with a huff. "Plus, I don't really care that she's older. If anything, it turns me on."

Dad throws his hands up in surrender. "Okay, you don't

need to say everything that floats through your mind when I'm here."

I direct my focus to Dane. "What do you mean she's out of my league? She's hot as hell, and we'd be hot together. God." I sigh wistfully. "Can't you picture it?"

"No, and don't ask me to do that again." His lip curls up as the pause lingers between us. "She's way smarter than you, bro. Like, leagues smarter." He gestures with his hands like he's scaling a ladder. "Granted, most people are, but she's still smarter than most people."

Dad lightly shoves his middle child. "Don't say that about your brother."

My brother doesn't apologize; instead, he shrugs like, *You know I'm only telling the truth.*

He is. I am dumb. Who needs smarts when you've got pretty privilege?

Dad sighs and levels me with a trademark Dad stare that tells me he means business. "Renée is not some hot young thing who can be spontaneous with you—"

"I'm not that spontaneous."

Dane throws a blanket he was folding over a railing before he turns to me. "You drove to Orlando six months ago after watching a viral video about a restaurant that makes elote."

That elote was fire.

But he has a point, so I shut my mouth.

"Son, she's a single mother. Her priorities are very different from yours."

I scoff and rub Ginger's velvety nose that's so darn soft I could melt. I've always been able to get what I want. Heck, I've always been lucky enough to fall right into things I didn't ask for, but made my life easier. Good looks and charm have given me everything, so if I want Renée Wilde, it's only a matter of time before I have her.

Her feistiness from earlier will only make our inevitable

bedroom tangle that much sweeter. She can't run away from this for long. I'm too fast, and she's too mouth-watering.

I smile when the best idea ever springs forth. "I bet she'll come with me to Isaiah's wedding next month if I ask her."

Dad turns to Dane. "Did he hear anything I just said?"

My brother's lips flatten. "Unlikely."

"So you take her to the wedding," Dad says. "Then what?"

"I don't know."

"Exactly. See, that's something you've gotta sort out. She doesn't seem like the type who's just in it for kicks when it comes to weddings."

Dad's words settle in while I detangle Ginger's mane. He might have a point. I haven't had any serious relationships since college because I was always a stepping stone before my exes found their better match. Like I was a detour on their way to their destination.

I've pretty much always been Good Time Jonah. Partly because I do genuinely enjoy a good time (who doesn't?), but mostly, if I'm honest, it's because I don't want to get hurt again. Breakups are brutal. Like when your college girlfriend breaks up with you the day before finals, moves out, and takes the dog you bought together two months earlier!

It's not that I want to stay single forever—I just figured the right person would fall into my life one day. Like—boom—here's your wife. She's gorgeous and thinks you're funny. That's how most good things happen to me.

But Renée's not exactly falling into me the way I thought The One would. If anything, she tries to leave as soon as possible when we're together. Which is weird because, did she not feel our connection that night at Strip Tease? We were so in sync, our bodies like a duet. Or magnets. I don't know; I'm not good with metaphors.

I've hooked up with enough women in my life to know

one-night stands are never *that* good. What we shared was more memorable than any try I've scored, and more beautiful than any place I've been, and I've been to France... or maybe it was Greece? Either way, there was ice cream and pretty ocean views, so like, really romantic.

Perhaps Dad is right, and she's not spontaneous. But what could be spontaneous about attending a wedding with me? She'll have a few weeks to prepare, and I can show her the side of me that dances with my clothes on. Well, clothes that *stay* on. Eh, who am I kidding—if I can get her to that wedding, I'll charm our clothes off and we'll just have to fall into my bed to stay warm for the night.

I am but a simple man with simple needs.

Chapter 9
Only One Garden Bed
Jonah

After Renée left yesterday, Dane showed me how to take care of and ride Ginger. I had this image of dashing through a field of wheat with her, climbing over rolling hills at breakneck speeds, throwing my hands up in the air. But apparently, those days are in the old girl's past. She prefers a simple life. Long walks and maybe, if she's feeling frisky, a trot or two. That's probably for the best anyway, because riding a horse is nerve-wracking.

Ginger and I wind through my property with a muddy Rugger beside us while Yogi stays back with his ducks by the pond. I couldn't even get the boys to come inside with me last night. They usually sleep in my bed, but with Ginger here, they both refused to come inside. Instead they slept in the barn with their goats, ducks, and new horse.

I took pictures when I found them this morning, all cuddled up. So cute.

As we make our way back toward the barn, I peek over at Renée's house. That house can't be over eleven hundred square feet, and I'm not entirely sure it has a basement. Her yard is small too, and I notice the itty-bitty garden in her backyard.

That's a shame. I know she loves plants. She filled her classroom, biology lab, and even her office with plants and displayed dead bugs with precision and elegance. There were owls and birds and a bobcat scattered throughout, and I was never sure if they were taxidermied or fake.

Maybe I could give her some space over here for a sizable garden. I'm certainly not using most of my property, and there's a great big open area between our houses she could have. This area must have been a garden at one point because there's an empty gardening shed not ten yards away. There's a slight hill, but we could work around that.

Ginger and I stray dangerously close to her house when she pulls her old Subaru into the driveway. A smile stretches across my face when I catch Delta in the backseat with her hands plastered to the window. I can hear her squealing from all the way over here. I'm not sure if she's howling for me, the horse, or the dog, but I enjoy being mixed into consideration.

Renée catches my eye and rolls hers before parking.

"Mommy, can we pet the animals?" Delta chirps as soon as her feet hit the ground.

"Yes, but not Jonah."

Lo catches up with her sister as I dismount. "Well, howdy girls!"

Rugger takes a seat and accepts his fate before Delta's hands are all over him. "Where's your cowboy hat?" she asks.

"I don't have one."

"But you were riding a horse. You need a cowboy hat if you're riding a horse."

Renée saunters toward us and picks Lo up so she can reach more than just Ginger's legs.

"I suppose I should get a cowboy hat then," I say. "What do you think, Professor Wilde?"

She sighs. "Just call me Renée."

My heart skitters at the gigantic door she's flung open for me. *I can call her by her first name? To her face?!*

I fight back the strongest grin with valiant effort. "Would you like to see me in a cowboy hat, Renée?"

There is no reply, just a flat look.

That's not a no.

Lo silently gestures to be lifted into the saddle, and her mother asks, "Can she sit up here?"

"Of course! She won't go anywhere."

As the youngest Wilde fixes herself atop my horse, a wave of happiness crashes into me. This is the first time Renée hasn't fled my presence, so I take it as a sign to shoot my shot.

I clear my throat and nod toward her backyard. "I noticed your garden over there. It's nice."

"It's small," she sighs, stroking Ginger's rump without a look back to her yard.

"But it's really nice."

She flashes me a look of indignation as her only reply.

"Would you like a bigger garden?"

She lifts a nonchalant shoulder. "Of course."

"I could give you this space right here," I gesture around us.

She furrows her red eyebrows. "This is your property."

"I'm not using it. You could plant whatever you want here."

A long pause stretches out as she studies me. "Why are you offering this?"

"Cuz I think it would make you happy. Would it?"

"Jonah," she sighs. "This is too much."

"But would it make you happy?"

Her hand stills on Ginger as she takes a moment to respond. "Yes."

"Then it's yours. How many garden beds do you want?"

"No, no, no. You don't need to create garden beds. I can just work with the land."

I point to her backyard. "But you have a raised garden. Is that what you'd prefer?"

"Yes, but—"

"Consider it done. I'll take care of installing them, and

you'll keep everything you grow. You'll have access to them and the gardening shed whenever you want—they're yours. How many beds do you want?"

Blush creeps over her neck and spreads across her face, and I kind of love how it doesn't stay confined to her cheeks. Her entire head and neck turn red, and it's the cutest thing I've ever seen. Renée Wilde has always been all woman to me—sophisticated, and sure of herself. But watching her become speechless and blush like a little girl has me itching to see more of it.

All of it.

"Just one."

I shake my head. "That's not enough. Sky's the limit."

"Mom, can we plant sunflowers?" Delta asks as she rubs my dog's hairy belly.

"I love sunflowers," I reply.

"Fine," Renée concedes. "Four beds. I can pay—"

"Oh, no. You're absolutely not paying."

"Jonah..."

"Fine. You can pay me in baked goods. I like cookies and cupcakes. Ooh, I also like Jell-O and pie."

"We can do that!" Delta beams.

I point at her and give her a serious look. "You have pretty high standards to live up to, miss. Those no-bake cookies were incredible. I expect nothing but the best."

"We are awesome bakers!"

"It's settled then."

"It is not," Renée pushes.

"Fine." I shrug dramatically. "I guess... you could come with me as my date to my brother's wedding three weeks from Saturday."

Her eyes roll the same way they did when I was her student. "There it is."

"I'm only kinda joking. This garden has nothing to do with me actually wanting you to be my wedding date. The garden has absolutely no strings attached."

"You promise?"

"Cross my heart and hope to die."

"Why on earth would you want to take me to a wedding?"

"Because I like you."

"Take someone younger, someone your own age."

"No."

She lets out an exasperated huff. How do I sweeten this for her? I've gotta lock her in.

"There will be great music, dancing, a plated dinner, and champagne. Oh, by the way, my brother is marrying two people. I should probably mention that."

Her eyebrows raise up because, yeah, I get it. How often do you get to attend the wedding of a throuple?

She crosses her arms. "And it's local?"

"Yes!" I suddenly remember where the wedding will be and know this will be the thing that will lock her in. "You're going to love the venue. It's at the Fairmount Park Horticulture Center."

Her eyes go wide. "I've never been there for a wedding. Oh, it's so beautiful," she says, her voice a mix of wistfulness and hesitation.

"So you'll come with me?"

"If you can promise me there will be nothing more *after* the reception," she breathes, and I catch her meaning. "We will leave the venue and come right back to our respective homes."

I place my hand over my heart. "I wouldn't dream of it," I lie.

She looks like she barely believes me, but when she sighs, I know I've got her. "Fine."

I take her reluctant, defeated acceptance and bathe in it. Mark my word: I'm gonna wear her down to her panties soon enough.

She plucks her phone from her purse. "When is it?"

"Oh, um… I don't remember. I'll text you about it."

"You'll tell me right now."

I wanted to have an excuse to text her, but her eyes tell me to obey and—*whoa Nelly*—do I want to. Pulling my phone from my pocket, I nod. "Yes, ma'am. Wedding is at 3:00 p.m."

After taking a few moments to type, she tucks her phone back in her purse. "I'll see you then," she says curtly. "C'mon, girls." She lifts Lo from the saddle, and Rugger gets up from his lounging position to make sure Lo is safely put down. "We have to put the groceries away."

"Bye, Jonah!" Delta hollers, before running back to their car and opening the hatch.

"Bye!"

Lo takes her mom's hand and waves to me with the other as they walk away, too.

Rugger rubs his head against my thigh like some kind of post-game handshake, and I lift all one hundred eighty pounds of him into my arms. "We got her!" I whisper. "We got her, boy! C'mon, let's go." He leaps from my arms and runs toward the barn with Ginger and me trailing behind him.

Time to call a landscaper, because I'm about to have the most beautiful garden in the state of Pennsylvania.

Chapter 10
Planting Seeds

Renée

H e had ten garden beds installed. Big ones. I stood there stunned, watching the landscaping crew tear out everything that used to be there. Then, one by one, they built ten large raised beds in a neat five-by-two grid. Despite being set into a hill, every single bed was perfectly level.

Oh, but it didn't stop there. The next morning, the crew arrived again and put up a beautiful fence around the entire garden—tall enough to keep the deer out. Then came the dump truck, rumbling up the drive, and it unloaded a mountain of pea gravel. They spread it carefully between the beds, raked it smooth until it looked like something out of a magazine.

The whole thing looks like Martha Stewart herself designed it.

I'll pretend I'm mad about the over-the-topness of it all when he's around, but secretly I'm glowing on the inside. A garden like this has always been a dream of mine. I had one about half this size when I was first married, living in Nashville. But with studying for my master's and doctoral degrees, I didn't have the time to really take care of it. When we moved out here, a little slice of me fell away.

The girls and I went to the garden center to pick out all the seeds we wanted. It's too late in the season to plant everything we wanted, but a late summer/early fall harvest should turn out plentiful with pumpkins, butternut squash, kale, beets, cabbage, and Brussels sprouts. But that's just six of the beds. The other four are going to be a mix of daylilies, foxglove, cosmos, zinnias, dahlias, and of course, sunflowers (because my daughters love them, not because Jonah does).

The three of us are preparing the garden, Delta asking me a million questions, and Loretta silently by my side, waiting for the next direction, when Jonah's SUV rolls down the street behind us, well under the speed limit.

A couple of minutes later, his pair of Great Pyrenees are bound for us and bark to be let inside the fence line. God, they're adorable. I want to rub my face in their fur.

Jonah catches up with them. He's wearing rugby shorts, sandals, and a cut-off T-shirt that exposes his tattooed, muscular arms and the sides of his defined torso. I quickly tamp down the horny little gremlin inside of me who is begging me to remember what his arms looked like hooked around my legs and his face between my thighs.

"Looks like you've put in a lot of work already," he says, but makes no move to open the fence gate, his hands firmly placed on his hips.

"We planted sunflowers," Delta replies, before running to open the gate.

When it's opened, he hesitates and looks to me for approval—which is both comforting that he's respecting my space, but also infuriating because it turns me on when a man waits for what he wants.

Even his dogs wait there until I give him the okay. Each of the girls hugs a dog as Jonah strides in, inspecting our progress with a smile. "Can I help with anything?" he asks.

"That's okay; you don't have to. You probably wanna shower and rest up."

"I'd like to help if you don't mind. If you can handle how much I smell," he chuckles.

"We've been elbow-deep in compost today, so I think we

can handle your body odor."

That makes him grin. "What do you need?"

"We're just finishing up with beets right here. Hand me that little plastic container." I outstretch my hand, and he passes the tiny, jagged beet seeds to me. "Now take that spade and dig half-inch holes, each hole two inches apart."

"Yes, ma'am," he says, but it's not in a flirtatious way. It's studious, and it burns me with unexpected pleasure.

The girls are far from interested in helping me now that the dogs are here, and they're rolling around on the gravel with them without a care in the world.

There's not much left to do other than wait for each hole to be scooped and plant a single seed in each, which gives me time to sit on the wide edge of the garden bed and watch as Jonah carefully digs each half-inch hole. To be quite frank, I've never seen him apply so much focus to anything.

I could take another spade and dig along with him, but after a long day of gardening, sitting here and watching a pretty boy do my work feels luxurious.

He digs a hole a little too deep, but fills in back in at the right depth. "Sorry," he says.

Fuck, he's cute. I want to punish him for it.

He's so concentrated on his task that it gives me space to study his body. His golden hair is tied back in a bun, flyaways framing his head. His jawline is strong and defined, giving way to a pronounced Adam's apple. He has the most random assortment of tattoos covering his arms and peeking along his ribs—all different styles. Some colored, some not. Animal from *The Muppets* sits behind a drum set along his left-side flank.

Jonah is kneeling on a pad in front of the raised garden bed, and my gaze skates over his thighs, which are very exposed in his small black rugby shorts. Dark blond hair dusts down to his ankles. There's a crest inked on this right thigh with the words *Philadelphia Men's Rugby Team* in a banner at the bottom.

"You still play rugby," I say.

"I do," he replies, still focused on his task. But something triggers him, and he looks up at me. "You knew I played in college?"

I drop a seed into a hole and cover it up. "You pretty much only wore Keystone State rugby apparel. And your brother had mentioned a time or two that you played together."

"You ever see one of our games?"

"No." Though suddenly I'd love to see him running around in those hot little shorts. "Is post-college rugby much different?"

"Kinda." He lifts his shoulder once and resumes his careful digging. "Less singing, more seriousness. But it's still fun. Always is."

"Singing?"

"Yeah, ruggers have a bunch of drinking songs. And team songs. It's a thing. That's how Yogi got his name. It's based on a rugby song about Yogi Bear."

I plant another seed and hum. "And the other dog?"

"That's Rugger."

"They're cute. Good with kids, too."

"They've been around my family since they were pups. They love babies." He smiles. "And ducks, and goats, and horses, apparently."

I glance over at Loretta, who is inspecting one of the dog's ears like she's playing doctor, and my heart warms.

Jonah adjusts his kneepad further down the garden bed to reach fresh territory. "But the team is definitely more serious. I play Division 1, but we're trying to level up to the Premiership League. That's like, the level between where we are currently and profesh."

"What do you have to do to qualify for the next level?"

"Score a lot of points. Act like we want it."

"And do you want it?" I ask, and cover another seed.

"Honestly, I don't really care what level I play at. But my brothers and teammates really want it, so I'm gonna do everything I can to get us there."

That's... a little surprising. Jonah always seemed like the kind of person who thought little outside of his own bubble, if at all.

"We just made an offer on a building we're turning into a training facility. I'm really excited about it. And we're gonna work with community organizers to see what we can offer to the neighborhood folks."

"Like what?"

"Like, I don't know. Cleaning up their yards or streets for free, or letting people use the facility for events. Something like that. We haven't figured it out yet."

"That's very generous of your team."

He shrugs, and even under that bit of a sunburn, a blush creeps to the surface. "So, um," he starts, "what all have you planted?"

"Mostly vegetables and flowers that will bloom in late summer."

"What are we planting now?"

"Beets."

"I've never had a beet."

A smile grows fat and lazy across my face. "You'll have to try one when they're harvested."

My pulse picks up when his big blue eyes find mine, and I'm suddenly frozen. He looks so good, so fuckable on his knees, waiting for me.

"Promise?" he asks quietly, and there's nothing sinister or bratty about what he says. In fact, it feels filled with meaning—about our history and the future.

There can't be a future between us, though. We're in different parts of our lives. He's young and carefree and has his whole life to screw up. I'm a thirty-eight-year-old mother of two with baggage so heavy and dark no one would ever touch it. I certainly don't.

And I don't want to lead him on. "I make no promises," I say.

He side-eyes me, and the corner of his mouth turns up. "Alright, keep your secrets."

A comfortable silence settles between us before I ask, "You never told me what the dress code is for this wedding. I need to buy a dress." I don't reveal that no matter what the dress code is, I'd have to buy a new one because none of my dresses fit anymore. My weight has fluctuated in the last year, and I'm rediscovering my body in this unfamiliar size.

"I don't know," he offers. "Just wear what you'd normally wear to a wedding."

My eyes find the back of my skull. "Jonah, I've been to weddings in a forest wearing hiking boots. I need to prepare properly. Do you have a wedding invitation you can show me?"

"Oh, yeah." He sets down the spade and pulls his phone from beneath his compression shorts. "We cordially invite you... blah blah blah... black tie."

I gasp. "Black tie?"

"That's the fancy one, right?"

I huff a humorless laugh. "Yes."

And just like that, I'm painfully aware of my bank account and its sad little balance. A black-tie dress would wipe me out. There's still time to back out, right? If I rescind my offer to be his date, he might be disappointed, but—

A gentle hand lands on my knee. "Renée?"

I blink back to reality. He's watching me, concern written across his face. "You okay? You kinda zoned out there."

I lift his hand off my knee. "I'm fine. You know what, Jonah, I don't think—"

He cuts me off. "Would it be okay if I bought your dress?"

"No."

"Why not? I'd love to. I've always wanted to do that."

"You have?"

He nods, earnest as ever. "I always wanted to ask a girl out, buy her an entire outfit for the occasion, and set up a hair appointment for her too."

I don't miss his choice of words—*girl*, not *woman*. It's a painful reminder: he probably hasn't dated many grown women. College girls, sure. Yes, they're technically women, but they're still budding into womanhood at that point.

But there's something undeniably sweet—and yes, a little intoxicating—in the dreamy, boyish way he offers.

Oh God. How does he keep persuading me?

"Why would you do that?"

He shrugs. "I don't know. I guess it would make me feel good. If I knew you were pampered and looked and felt incredible, I would feel like the luckiest man in the world."

And just like that, it clicks.

He's a service sub.

I hate that Amber's right. He is *exactly* my type, and he'd perfectly match my freak. Why did he have to move in next door? This is bullshit.

"Please?" he adds, softly now. And *God*, I have to bite my tongue.

I won't date him, and we're not hooking up, so there's no future here. But that doesn't mean I can't have a little fun toying with him... right?

I drop a few more beet seeds into the soil but don't cover them. "Finish planting these, and if you do a good job, I'll let you buy me a dress."

He smirks. "Oh, you'll *let* me?"

I arch an eyebrow, and he tracks my gaze to the holes I just dropped the seeds into, and he catches my meaning. Jonah efficiently covers them in the same manner I did, before continuing the row.

"You're doing great," I murmur, and a dark little thrill rushes through me.

He works with quiet focus, every hole exactly two inches apart, a half inch deep by my eye. I drop in the seeds, and he seals them with care, grinning like digging in the dirt for me is the best thing he's done all week.

When he finishes, he stands without a single knee crack and brushes off his hands. "How'd I do?" he asks, before spotting a watering can. "I should water them, right?"

I nod, but don't move. "Just a little drink over each."

With more focus than anyone has ever needed to water a garden, he showers each seedling for a second or two until the can runs dry, and refills. When he's finished, he surveys his work like a Midwestern dad admiring a perfectly mowed lawn—hands on hips, scanning for last-minute flaws. But there are none.

"You did very well, Jonah. Thank you."

Pride puffs out his chest. "So, I can take you shopping?"

"A deal's a deal."

Chapter 11
New Dress

Renée

I knew Jonah wanted to purchase my entire outfit, but I didn't know that he wanted to take part in today's shopping activities. So color me surprised when he showed up on my doorstep and offered to drive us. I said no, so he hopped in my car and I drove.

I figured he'd transfer funds electronically to me, not be the one who swipes the damn card.

I also thought we'd just go to the King of Prussia Mall and find something in one of the high-end department stores, but nope. Jonah has directed me to a store in Conshohoken that I've never heard of.

As soon as we step out of my car and face the building, I know why. This is a dress boutique. The only time I've ever purchased a dress from a store this sleek and sophisticated was when I bought my wedding dress.

I'm suddenly painfully aware that I am no longer a size six. After babies, after Greg, after... everything, I've settled into a size twelve. And when you're short like me, a size twelve fits a lot differently than it does an average-size woman.

I'm wracking up the timing constraints for alterations versus the wedding deadline when Jonah places one hand on my shoulders and opens the glass door with the other hand. "Come on," he beams, completely unaware of the stress I'm already under. I'm not even paying for this, but I know this will not work out. Boutiques like this might—*might*—go as high as a size twelve. Even if I find a dress, will I even like it, or will I settle because it's the only option? What if they're rude to me? What if we're turned away because they don't have my size? What if there isn't enough time to alter the dress?

"Welcome." A bright smile greets us. A middle-aged white woman with a brunette ponytail, dressed head to toe in black and wearing bright red, wide-brimmed glasses. "You must be Renée and Jonah."

He extends his hand without pause. "Yes, we are."

I shake her hand on autopilot. "Hi."

"My name is Paula, and I'll be assisting you today. May I bring you something to drink? We have sparkling water, champagne, wine, soft drinks of any kind..." She trails off and waits for us to answer.

I can already tell this place charges a lot.

I used to have money. I *came* from money. But when our financial situation took a nose-dive and Greg moved us here, my priorities had to change. I adapted.

If I'm going to be out of here in ten minutes because they have nothing that will work for me, then you better believe I'm taking some bubbly as a consolation prize.

"Champagne, please," I say cooly, because I will not show fear.

"Make it two," Jonah nods.

Paula narrows her eyes at Jonah. "Would you mind showing me your ID?"

I fight back a snort of laughter, but he seems unfazed as he whips it out of his wallet and shows her that he is just barely old enough, in fact, to legally drink.

I snatch the ID from him before he tucks it away, and I look for myself. *God help me, he's twenty-five years old.*

"I'm a Taurus," he says with a wink.

Another staff member comes along with two flutes of champagne (how did they get here so fast?). When the brim of the glass touches my bottom lip, I survey the space.

There are large canvases displayed with abstract, but distinctly round, womanly figures. And when I take in the mannequins, they're all... large. Larger than me, even.

"Now tell me about the event," Paula says, flicking her fingers like she's digging for gossip with a friend. "What are we going for?"

Too struck by what I see to actually register what she says, I blink in shock. "Excuse me, Paula, was it?"

She offers a courteous smile and nods.

I cuff a hand around Jonah's arm and lead him. "Can we have a moment?"

"Oh, sure. I'll just be right over there by the register when you're ready."

When she's far enough out of earshot, I turn on him. "Why are we here?"

A befuddled look paints his face. "Because... I'm buying you a dress."

"No, I get that. Why here, specifically?" I gesture around us.

He shrugs, the picture of cluelessness. "My sister Angie recommended it."

I can't stop my face from scrunching up. "You told her about me?"

"Well, yeah. She would have found out eventually. She has a way of knowing everyone's business."

"And you told her you were buying me a dress?"

He nods. "And then she asked what size you were, and I didn't know, so I just said you were thick." His eyes widen with delight when he says that last word. "My sister is a big girl, too. She's a lot taller than you, though. She recommended this place; I don't know."

His expression sours. "Did I do something wrong? I'm so sorry. Whatever it is. We can go somewhere else."

"No," I say quickly, and place my hand on his arm again (to soothe him, *not* because he's nothing but firm, warm muscle underneath). "This is—I just—" I huff before collecting my words and taking a deep breath. "I didn't know stores like this existed. Ones that cater to larger bodies."

"But you're really short."

I roll my eyes, but the corner of my lip curls up. "We will see what their alterations crew can do."

Hope washes over me, and as it recedes, my inner Dominant is exposed. So with a sly grin and my fingers still on his bicep, I erase his worry when I ask, "Is there a budget I should be mindful of?"

His pupils seem to dilate, and his effervescent smile returns. "No, ma'am."

I should feel guilty, but this guy has an eight-million-dollar estate. A couple thousand dollars will not hurt him.

"Good," I say, and bat my eyelashes for good measure. "Let's find a dress."

Paula notes the styles I gravitate towards and picks a few for me as we go. She explains that, from cocktail hour to the Oscars, they can dress anyone from a size ten to a thirty. I'm almost misty-eyed at that. I haven't even tried on the dresses yet, and I'm blinking back the emotion at this whole situation.

I haven't been spoiled like this since I was first married, and it's grating to think about. I don't need or desire expensive things. My forty-dollar handbags, knock-off Yankee candles, and ten-year-old SUV are fine with me.

My daughters are fed, loved, and happy. That's all I need.

But I didn't realize until just now how much this extravagant little excursion means. I was unknowingly starved for just a little something extra—a little something unnecessary. I'm hit with the sudden urge to walk out of this store with a dozen bags in my arms like Julia Roberts in *Pretty Woman*. Except now that I think about it, I'd like Jonah behind me, carrying my bags.

A tingling sensation races up my spine at the thought. *Are my nipples hard?*

After Paula gathers several options, she leads us to a lounge area centered between two dressing rooms. We take a seat on a circular, dusty rose velvet couch while Paula gathers more items.

Someone refills our champagne within seconds. I sit back and enjoy my mood.

Jonah can't sit still though. "Do you like what you've picked out so far?"

I arch one eyebrow and take a sip before answering. "Yes."

"Can I, um…" He wipes his palms down his jeans. "Can I pick some?"

"You wanna shop for me?" I ask, bemused.

He nods vigorously.

"Knock yourself out."

He pulls gown after gown, bringing each one back to me to gauge my approval. At the slightest look of displeasure, he tosses the dresses onto the nearest rack like they offend him far more than they offend me. I have to school my features before he catches me… I don't know… enjoying myself around him? How is that even possible? I'm repulsed at the thought.

I did not expect Jonah to be so involved in today's purchase. Now that he is, I see the truth in his desire. He really does want to outfit a date. This is *actually* bringing him happiness.

If you had told me two years ago that my student, Jonah Johanssen, would take me shopping with his own money, I wouldn't have believed you. Not even after that night at the strip club. No part of me would have believed you until this very hour.

Paula graciously accepts Jonah's picks, and before I know it, she's tying me up in a strapless evening gown. Silky smooth and midnight black, it's cool to the touch and structured in the bodice.

"There's also a high slit," Paula says with a little mischief in her tone. She pulls the skirt slightly to reveal my pale leg, almost completely exposed. "If it's too much, we can lower the slit in alterations," she says. "Shall we show him?"

I'm lost at the sight of my cleavage. Unless I'm at the beach or in my Domme outfits, I never show this much. I don't think I've ever shown this much of my chest in public before.

Paula guides me out, sweeping away the fabric of the too-long skirt so I can walk easily. Jonah's eyes pop out of their sockets and lock in the second he sees my breasts.

I'm helped onto the round step surrounded by mirrors. "Does he need a towel for the drool?" Paula murmurs from behind me.

He's up off the couch, striding toward me to get a closer look.

He beams. "I love this one," he says. "You should get this one."

I arch an eyebrow. "I thought it was my choice."

"Of course, it is! I just mean, do you like it?"

"I do," I say with a sigh, as I admire the way the silk glides under my palms. I bunch up the skirt in my hands and spin on my heel before stepping down and leaving him in my wake. "But I think it's too revealing for a wedding."

"I disagree," he says while skipping next to us. "I think this is *exactly* what you should wear to a wedding with me."

"Sit down and wait for me."

He stops. Nods. Sits.

There's a curse on the tip of my tongue because the urge to call him a good boy is so overwhelming I could choke on it.

Paula puts me in six more dresses, each of them beautiful in their own way, but just not right. Jonah is, unsurprisingly, gaga over each one. The last one I try on has a double-high slit and a V cut so low it almost reaches my belly button.

It's red and flowy, and Paula confirms it was a Jonah pick he snuck in without my approval. Wholly inappropriate for a wedding. The satisfaction of not showing him is too great, so I snap a picture inside the fitting room for myself. I look hot as sin, and I want to memorialize this moment.

When I step out onto the platform and show him the eighth gown, deep indigo and velvet with long, tight sleeves, I'm sweating in the way I always do when trying on clothes for more than ten minutes. As pretty as this dress is, it doesn't fit right, and I can't envision myself in it even with heavy alterations. What I see before me is blotchy skin underneath a face full of freckles. Sweat trickles down my neck and forehead as I throw up my mane in a hair tie I had around my wrist.

"Are you okay?" Jonah asks. "You don't look like you like this one."

I finish tying the bun at the top of my head before I sigh. "I'm just warm."

Somehow the boy materializes a bottle of water, and I'm downing the ice-cold refreshment in a few gulps.

"Is there a fan we could set up?" he asks Paula.

Today, for the first time, Paula looks unsure as she thinks. Before she can even say um, Jonah's racing for the register and asking the staff.

Within a minute, he's carrying a standup fan that has clearly seen better days. "They found this in the storage room," he smiles brightly.

"Here," Paula gestures. "Let's get you out of this dress and cool down in the fitting room."

I hike the skirt up all the way to my knees so my legs can breathe, and sigh. "Thank you," I say to both of them, lingering a little extra on Jonah.

Paula plugs the fan in, and I pray the relic turns on. She pushes a button, and it whirs to life in the spacious room. I take off the dress faster than on prom night, and the breeze washes over me, giving sweet relief.

Paula apologizes for the warmth of the room, but I reassure her it's fine; sweating is just something I expect in fitting rooms.

She busies herself with hanging the dress and organizing the others while my body temperature returns to normal and the sweat evaporates. I check my underarms and find they're dry as a bone thanks to my extra-strength deodorant, and I chuckle to myself.

I shouldn't be so happy over a fan. It's just a fan. It's just a little relief in a situation I could have easily ignored. But it's not about the relief; it's about the act itself. I was hot, and Jonah just... fixed it.

I didn't have to ask him—he saw I was uncomfortable, and he... *Why are there butterflies in my belly?*

With skin back to a more pleasant level of moisture, Paula helps me into a variation of the first dress. Same high slit, silky black fabric, and structured bodice, and I stop breathing. I am genuinely stunned, not because the dress cinches me too tight. Instead of my boobs being on full display like a Vegas headliner, they're tastefully framed, the fabric sweeping over one shoulder in a way that feels almost... regal. I've always avoided one-shoulder dresses—my tits are famously asymmetrical and usually need more targeted support. But this dress? The dress holds them perfectly, in harmony, as if it were made just for me.

"Renée," Paula drawls with a smile and fluffs my skirt. "This is..."

"Perfect." I finish. "How much is this?"

"He told me I couldn't tell you."

My eyes meet the back of my head.

She smiles. "Let's show him."

When I step out, I can't help but match Jonah's wide grin. He covers his mouth and bites his knuckles when I step onto the platform. "Come on," he exclaims. "This has to be the one, right? Oh my God, I can't even look at you, you're too pretty."

My dumb heart races like a schoolgirl who holds a valentine and a pink carnation from her secret crush she's been writing about in her diary.

How dare he do this to me?

But I do feel pretty. With sweaty, coiled strands of hair springing around my neck, I feel so damn pretty.

"I love it."

Marveling, Jonah stands beside me, and even though I'm standing six inches up, he still has at least another six inches on me. "I love it too," he says. "But if you can't decide which one, we can get them all."

A surprising little giggle bursts from me. "You are not buying me more than one dress."

"Please?" he begs.

"No," I say in a firm but well-meaning tone.

"Is this the one?" Paula asks.

"Yes, I think it is. It just depends on whether they can alter it fast enough. I need it by next Friday."

Paula grimaces. "Oh, alterations usually take a month, but we can always add a rush charge—"

"Do that," Jonah says, cutting her off. "Whatever it costs, as long as she has the dress by next Friday."

Within twenty minutes, I'm measured, and the dress is marked and pinned until the in-house tailor and I are both satisfied with the new length and adjustments. By the time I'm done with them, Jonah is waiting for me at the front of the store with a grin.

"Are we all paid up?"

"It's all taken care of," he says. He holds the door open for me. "Now let's go get you some new shoes and a lingerie set."

"Don't you fucking dare."

He gasps. "Professor Wilde, that's a bad word."

"You're not buying me lingerie. We agreed on a dress and my hair."

"We agreed on an outfit," he argues.

"What's the point of buying me lingerie if you're never going to see it?"

He taps his temple and narrows his eyes at me. "I'll know you're wearing it under that dress."

"I'd sooner burn it."

"Yeah, but you'd be thinking about me when you watch it go up in flames."

"And wish you were roasting over said flames."

He flashes a devilish smile. "Kinky."

Chapter 12

Isaiah's Wedding

Jonah

"**D**amn, I look good," I say, inspecting every inch of myself in the mirror. I once heard a fitted suit, or tuxedo in this case, does to a man what lingerie does to a woman, and they were right. I'd fuck me.

Gosh, I have to stop saying swear words even in my head. I'm always being chastised for swearing in front of my niece and nephews. I have to get better about that.

But maybe I can make an exception because I look fine as hell. Hair pulled back into a respectable bun, clean-shaven, and… dog hair on the back of my pants. Shoot.

I search for the sticky roller, which has to be around here somewhere. God, I wish everything was in a specified place. It's been more than a month since I moved in, and I still haven't unpacked everything. There are entire rooms in my home that are still empty. There are boxes that I rifle through every morning for socks and T-shirts. But at least I have a bed frame and a nightstand.

The nightstand!

I locate the sticky roller in the top drawer, where I also find an empty and expired bottle of ADHD medication and a box of condoms. I remove the offending white dog hair from my pants as I consider using those condoms tonight.

So what if Renée told me nothing would happen between us? I don't believe it for a second. I think she's going to see me in this tuxedo, standing tall with my brothers, and she's going to experience Good Time Jonah for the first time.

She already knows what I'm capable of if she just lifts her skirt for me; all I have to do now is show her my charming, devilishly handsome, and irresistibly touchable side.

I look like I could play in the next 007 movie!

I wonder how much an Aston Martin DB5 costs...

I toss the sticky roller back in the drawer and fluff the pillows on my freshly washed and made bed. I rarely make my bed, but I make it look like I have my life together when there's a chance my very attractive older professor will be in it later.

In the center of my bed is a black and gold-trimmed box I can't help but peek into one last time. It's the lingerie set Renée told me not to buy her. I may have called up Paula at the boutique and asked for Renée's exact measurements so I could get the right size. It goes against her express wishes, so the least I could do is make sure the skimpy little garments she's going to ride me in fit perfectly.

When the driver I hired sends me a text that he's twenty minutes away, a surge of excitement courses through me like white water rapids. It's happening. My brother is about to get married, and I'm taking the sexiest woman as my date to his wedding.

I'm striding across my yard on cloud nine, thinking about Renée wearing the dress I bought her, imagining what her hair will look like, what she'll smell like, and if she'll like my cologne.

When I step onto her front porch, I realize I've never seen inside her home and I'm giddy in anticipation. With a deep breath, I knock and step back before straightening my jacket and bow tie.

When there's no answer after thirty seconds, I knock again. Before I knock a third time, Renée answers wearing... a robe. Her shiny red hair cascades over one shoulder in large, classic Hollywood curls. I've never seen her wear makeup quite like this. She painted her pouty, inviting lips the perfect shade of red, and I suddenly want to see evidence of that on my white shirt collar. Her freckles are still on display, but her eyes are sucking me in like a black hole. She clearly had a successful trip to the salon appointment I made for her earlier. Even in a bathrobe, she's a vision.

A tantalizing idea pops up, and I smile. "Did you need some help getting dressed?"

Barefoot, she abruptly steps onto the porch and shuts the door behind her. "Jonah, I'm really sorry, but I can't go tonight."

Her words hit me like a cold bucket of water over the head. "Why not? What's wrong?"

"Delta got really sick today," she sighs. "She's been throwing up and has a fever. My sister was supposed to watch them, but she just started throwing up herself ten minutes ago."

My mind reels with ways to fix this, but I come up with nothing. Everyone I know is going to be at this wedding, and I've been imagining this evening with her since she reluctantly agreed to be my date. This was my big shot with her. This was the moment I was going to prove to my dad and Dane that I could pull her. That our age gap and differences in our life stages didn't matter. I was going to twirl this woman on the dance floor and make her forget about the outside world for a while.

"I'm so sorry, Jonah, but I can't go." She sighs. "I don't have anyone else to watch the girls, not this last-minute. In fact, you should probably take a step back because I'm sure I've caught whatever they have."

I have to look away from her to focus on solving this problem. The warped wood beneath my leather dress shoes provides a blank canvas for my mind to work.

Renée must sense I have no answer to this, the same as her. "I'm sorry. We can return the dress."

My head jerks up at her ludicrous words. "No. Please don't

return it. It's yours." Before I can say anything else, the sound of tires pulling into her driveway has me spinning around to find the hired blacked-out Escalade coming to a stop.

"You hired a car service?" she asks.

I face her once again and pull at the back of my neck. "Yeah."

For a too-long moment, we stand there, unable to fix this. The clock has run out. There will be no overtime. I lost.

"Go on," she says with a smile that doesn't reach her eyes. "It's your brother's big day. Go make sure he has the best wedding ever."

I'm not entirely sure how our conversation ends or how I got into the SUV because my thoughts are shrouded in a fog.

For my family and friends, I put on a brave face. I smile brightly for every camera shot the wedding party takes. I joke with my brothers and teammates, but inside, I'm bummed.

Renée would have loved being here. I saw the way her face lit up when she found out the wedding would be at the Horticulture Center. Floor-to-ceiling glass windows surround us, as well as endless plants and twinkling lights. There's a floral scent I can't place, and I wish she were here to tell me what it is.

At the altar, I stand in a mix of Isaiah and Dell's grooms-men while Robyn—more beautiful than I've ever seen—and her bridesmaids stand on the other side. I teased my broth-er for years that she was my dream girl, just to ruffle him up so he'd admit that he loved her. In the end, it wasn't me who got him to admit his feelings—it was the big blond personal trainer standing between them.

The wedding has only just begun, and all three are fight-ing back tears, which causes me to well up. I can't help it. I'm so happy for them.

I want what they have someday.

The officiant asks Angie to read a passage a few minutes into the ceremony. Our family isn't particularly religious, but maybe Dell's family requested a Bible passage. I cock an eyebrow as my sister takes the microphone. I do not remember this from the rehearsal.

She clears her throat. "Our mother, Zofia, left each of us Johannsen children a journal where she documented our first years of life. I thought this entry was perfect for today." Angie swallows, and she glances at Isaiah before he gives her a nod.

"Hello my little noodle," she reads. "Today, you are ten months old. You've just learned to stand—wobbly, proud, and completely undeterred by gravity. You looked so pleased with yourself when you fell on your butt that I laughed until I snorted. Isaiah, you are brave, joyful, stubborn, and absolutely certain the world should be explored.

"I don't know who you will become, but I already know your heart. It's gentle and bright and far too big for your little body. You reach for people the way most babies reach for toys—with curiosity, with trust, and with both hands.

"Wherever life takes you, my little noodle, stay that way. Laugh when you fall. Stand tall when you can. And know that from the very beginning, you were a joy to love."

When Angie closes the journal, I realize I haven't thought about my mother in a long time. I was only three when she died, and I barely remember her. I've relied on pictures and the memories Angie would share with me when we were alone. We never spoke about her growing up because Dad had such a hard time with her passing. At any mention of her, he'd disappear into his workshop.

When we all became friends with Rafael and Joaquín, their moms adopted us in a way. I clung to their family like it was my own, desperate for more motherly attention. Ana and Christina fed us, taught us Spanish, and we celebrated every Día de los Muertos with them. We never told my dad, but all of us Johanssen kids looked forward to that day more than any other. Angie had found a picture of our mom in a photo album and brought it to their house where it stayed, in a new frame, amongst all the deceased relatives of their families.

It was the one time a year we openly talked about our mom. Angie fed us scraps when she could throughout the years, but we feasted on Día de los Muertos.

I think about Renée's daughters and how lucky they are to have her. I'm sure they miss their dad, though. Maybe they're in the same boat I was as a kid—missing a whole parent. At least they have their mom, who seems much more involved in their lives than my father was for me.

The next thing I know, rings are exchanged and kisses seal life-long vows. Music swells as we walk down the aisle. Soon after, a glass of good whiskey rests in my palm.

There were so many people in the wedding party that the bride and grooms forewent a long table, and just the three of them sat at a small one.

I take my assigned seat with my family and Joaquín. Before dinner, a waiter asks if someone is sitting in the empty seat next to me and asks if I know what they ordered.

"No, she wasn't able to attend," I reply.

The waiter gives a polite nod and efficiently clears her plates, silverware, and glasses. With each item removed, I sink a little further into my chair. My whiskey doesn't taste as good, and the invincibility I felt in my tuxedo a while ago fades.

Angie places a hand on my shoulder. "What happened to Renée? She couldn't make it?"

I shake my head.

"I'm sorry. I was looking forward to meeting her."

"You were?"

"Well, yeah," she smiles. "You sounded so excited over the

phone when you told me about her. And from the way Dad was talking"—she shrugs—"I just... had to see for myself."

"She's really pretty," Joaquín adds from my right side. He scoots over a little more, making up the room where the waiter pulled the extra chair. "I met her when he moved in."

"She was there that day?"

I nod. "You were all heading inside after our hike, and she was in the front yard."

"With her daughters," Joaquín smiles. "They made him cookies."

"Aww," Angie coos, her face tilting and eyes softening. "So she couldn't make it?"

I take another swallow of whiskey. "One of her daughters got sick today, and her sister, who was supposed to babysit, got sick right before we were supposed to leave."

"Oh no," she says, frowning.

I don't know what causes me to say what I'm about to say, but I can't stop it. "She doesn't like me anyway."

Joaquín rears back. "That can't be true." Bless my best friend for being confused that someone doesn't find me likeable.

"No," I sigh. "It is. I wasn't a very good student when she was my professor. And she's always, like, pulling away. Usually. She's probably relieved she didn't have to come here with me."

"Don't say that," Angie says with a pinch between her brows. She turns fully in her seat to face me head-on and places her hand on my forearm. "What do you want with her? Something casual? Something serious?"

"I..." I have to stop myself because I don't want to admit the truth. I'm not even sure what the truth is anymore. All I wanted was to sleep with her. Preferably many times in many positions on many surfaces. I wasn't thinking about how it would all shake out, and I can't tell my sister I was only thinking with my dick. But tonight has shown me what

I want is a lot more than living out my naughty professor fantasies.

"I just want her." I shrug, and it hurts to admit that boiled-down fact, because I really don't think she wants me the same way. "I think Dad was right. She and I are at different stages of life. I'm just this... young dude who didn't pay attention in her class, who probably made her life harder because of it. And she's annoyed that I live right next to her and she can't do anything about it."

"I think you're being too hard on yourself," Joaquín says. "I know I'm your best friend, but I truly mean it when I say you're a very lovable person, Jonah. It sucks that she couldn't come tonight, but I think she would have had a lovely evening with you."

"You weren't planning on taking your shirt off at this wedding like you did at mine, though, right?" Angie asks because, valid.

I roll my eyes. "No. Zay specifically told me to keep my clothes on."

"Look at that." Joaquín grins and throws his arms out wide. "You are capable of maturity! Renée will love that."

"Yes," Angie says. She points a finger at him like he's onto something, then looks at me. "Baby brother, if you wanna date this woman, a single mother, you need to show her how dedicated and responsible you can be. Keep showing up. Don't give her any reason to think you can't handle your own life. Then, she might consider letting you into hers."

The notion that I could be someone who has their life together enough to win over a woman like Renée is laughable and daunting. I don't always think things through, and I have never been someone with much responsibility. Hell, just last year I lost my phone in a lake, jumped in, and asked my friend to call it so I could hear it ring under the water.

But my life feels different now that I'm a homeowner—now that I have animals that rely on me. Caring for them hasn't been too difficult; it's been rather enjoyable. I love getting up in the morning and kissing their happy faces. I don't even mind the chores that go along with having animals and all the property.

Maybe showing more responsibility is not so far-fetched.

It's not unlike what I'm doing with my rugby team and building the training facility. The meeting I had with Raf and Joaquín the other day comes to mind—how doing things the right way often takes more time.

And I realize with new-found clarity, that I *want* to do things the right way for her.

"You think so?" I ask. "You think she would let me in?"

"I can't know for sure," Angie says. "She might be too badly burned to ever want something serious again. I don't know her story. But if you want her, and you want more than—I'm assuming you just wanted to sleep with her?"

I nod. "But I think I want more than that now."

"You're sure?" she asks.

I suck in a deep breath. "Yes."

"Then you need to show up for her without a dick agenda. Can you do that?"

I sit up a little straighter now. "Of course I can. I really do just want to spend time with her." The words come tumbling out before I even register them. *But they're... true,* I realize with complete clarity. I've been so focused on getting her underneath me, I didn't notice my priorities shift. Don't get me wrong, I want to know what her tits look like, but I also want to know what songs she listens to on repeat, and what problems keep her up at night.

"And what about her daughters?" Joaquín asks.

"They're so cute. And like, really cool." I smile. "The little one, Lo, she doesn't talk, but she's so sweet."

Joaquín points at me. "Then make them a priority, too."

"Yes," Angie smiles conspiratorially. "Respect her boundaries, but make sure she knows you value her daughters just as much."

All at once, the extinguished flame of my hope flickers to life once again. "I can totally do that."

"You're already so good with my kids," Angie says. "Just be yourself, turn up the volume on responsibility, and she'll see what we all see."

A genuine grin returns to my face for the first time since I left my house today. "Yeah! You're right. God, you two are way more helpful to talk to than Dad and Dane."

My mood returns almost to normal as the rest of the evening passes. I eat an incredible dinner. Drink a couple more whiskies and meet Dell and Robyn's families. I dance with Joaquín and Robyn and a few of her teammates, all the while wishing Renée could be here. My determination to win her has taken over, and I can barely think about anything else.

I was stupid to think she would simply fall for my charm—that I could flash her a smile and she'd be in my arms. If she needs to see how responsible and dedicated I am, then that's exactly what I'll be. I've delayed becoming a real adult for too long. Renée Wilde deserves a man who knows what he's doing, and I'm gonna be that man.

At the end of the evening, I stop one of the waiters and ask if they have any entrees or cake left that they could wrap up for me. To my delight, they do. As I wait for them to return, I spot Dane sitting with his legs wide and a glass in his hand, talking to Rafael.

It starts now, I tell myself as I walk up to them.

"I'm gonna give the team my all," I interrupt. Dane and Raf both look at me in surprise. "You were on the fence about me supporting the team enough, but I'm gonna stick with it. I'm going to be the first one there and the last one to leave. I'm gonna remember the plays. I'm gonna do this right."

I expect my brother to give me some asshole reply or sigh like he doesn't believe a word coming out of my mouth.

What I don't expect is for him to smile, stand, and wrap me in a hug.

"I know you are," he slurs.

Oh, so he's drunk. Great.

Rafael chuckles behind him. "I'll make sure he remembers this."

The waiter returns and sets a paper bag on the table and nods to me.

"Thank you," I whisper over my drunk brother's shoulder, who is still fiercely hugging me.

Rafael laughs some more because this embrace is lasting way too long, but soon enough Joaquín is peeling him off me. "Ven conmigo, güey."

"Oh God," Dane groans. "I can't think in Spanish right now."

"You got him?" I ask Joaquín.

"Oh yeah," he smiles. "Come on, drunky, let's go home."

"Can we get Wawa on the way?"

Joaquín leads him to the lobby and rubs his hand over Dane's back. "Of course we can."

"I think I drank too much," is the last thing I hear before they disappear around the corner.

On my drive home, I have the driver pull into a twenty-four-hour grocery store. The harsh fluorescent lights assault me when I step through the sliding doors, and the reality of what I'm doing hits me, but in a good way. It's like the hit you receive from your teammates when you score. The back slaps and body slams of a job well done.

I made a list in the car of all the things that might be nice in a get well soon care package for Delta. But as soon as I put the first stuffed animal in the cart, I realize I need to double everything. I can't leave Lo out. Even if she doesn't get sick, she deserves a little something too.

That's how I end up with two pink baskets, each filled with a Squishmallow, children's upset stomach medicine, hair ties, nail polish, ice packs, electrolytes, coloring books, and soup.

I also made a basket for Renée's sister. Everyone loves Squishmallows, right?

Twenty minutes later, the driver pulls into her driveway, and I text Renée for the first time. I triple check that I spelled everything right and used the correct punctuation before I hit send.

> Me: If you're awake, come to your front door.

I'm already waiting there when the door unlocks and the porch light washes over her.

She shuts the door behind her, still in her robe, with no makeup on her face, and her hair pulled back into a pony. She stands there, fiddling with her robe.

"Did you have a good time?" she asks.

"I missed you."

The corner of her mouth twists up in a way that tells me she doesn't quite believe me. "I'm sure you got on just fine."

"I really did. I wish you could have been there. There were so many plants, and... I thought about you a lot. I wanted to ask you what each plant was."

"Jonah, I've seen pictures of that place. That would have taken all night."

I can't stop the little smile on my face. "Okay. Another time then."

Renée studies me for a moment. "What is all this?" She nods at everything I'm carrying.

"Oh," I laugh. "I brought you leftovers. I got the pasta that you ordered, and some cake slices. Then I made some care packages for Delta and Lo and your sister. What was her name again?"

"Amber..."

"Right. Amber. I hope that's okay. I felt bad that I was... well, I felt bad. The pasta is still warm. It wasn't sitting out or anything."

"Thank you," she says. "That's really nice."

"How is everyone feeling?"

"The vomiting has stopped for now, but Delta and Amber are still running mild fevers."

"But Lo and you are okay?"

"So far."

"Well, I don't want to take up the rest of your night. I just wanted to stop by and give this to you. Do you want me to carry these inside?"

"No, I got it. Thank you, though."

"Sure." I let a soft smile linger before I step away. "Have a good night. Let me know if there's anything I can do to help."

"Okay," she says tentatively and gives me a small wave. "Goodnight."

· · · ● · ● · · ·

Renée

I'm on autopilot when I shut and lock the door behind me. The care packages make their way in—they're somewhere now—but all I can think about is what just happened on my front porch.

When I first stepped outside, all I could hear were crickets chirping and the engine of that big black SUV. Somewhere between then and now I lost myself.

I flick on the living room lamp before poking through the care packages. The children's medicine isn't for the right age, but that doesn't stop my chest from cracking in half at just how thoughtful this gesture is. Art supplies, hair accessories, chicken noodle soup with the little stars...

Part of me expected him to get college-level wasted

at the wedding. Instead, he thought of my daughters. He thought of Amber, and he hasn't even met her yet. Maybe I had Jonah all wrong.

With an unexpected smile, I pluck the Squishmallows from each basket and carefully open the door to the girls' room. A soft purple light casts low from the unicorn night-light, just enough for me to see two sleeping beauties, one with a sick bucket next to her twin-size bed. I gently lay a stuffie next to each girl.

Delta sleeps like the dead when she's sick, so she doesn't even stir when I scan her forehead with the thermometer. Ninety-nine. Better. I check Lo for good measure, and she's still holding strong.

Her eyes crack open as I pocket the thermometer, and she reaches for me. Her little body is warm against mine, and the scent of watermelon shampoo stirs something tender and fiercely maternal in me.

"Go back to sleep," I whisper, and kiss her on the forehead. "I love you."

When I get back into my bed, I stare at the expensive gown hanging on the back of my door. At the pretty shoes tucked against the wall—shoes I've only ever worn to dominate in. Tonight was going to be my first time wearing the black, pointed-toe heels outside of that capacity. I chose them for tonight because they've always done right by me. They're sharp and elegant, and I can wear them for at least a few hours without hurting my feet.

I would have loved to wear them dancing tonight, though. I doubt that even pinched toes could have spoiled the night. Not in the least.

Chapter 13

Rugby's Not For The Weak

Jonah

I t's a blistering summer day. I spent most of the morning outside with the animals before I arrived at rugby practice—early! *Man, I am nailing this responsibility thing.*

Despite my internal pep talk, I'm buzzing with nerves, which is weird because I haven't been nervous about rugby since I started playing in high school. I've also never had to prove my dedication to a team. Showing up at some point and scoring points was always enough for me to earn my spot in the A-side starting lineup.

But being late is old JoJo. My brother's right—if we're gonna level up as a team, I need to do the same. I had to beg him to let me train this summer, and I don't want to continue disappointing our family and teammates.

"As I live and breathe," Wheels chuckles, before plopping his kit next to me on the ground. He plays fullback and has thighs the size of tree trunks. Wheels glances at his watch. "Did someone tell you practice started an hour earlier or something?"

I finish lacing up my boots. "No, I just wanted to get here early. I'm excited about the season."

"You know the season doesn't start until fall, right?" he teases, but there's a very real possibility he's not. He gestures around the empty field. "This is only summer training."

"I know," I smile. "Bring it on."

When the rest of the team arrives, I receive much of the same teasing. They've always ragged on me for being late, and though it never bothered me, it's kind of nice to be teased for my punctuality. I'm taking this seriously now, and they're noticing, even if they're laughing about it.

Warm-ups go the same as they always do—a couple of laps around the field followed by dynamic and static stretching. Then we launch into partner drills. We match up with someone of equal size, so Dane and I naturally gravitate toward each other. We practice tackling and racing with the other piggyback. He doesn't say anything about me being on time to practice, and the more time we spend together on one-on-one drills, the antsier I become for acknowledgement.

When we go into a scrimmage, my legs and core are shaking. It's an inferno on the field. Despite the heat, the team's tempo is unbelievably fast. It's hot as hell, and we're all sprinting like we're being chased by Satan himself.

The forwards split away to do their own thing, and I join the backs. Our quick hands turn into tried-and-true plays, and I feel like a gazelle tearing through gaps in the B-side. That is, until I collide with someone and a chorus of inaudible gasps and *Oh damn*'s break out.

He called my bluff when I tried to juke him.

Sugar, that hurt.

After that, nothing goes right. I trip over my own feet and miss a perfect pass. I get too greedy near the end zone and try to score, only to get tackled again and reprimanded for not offloading the ball to the player who was yelling, "With you on your right." To make it all worse, every time I look at the forwards, I catch my brother, El Capitan, watching me like a hawk.

Ughh, that's not helping. Why's he so obsessed with me?

It's freaking me out, and I already feel like I'm on a razor's edge here.

"Get your shit together, Philly," Coach hollers at the back-line, but I know it's directed at me. He blows the whistle, and barks at us to sprint seventy meters to the try line and back. Then three more times because I'm pretty sure he's sick in the head. Listen, I'm in shape, but even I'm heaving.

"You think we're gonna make the Premier League lookin' like this?" he yells. "Get your heads out of your asses and run the loop again."

The groan I suppress is on the tip of my tongue, but Coach is right. This next level will be more demanding than what we're used to. If we want a chance to compete with the big dogs, we have to play harder—and train harder—than ever before.

Coach shows us mercy once he's satisfied with our progress, and we all gather by our bags for a water break. I dig through mine, sweat pouring from my hairline and shirt half-soaked. I freeze when I realize I forgot to bring water. It's not uncommon for someone to forget their bottle and to ask another player for a swig of theirs, but with the way my brother's been watching me like he's waiting for me to fail... yeah, I'd rather eat rocks than admit I didn't bring any water.

Luckily, I find a plastic bottle hidden at the bottom of my bag with just enough water to wet my whistle. I open the tiny cap and throw it back before spewing it on the grass—coughing and sputtering. *That's disgusting!* How long has that bottle been in my bag?

Two guys laugh at my misfortune. "I remember my first beer," one of them says.

"You okay, JoJo?" Raf asks, and extends his water to me. "You want some of mine?"

I clear my throat, but the rank taste lingers and now it's crawling up my nasal passage. "I'm fine. Thanks though."

"D'you guys hear our Daddies won Beachside Sevens?" one teammate asks, referring to our summer tournament team—the team I would have been playing on this summer if we weren't trying to level up.

My heart twists as I remember my experience at Beachside Sevens. All the drinking songs and partying… I miss that. Summer sevens is not serious, and the games don't count for anything other than a wacky trophy and bragging rights. You can sub out whenever you want, drink a beer on the sideline, and yell at the ref if you're feeling saucy. Heck, the ref is drinking their own beer at halftime.

I could have been there—carefree, drunk, playing mermaids in the water after each game.

A few teammates continue their summary of the tournament, and Dane laughs along with everyone else. He's so confident in his choice to be here that he can joke around and not miss the same games we once played together.

Why am I doing this to myself?

Do I even belong here?

Coach cuts the Beachside recap short when he whistles for our return. Like always, we split into A-side and B-side for a scrimmage, but when I join the A-side, Coach stops me. "JoJo, switch with Pacha."

Excuse me?! Pacha is a rookie and has never been in the starting lineup. He's B-side for a reason!

I'm flaming hot, ready to question Coach when Dane forces himself in front of my face. "Do what you're asked," he says through clenched teeth, his eyes the same Johanssen blue as mine but with an intensity I rarely have. "Just go," Dane murmurs, and he shoves me in the opposite direction.

Pacha runs past me grinning from ear to ear.

Lucky him.

Saltier than a pretzel, I slot into the defensive backline and flip my mouth guard into place. Play begins. A-side's scrum half feeds the ball into the tunnel of the scrum, and every forward engages—every muscle tight, every player locked into each other like a Chinese finger trap, fighting for advantage.

To my surprise, our B-side hooker snags the ball. I make the split decision to run a 10-loop so I can prove to Coach I know what I'm doing and don't deserve to be on this side.

"Winning, winning, winning," I holler to my backline, and throw my arm out to remind them to get steep.

When our scrummy has his hands on the ball for the pickup, I'm already in a dead sprint in the opposite direction, looping behind the two closest players. This trick play exploits the gaps in the opposing team's backline. The inside center should replace me, fake to the outside center who's the most obvious choice, then whip it out to me.

But before I can take my place, my winger shouts, "Losing! Losing!"

I gape as the rookie who replaced me on A-side retrieves the fumbled ball.

"What the fuck was that, JoJo?" my scrummy chirps.

"I was running a loop!"

"Then warn us next time!"

Seconds later, our players force the A-side ball carrier out of bounds, and I take a second to recoup. That was a dumb thing on my part not to communicate that to my team. As fly-half, it's my responsibility to call the plays for the backline.

Of course I catch my brother eyeing me, but it's less observational and more like he's trying to figure out what's wrong with me. I shrug because... I don't know either. I've had bad practices before, but this one is different—I feel like an outsider on my own team.

Swallowing my pride, I apologize to the backs and set up for a lineout. Taking a deep, dehydrated breath, I channel my frustration into focus. I signal to my backs that in the unlikely case we win the lineout, we'll run a simple quick-hands. There's nothing fancy about this play—run forward and pass the ball to the person next to you as fast as you can. It's basic, but after a failure like the one I just caused, it's necessary.

The jumpers are lifted into the air, and as I predicted, the other team takes possession. The lineout is faster than I expect, and the jumper tips the ball to my brother-in-law, who is taking off for the try line.

He's zoned in, but so am I. He's searching for real estate, but he knows his pack is supporting him, ready for his next move.

This is just a scrimmage, which means the intensity of play is around seventy-five percent that of an actual game. But there's a bloodthirsty victory gleaming in his eyes, and we're both at full tilt when I wrap around his waist and take him down.

Both of us grunt when we hit the ground.

Dane and another player ruck over us, and I scurry out. Raf compliments me on a good tackle while he feeds the ball to his side.

"Good job, bro," Dane grits out while someone rucks against him.

It *was a good tackle.* Nothing groundbreaking about it, just a textbook takedown. Yet, a surge of confidence makes my chest puff out at the encouraging words from my brothers.

I'm pleased to find my backline is already in place when I join them. Meanwhile, the forwards battle out several more phases.

Maybe it's the quick breather, or being out here with the guys, or that sweet thrill of seeing your hard work turn into something real—but something inside me clicks.

I *want this.*

Not just for Dane and the team—I want this for me. I

want to work hard to get this team to the Premier League because I want the satisfaction of earning my elite rugby position.

When practice ends and the sun sets, everyone's dead with exhaustion. During the cooldown stretch, everyone discards their shirts and socks, left covered only in shorts and sweat. I collapse when I reach my bag—my jelly legs unable to support me any longer.

I close my eyes and listen to the hard breathing of my teammates and their continued tales of Beachside Sevens. There's a nudge on my shoulder, and I turn to find Dane standing tall, holding out a blue sports drink for me—*a full one*. My mouth would water if I weren't so dehydrated. I hesitate. He says nothing, but there's a hint of a smile. No big speech, just quiet... approval?

I take his peace offering with a tired but genuine grin—feeling like I've earned something more.

Dane sits next to me, and I down the entire bottle in a couple seconds. I lay back and relax, listening to my teammates laugh about the antics of our social sevens team—my earlier envy gone.

For once, the fun can wait. I now have something better—a shot.

Chapter 14

The Storm

Renée

"**H**ave you seen the sky today?" Amber asks, kicking off her work shoes when she gets home for the day.

"No," I reply absentmindedly from the couch, where I've been grading online assignments and prepping next week's lesson for the last few hours. I can't wait to return to in-person courses in the fall—biology was not meant to be taught virtually.

Delta and Lo are both in their room playing. It's nearly one hundred degrees today, so playing in the air conditioning is the only way to go. To keep the house cool, I drew all the curtains so our two little window units wouldn't have to work any harder than they already do. Every fan we have is blowing cool air through the rest of our small home.

My sister crosses the living room and pushes open the curtain to reveal an ominous sky. It's only 3:00 p.m., yet the sun is nowhere to be found.

"Makes me wanna watch *Twister* and get it on with a hot tornado chaser," Amber says, waggling her eyebrows.

I pick up my phone and open the weather app. "Yikes. Not a tornado, but we're about to get hit hard. We're under a severe weather advisory."

Amber is already hightailing it for the back door. "I'll double-check all the windows and secure the lawn chairs."

"I'll find the candles."

Before I even open the closet, a sudden, roaring downpour hits the house like a tidal wave, drowning all other sounds.

"It's raining, Mom," Delta hollers from her room, excitement lacing her tone. "All the plants are going to grow better now!"

My heart pitter-patters whenever she talks about nature like that. Does she care if there's a massive storm? No, she cares about the flowers in our garden, and I hope I can keep her view of the world like that as long as possible.

As soon as a drenched Amber makes it back inside, the lights flicker once, twice, three times before everything goes dark and the air conditioning cuts out.

Shit.

To make matters worse, I just bought groceries. So help me, if the power doesn't come on soon, I'm billing the electric company.

"Mom, the lights turned off."

"Yes, I know, sweetie. The storm made the power go out."

She takes a candle from me, and her eyes widen. "We could tell ghost stories."

"Yes!" Amber hisses as she towels off her hair. "Did I ever tell you about the time I stayed in a haunted mansion with the heiress of an orthopedic shoe empire and the cast of Cirque du Soleil?"

There's no way Delta knows what most of the sentence means, but she clutches her little sister and gapes at her aunt. "No."

"Let me get changed, and I'll tell you everything." When I give her a knowing look, she rolls her eyes and whispers, "I'm obviously not gonna tell her about the orgy part."

A couple of hours later, the four of us are in tank tops and shorts. The sun is gone, and the indoor air temperature is ninety degrees. Although the rain has lessened, the wind persists, and according to the electric company's outage alerts, power won't be restored until at least tomorrow night.

When I check my phone again, I'm surprised to find a text message from Jonah.

> Jonah: I know you said not to text you, but are you ladies alright? Do you have power? I don't see your lights on.

Well, that's... kind of him to check on us. A little invasive, but neighborly, I suppose.

> Renée: No power. It's going to be out for a while.

> Jonah: <Ten alarm emojis> OMG SHE TEXTED BACK

> Jonah: Sorry that last one wasn't meant for you. Do you have a generator? I could set that up for you if you need.

> Renée: I don't have one. We'll be fine.

When he doesn't reply right away, I think little of it until there's a loud knock at my front door.

Amber and the girls are hot on my heels when I peek through the side window to find none other than the man himself—drenched—standing under our porch roof, wearing barn boots, rugby shorts, and a cutoff T-shirt. For the first time ever, there's an emotion on his boyish face that I've never seen—worry.

"What are you doing here?" I ask as soon as I open the door.

"Hi Jonah," Delta cheers.

"Hey Ladybug," he says to her, then scans our home past our heads and back to me. "It's hot in here."

I shrug. "It's hot outside. The rain isn't cooling anything."

"Stay with me."

"Pardon?"

"I have a massive generator, so I have power, and air conditioning. It's too hot to live like this," he says with a gesture to our living room. He spots my sister just then. "Oh, hi. I'm Jonah. You must be Amber."

"Hello," she croons the way I'd expect if she ever met someone like Pedro Pascal.

They shake, and I slap it away. "No, none of that. We will be fine."

"It's no trouble," he says. "I have spare rooms, and they all have locks. And you can bring all your food over so it doesn't go bad. There's also an extra refrigerator in my garage."

"Can we, Mom? I'm so hot," Delta whines, and Lo nods her head. They both have their hair braided and off their faces, but curly wisps cling to their necks. There's nothing I can do to cool them off other than put them in a cool shower.

I inwardly sigh because I'm being presented with a tremendous gift—one that will save me money and provide us a safer environment—but I feel uneasy about it. Their father—may the devil torture his soul—was the last man we shared a house with, and I was planning on keeping it that way forever.

As if he can read my mind, Jonah says, "If you want, I can give you the keys to my house and I'll sleep in the barn."

"Don't be ridiculous," I huff, but I know deep down if I said yes, he'd do it in a heartbeat. I study his wet face for a moment longer, gauging whether I can trust him. He wouldn't do anything malicious; he's too pure and too clueless to even think about it.

"Fine."

"Yes!" He pumps his fist in the air. "I have coolers in the back of my SUV for all your food." Before I can reply, he's running to grab them.

"Girls, go pack your bags with a change of clothes and pillows."

"Sleepover!" Delta shouts, before taking Lo's hand racing to their room.

Sensing my trepidation, Amber places a reassuring hand on my bare shoulder. "We'll be okay. You know he's nothing like Greg."

Exhaling a shaky breath, I nod. "Still doesn't negate my feelings."

Jonah carries two large coolers back to the porch and tries to enter our house, but I stop him and grab for the coolers. "I'll load these up."

"I can do it! You go pack your stuff."

"You're not allowed in here, Jonah. I'm sorry, but this is my space."

"Oh," he says, and pulls at the back of his neck. "Okay. I'll just... wait here on the porch then. Bring everything out, and I'll load up."

True to his word, he stays put while we pack. He loads the coolers and bags into the SUV and helps the girls up to their seats in the back. I'm a stickler for car seats, but we're driving down a country road to the house next door, so I don't bother worrying.

My focus halts on the little window decals at the corner of his back window. It's one of those stick figure families you'd see on the back of a minivan, but it's just... a man, a horse, two dogs, two goats, and eight ducks.

Who is this man?

Jonah hops in the vehicle last and has a big smile on his face, seemingly unaffected by the maelstrom outside or by how wet his car's interior has become. "Alright, let's do this! Who likes pancakes?" he asks as he puts the vehicle in drive.

"Me," Amber and Delta say from the back seat. Lo raises her hand.

"Perfect. That's what we're having in the morning." As soon as he pulls out onto the road, there's an incoming call, and the name Angie Pangie pops up on the dash screen before he accepts it. "Hey sis."

"Hey, sorry I missed your call."

"That's okay. I was just checking on you guys with the storm and everything. Do you have power?"

There's a long pause before she speaks. "You... you're checking on us?"

"Yeah."

"Oh, um... yeah, we're fine. We lost power, but Raf got the generator running. We're okay. Oh, and Ivy is with us. She's sleeping off a long delivery from yesterday."

"Okay, that's why she didn't answer when I called. Good. You're welcome to stay with me if you need to. I have plenty of space."

"Thanks, baby brother. That's... surprisingly sweet of you."

He guffaws as he turns into his driveway. "I'm a sweet guy."

"I know."

"I gotta go. I have some Wilde ladies in my car, and we're gonna get settled in at my place."

"You what?" Angie exclaims.

"Call me if you need anything!" He hangs up and pulls into his attached four-car garage. "Alright, you ladies head on inside. All your bedrooms will be on the second floor. Pick whichever one you want. I'll unload everything."

"Are Yogi and Rugger inside?" Delta asks as we all exit the vehicle.

"Yogi is. He's a big scaredy dog with storms. Rugger's in the barn with everyone else, keeping them safe."

Delta's face falls. "He sleeps in the barn? Is he scared?"

I pick her up and head for the side door of the house. "That's normal for a dog like him, sweetie. He's a guardian. His job is to protect his family from coyotes and other predators."

"And he loves his job," Jonah adds, and follows us into the

house.

Once we find a room and Jonah drops our bags, he leaves us to finish unpacking the SUV and stock the fridge, and I gawk with Amber at the beauty of his home. We had a sense of what it would look like from the outside, but it's even more incredible inside. Fieldstone walls and original wood features mark every inch. The custom doors and trim look like they've been here since it was built over a hundred years ago. Intricate floors with beautiful, timeless designs flow through every room. Even the ensuite to our guest room hosts marble tile with a black, swirling mosaic design.

The only thing missing from nearly every room we've seen is furniture. There are mattresses and bedding in the rooms, but not much else.

"Okay," Amber drawls, stepping from the Jack and Jill bathroom into the bedroom I'll be sharing with my daughters. "So he hasn't furnished much. At least it's clean."

"And cool," Delta sighs before flopping onto the made floor bed. I'll give her that. It's so much easier to breathe now that the humidity and temperature are at a comfortable level.

When there's a brief knock at the door, I turn to find Jonah peeking through the crack. "I have towels for you." Delta opens the door, but he stays right where he is and hands her the stack. "Use the tub and shower. Use anything in my home. Seriously."

My daughter carries away the tower of towels, and I step closer. "Thank you. This is very kind of you."

The way his lips turn up causes a deep dimple to appear. He scrunches the fabric of his black rugby shorts in his fists, and if I had a little privacy, a little more time, I'd let my eyes wander down his colorful floral arm tattoos and admire the rain-made sheen coating his tan skin.

"Anything for you," he says. "I mean, anything you need, or want, just let me know. Or just take it. I'm gonna go check on the animals one last time tonight and then I'll be right back."

"Thanks, Jonah."

He leaves, but calls back from down the hall, "If you see Yogi puttering around, be extra nice. He's drugged up."

After showers and rebraiding of hair, we slip into pajamas. Since I'm staying in someone else's home, I opt for a comfortable sleeping bra under my light blue summer pajama set.

The entire time I am readying myself for bed, I think about him. How he just showed up with his SUV and coolers and took charge. It's been a long time since I let someone else do that. *Let.* For many years when I was married, I had no choice and no control. I crave it now. I expect it now. I rely on myself, and sometimes on Amber, but never another man. But tonight, unexpectedly, it feels good. I'm still on alert; I'm still in mama bear mode, but I breathe a sigh of relief at someone else doing something helpful for me.

I think about how he respected my wishes. He waited on my porch and didn't try to enter my home. Even when he stood at the guest room door, he didn't make a move to come inside. He just handed over the towels and gave us our privacy.

That's not the same Jonah I had as a student. Student Jonah never respected my boundaries.

When he called Delta Ladybug, my stupid heart fluttered, and it made me want to let him in where I never thought I'd let another person go—where *no one* should have access.

And then there's the way he checked on his family—offering them a safe place to stay, just like us. I would have never thought that Jonah, the irritating, careless boy I knew from my class, the one who thought the world revolved around him, the one who could charm his way out of any circumstance, would be here offering my family his home.

For someone who seems to wear his heart on his sleeve,

he's a weird little puzzle I'm having a hard time piecing together.

By the time I'm ready for bed, I make my way downstairs and find everyone sitting around the large kitchen island, poking at a strange charcuterie assortment.

Jonah flashes his pearly whites when he spots me. "Delta said you already had dinner, but I thought you might like a snack before bed." He gestures to the spread of cheddar cheese, apple slices, lunch meat, mustard, pretzels, and some kind of ball about an inch in size. "These are chocolate protein bites. I eat them after a workout."

"They're fantastic," Amber mumbles through a mouthful.

Lo doesn't seem to care about the food, opting for a spot next to Yogi on the floor. She rubs her finger through his long white hair and lays her head on his side, as if this giant guard dog is just another one of her stuffies.

I pluck an apple and cheese slice from the cutting board. "Thank you again."

"I didn't have much in the fridge, but I can go into town tomorrow and get more."

"It's okay, Jonah. We'll be out of your hair tomorrow, anyway. Your animals are good?" I ask with a nod toward his back door.

"Oh yeah. Ginger's happy with Rugger close by and fresh hay. The ducks have settled in. I gave them watermelon to munch on, and they are loving it."

"Ducks eat watermelon?" Delta asks.

"They love fruit and veggies. I also learned they eat bugs! Isn't that gross?"

"Like Timon and Pumbaa," she replies with a smile.

"Exactly. Hey, would you ladies like a tour of the house?"

"Yes," Amber replies in haste, like she's been dying to accept the offer. And, truth be told, I am too. I will not deny myself the pleasure of snooping through another person's home.

Jonah leads us through the six-bedroom, six-bathroom estate that was built in 1880, with additions done in the 20s and 70s. Incredible stonework and arched ceilings are everywhere, and there's a magnificent fireplace I would kill to curl up next to with a good book and a piping hot mug of Earl Grey.

A drugged-up Yogi follows us from room to room where Jonah lights up, explaining everything. I can't help but wonder where he got the money for this place. I want to ask more questions even more than I want to use his decadent soaker tub, which appears unused. *Ugh, men!* They don't deserve tubs like this—deep, and wide enough for big hips—with a gold freestanding faucet.

Throughout the tour, it's clear he doesn't have a clue what he's going to do about furniture. Our bedrooms tipped me off he had done little in the way of decorating, but entire rooms sit empty. There is no dining table, no comfortable chairs, no TV stand or artwork.

What he has are boxes, a seventy-inch TV sitting on the floor, and a couch that, if he told me it came from his college apartment, I would believe him. I glimpsed into his bedroom and found at least some matching furniture in there. I dared not linger. The last thing I want him to catch a whiff of is my interest. It would be stupid of me to let a man of his age think there's anything between us.

Ugh, look at me, thinking there's even the possibility of something between us. Who the hell do I think I am?

Despite the lack of furniture and decor, his rough-hewn, winery-like home is beautiful and comforting all on its own. Even as the wind and rain blow outside and the storm's hum muffles the sound of everything else, there's an undeniable sense of safety here. Like even if a *Wizard of Oz*-style tornado tore in and picked up the house, there'd be nothing to fear.

What the hell is that about?

"There's one more thing I want to show you," he says, before sweeping open a glass door in his basement. It's then that I realize where Jonah has focused his furnishing attention. "This is my studio."

Delta's jaw drops at the sight of the control panel. "Whoa. It looks like a spaceship in here."

All at once, my sense of safety feels both brittle and reinforced, and I have to stop in my tracks. I grew up in rooms like this. Fell asleep on control room couches as my parents sang me to sleep. Watched in rapture as a song found its roots and planted itself in my soul. I lit up like fireworks the first time they invited me to record with them. I can still feel the press of mandolin strings tight beneath my grip as I tried to reel in my unbridled joy.

But though these are wonderful memories, they're intertwined with ones of Greg. An alluring man, he was once revered in music producing and trusted by everyone. A wolf in sheep's clothing.

Studios were once a place I felt at home—I felt special and cool and powerful. Greg extinguished that. He disposed of the evidence and covered his tracks, oblivious or uncaring of what these rooms meant to me.

"Are you"—I start, but have to clear my throat of the crack—"some kind of music producer?"

"It's just a hobby. But music management was my major in college."

I lower my brow. "And you took a nature study course from me?"

He lifts a shoulder. "It was a cultural enrichment. It was either that, which my brother had all the notes for and could pass them along to me, or take something like philosophy."

The image of Jonah Johanssen partaking in meaningful, philosophical discussions is slightly more unrealistic than a biology course, I'll give him that.

"You know, I knew when you turned something in that was Dane's work, right?"

He pulls at the back of his neck and groans. "*Ugh*, yeah. You threatened to fail me multiple times. And then you did fail me at the end of the semester for plagiarism."

An affectionate smile lifts the corners of my lips and my mood. "Oh yeah. Good times."

"Did you know Renée is an incredible singer?" my unhelpful sister asks. "She also plays the mandolin."

Jonah's eyes round and he beams. "I have a mandolin in here!" He opens the door to the tracking room, where I fight back a gasp at all the instruments lined up and hanging on the walls. Even though most are covered, I can easily spot a mandolin case.

The girls head straight for the keyboard.

"Why do you have so many instruments?" I ask.

"I can play most of them. Music is everything to me. It's like an itch that needs to be scratched every day." He turns to Amber, who's gliding her hand against a symbol. "Do you play?"

"Oh, no. Renée got all the talent from our parents, sadly. What I got was a crippling sense of stage fright."

"Your parents are musical?"

I bob my head. "Mom is, and Dad was. He died."

"I'm sorry."

"Mom used to perform on stage with them," Delta says from her bench seat next to Lo. "But she doesn't sing anymore."

My heart twists in an uncomfortable knot as Jonah's stare flicks between Amber and me.

"Have you ever heard of David and Ophelia Wilde?" Amber hedges.

"Yeah..." he drawls, like he's trying to coax us for more information. "They were major players in country and bluegrass. Heck, I remember studying them in my music history classes."

"That's Mom and Dad," Amber shrugs.

"Oh my God," he says, digging his fingers beneath his pulled-back hair. "I've been in the presence of bluegrass music legends this whole time?"

Amber preens. "You have."

"That's a stretch," I say flatly.

He's leaping for the mandolin case before I know it. "Would you like to play? Or sing?"

"No. I don't do that anymore."

Ignoring me, he places it at my feet and busts open the latches, revealing a regal, mustard yellow velvet interior. The instrument itself is maple and rosewood with an open scroll F-style construction, and a rounded V neck profile. She's remarkable. Memories long buried rise to the surface, and I feel a pang in my chest, all words lodged behind my throat.

Delta races to stand next to me. "That's so pretty," she coos. "Mom, please, can you play for us?"

"Yeah, Mom," Jonah adds. "Please?"

"No, I'd be too rusty anyway. Jonah, why don't you play them something?" Lo walks over, and I lift her in my arms before taking a seat in the corner, showing that I do not want to take part.

"I can do that," he says, and points at Delta. "But only if you sing with me. I'm not a talented singer. What songs do you know?"

"Can you play 'Blackbird?'"

"By The Beatles?"

She just shrugs, because no, she wouldn't know the artist. All she knows is that it's the song I sang to her almost every night for years. It's breaking my heart to realize I haven't sung to her since before her father died. Now here she is, eager to sing the first song that comes to mind—one of comfort.

"I'll need my guitar for this one, then."

Jonah closes the mandolin case and replaces it before plucking an acoustic guitar from the rack. He throws the strap over his broad shoulder with the ease of a seasoned musician and tunes as he meanders back. When he's finished, he lets loose a fervent strum and smiles. "Lo, would you like to join?" he asks.

My silent daughter shakes her head, but doesn't tuck herself away in my chest. She watches; she waits. And there it is again, my stupid heart pumping harder because he *knows* she doesn't talk, and he still asked if she wanted to join.

"Alright, Shortcake, but if you feel the urge, just join in, okay?"

Lo's brief nod is quick, and I know she won't sing, but hope is a powerful drug. And *oh God*, now he's calling her Shortcake? I'm cooked.

Yogi lays at my feet, ready to enjoy the show. Lo takes that as her cue to wiggle free from my arms and sit next to him, shoving her hands through the hair at his neck.

He takes a few measures[1] to connect the tune in his mind to his fingers, but when he does, Jonah flashes his wide smile at Delta and nods along with each beat. His fingers don't stumble; it's like he's played this song a thousand times before. He said he can play most of these instruments, and if that's the case, he must be one of those people born with a golden ear.

My daughter waits for his cue, and when she releases her first note, I'm soaring. Delta sings in the car with Amber sometimes, but when we're home, she sings quietly in her room when she thinks I can't hear. But this... this is different. Tears well in my eyes, and goosebumps cover my skin

---

1. Blackbird by Delta Rae

before she's even finished the first verse. Amber's hands settle on my shoulders, but I can't look away from the two of them—watching each other, waiting for the right beat and the perfect note to meet and fly away together.

When the song ends and the last note lingers, I have to wipe away my tears. Delta launches herself at me with a satisfactory grin, and I hold her for as long as she lets me.

"That was amazing, sweetie."

"I knew all the words."

"Are you proud of yourself? Because you should be."

She pulls back enough for me to study her face—round, freckled, brighter than the sun—and she nods.

"Good."

"Why are you crying?" she asks.

"Because that was beautiful."

My daughter smiles—hope swelling in her eyes. "I can sing it to you again when we go to bed."

My heart can't take this sweet torture, but I nod tightly. "I would love that."

"Speaking of which," Amber says, glancing at the clock on her phone, "it's well past their bedtime."

"Oh." I blink away the last of my tears. "Let's get you girls tucked in."

True to her word, Delta sings 'Blackbird' again once they're in bed, and Loretta is out by the second round. My sister settles into the adjoining room, but there's one last thing I need to do before I turn in for the night.

I sneak out and head for the main floor with feather-light footsteps. When I get to Jonah's room, the door is ajar, and warm lamplight spills out. I knock softly and he's there, changed from his rugby clothes to just a pair of pajama pants.

Part of me expects a smug reaction—like he knew I'd be here—but that's not what I find on his handsome, boyish face. It's concern.

"Is everything all right?"

"It's fine." I take a deep breath to keep from fidgeting. "I just wanted to say thank you for letting us stay here."

He leans against his door frame. "It's no problem at all."

"It's... kind of... hard for me to accept help sometimes. Or, most of the time. So... thank you. Again."

"There's no need to thank me. All I wanted was to make sure you were all safe."

The moment lingers too long, and I pray he can't hear the way my heart hammers. His blue eyes are dark, just as I remember them from the night at the club, and I'm hyper-aware of the flare of his nostrils and just how full his lips are. And he's so tall and he's so here and I want to push him against a wall and kiss him for being so nice to my girls and for having this ridiculous body that would look so good kneeling for me.

But I push all of that aside and choose the next most vulnerable thing to say. "You're not who I expected you to be."

"I'm trying to be something better." His tone is steady and sure before he leans in close, so close that his body heat warms my face. "And someday, I'm gonna be worthy of you."

I'm flushed, and my heartbeat throbs between my legs. "You shouldn't wait for me."

"As much as I love it when you tell me what to do Professor, I'm not accepting that."

My throat tightens on a contradictory response, and I mentally kick myself for not replying faster—for not shutting this down with finality.

That's when he steps back into his room, one hand on the door, and a slow, knowing smile grows on his face. "Goodnight, Renée."

And he closes the door.

Chapter 15
Nature Study

Renée

I'm an early riser; I always have been. Before the first crack of sunlight breaks over the world, I'm usually up and ready.

While Amber and the girls sleep for a while longer, I check on my house and garden for any damage last night's storm may have caused. But as soon as I step out of our guest room, the tantalizing aroma of fresh coffee guides me to the kitchen. A full pot waits next to a couple of clean, mismatched mugs and a note written on the back of a piece of mail.

> *Good morning! Help yourself to coffee. I'm checking on the animals.*

On the bottom of the note he drew a little sun with a smiley face next to a cup of coffee with tiny heat squiggles. It's poorly drawn, but what he lacks in artistic skill, he makes up for in charm. I'll give him that.

Coffee in hand, I step outside to a dark, muggy morning. It's still unbearably hot even at this hour, and I'm thankful once again for Jonah's generosity. We would have sweltered in our house if we had stayed.

I have to weave through several downed tree limbs scattered between our homes before I reach the garden. My yard has nothing but puddles and twigs. Nothing a rake and a controlled fire won't fix.

Thankfully, everything in the gated garden is fine, and nothing should be thirsty for the next several days at least.

When I get back to his house, Jonah's walking from the barn with the dogs and slows down to meet me. He twirls something small between his fingers. He's in fitted jeans, barn boots, and a crisp white T-shirt. No one has any business being that attractive this early in the morning.

"I see you got my note," he nods to the nearly empty coffee cup in my hand.

"Thanks. Are the animals okay?"

"Seems like it. Everyone's accounted for and eating their breakfast." A slight pause hangs between us before he lifts his hand to offer me...

"A four-leaf clover?"

"I always find them. I used to stick 'em between two pieces of clear tape to preserve."

My fingers spin the delicate trefoil. As a biologist, I know four-leaf clovers aren't that rare. Yet, I still feel childlike wonder when I see one.

"Used to?" I ask.

He shrugs. "Haven't done it in a while. I had hundreds. After a while, I just gave them away. Watching people get excited over it was more enjoyable than keeping them."

Oh, for the love of God. Why does he have to say things like that? Now my insides are goo while I pretend I'm not the kind of woman who liquifies over sentimental nonsense.

He finds four-leaf clovers everywhere? Of course he does. Of course the universe just sprinkles little symbols of good luck at his feet like he's some kind of whimsical forest prince. Meanwhile I'm over here stepping on the cracks in pavement and assuming every man is a walking red flag.

And the audacity to say he gives them away because he likes watching the joy on their faces. *Ughh.* I mean what kind of guy spreads good luck around just because it makes other people happy?

Certainly not Greg. He was the kind of guy who leeched off other people's good fortune. He was more I *found something valuable and I'm gonna bleed it for all it's worth*, not *Here, take this tiny miracle, I like your smile.*

Ughh. No. No smiling. I refuse to smile.

...Okay, perhaps a tiny one. Internally. And buried deep.

There's a cynical part of me scrambling for something snarky, anything to reestablish the correct amount of distance, but it's like trying to hold back a tide with a tissue.

Hands on his hips, he turns to gaze out on his property. "I'll need to take the tractor out and clean up the fallen branches."

"Do you want some help?" I ask because it's a knee-jerk reaction to offer, but also, he helped us and I should return the favor.

He's a bit stunned for a moment. "You don't have to do that. I got it."

"It's no trouble. Truthfully, I've always wanted to hike around your property and explore."

"Well, you have my permission to do that at any time."

His open invitation warms something inside me, and I fight back a smile as my stomach swoops.

When Amber departs to prepare for work twenty minutes later, she brings Delta and Lo to join us outside. We walk with farmer Jonah and his tractor. He's desperately trying to look like he knows what he's doing and it's not working. As he's figuring things out, we walk with him, gathering small branches and tossing them in his trailer.

We mainly stay on the path, which is flanked by flowering dogwood trees. By my estimation, the deciduous trees were all planted about sixty years ago. While they're native to this part of North America, most are planted for their beauty. Between their springtime greenish-yellow flowers, pink bracts, and distinctive bark, it's one of my favorites.

As we reach the top of the hill, a huge dogwood tree, split in two, lies across the path roughly fifteen feet away. Yogi and Rugger check it out first, with warning barks to stop Jonah. He kills the engine and hops down to retrieve the chainsaw in the trailer.

"Is that a saw?" Delta asks, following Jonah like he's the most interesting person in the world.

"This, Ladybug"—he starts, placing one foot on the fallen trunk and displaying the dirty tool like it's on a showroom floor—"is a Husqvarna 450 Rancher 20-inch gas chainsaw, with 3.2 horsepower and a 2-cycle X-Torq engine."

Lo runs up to touch the handle.

"Can I use it?" Delta asks.

He shrugs and takes the safety glasses from his head to hand over. "Sure."

"No!" I bark. "Girls, you can drag the pieces he cuts off into the trailer."

"Oh man," Delta whines.

"She's gotta learn sometime," he says.

"She's nine years old, Jonah. Cool it."

"I'll be ten soon."

"Perfect," he smiles. "I know what I'm getting you for your birthday. Alright, now stand back and watch me be really cool and manly."

He rips the machine to life, and the girls cover their ears. They look so cute in their little gardening gloves and jeans. He cuts limb after limb as the dogs help us drag everything to the trailer.

After five branches though, the girls give up and leave us to search for nearby fairies. Yogi tags along with them while Rugger stays back and helps me haul limbs in exchange for butt scratches.

Jonah and I swap jobs midway, as he handles the heavier wood pieces. Whenever he turns his back to me, for only a couple seconds, I watch his broad shoulders taper into narrow hips. Strong back muscles work underneath his white tee, and both his shirt and my mind are becoming dirtier with each passing minute.

I want to ride this man hard and wet. I want to drive him like a fully insured rental car.

The imagery holds me captive, and the next thing I know the tree's finished. When I kill the chainsaw, Jonah hands me a bottle of water before taking the last few pieces back to the full trailer.

As he gets on the tractor, I gather the girls so we can go to the designated burning area. When the tractor doesn't start up, heat floods his face as he attempts to fire it up again and again with no luck.

"Shoot," he mutters, and jumps down to open the engine hood.

"Do you have any idea what you're looking at?"

"Nope. But my dad does." He takes a picture before shooting it off in a text. "Girls, did you find any fairies? I could really use some of their magical dust right about now."

Lo shakes her head and Delta sighs dramatically. "We didn't see any."

"They must be hiding. Okay girls, looks like we're hoofin' it. I'll come back later for the tractor."

As we walk around his property together, Jonah and I clear away the easy debris, and the girls continue their fairy hunt with the dogs.

"What kind of tree is this?" Jonah asks, pointing to the same kind of tree we chopped up moments ago.

I shoot him a side eye. "You learned about it in my class." The wince he gives is so cute I can't help offering him a little help. "Its binomial name is *Cornus florida* and it's monoecious."

His pace slows and he rubs his neck. "Um... what does monoecious mean again?"

"It means it has both male and female flowers, so every one of these trees can produce fruit."

"Trees have different sexes?"

I sigh. "Yes. We covered this a lot in class. Did you do any of my assignments?"

He shoves his hands in his pockets and kicks a pine cone off the trail. "I did some, but... I'm sorry. It's probably pretty frustrating having students like me."

"Have them every year. I'm used to it."

"So, I wasn't exactly memorable, huh?"

"I wouldn't say that. No one tried charming me as relentlessly as you did."

Out of the corner of my eye, I spot his face-splitting grin. He replies, "Oh, really? Well, you're a tough one to crack. You're the only person I've never been able to win over."

"I have a hard time believing I'm the only person who has ever told you *no*."

He pauses, checking how far away my daughters are before leaning in. "You may have told me *no*, but when I'm alone, I think about you screaming *yes*."

Despite the summer heat, every hair on my body stands up and my downstairs region tingles with electricity. I have to remind myself how to walk and breathe after a statement like that. *Jesus Christ.* I inhale deeply to calm down and try to navigate through the lust-fueled images.

He always danced around explicitly saying it, but it was clear when he was in my class that he was willing to offer his body in exchange for passing grades. In the privacy of my depraved mind, I consider what would have happened if I gave in back then. He'd lock my office door before getting on his knees. I'd punish him and make him earn my forgiveness. He'd earn those grades all right, and based on our encounter at the strip club, I know he has the mouth to back it up.

I have never considered a student like this, but the

naughty professor fantasy is popular for a reason, isn't it? It's wrong and there's a power imbalance and so fucking hot I'm sweating just thinking about it. I've dominated other people in far kinkier, far more licentious ways, but for some God-forsaken reason, none of those situations compare to the irritating sexual tension between myself and this stupid fucking boy.

A wiser version of me would contact one of my trusted subs to fuck away these ridiculous feelings for my too-young-for-me former student. But I don't want to. I have no urge. Unfortunately, all my urges are flowing toward this jock with a too-wide smile and a soft spot for animals and the ability to make my daughters happy. It doesn't make sense, but I'm learning nothing about Jonah does. He's blissfully ignorant and totally delusional about me. He doesn't know what being with me means, and despite that... I want him.

It wouldn't last. It couldn't. He's too involved in my life, and he's only my neighbor. For Christ's sake, he gave me a gated garden and played guitar for my girls. If I gave in, how could I keep him at bay? It's getting harder every day with him. How could I protect myself and my daughters' hearts from inevitable destruction? Because I don't have it in me to do this again. A life with someone; partnership, marriage.

Kill me.

But there's a thrilling patter in my heart and an insatiable desire to watch him submit that makes me look for any detour in my ironclad life plan. Maybe I could scratch this itch differently. Domination feels good in many forms. Maybe this doesn't need to be sexual at all.

Once the idea takes root, I take a deep breath and plunge into uncharted waters.

"Jonah, you should better understand your property and what grows on it. Especially with all your animals roaming around. If they ate anything, you should know what's safe and what's not."

He furrows his brow. "I guess you're right. Yeah, I could do that."

"You *will* do that."

He looks surprised at my blatant command, but it morphs into a tiny, wicked smile. "Would you like me to report my findings, Professor Wilde?"

His brazen reply throws the thrilling little patter in my heart into overdrive. Heat curls around my core and seeps into my blood. "I would."

"Will you grade me?" he asks.

"Would you like that?"

"Oh," he drawls, with a salacious gleam in his eyes. "I would very much like that."

"And you think you deserve all that attention from me?"

"No. But I want it. Any of it."

"And what would you do if you had my full attention?"

For a long moment, he studies my face before his focus drags down my body and lands on my hiking shoes. Then, right there in the grass, he lowers himself to one knee and begins fixing a shoelace that's come undone.

"You can have your way with me, Professor. You can tell me what to do, what to say. I'd like to know how to please you."

Like a live wire, I'm buzzing with the intense desire to show him exactly that—to teach him. But my reply dies upon my tongue when this kneeling, pretty boy wraps his large hand at the base of my calf and glides his fingertips across my skin.

All at once, everything resets when I hear the high-pitched squeal of my oldest. "Mom, look!"

I step back as if he just tried branding me, and do my best to collect myself.

"We made necklaces for the dogs," Delta cheers.

Sure enough, a daisy chain is dangling from the neck of

each Great Pyrenees. It's literally one of the most adorable things I have ever seen, but I struggle to appreciate it while catching my breath from Jonah's last remark.

Lo tugs at my arm, so I bend down and she places a daisy in my hair. "Thank you, sweetie. I love it."

"We got one for you too, Jonah."

Lo nods and prances over to him. He's still kneeling on the ground, so she takes no time to tuck the flower above his ear, nestled against a bed of sunshine hair.

"Cool," he grins. "Does this make me part of your club now?"

"No," Delta replies on Lo's behalf. "Our club is only for redheads."

"Dang."

I can't do this with him. I'm now incredibly grateful for the girls' interruption because I took this—whatever this was—way too far. What was I thinking? I obviously wasn't, at least not clearly or level-headedly. I don't do this kind of thing, not outside the play parties where rules and structure reign supreme. Where I can enter and satiate my domination craving before returning to real life. What I'm doing with Jonah is dangerous. Against my best efforts, he's woven into life. I can't open the door to my body for him—*again*.

Well before Greg died, I told myself I'd never let in another man. Not into my house and never into my heart. No one will manipulate me like that again. I won't be someone's target.

That's why I keep things separate. My feelings have no place in sex, and sex must be pushed to the outskirts of my life—accessed only by careful planning.

We spent the rest of the cleanup tour in relative silence. By the time we're done and head for his house, I receive a notification from the electric company that our power has been restored.

Jonah loads our stuff into his Yukon while talking with Delta and asking Lo questions regardless of her silence. He responds to her facial expressions in the same way he responds to Delta's verbal replies.

There's a war for balance inside me. I want to shoo him away because I can't stand the tension we created, and I want to politely thank him for taking us in during the storm.

Eventually, I'm able to shut the door on him. I stand in front of our window AC unit and close my eyes as the cold air heals me.

I was not weak for accepting his help—I did what was right for the safety of my family. Now I need to be more careful with myself.

I finish grading the online assignments from yesterday and pour a glass of pinot grigio before dinner prep. Before I can take a sip, a text message comes in.

Jonah: <Image of a daisy held between his fingers> Kingdom: Plantae. Order: Asterales. Family: Asteraceae. Genus: Bellis (please pretend this word is in italics bc I can't figure out how to do that in text). Species: B. perennis (also in italics). It's native to Europe, and even though it's technically invasive to America it likes to grow in fields. Humans and ducks can eat the whole thing but they're toxic to dogs and horses!

Jonah: <panic emoji>

Despite his worry, I can't stop the bubble of pride that floats from my stomach to my throat. A stupid grin pulls at the corner of my mouth as my thumbs hover over the keyboard.

Renée: Very good.

Chapter 16
Dr. Brother, DVM

Jonah

There are too many plants on my property that could kill my animals. Thelma, Louise, and the ducks can eat just about everything, but I'm worried about the dogs and Ginger. Apparently, I have many red oak trees, and their fallen leaves are poisonous to horses. How the hell am I supposed to watch everything she eats? How can I sleep knowing there's water-hemlock growing and it's fatal to my babies?

That's why after two days of walking around my land with my phone and a notebook in hand, scouring the internet, I'm here, at my brother's veterinarian office with anxiety pits and the dogs in tow.

I walk through his office door one minute before they close and Kendra, the receptionist, is already packing up. Dane is fiddling with a file next to her.

He's already annoyed, but my dogs chase away his frown when they jump up on him. "What are you doing here?"

"My land is full of dangerous, animal-killing plants, bro. I'm freaking out." I throw my notebook on the counter and flip through the pages I've scrapbooked together with printed images of the offending plants and angry red exclamation points all over. "What do I do?"

He glances over to Kendra. "You can leave. I'll finish up here and lock up."

"You don't have to tell me twice," she says.

"What do I do?" I ask again once she's gone.

"First of all"—he sighs, then tosses a small bit of treat to each dog—"an appointment would have been nice."

"Okay, sure," I rush out, eager for him to skip all the brotherly jabs and get to the answers I need.

Dane flips through the pages before he speaks. "You can always try to remove the offending plants, but many of these are stubborn and will come back year after year."

"Shoot."

"You can also try barricading some of them off if you find them grouped together. You could spray them with diluted vinegar solutions, but with the size of your property and the amount of vegetation you have, that's gonna be a full-time job and still might not even guarantee your animals won't eat them. I once had a Labrador in here who would eat anything. The owner tried putting hot sauce on the legs of their dining table, but he still ate it."

"This is not reassuring."

"Just make sure your animals eat at the same times every day and receive physical and mental stimulation. Dogs chew things they're not supposed to when they're bored."

A flashback plays in my mind of what Yogi and Rugger were like in my old rowhouse. They literally ate the bunk beds we made them, ripped our couch to shreds, and knocked over my television while wrestling. But they haven't done any of that since moving to our new place in the country. Not that I have much furniture for them to destroy anyway.

"They haven't given me much trouble since we moved," I say. "I take them on at least one long walk every day, and they like to run with me."

"And with the horse and the ducks and the goats... these guys are always working."

I suck in a deep breath for the first time since my research started and smile to myself. "The girls too."

"The girls?" Dane asks.

"My neighbors. Professor Wilde's daughters. The boys *love* them."

Dane crosses his arms and smiles. "Hey, goat, horse, child, it doesn't matter. Guardian dogs like this don't discriminate. I wouldn't worry too much. Keep 'em busy and they probably won't eat stuff they shouldn't."

"But what if they do?"

"Then you call me. Take a picture of what they ate, if you can. And if I don't answer, call poison control. You should probably program the number in your phone, regardless."

"And you won't get mad if I call you?"

"If it's about the health and safety of an animal? No."

My arms are around him in a bear hug before I speak. "You're the best."

Before he can reply, a chorus of barking from down the hall echoes off the laminate floors and wood panel walls.

"Damn it," Dane mutters as he pushes me off and heads back toward the sound. I follow him to the kennel ward where my dogs are wagging their tails and barking at a German Shepherd.

"Sorry," I say, and hook each dog on their leash. "What's this guy doing here?"

My brother runs his hands through his sandy brown hair and sighs. "His name is King. His owners dropped him off for a minor procedure and never came back."

I gasp. "What? Just today?"

"About a week ago. Between the staff, we've been taking turns bringing him home every night to care for him."

"What happens if they never show up?"

"We press legal charges. And if no one on our staff can take him, then he'll have to go to the animal shelter."

I lower myself to get a better view of King. He's old judging by the white around his face, but he still has that puppy-dog quality about him—like he's always ready for a fetch and scritches behind the ear. He can't possibly go to an animal shelter! Those places are all cinderblocks and noise, tough little cots and a singular sad blanket for each poor animal. My heart hurts just thinking about King in one of those places.

"I'll take him," I say.

"Dude, what? You already have two."

"So? I have the room."

"Yeah but... he has medical needs."

"Like what?"

"He just had a small mass removed from his chest, and he has diabetes."

"Okay, that's no big deal."

Dane's eyes widen. "No, that's a very big deal, dude. He needs insulin injections every day. No matter what."

"I can do that."

"Is this what you wanna do with all your money? Start a farm?"

I shrug. "I don't know. I haven't really figured out what I wanna do yet. But... I know I can't let this dog go to jail."

"It's an animal shelter."

I roll my eyes. "Tomato potato."

"The phrase is tomato tomahto."

"What the fuck is a tomahto?"

"It's about comparing two—you know what"—he throws his hands up—"Never mind. It's not gonna help."

"Please," I whine. "You've seen how good I am with Ginger, and I had no idea how to care for a horse before I got her. I'm mature as heck now."

"Mature as heck?"

"I'm trying not to swear. Between Ana withholding churros for swearing in front of our niece and nephews, and the Wilde girls next door, I'm trying to stop."

My brother takes his time assessing me before looking down at King, who's smiling in his kennel.

"I will admit," he drawls, "you have shown *some* increased

maturity lately."

I remind him of the facts. "I've been on time for every practice this summer. I've been to every training facility renovation meeting, aaaand I've kept my mouth shut about my lottery winnings."

That last one has been the hardest of all. I want to scream it from a mountain and buy everyone everything. I want to buy a generator and central air conditioning for Renée. Matter of fact, a whole new house would be ideal.

Dane plucks a dog treat from his scrubs pocket and feeds it to King through the metal grating of the kennel door. "Promise me you'll give him back if he's too much work?"

"Of course. But there's nothing to worry about because he's gonna be spoiled rotten."

• • • • • • • • • •

After the dogs become acquainted in the clinic, Dane sends me off with the new addition to my herd, diabetes medication, special food, and wound care for King's chest. As soon as we get home, we all take a hike out back so our new buddy can scope out his new home. King stays on his leash so he doesn't run, which would damage his stitches, but I can tell he's excited for the day he can run.

When the sun sinks below the treetops and the temperature drops, I take care of Ginger and the Quack Pack in the barn and leave Yogi and Rugger to their guardian business.

Once we're inside, I give King his evening insulin injection exactly the way Dane showed me. By the time I set a recurring reminder on my phone for his morning and evening shots, King is exploring every square inch of his new home.

I take a picture of him sniffing my hand and shoot it off to the family group chat.

Jonah: Meet the newest member of the Johanssen family: King!

The texts are flying in within ten seconds.

Ivy: Look at that sweet old man face!

Angie: OMG HE'S ADORABLE

Angie: Also, WTF, another one?

Jonah: Blame Dane! He gave him to me.

Dane: He needed a new home. His last owners left him at the clinic.

Robyn: That poor angel baby! <ten sobbing emojis>

Dad: Why does he have a cone on his head?

Jonah: He had a b9 mass removed from his chest

Rafael: B9?

Isaiah: B9?

Dane: He meant benign (non-cancerous)

Dell: You almost got yourself a proper farm, bro. All you need now is a barn cat.

Isaiah: Don't encourage him.

Robyn: GET A CAT

I pocket my phone while the group chat blows up and search for King. When I find him upstairs in my room, he's sniffing around a couple of unpacked moving boxes. I scratch his neck. "That smell good, buddy? Here, lemme see."

I plop on the floor of my walk-in closet, and he does the same—curious to see what's inside. The first thing I pull out is the diary my mom kept for me. The one she wrote in from the time she was pregnant with me until I turned one. Angie didn't let me have this physical copy until I moved in here. She scanned each page and sent me an electronic copy that I... never opened. I don't really know why. I was so young when she died, and I've always felt bad that I never had a strong connection to her like my older siblings did.

Now that I look through this box a little more, it's all stuff Ang packed for me. Old trophies and pictures, sheet music to the first song I wrote with my brothers (long live Agony Nectar). All kinds of sentimental stuff I haven't seen in years, if at all.

When I open the diary, there's a pink sticky note on the first page written in my sister's handwriting.

Congratulations on your new home, little brother. Please take good care of this. You may not find it meaningful now, but someday you will. —Angie

King sniffs around the closet some more while I settle against a pile of clothes and begin on the first page.

December 4th
Hello Loin Fruit #4! Welcome to your new home inside my

womb. If you're anything like your siblings, you'll find it quite comfortable and won't want to leave. But I'm going to need to kiss that squishy little face of yours and sniff your head when you get out, so don't take too long, okay? But right now, you're the size of a grain of rice, so we have lots of time.

My, do you have a hored of people who will be excited to meet you! Angela, Isaiah, and Dane will be thrilled when they find out about you. I'll tell them when I start showing. Angela has been begging for a sister because the boys "don't play nail salon right." So I'm afraid whether you are a boy or girl, she will make you learn.

Your father and I can't wait to meet you, baby.

Love,

Mama

I have to laugh because Angie made me do all kinds of things that Isaiah and Dane wouldn't. Like nail salons and tea parties. Whatever, their loss. I had a great time doing those things.

My brothers mostly used me as their test dummy growing up.

"Hey Jonah, try out the new bike ramp to make sure it doesn't collapse."

"Hey Jonah, we're pretty sure you're Peter Pan, so jump out of our bedroom window and fly."

"Hey Jonah, attach these frisbees to your feet and skate on the icy driveway."

Good times.

I turn the page in Mom's diary and read on.

December 10th

My Little Loin Fruit #4 — Today we hunted for a Christmas tree. The key to picking a good tree is all about the shake. If a lot of pine needles fall off, it won't last. You need one that can withstand toddlers and gobs of tinsel. One as strong as the man hauling it to the roof of your minivan and strapping it down while you sip the hot cocoa from the Thermos and dream of sugar plums.

That moment lasted for all of twenty seconds before Isaiah was crying that the tree was going to fall off the roof and Angie spilled her hot cocoa down her coat and Dane tried to get in the car of another family. But I wouldn't trade today for any other. Soon, you're going to enter the best family ever, and it's only going to get better with you in it.

Love,

Mama

I think back to Christmas as a child. I don't remember any of them with my mom. Nothing as magical and chaotic as what she described. I remember gifts and the excitement around Santa Claus, but TV and school created most of the magic. Angie always did her best to decorate, but I never remember getting a real tree. Dad would just haul one up from the basement and we'd do our best with the ornaments.

Every year I tried giving Dad the best gift I could. When I was a kid, they were gifts that made me happy, so I thought they'd make him happy. He'd smile, but it never lasted. When I was old enough to realize he probably wanted a present that *he* liked, like a new tool belt or a Philadelphia Eagles hat, I'd get met with the same smile and thank you, but a clear sign that he didn't need anything from us.

It stung, but I never gave up. I just wanted him to be merry and bright for one day, and I wanted to be the person that made that happen. I wanted him to see me as someone worth loving.

The last couple of years, we've all seen a positive change in him. He's more present with us, and he's opening up. Maybe others wouldn't be so welcoming of an emotionally closed-off father just now coming around—just now showing affection and meaning it—but I've been waiting for this, praying it would happen.

And I need more of it.

I set Mom's diary aside and pull out my phone to call him.

"Hey, bud. What's up?"

"Can I host family dinner this Sunday?"

"Um... sure. I don't see why not. You certainly have the space."

"You would come if I did? Because I could host all of them."

There's a soft chuckle from his end before he speaks. "Of course I'll be there. But maybe see how the first one goes before committing to hosting all of them."

"I could though!"

"Bud, no offense, but you forgot about your own high school graduation."

"That was the old me. The new me has a farm and animals to care for and a rugby team to level up."

"Alright," he concedes, but doesn't sound convinced. He sounds like a father who knows his kid might fail, but is willing to let him learn that lesson.

But I'm gonna prove him wrong.

After we hang up, I text the whole family, including Joaquín and his moms to let them know dinner is at my house this week and that I'll provide everything. There's an extraordinarily long pause before someone responds—almost like they're having side chats about this.

> Angie: Sounds like fun! Would you like any help beforehand?

> Ana: We will bring the enchiladas.

> Jonah: No I can do it! Dont bring anything but urselves

> Ivy: <salute emoji>

> Dane: This I gotta see

Once I'm showered and ready for bed, I coax King to join me. He's unsure if he's even allowed, but with lots of praise and petting, he takes a spot curled next to me.

Normally, I doom scroll before bed, but I remember the pictures I took on my property today and start investigating each one before sending them off to Renée.

I send her a picture of a bird.

> Jonah: The tufted titmouse (lol that's really the name) also known as Baeolophus bicolor is a songbird. It's part of the tit and chickadee family.

I smile when I hit send and lay back with one arm behind my head. *She's gonna be so pleased.*

> Renée: I'm going to need more than the first line Wikipedia gives you. Tell me about their ecology.

Swing and a miss.

I have to look up the definition of ecology before doing more research and responding.

Jonah: Ok so the tufted titmouse (or titmice if you're talking more than one) is a total savage despite its cutie patootie looks. It snacks on bugs, berries, seeds… whatever it finds on the ground or in trees. In the summer it's all about munching on those caterpillars. Bro's a total simp for a bird feeder too. He loves to stash food like a sneaky little hoarder. With 4 siblings I can relate.

Jonah: Also? Lowkey the titmouse is a curious guy. Might roll up to your window and be like "what's up?" The internet makes it sound like he's harmless but that sounds like a peeping Tom to me.

Jonah: And this bird is loud! Chirps more than hockey players in a locker room. Especially when other birds are freaking out.

Jonah: Oh, and if one of the dogs ate a titmouse (lol I still can't get over the name of this bird) the risk of harm is really low.

Jonah: OMG I got a new dog! <picture of King wearing his cone of shame from earlier> He's got the sugarfoot, so let the girls know he can't have any extra treats. They're gonna be sad but it's for his own good.

Renée: Okay… first of all, that dog is very cute. Do you know how to say no adopting animals?

Jonah: why would I want to?

Renée: Second, that was one way to present bi-
ological findings, I guess.

Jonah: Do I get a good grade?

Renée: You're going to need to give me a little more. Did you find anything on their nesting
habits?

Jonah: Hmm... it's getting pretty late. Maybe I
could come by tomorrow and we could discuss
nesting habits during your office hours.

Renée: <unimpressed emoji> No.

Jonah: But the titmice!

I suddenly remind myself that tomorrow is Saturday and
I not only have a rugby game, but I have to go grocery
shopping for the family dinner I've demanded to host the
following day. So I text her back and look like a moron.

Jonah: Wait, I have a game tomorrow. I'm sorry Professor Wilde, but I won't be able to make
your office hours. Another time then.

Renée: <unimpressed emoji>

Jonah: If you're not too busy tomorrow... would
you and the girls like to come to my game?

Renée: I don't know the first thing about rugby.

Jonah: That's ok! No one does. I don't actually think there are rules. It's all vibes.

Renée: lol I highly doubt that

My heart soars like an eagle—no, a titmouse—when I process the incredible fact that Renée Wilde just lol'd at something I said. A screenshot is hastily fired off to Joaquín with a million exclamation points before I return to my text chain with Renée.

Jonah: I'll learn about the nesting habits of titmice, and you can learn about rugby.

Renée: I don't need to attend a game to learn about a sport.

My soaring heart deflates a little—she's right. Why would she want to watch a sport she doesn't care about? I'm still just her neighbor, an irritation that she sometimes lols at. For the first time since we began texting tonight, I set my phone down, and I curl up against King. His plastic cone isn't exactly comfortable against my cheek, but he lets me hold him close. My fingers sift through his warm fur, and he grunts before relaxing into it.

"You would come to my game, right?"

King doesn't respond, but I imagine he would. We lay there for a few minutes while a pile of dog hair falls to the comforter with each stroke of my hand. When I reach for my phone to add deshedding shampoo to tomorrow's grocery list, I double-take when a new text comes in.

Renée: Maybe it would be nice to get out and do something we don't normally do. What time is the game?

I'm scrambling to sit up and double-check the team's schedule.

Jonah: Noon at Fairmount Park. I'll be there by 10:30 for warm-up.

Renée: We have a couple things to do tomorrow, but if we have time, we'll try to stop by.

Jonah: I'll let my sister Angie know to look out for you. She'll be the one on the sidelines screaming at the ref.

Renée: I can't promise I'll make it. But I'll try.

Jonah: <fingers crossed emoji> I hope you do.

Chapter 17
Shut the Fuck Up, Children Are Here

Jonah

N o matter how long I play, nothing beats waking up on a Saturday with game day excitement. At least that's what I thought until this morning. Now that Renée and her daughters might be there, I'm struggling to stay calm.

When I leave my place for the city, Renée is out in the gated garden I gave her. As bad as I want to see her, I remind myself I cannot be late to warm-up. Dane would have my head, and I'm trying to show up for the team.

I double honk and wave before yelling, "See you there!" I hope like hell she comes. I mean heck—I hope like *heck* she comes. I have to watch my mouth on the pitch today if the girls are going to be there. It's easy to get caught up in the moment and cuss like a sailor. We're all juiced-up on pre-workout and slamming into each other—the testosterone level is through the roof.

When I get to our field at Fairmount Park, that's the first thing I tell my team.

Everyone's bootin' up, taping ankles and ears to prepare for the game against New York when I join the mix.

"Everyone listen up," I announce, but am cut off by our tighthead prop.

"Holy shit, I don't think you've ever been early to a warm-up in your life, JoJo."

Our scrummy pipes up. "Fuck! Which one of you fuckers do I owe fifty bucks to?"

"That'd be me," Raf says with a smirk. Well, now that we're amongst rugby players, he goes by Jimmy—a play on his last name Jimenez.

I forget what I was trying to say for a moment. "You bet I would show up on time?" I ask him.

"Of course," my brother-in-law says, as if it's totally normal for anyone in my family to believe in me. "You said you were trying to step up, and I'm going to hold you to that."

A couple of the guys give us teasing remarks and shove at Raf's shoulder as he laces up. I can't believe he would stick up for me like that. I mean, there's no doubt in my mind Raf has my best interest at heart—he's always been my older, cooler friend who always had my back, yet he's never missed an opportunity to make me look like an idiot. Based on my track record, it would have been safer to bet against me showing up on time.

I'm so used to the disappointing sighs and dismissive eye rolls that having someone rooting for my personal success feels new—and pretty awesome. It actually makes me think I have a fighting chance at leveling up to Premiership...

And impressing Renée.

Oh, shoot, Renée!

"Wait, that reminds me!" I shout over everyone again. "I need you all to be on your best behavior today."

"Fat chance, fucker," TumTum laughs. "This is a game for hooligans. New York's second row punched me last season and I've been planning my revenge."

I shrug. "That's fine. Just make it look like an accident."

"As your captain," Dane says, "I'm going to pretend I didn't hear that." My brother bites into his ritual pre-game apple—the source of his rugby nickname, Pony. The irony is not lost on any of us that Pony turned out to be a veterinarian.

On the field, Dane becomes Pony, and Raf becomes Jimmy. If Isaiah were still playing for the team, we'd call him Icey.

"But no, I'm not talking about that," I say to the team. "I have someone special coming today and she has two young kids. So everyone watch your language. Please."

Half of the guys groan while the other half rib me for details.

Dane and Raf take me aside. "Professor Wilde is coming today?"

"Your new neighbor?" Raf asks.

"You know about her?" I ask.

My brother-in-law looks offended. "Of course I do. Angie tells me everything." He crosses his arms but flicks his hand like he doesn't need reminding. "She was supposed to be your date to Isaiah's wedding..."

I suck in a deep breath and nod. "That's the one."

Dane's face screws up like he can't process any of this. "And she's coming here... today? To watch you play rugby?"

The knot forming inside my stomach all morning twists a little tighter and even though it's a cool morning, sweat forms. "Yes. Well, maybe. I don't know. She said she has other things to do today, but she said she might."

Raf's unblinking gaze does nothing to calm me. "I don't think I've ever seen you nervous before."

He's not wrong. I really don't get nervous often. Things always find a way of working themselves out, and if nothing less, a broad smile and a wink can get me pretty far. But as I've seen with Renée, my old tricks aren't going to cut it.

"I'm so far out of my league with her," I admit.

I expect them to agree and tell me I'm on a fool's mission, that I need to focus on the game and worry about this later. Instead, my brothers exchange a look.

To my utter surprise, Dane pats me on the shoulder. "I'll do my best to make you look good out there today."

"I will too," Raf nods.

"But we gotta win this one, JoJo," Dane says. "Every try, every point counts if we're going to the Premiership. I need you to rack up those points."

"You know I'm good for it."

"How many tries do you think you can score today?" Raf asks.

"If I'm playing the full eighty... six."

Dane turns around and reaches into his kit bag. When he pulls out a hat and places a few bills in it, he announces to the team, "The player that scores or assists the most tries today wins the pot."

The front row players grumble because they know it won't be them, but everyone else cheers before people pass the hat around like a collection plate.

Dane turns back to me. "You'll be donating that money to the team."

· · · • · ● · • · ·

Warm-ups are uneventful, aside from the fact that I'm constantly watching for Renée's arrival. Dane reminds me to keep my focus on the field when he notices me scanning the sidelines before kickoff.

Before he jogs away to take his spot on the other side of the kicker, he pats me on the back and says in a low voice, just low enough that only I can hear it, "We're counting on you, Jonah."

And for a second, it's alarming to hear him call me by my real name in a rugby environment. Did he do that on purpose? Maybe he believes in me, or at the very least, he's trying to. He's never had much reason to trust or rely on me.

There's no time like the present to turn a new leaf.

A shrill whistle is blown and within a couple seconds, we kick the ball toward the other team. Jimmy makes the first tackle, but New York's ball carrier gets the ball out to a supporting player before his shoulder hits the ground.

Our forwards rotate through a few rucks as the rest of us line up in a defensive flat line. But once our tighthead strips the ball from New York, our backline angles, ready to strike.

Small Fry is immediately behind the offside line with his hand hovering over the ball. He's been our scrummy longer than I've been on this team, so his timing and throw is second nature to me. By the time he passes it to me, I'm already sprinting. There's no gap in New York's D line for me to exploit, so quick hands it is. I throw the ball to Timmer next to me, and by the time it reaches our winger, we're just past the twenty-two-meter line and getting closer to our try line.

But New York tackles our ball carrier out of bounds and the flags go up.

It's their lineout, so I watch from the backline as our forwards match their numbers and lift Pony in the air by his knees. I'm roaring when he aggressively wins possession and suddenly, all I can visualize is crossing the goal line.

Before he's even on the ground, my brother is throwing the ball over his head in a direct spiral to me. No, even better—it's falling about six feet in front of me—just far enough away that I can get a running start and hightail it between New York's unprepared, too-steep backline.

Timmer's ready for my pass, but I can hear Jimmy and a couple other teammates bellowing for me to take it all the way in. Heck, I can hear Angie from the sidelines, louder than anyone, demanding I do the same thing.

But when I try to juke, one of their beefy props—a man who looks like he's been to war and seen things he'll never repeat out loud—catches me off guard. He calls my bluff and tackles me with only a foot to go before the goal line.

For the next several minutes, we battle over the remaining inches that separate us from our first try. But when our hooker develops a severe case of butterfingers and loses possession, New York is there to scoop it up and kick it out of bounds.

God da—*bless it.* We just lost all that ground and will have to restart play at the twenty-two. The groan I release is the only thing I can utter without cussing. We're not even five minutes into this game and I'm failing us already. I'm one of the fastest players on this team; I should weave in and out of big players like that no problem.

I cannot let my team down.

As we jog to our new positions closer to midfield, there's a hand on my shoulder that takes my attention away from the frustration that's beginning to boil.

Pony's voice is clear and even. "She's here," he says.

That's when I spot her—with all that red hair piled up high, sunglasses on and her bangs blowing in the breeze. I really should pay attention and get set up for the lineout, but my racing heart seizes control of my body. Without thinking, I extravagantly wave at the Wilde girls. Lo and Delta each stand next to their mom and point at me, begging her to "Look, see! That's Jonah right there!" Even quiet little Loretta is jumping up and down, tugging at Renée's arm.

With a curl on her lips, she sends a tiny wave back... to *me.*

"You got what you wanted, bro," Pony says. "Now get your head in the game."

The next thirty-five minutes are a slog. Not for me so much, but for the forwards who have been playing a scrum-heavy game—they're feeling it. The props are subbed out for fresh legs at half time, as well as a lock. We haven't been able to put a single point on the board, but neither has New York.

When Coach finishes his half-time pep talk, I take one more drink of water and pass the bottle off. The entire team circles up with arms locked around shoulders for Pony's last words of encouragement. He reminds us of the jackpot waiting for the highest-scoring player.

My gaze drops to the circle of open grass between us, and something familiar catches my attention. So much so that I slip out of the huddle and pluck it from the ground while Pony is still talking.

A four-leaf clover.

Pony chortles. "Well, if that's not a sign we're going to win, I don't know what is. Okay everyone, hands in and touch the clover."

We break and head for our spots on the field for the second half. I pocket our good-luck charm and send one more wave to Renée and the girls.

On New York's first kick to us, I catch it and take off like a bullet. Several players try to snag me, but I'm fast as fuck, boiii. Within seconds, I slide into the try zone just left of the uprights. The comforting smell of cut grass and spray paint greets me like a second home.

Five points for Philadelphia.

Cheers and butt slapping await me as all my teammates funnel into our end zone. Wheels kicks for an easy two-point conversion, and for the rest of the game we keep our lead.

With only a few minutes left in the game, most of us are bone-tired, but with try after try after try awarded to Philly, some of us are running on pure adrenaline. New York only squeaks in a single try and a conversion, but the energy on this field seems almost unfairly matched. We're smoking them like a Kansas City barbecue. Heck, we could walk off the field and let New York try to catch up with no opposition, and they still wouldn't be able to rack up enough points in these few remaining minutes.

But I've only had five tries and one assist—and I made a promise I intend to keep.

In the last few seconds, at the five-meter and fifteen, the forwards scrum down, all of them looking desperate for an ice bath and painkillers. But I see the special tap Jimmy gives his strongside flanker to indicate he's going to shoot for an 8-man pick.

Weird he's going strongside. He'd have a better chance at scoring if he went weakside. Unless...

Jimmy shoots me a wink before he crouches down and shoves his head between the locks' hips.

Once the scrum sets, Small Fry feeds the ball through the channel, hurries behind Jimmy, and acts like he's going to grab the ball and throw it out to me in the backline. Except he fakes, drawing the attention of New York's backline away from the scrum. I pretend to catch the ball and whip it down the line, all while Jimmy picks the ball from the back of the scrum and beelines for the endzone. Our strongside flanker follows as support, essentially using Jimmy like a jousting stick to break through the defensive line. But the play isn't successful (or maybe this was always Jimmy's plan) and he takes it to the ground. His flanker doesn't even set up a ruck. He just plucks the ball, and without looking, tosses it perfectly to me, before I zip through a narrow gap and over the try line.

My chest pounds as I lie there and listen to the screaming whistle of the sir awarding my try and announcing the end of the match.

Six tries.

One assist.

Not to mention the two tries Pony and Timmer scored and the points Wheels kicked for us.

The high I'm riding as we shake hands with the other

team feels better than any drug I've ever taken. I'm proud of what I could do for our team. Proud I could keep my promise to my brother—to my captain. I don't think I've ever seen Dane and Rafael so pleased with me. I've always chased approval from my older siblings, from Dad... but this game today was some kind of switch.

Maybe they're finally seeing something in me worthy of believing in.

But there's someone else I'm dying to hear from.

Three someones, actually.

Dad and Angie try to grab my attention, but I hold a finger up and slip away from the hoard of bloodied and bruised, half-naked ruggers on the sideline.

"Jonah!" Delta squeals as I approach them.

"Hey Ladybug." I'd love to hug her, but I'm not sure where Renée stands with that. She's so protective of her daughters and their space, so I don't want to assume anything.

Lo hands me a plastic container served with a smile as Delta explains. "We made you cookies again."

"You did? Thank you! This is the best day ever."

Lo takes the container back from me and opens it, as if I weren't a split second away from doing it myself.

"I hope you're not allergic to pecans," Renée says sheepishly.

The aroma of sweet pumpkin and cinnamon floats to my nose, and I'm certain this is what Heaven smells like. "Oh my God, if I were allergic, I wouldn't care. These are worth dying for."

"The recipe was all Loretta," Renée says, right as I pop an entire cookie in my mouth.

"It's just like another pumpkin cookie we make," Delta adds. "But Lo wanted to add nuts and a maple icing."

I squat down so I'm eye level with the littlest Wilde and speak before I'm able to fully swallow. "This was your idea?"

Blush blooms bright red across her entire freckled face

as she nods vigorously.

"You're a master chef, Lo. These flavors are insane." I point one finger at her nose. "You, ma'am, are talented."

All at once Renée's quiet little ginger snap leaps forward and wraps her arms around my neck.

I can't breathe. Not because she's blocking my airflow, but because I'm too stunned. She's... she's *hugging me*. Adorably shy Loretta, who likes to hide behind her big sister, is hugging me!

As I squeeze her in response, I look up to Renée. She's just as surprised as I am, but nods that it's okay.

I once heard that the people who work as characters at Disney are never supposed to be the first to break a hug from a child. The cast member must remain there until the child is ready to let go. Lowkey, I sort of cried when I heard that.

If she keeps hugging me like this, I'm gonna lose it right here in front of my team.

"I thought we weren't supposed to touch him," Delta says, and Lo releases me before looking up at her mom.

I stand and take another cookie. "Yeah, I distinctly remember you setting that rule."

The breath Renée inhales is long, like she's reluctant to respond. "I guess you're growing on us."

A charming reply dances on the tip of my tongue, but Delta delivers her interruption like a seasoned heckler. "Yeah, like a fungus!"

The jab is so out of left field it has all four of us giggling. Ecological humor—yep, she's Renée's child.

When I collect myself and swallow the second cookie I nearly choked on, I remember the four-leaf clover in my pocket and gently remove it. It's wilted from the game, but all four leaves are intact. I hold it out to the girls. "Look what I found."

"Those are lucky!" Delta gasps and snatches it.

"That's how we won the game. Found it right there on the field."

Renée rubs the tops of their heads. "Girls, why don't you go look for some while I talk to Jonah for a little bit."

They're on the hunt in a matter of seconds without so much as a wave.

For a long, comfortable moment, we stand there watching the pair crawl along the twenty-two-meter line, on their hands and knees like they're mining for gold.

"You played well today," she says gently, and shrugs. "Obviously I know nothing about rugby, but you..." she trails off, playing with her fingernails. "You certainly looked like you knew what you were doing."

Is she... blushing? Oh God, I can't hear anything over my heartbeat. Did she really say I played well? I thought nothing would top the approval of my family and team, but hearing Renée compliment me feels like I've hit an entirely different, entirely better jackpot.

"Did you enjoy yourself?" I ask. "Even though you didn't know the rules?"

"I did."

"Cool," I say in a way that's entirely not. And for good measure, I repeat it several times because I can't think of a better reply.

"It was an exciting game."

"Would you like to come over for dinner tomorrow?" I ask too fast. "My whole family will be there."

"Oh... um, I don't know about that."

"Yeah, you're right. That was dumb. Sorry. But if you change your mind, my door is always open."

"Okay." The soft smile she flashes helps to tamp down my embarrassment. "Will you have any more games?"

"Yeah! We have a few more home games this season and several away."

"Would it be alright if we came to another?"

"Absolutely," I beam. "I'd *love* it if you did. I can send you my schedule."

"See that you do."

"JoJo," Coach Batsakis yells over a crowd of ruggers. "Get over here. We need you."

"I'm sorry. I gotta go." And I really am. I don't want to leave this moment we're in together, where it feels like your middle school crush finally knows who you are and it's both electrifying and embarrassing and you want to tell the entire world what happened, but also tell *no one.*

Her soft smile grows wide, and it might be the biggest I've seen from her. "It's okay. I've probably taken up too much of your time anyway."

She steps away, but her eyes don't leave mine. Without thinking, I step closer and reach for her but stop when I realize what I'm doing—or *trying* to do. Renée clocks my hand stuck between us midair. I retract it, and she looks away, both of us pretending like I didn't just try to pull her into a kiss.

To keep my hands from roaming like a hound dog on a scent trail, I clutch both around the plastic cookie container and clear my throat. "You could never take too much of my time."

I wish I could read her mind in the moment that follows because I can't gauge her expression. Is she holding something back, or showing all her cards?

This time, she commits to walking away toward her daughters still scouring the field for luck. "Good game today, Jonah. I'll see you later."

For the rest of the day, through the social and grocery shopping for family dinner tomorrow, I replay her words like they're the only ones I'll ever need.

"You played well today. You certainly looked like you knew what you were doing."

Chapter 18
First Time Host

Jonah

Turns out, hosting the entire family is a lot more work than I thought. By the time people arrive, I'm not even close to having everything ready. I thought keeping it simple with steak tacos would be easy, but I'm a dumbass and forgot to buy onions. Not only that, but the cilantro I grabbed from the store turned out to be mint, and now I'm spitting out the weirdest chimichurri into the sink.

Mint does *not* go with garlic, oil, and salt.

Unfortunately, living out here in the country means the closest grocery store is twenty -five minutes away, so that's not happening.

Thankfully I realize my cilantro mixup before making the guac.

"What do you need?" Joaquín asks, already tying back his long, black curls. He's the first one here and I'm eternally grateful. I don't want anyone else to see how much I've messed this up. This is best-friend territory only.

He's wearing ripped jeans and an old Agony Nectar T-shirt. If I weren't so frazzled, I'd comment on how old and too small that thing is. He's had it since middle school.

"I was trying to make carne asada tacos, but I have no onions. I bought mint instead of cilantro, and I don't have time to run to the store."

"It's okay, amigo." He smiles like he's trying to calm a skittish animal and takes an inventory of all the fixings littered on the counter. "Don't say we're having tacos," he says. "We'll just say we're having botana."

My mouth drops. "You're a genius."

Botana can be a lot of things, but I like to think of it as charcuterie. It can be a little snack or something fancy, but it's perfect for feeding a crowd. The best thing about it: I don't have to worry if all the flavors go together. People can serve up whatever they want from the spread.

"I'm surprised you wanted to host," Joaquín says as we work side by side plating up each ingredient. "You have the insane ability to be the life of a party but I've never known you to be so..."

"So what?"

"Domestic."

I rip open a bag or tortilla chips and dump them into a bowl. "I was reading my mom's journal a couple days ago and it got me thinking."

"Jonah, what have I told you about thinking?" He pauses, and I stare at him. "That's right: don't."

I roll my eyes and laugh. "Ass."

"I'm fuckin' with you. What did it say?"

"She just... seemed so happy with her family. Like, even though it was messy, she was so proud of it."

"Angie told me your mom was a wild child back in the day," Joaquín says. "She used to hitchhike and play piano in rowdy bars. She went horseback riding in Morocco when she was nineteen."

"Really?"

He nods. "Angie read about it."

"That's so cool," I say. "See that's what I mean. She had all these experiences, she traveled... and yet, we were the ones she wanted to spend time with. I don't know. I guess I wanted to feel what she felt. I wanted to make an effort for the family she was so obsessed with."

"Do you think this has anything to do with your need for approval?"

"Probably." I sigh. "I do want to show everyone that I can be responsible."

"Well, I think hosting a family dinner is a good move then."

"I just wish it wasn't so hard. I don't know how you do it all, dude. You have your whole life together and I... have no idea what I'm doing most of the time. I thought buying this huge place with all this property would make me feel accomplished, like I was a real adult... but I don't feel that."

"Not yet," he says, nudging my shoulder with his. "And don't stress about it. I don't think feeling like an adult comes at any specific time or threshold. I think one day, it's all gonna hit you at once. You're gonna see everything you have, everything you made, the people you love happy... and you'll know."

"But what if I lose all my money like I've... y'know... done before?" I ask, my voice small and unsteady. The ten grand I blew in less than six months—spent on nothing meaningful. The sad reality is, I don't even know what I spent it on. Probably beer and burritos.

"First of all, I don't think Raf is going to let that happen." I chuckle and he continues. "He's made sure you're set up with too many barriers in place for you to lose it all. And second, so what if you did? Then you'd be back to the grind like the rest of us. People who don't have money can still feel like adults. They're rich in other ways."

"You think so?"

"Look at the way your mom talked about your family. All of you crammed in that tiny house and she adored her life. That's *rich*-rich if you ask me."

My hands are on autopilot as I slice an avocado and think about what he means, about the words Mom gave me. I wish I could ask her when she knew she was an adult. Maybe she was like me, and never got to that moment. Or maybe she knew from a young age.

Dane is the first to arrive as we finish up the botana, all

the dishes now scattered over the kitchen island. Angie, Rafael, and their three dark-haired mini-mes arrive just as I'm stepping outside to light my brand new grill.

The ignite button *click-click-clicks* and… nothing. My second and third attempt have the same result. Dane steps out. "Need some help?" he asks.

"I got it," I say, a little too defensively.

My brother stands there with his hands in his black shorts, tattooed legs stemming from his Vans, and rocks on the balls of his feet. He says nothing as I click through a fourth, fifth, and sixth attempt.

"C'mon," I huff. "I just bought this." I fling the grill lid up and inspect it like it's magically going to tell me what I'm doing wrong.

I hold out my hand. "Gimme your Zippo," I tell Dane in a tone that's reserved only for siblings. He gave up smoking a couple years ago but he always carries a lighter in his pocket. I guess smoking was an easier habit to give up than carrying a flame. I locate a twig on the ground and light the end of it.

"Did you see Green Day is coming to Philly in a few weeks?" he asks. Green Day was a huge influence on us as kids. A lot of bands shaped us, but it was that particular political punk rock band that had us believing our family band, Agony Nectar, could follow in their footsteps. Their lyrics are inked on my skin. And on his.

Most of my focus is on lighting the grill and not singeing my eyebrows, but I answer. "Yeah, but we have a game the next day in Baltimore."

"That's never stopped you before."

There's a soft *woosh* of the slider door. "Why is there no furniture in your house, Jonah?" Rafael asks. He stands next to Dane and has my youngest nephew, Mateo, strapped to his chest. If I weren't so busy worrying about how I'm going to grill the giant flank steak, I'd be taking that curly-haired bambino from his father. "What's going on here?" he asks before I can even process his first question. "Did you—"

Dane cuts him off. "He said he didn't want any help."

Raf leans to the left to inspect my busted chrome monstrosity and points to something. "But—"

"I know," Dane hums.

"I know how grills work," I say through clenched teeth. The flame extinguishes on my twig and I light it again before shoving into the belly of the grill.

"Not to be that guy," my brother says, "but you once asked me how wind works."

I still don't know the answer, but I ignore him to focus on my task.

Dane and Raf stand there chatting away while I try harder than an old prop on a breakaway. When I pull out my phone to search the internet for a *how to fix your grill* video, Raf and Joaquín's step-mom, Christina, joins us.

She studies me for a moment, her hands stuffed into her cargo shorts the same way Dane's are. "You know, most gas grills need gas."

Cold, bright relief flicks the bulb on in my brain, immediately followed by creepy-crawly embarrassment that starts in my belly and climbs up my torso until my cheeks are burning. My palms are on my face a split second later, muffling my groan.

"It's okay," Christina says, attempting to soothe my embarrassment. "Just tell me where the tank is and I'll hook it up. Is it in your garage?" She's already turning in that direction but I have to stop her.

"No," I sigh. "I forgot to get a tank."

Why am I the way that I am? I bought a *gas* grill. You literally only need two things for it to work: gas... and a grill.

"Mijo, where is your furniture?" Ana asks as she joins the crowd that's formed to watch my downfall. She hugs me smelling like citrus and fresh laundry, and it's a small comfort that transports me to my childhood.

"I'm still working on that," I say with no small amount of defeat. "God, why did I think I could host? I don't even have a place for everyone to sit. I've been here for months, I should have furniture by now! I should have a gas tank for my gas grill and I should take an extra moment to make sure I'm buying cilantro, not mint!"

"First of all," Ana says, still holding me like a broken child and not a full-grown man who's nearly a head taller than her, "don't use the Lord's name in vain."

I can't help my tiny, hidden smile. Ana may be an out-and-proud lesbian, but she's a Catholic above all else. Even though I'm not particularly religious, it's a nice reminder that this world does not revolve around me.

I release her and grimace. "Lo siento."

"Second, it's going to be fine. It's a beautiful day," she says with a dramatic arm flying wide. "We'll have a picnic. You have blankets, yes?"

I nod. I don't tell her the only ones I have are the covers currently on my beds and the one Rugger drags around with him and dry humps. Definitely not the time to tell her about that one.

"Perfecto," she says.

"But the grill," I sigh. "I have a flank steak marinating."

"Jonah," Christina says gently, placing a hand on my back and rubbing it. "You have this amazing thing called a stove. How about I take a crack at that." She's telling me more than she's asking.

I'm far from a perfectionist, but I wanted this family dinner to be just that. I thought I prepared enough—heck, I made a grocery list. If that doesn't scream *I'm half-way to having my life together*, I don't know what does.

But I don't want to appear ungrateful, so I accept her offer. I gather the four blankets I own, leaving Rugger's special blankie lover balled up in the corner of my room, and Ana helps me arrange them in the yard.

By the time my dad, Robyn, Dell, and Isaiah show up, Christina's slicing the medium-rare seared steak in strips and loading up their plates. Everyone's distracted with kids and catching up when Joaquín stands next to me. "Here," he says, handing me a bottle of beer. "Relax, Jonah. Everything's okay. People are eating."

"And sitting on the ground," I grouse, but accept the beer and take a swig.

"You know what would make this family dinner *great*?"

"Hm?"

"If we had a little live music." He grins.

I swear my best friend knows me better than I know myself. Only a moment ago I was sulking, unable to even enjoy the day. Now I'm sprinting for my studio and hauling instruments outside by the handful with a happy little patter in my heart. It's been too long since I played outdoors, and my flabbers are gasted as to why I haven't played yet on my new property.

Once I have everything set up and plugged in on my porch, I wolf down a few bites and fling myself behind my drum set. Joaquín warms up on the keyboard. Dell pushes a reluctant but smiling Isaiah to the stage and hands him his bass guitar, while their wife Robyn is grinning like a maniac as she records on her phone.

"Long live Agony Nectar," she hollers like a superfan in a crowded basement bar, ready for her favorite band to blow her away. She acts like we're literal rock stars instead of a few dudes who never grew out of our emo-punk-band phase.

And you know what? I hope we never do.

When Dane finishes tuning his guitar, he whispers to each of us the song he wants to play first, and my smile grows even bigger. "This one goes out to our niece and nephews," he says into the microphone.

Because we've never played this song before, I take the lead and establish a beat that speaks to me. Isaiah joins next, layering in mellow reverberations. Joaquín finds his melody on the keys shortly after. Finally Dane, our front man and lead guitarist—covered in more tattoos than any of us with black gauges in his ears—lets it rip.

The second the lyrics of Old MacDonald hit them, Zo and Nico get up and dance the way toddlers do. Squatting up and down, throwing their hands out, and clapping out of rhythm. I watch as Raf bounces to the beat with Mateo in his chest carrier, Mateo's little hands clutched around his father's index fingers.

God, they're cute.

Of course, the version we're playing is nothing like the simplistic nursery rhymes these kids have heard. Agony Nectar is hard core. And Dane's voice—rough and low, but always in control—conveys that, even when the lyrics are "with a quack quack here and a quack quack there."

Angie, Robyn, and Dell dance and sing along, each holding a beer like they're at a real concert.

We play a couple more for the kids before playing requests from our parents—all songs from their youth, as nostalgic and warm to them as The Black Keys or Cage the Elephant are to me.

But we can only play covers for so long.

When the sun starts to set, Angie and Raf take off with the kids to make it home for their bedtime. After hugs and see-ya-later's and wet toddler kisses, Agony Nectar revives. We're pulling out classics like *My Hoodie Still Smells Like You*, *Nothing Hurts When Everything Does*, and my personal favorite, *Graveyard Date Night (Acoustic Version)*.

When the automatic porch lights come on, we call it a night as our remaining fans whoop and holler from their picnic blankets.

I'm buzzing like a live wire, free of whatever mess I was

feeling earlier, and overall, incredibly pleased with how this evening shaped up. Together, my bandmates and I disassemble our equipment and carry it back in the studio. All the while, we poke fun at each other's missed notes and wrong lyrics.

Someone has connected their phone to the surround sound, and judging by the country music selection, I can assume Dell is the culprit. When we stride into the kitchen, we find everyone wiping down the counters. Dad closes the dishwasher.

"You guys didn't have to do that," I say.

"You hosted," Dad replies, like that's a whole answer. He comes in for a hug, his tall frame so similar to mine, but far less muscular. His short beard is softer than it looks, and it rubs against my ear when he whispers, "And you did a good job, son."

There's something uncomfortable in the way those words settle into me. Uncomfortable because I grew up without such acknowledgement from him, and yet... my chest expands with a lightness that rivals the time I went cliff diving with Joaquín. It was technically illegal and we were technically arrested (and I don't think I'm using the word technically right), but the adrenaline rush was off the charts.

I play it cool in front of Dad though, like his praise is not breathing life into me.

Despite my lack of furniture, no one seems to be in a rush to get home. Dane and Dell lay on the floor and play with the dogs while hair falls to the floor like snow. Robyn sits on the one stool I have while Isaiah stands behind her, snuggling his wife like a pillow as she regales us with stories of the Olympic Village. It does not get old that my sister-in-law is an Olympic rugby star. God, she's awesome. I want to be her when I grow up.

Seeing my older brother like this, no trace of his usual

irritability, a man totally in love and happy in a way I never thought he could be... well, it's admirable. And I want that.

Joaquín leans against the counter with a beer in hand, and I tuck myself into him. He's five-nine, so it's more like I'm falling into him, but he doesn't hesitate. He wraps his arms around me, and I soak in the comfort I'm suddenly craving. I wish like hell it was Renée, though. Joaquín is all lean muscle and hard planes, but Renée... oh, she'd be soft. She'd absorb me.

I don't know when my imagination started veering this way—to what it would be like to be hers. To feel the weight of her affection and not just the filthy professor fantasies I have password protected in my spank bank. But I want both.

She's a prickly one, but I'd wager anything she's tender and sweet on the inside.

When Christina tells us about the upcoming bluegrass festival she's organizing, my ears perk up because Renée would *love* this. Wouldn't she? She did say her parents were bluegrass legends.

"How much are tickets?" I blurt. Not that I really care now that I'm rollin' in the dough, but it's a gut-reaction to wonder.

"Forty bucks for general admission," she replies. "Seventy for VIP. I have some tickets I can give away if you want them."

"Yes! Wait, are kids allowed?"

The look Christina gives me is quizzical. "Yeah..."

"Perfect," I say. Then I check the calendar on my phone to make sure we don't have a game or team event that day. "I'll take four tickets."

"Who the hell are you inviting?" Isaiah asks. "And since when do you like bluegrass?"

up to it. She cuts back to weekly reminders in the eleven months after.

"We were wondering," she murmurs, "if instead of the roller rink, could we have my party at Jonah's?"

My brain takes a moment to buffer. "Wait, what?

It's Amber's turn to chime in. "But you've been looking forward to the roller rink with your friends all year. I got us sparkly disco outfits. Do you know how hard it was to find matching halter-top jumpsuits that would fit all four of us?"

"We can still wear them," she says, enthusiasm oozing.

"We better." Amber huffs. "I had to meet up with a seamstress named Madame Featherhole I found on Craigslist who kept trying to sell me her homemade bookmarks made of *human* hair. But"—she sighs—"that's the price you pay for quality. There's not a stitch of polyester in those suits. You know how cheap fabric gives me panic attacks."

I ignore my sister. "Why do you want to have a party at Jonah's?" I ask.

"We want to play with the animals."

I huff an amused laugh. "Sweetie, we could just have your party at the zoo instead. There are way more, way cooler animals at the zoo."

"But we want to ride Ginger and play with the Quack Pack."

"Is that what he calls his ducks?" Amber snorts. "Brilliant."

"And all my friends would love it!"

My scheming, doe-eyed offspring has me pinned. If I deny her request, she'll be heartbroken, and there's no way she's going to be happy with the roller rink party when it wasn't her first choice. I may be a stick in the mud sometimes, but not when it comes to her birthday. I close my eyes and take a deep breath, imagining how awkward it's going to be when I ask him for this insane favor.

"I will ask him..." I say as slow and calm as I can before

the girls start twirling, their faces brighter than every star in the galaxy. "But, but, but... he might be busy that day, we don't know. I need you to understand he has the right to say no, and then it's back to our original plan at the roller rink, okay?"

"Thankyouthankyouthankyouthankyou!" she screams, before the pair of them hug me with all their might. Their little arms, which aren't so little anymore, are like a vise around my neck, and their unbridled joy infuses into me.

The girls bound for the living room, turn on the TV, and take out their coloring supplies to hatch party plans while Amber and I finish getting ready for tonight. It's my monthly allowance afterall, going to one of these play parties. But as the date crept closer on the calendar, the unease in my stomach amplified. I've never been this unsure about going—not even the first time Amber took me.

My first time was based on curiosity and research more than anything. And the following parties? Education turned to realization which turned to pleasure. But as I stand in my bathroom, fixing my hair into a slick-back bun, there isn't excitement drumming through my veins like there used to be.

I'm determined to push through it, however, because there's no way in hell that man next door is having this effect on me.

I'm going to get to the party, find a pre-approved submissive, and have them eating out of my palm in no time. Judging by the texts I've received from a few of my favorites, I'll have the pick of the litter tonight. Maybe more than one.

Then... *then* this weird feeling will disappear.

The wrap dress I throw on gives no indication I'm wearing a leather and lace bodysuit. The dress is elegant and professional, but I'd never wear it to class. I don't need my students focusing on my cleavage instead of their lesson. Though covering up never really deterred Jonah, did it?

Argh, stop thinking about him!

The bodysuit pushes my tits higher than they have any right to be, and my waist is snatched in thanks to a corset back. Well, as snatched as a petite, chubby woman like myself can be. This is my armor... yet I'm questioning if it's strong enough to withstand my turmoil.

When Tracy arrives to babysit, I check my reflection one last time before I greet her at the door with a hug.

"Thanks for coming," I say before releasing her.

"You know it's no trouble." She smiles, and the wrinkles around her mouth and eyes deepen. Tracy is a white woman in her late sixties with wavy brown-gray hair that she stopped dying when she retired a couple years ago. A professor of chemistry, she was my colleague at Keystone State. Our offices were right next to each other in the science building, and even though I saw her often, I never really knew her until right before she retired.

Whatever made her strike up a conversation with me that fateful day, I don't know. But I'm grateful for the way she changed my life.

As always, Lo and Delta geek out over Tracy like she's Santa. Probably because she always brings gummy worms and peel-off face masks.

Amber gives Tracy a warm welcome. "Thanks for letting me take my sister out of the house." She winks.

"Lord knows she needs it," Tracy replies, mirth pulling at the corner of her mouth.

My sister raises her eyebrows and rolls her eyes, communicating something only the three of us know. We give the girls a goodbye hug, and promise we'll be back when they wake up. Amber leads us out, swinging the front door open and leaving it for me to follow.

I'm about to move out when Tracy stops me on the porch, her voice just above a whisper. "How are you?" she asks, her tone serious and knowing.

"You know." I shrug with casual indifference that I know she knows is a lie.

"Are you sleeping?"

"It's getting better. I still wake up in a panic sometimes, but it's not as often." A long pause stretches between us as she studies me and holds my hands in hers. I don't squirm. I don't look away.

"You made the right choice."

· · · • · • · · ·

Thirty minutes later when Amber and I arrive at the party, my nerves are no more at ease. The party is being hosted by a former mayor and her partner in their ostentatious estate situated on four acres of manicured lawns. As gaudy as their decor may be, I do like them. Our kinks don't align, so I've never played with them, but they are stunning together.

A soft, male voice from behind takes my focus away from people watching. "Hello Mistress." It's Victor, a man of fifty with olive skin, perfectly coiffed hair, and the CEO of a Fortune 500 company. I'm not supposed to know that, but he's a member at the country club Amber works at, and she told me.

He hands me the single glass of champagne he's holding, full and untouched, like he was waiting for me. Victor has been one of my favorite submissives and he's been a frequent partner of mine since I started coming to these things.

"You look beautiful tonight," he says a little breathlessly. I can tell he's already uncomfortable standing here, towering over me. I can see it in the way his eyes can't settle and the way his throat works.

"Thank you," is all I say in reply.

"Can I get you anything, Mistress? Anything to make you more comfortable?"

My gaze floats down to the bubbles in my flute. Why aren't my thoughts in the right place? "I don't know if I'll be good company tonight, pup. I think I'd rather watch than play." I don't ask if that's okay with him. I don't have to.

"Oh." The look on his face could kill me if I was in love with him, but that's not how we operate. Nonetheless, guilt finds me.

I offer alternative Dommes for him. "Princess Porsche and Mistress Noir are both here."

Victor finds each of them and lets out a slow breath before smiling. "I know."

"Tell you what, pup. I'm going to have a seat and watch my fill tonight. If you'd like to join me, the floor at my feet will be open for you."

Besotted with the invitation, he gleefully kneels once I sit. My legs are crossed, one foot bobbing in the air slightly, and I know the shiny black leather taunts him. He lays his head in my lap, and I know he's dreaming of the way my heel would feel against his chest.

Despite all of my distractions—my pup's soft hair that I've been running my fingers through for hours, and his quiet, appreciative sighs... the women I watch in front of me, one writhing in pleasure so deep she's sobbing through her twentieth consecutive orgasm, the other looking like she's not even half way done with her little pet—despite it all, I can't stop thinking[1] about Jonah Johanssen.

We pull out of the driveway of the mansion, and Amber knows. She doesn't even look at me first—just eases the car onto the road, one hand on the wheel, the other drumming

---

1. Bad Things by Cailin Russo

against it. "Huh."

I brace myself. "What?"

"You left a sex party, and somehow"—she gestures vaguely in my direction—"you look exactly the same as when we arrived."

"I... did other things."

My sister hums. "Your hair is untouched. Your lipstick is intact. And I don't see a single drop of sweat." She gasps, because she lives for dramatics. "Oh my God, you didn't even *try*."

"I resent that," I mutter, staring out the window. "I tried very hard to mind my own business."

She laughs—a chaotic, delighted sound that usually means I'm about to regret my life choices. "Something is wrong."

The car fills with silence.

"Spill."

I sigh and sink lower in my seat. "I don't wanna."

"Real mature. It wasn't a request."

Streetlights flash past and I give in, because resisting Amber is a losing battle. I close my eyes and admit the most inconvenient truth. "I have... *ughhh*... feelings... for Jonah."

Amber full-body cackles. "You like Jonah!"

"I do not *like* him," I snap. "I am experiencing an unfortunate emotional response."

"That's liking. That's capital L liking."

"Please keep your eyes on the road. I don't want my tombstone to read, 'Died because her sister discovered a crush.'"

She wipes at her eyes, still grinning. "This is amazing. You left without hooking up. You probably didn't even flirt."

"I panicked."

"It means you liiiiike him. You really liiiiike him," she taunts.

"Shut up."

"Do you want me to invite him over?"

"No."

"Drive by his house real slow?"

"I will jump out of this moving vehicle."

Amber laughs, warm and loud, filling the car. She continues teasing me the whole drive home—asking if our couple name would be Renah or Jonée, if I've imagined where we will honeymoon.

I threaten her.

She dares me to text him.

I almost do.

Somewhere between the third red light and our street, the knot in my chest loosens. I feel lighter, like we're teenagers whispering secrets in the dark, daring each other to make the first move, and pretending this stuff isn't terrifying.

When we get home, we relieve Tracy of her babysitting duties and she rejects my money as always.

A hot shower isn't necessary because I didn't work up any kind of sweat. I didn't even take off my dress. Said dress is hung back in my closet and I peel out of my armor that did jackshit protecting me tonight. I pop on an old nightgown and slip into bed.

In the privacy of my room and steel vault of my mind, I think of my former student. Cocksure and irritating.

I think of the stripper. Magnificent and talented.

I think of my neighbor. Generous and kind.

Wetness forms at the crux of my thighs for the first time tonight, and when my fingers slide through, I dream of his tongue. Of his broad, muscular shoulders under my legs—steady and grounding.

The house is silent, but I can't hear anything over the blood rushing through my ears when I come fast and hard to the image of me riding him, teasing him, forcing his arms down and taking what's mine—mine—*mine*.

And when I come again, all I picture is that smile.

Chapter 20
A Small Request
Jonah

On the Monday morning after family dinner, I go out to the barn to feed everyone and freshen up their pens. When I see the space where the tractor usually is, I remember it's still dead and parked a ways back on the trail.

I'm about to call the first tractor repair mechanic the internet offers, but then I think of Dad. He probably knows exactly what to do. And even though he was just here last night, something tells me he wouldn't mind coming back. He stayed longer than anyone last night to talk to me. We sat on the porch, listening to crickets and talking. I would have stayed up all night if he wanted to. Something's changed between us. He spoke to me like a friend, man-to-man, not father-to-son.

It made me realize two things: He's not as concerned about where my life is going as he once was, and he's lonely. I'm sure it was hard enough when all us kids finally moved out, but now he's retired.

So, before I press the phone number for Mike's Deli and Tractor Repair (10.2 miles away with a 4.4 out of 5 star rating), I call Dad instead. He may be retired from his corporate life, but he still takes odd engine repair jobs.

Two hours later, he pulls into my driveway.

The dogs mill about the trees in search of squirrels while the pair of us stand over the front wheel wells. Dad knows what he's looking at. I do not.

Shocking, I know.

"That's what I thought," he sighs, but he doesn't sound grim. "It's overheating," he explains. "You've gotta be careful with these older tractors. Your coolant is low. I'm guessing you haven't topped it off with any new fluids since you bought this place?"

I shake my head.

"That's alright. You know now. I'll write down what kind of oil, coolant, hydraulic and transmission fluid you'll need, as well as a schedule. See that you stick to it."

"So, I don't have to buy a new tractor?"

"No," he drawls, amusement pulling at the corners of his mouth. "This girl's old, but she's still got plenty of life left in her. Just keep her tuned up and take her out now and then."

"I can do that," I reply. I feel like an idiot for even thinking I needed a new tractor.

"You've also got a clogged radiator," he says, pointing to… what I'm gathering is the radiator. "All you've gotta do is clean it out with a leaf blower or some compressed air."

See, these are the kinds of things I should do myself. This is what a farmer would do, and I live on a farm! It's small, and I have no crops, but I have a barn and animals that depend on me.

I am Farmer Jonah.

We hop in the Yukon and head back to the house to grab a leaf blower and search the barn for coolant that we hope the last owners left behind. I park between the barn and garage when movement from the side yard catches my attention.

The curly red hair of Miss Loretta Wilde is unmistakable as she bounds past her mother's garden, grinning a mile wide. For a second, I catch my breath because… is she going to say something to me? Hope builds in my heart like a volcano, ready to burst.

When she's only a few feet away, I kneel, and she wraps me in a hug.

I did not start this, and I want that to go on my record.

"Hey Shortcake."

The hope lava in my body retreats when she doesn't reply. When she releases me, she puts two hands up, indicating for me to stay right where I am, and takes off for her house, dogs following. I stay kneeling with my hands in my lap like I have nothing better to do today.

Dad chuckles and stands next to me. "Glad to see you can still make friends out here in the country."

Dad is busy searching the barn for what he needs when Lo comes back with the dogs. She's brought an equally exuberant older sister, and their foxy mama trails behind them at a leisurely pace.

It's Delta's turn to hug me—*again, I'm not initiating*—but I do hug her back when their mother doesn't seem off-put.

"What's going on, ladies?"

"Can I have my birthday party here with all my friends?"

I rear back and stare at Renée. She finally stops in front of me. "What? Here?"

"Girls, you can't ambush him like that."

"You said—" Delta whines.

Renée cuts her daughter off. "I said I would talk to him."

I stand up. "Of course she can have her party here."

"Jonah, you don't even know what you're agreeing to."

"Birthday cake," I say, counting off on each finger as I go. "Pizza. Funny hats. Balloons. I know what I'm agreeing to."

"I want to have a petting zoo," Delta cheers.

"Do you want me to get more animals?"

"Yeah!"

"No," her mother claps back. "She means she would like to know if she could invite her friends over to pet and play with your animals. We would host the party portion at our house. That is, of course, if you don't have any plans that day. You're also absolutely allowed to say no with no reason at all." She says that last part looking down at Delta, her stare laced with unspoken words. Probably something like, *Remember, we talked about this.*

I open the calendar on my phone. "When's the party?"

"September 19th," Delta replies. "It's a Saturday."

My heart sinks when I find the date. "Oh. I have a game that day." Joy drains from both girls' faces, and it's like a gut punch to know I did that.

Suddenly, I have another idea. "Is there any way you can have the party the next day? On Sunday?"

They twist to watch their mom, eyebrows raised.

Renée thinks. "Well, we haven't sent out invitations yet, so sweetie, if you're okay with having it on Sunday—"

"YES!"

"—then we can do it Sunday."

The girls and I are jumping and screaming while the dogs circle us, barking at us to either settle down or let them join in; I'm not sure. But when I cut out and let the girls run off with the dogs, I'm left staring at the pleased face of their mother. And now my heart's racing for an entirely different reason.

"You didn't have to do that," she whispers.

"I know. I wanted to. And I'd like to host the whole thing if that's okay. Have the entire party here. I have space. How many kids are coming?"

"I don't know yet, but probably eight or nine and their parents."

I flick my hand like that's nothing. "No problem. She can invite her whole class if she wants."

She chuckles. "You do not want that."

But I do. I want to make that birthday girl happy. It's not even about pleasing Renée—though yes, I absolutely want to please her more than I want to breathe. I really just want to bring a smile to the faces of these adorable girls. I know what it's like growing up with only one parent, and while I'm not trying to replace their dad, I'd like them to count on me.

For these Wilde girls, I want to be someone special.

"Hey, do you think I should get her that chainsaw as a present, or do you think she wants something else?"

Renée narrows her eyes, and I receive her silent answer.

I cross my arms and nod, but an even better idea pops up. "Oh my God, what about a Nerf gun?"

Chapter 21
Girlfriend

Renée

"Remember to complete your pre-labs before Thursday," I say to the small lecture hall of students as they pack up to leave. "No one's going to know what the inside of a rat looks like unless you come to the lab prepared."

Most of the students in this three-hundred level class are students I have taught since freshman year, and they are hoping to use their biology degrees for the greater good. Aspiring veterinarians, research scientists, marine biologists, what have you. At least they *think* they're in it for the greater good at this point. It's easy to romanticize what your life will shape up to be when you're young and hopeful—before the crushing reality of capitalism and greed and expectations of others set in. Oh, to be a kid just dreaming of saving the whales.

But the semester just started, and I would never purposely crush their dreams. Manage their expectations, yes. First-year students majoring in biology always hear the truth, and the unsure ones weed themselves out by the end of the year.

I do particularly enjoy this level, however. They ask smart, thought-provoking questions. There's more diligence in reports, drawings, and presentations. Unlike the next class I have—my one hundred-level Pennsylvania Nature Study class—which starts in twenty minutes. It's held in the largest auditorium-style classroom on campus because students from all different majors and programs take it as a cultural enrichment course. This class is a breeding ground for students like Jonah—though no one is or was ever as brazen.

The last of my students trickle out, and I pack up my bag and head back to my office for a quick pit stop before my next class begins. My office is private, which not every professor on campus can say. There's a large glass window overlooking the quad, and the walls are white with my framed degrees, a periodic table, animal anatomy posters, and ecological memes pinned to a corkboard (I'm fun, dammit).

Before grabbing a stack of workbooks for the next class, I check my phone to find a few new emails and a text from Jonah. An embarrassing heat fills my face when I ignore the emails and open his message first.

Jonah: <picture of a flower> This is white goldenrod (aka Solidago bicolor). Non-binary they/them. They have white flowers instead of yellow because they're not as flashy as their goldenrod cousin. The flowers are tiny and pop off the sides of the stem. Insects like <bee emoji> and <butterfly emoji> love them. Birds snack on the leaves too. They grow 1-3 feet (I can relate <winky face emoji>), and like chill dry areas like the edge of my property by the road. They grow all over Canada and the eastern half of the United States except Florida (what did Florida ever do to them?!)

Jonah: White goldenrod is non-toxic to dogs, but very toxic to horses and goats! <crying emoji> I'm beginning to see why Florida doesn't like them <unimpressed emoji>

Jonah: Scratch that... there's confusion around

> a plant with a similar name known as rayless goldenrod (Isocoma pluriflora) which is highly toxic to goats and other livestock, but that's not what's growing on my land <relief emoji>

Falling into my chair, I lean back and reread every word. Even with an eye roll or two, I smile. Not because of the toxic to horses and goats thing, but... everything else. Him and all his sunshine and goodness that pours out of him like a waterfall—unstoppable and unfiltered.

> Renée: <paper and pencil emoji> <the letter A emoji>

> Jonah: I got an A?!

> Renée: I can tell you're putting in the effort. You deserve it.

The typing dots appear for a long time and disappear. Then again, and again.

> Renée: Are you doing anything tonight? I was thinking we could plan Delta's party. But if you have to work then maybe another time.

His reply is immediate.

> Jonah: Yes! Come over! And I actually don't strip anymore (but I'll make an exception for you, just ask) <disco ball emoji> <man dancing emoji>

> Renée: I'll see you later then.

The memory of our private room all those months ago flashes behind my eyes and, yes, I very much want a private dance from all those glistening muscles. *Ohhh, what I would do if there were no rules, no bouncer, no time limit...*

My mind trails off on a delicious tangent before it's derailed for another reason.

How does he make money? The question flickers like a neon sign. Stripping can't be *that* lucrative. Does he even have a job? I need to sort this out because it's starting to bother me. Straight up, I'm going to ask him tonight. I know it's none of my business, but... it kind of is now. He's not some random former student; he's not a quiet neighbor who sticks to himself. My daughters are enamored with him, and I am growing a garden on his property. I kind of do have a right to know how he makes his money.

· · · ● · ● · · · ·

Jonah

With a light heart, I fall back onto the closest soft surface in the middle of the showroom floor. This couch is too firm for my liking, but it serves as my fainting pad after reading Renée's text.

My exhale is loud and high-pitched, and I'm certain cartoon hearts are popping out of my eyeballs. "She's coming over tonight, LaShonda."

The sales associate, who has been more than accommodating of my every whim and expertly reigns in my furniture choices, crosses her arms and studies me. "You look smitten."

"As a kitten," I sigh.

Joaquín turned me on to this fancy home furnishings store, and for the last two days LaShonda has been helping me pick furniture for every room in my home. She about fell over when I told her how much I needed. I showed her the online listing of my house, and she snooped through every picture and took notes on what I needed. Couches and chairs and bed frames and desks and rugs and lamps and blankets and... I'm dizzy just thinking about it.

She'd better get a huge commission check because she deserves it! What a pro.

Suddenly the reality of what I just agreed to hits me. Renée will be in my home tonight, and I still have no furniture. It's been weeks since she was over during the storm, and all I had then were beds and a couple of stools.

I bolt upright. "How fast can I get all of this delivered? Like, can I get it tonight?"

LaShonda's eyes round, and she laughs. "Mr. Johanssen, this is custom furniture. Even with an expedite fee, delivery will take at least a month.

"A MONTH?"

I have Joaquín on the phone in less than five seconds. "She's coming over tonight to talk about birthday party plans, and I still don't have furniture, dude. What should I do?"

"I assume you're talking about Renée?"

"Of course."

LaShonda steps away to fill out some forms while my heart pounds through my chest, waiting for my Joaquín to save me.

"Okay, here's what we're gonna do. Finish your furniture order, and on your way home, pick up the nicest outdoor patio set at a home improvement store. It's a beautiful day, so have your meeting with her on your porch."

My best friend is the *best* best friend that ever friended.

•••••••••

Renée

The rest of my classes flew by after we made plans for

tonight. Amber only had to work the lunch shift today, so she was already home with dinner halfway done by the time I arrived after work.

"You should just go over there now," she says. I cast a glance at her as I sip on my chardonnay while the girls do their homework at the table.

I bite my lower lip and stare out the window toward his place. "You don't think it's too early?"

She shrugs. "He's home. His vehicle is in the driveway. You know he's just waiting for you," she says, with mischief in her eyes. "He's such..." She waits for me to flick my focus to her before silently mouthing, "...a good boy."

My cheeks burn and I attempt to stare daggers into her eyes. It's not like my girls heard her or know what any of that means. Regardless, red-hot lust dances with embarrassment under my skin.

Maybe I should walk over to his place now. I take a calming breath and nod. Then I look at my clothes—the same clothes I wore to work. A navy blue and tan plaid skirt that stops mid-calf, with a white, collared blouse. It's nothing special, really.

"Should I change?" I ask Amber.

"Oh, no," she chuckles. "You're a hot professor. This is exactly what he wants to see you wear."

I swallow the last bit of my wine and roll my eyes. "This is not a hot outfit."

"Wait, where are your reading glasses? He'll lose his mind if you wear them. Oh, and you're going to need this." She hands me a paper napkin. "For his drool."

Laughter bubbles up, and I wad the tissue to throw at her. The girls are still engrossed in their homework as I grab my notebook from the table and head out the back door for Jonah's place.

Instead of the sensible heels I wore to work today, I opt for the well-worn sandals to trek across our yards. Passing the garden, I'm pleased to see so much is ready for harvest already. Some tomatoes, kale, and green beans look good enough to eat straight away.

And the sunflowers! I must have picked the wrong seeds because they're twice the size they should be. Most of them stand about eighteen feet tall, and I have to laugh because what the hell? They're completely ridiculous, but I kind of love how outrageous and unexpected they are.

When I step up to Jonah's back porch, I realize a little too late I should have gone around to the front. I'm about to change direction when I spot something new—an elaborate outdoor dining table and six matching chairs with thick, tan cushions. He didn't have this last time we were here or the night of the storm.

Curiosity gets the better of me, and before I know it, I'm peering inside his windows to find out if he's finally filling his home with more than a massive TV and a recliner.

That's when my heart stops altogether.

Right there, standing in the kitchen with long, damp blonde hair and even longer legs poking out of a man's T-shirt, is a young—*young*—woman biting into a piece of toast. Only her profile is visible when she closes her eyes and sighs, like there's nowhere more comfortable to be than right here in Jonah's kitchen.

Before she can take another bite, I'm flying back to my house with a lump in my throat and stupid, stupid tears threatening to escape.

Of course he has a girlfriend. Or maybe she's a hookup. A situationship? *Ughh*, it doesn't matter because *she* makes way more sense for him than I do. *Fuck!* Why did I let myself even imagine a world where I was part of his life like that? He's twenty-five and I'm a mom who's knocking on forty, for fuck's sake. What did I think was going to happen? And when did my perception of what we were change? The plan was to keep the irritating manchild who had never heard "no" at bay. When did I let him into my heart, and why the hell did I think he would want to be?

When I return, Amber is surprised to see me. "Everything okay?"

I shake my head, and she follows me to my bedroom so we can talk in private.

"He had a woman over. In his kitchen. Young, tall, gorgeous."

"So?"

"All she was wearing was his T-shirt."

"How do you know it was his?"

"I guess..." I start, but irrational anger takes over. "I don't know! I just... It was oversized. And her hair was wet, so she obviously showered there, and she ate at the counter as if she owned the place!"

My sister sinks into the same realization. "I can't believe this. He's been so obvious with his feelings for you."

"This is what I get for not following my own rules. Dragged along like I'm some plaything. I knew he wasn't mature enough."

"Well, maturity might not be his downfall." I don't love that she's playing devil's advocate right now. She continues despite my scowl. "What if he's polyamorous? Didn't you say his brother was?"

"I don't think I'm cut out for that," I answer honestly. "I'm not even cut out for monogamous marriage anymore."

Amber lifts her eyebrows and sighs because she doesn't need a rationale behind my anti-marriage stance. I'm too damaged for that, and it's no surprise why. What is surprising, however, is how susceptible my heart still is to being trampled on.

An hour later, when my heart rate returns to baseline and I've reminded myself one million times that I don't need anyone's attention or sappy-sweet feelings clouding my judgement, I make the call.

Jonah picks up right away. "Hi," he answers. His voice is bright, as always. "Are you ready to come over?"

"I'm not feeling well," I reply, the half-truth easily falling out. "Would you mind if we discussed the party plans over the phone?"

"Are you okay? Do you need anything? I can—"

"I'm fine. I would just rather stay home tonight."

"Oh," he breathes, and I can practically feel his dejection.

Whatever. I will not feel bad about this. I will not feel bad about removing myself from someone who can harm me.

"No problem," he says. "I have my pen and paper, ready for whatever ideas you have. What is going to make Delta happy, and does it include an inflatable obstacle course? Because I heard you can rent them."

My icy heart thaws the tiniest amount, and I shut my eyes. "She would love that."

Chapter 22
Delta's Birthday

Renée

The weather on the day of Delta's tenth birthday party couldn't have been better. Not a cloud in the sky and just warm enough for shorts—not that I'm wearing any. Delta insisted the four of us wear our matching sequined jumpsuits that were originally purchased for a roller rink party. Amber insisted on it, too.

Leaves have barely started turning into their autumn palette, and without fail, just as I have done every year since she arrived, I think of her birth. I remember all the trees were green before she was born, then all at once they turned. At least, that's what it felt like. It's entirely possible I was so focused on the tiny human that I was madly in love with that I didn't notice the world around me changing.

I prayed having children with Greg would be my answer to a better life with him. He wanted children so badly, and I hoped giving him children would change him, change our marriage. I thought... maybe I could feel safe again. Through no fault of their own, our kids were not the answer to a better marriage, but having them forced me to find my way—our way—to safety. A better life for all of us.

I finish refilling a bowl of chips inside Jonah's kitchen only to look up and find Thelma clomping her hooves through the door yet again. Some of Delta's friends have a habit of leaving the doors open when they're running in and out of the house, which has led to the occasional goat or duck finding their way inside. The Pyrenees are doing their best to keep every animal and child wrangled, but it's a hard job. On top of that, Jonah acquired an old alpaca named Timothy last week, so the dogs' protection services have grown.

I place the bowl of chips on the dining room table and chat with some parents inside. I have to explain several times, this is not my home, but that of our friend Jonah. It's easier that way.

Curious eyes and wandering feet meander through the main floor, and I don't blame them. I myself wandered about when I realized his moving boxes were gone, re-placed by upscale decor. Every room has beautiful new furniture, all of it looking like it's been there forever. Rich leather cushions the color of mahogany. Reds, creams, and dark green sprawling area rugs warm the rooms, and soft throws lie haphazardly across furniture. A solid wood coffee table, end tables, and desk—all stained the perfect shade to complement the home's stonework.

Very rough-hewn Pennsylvania-winery-core.

I guess he's really doing it—planting his life right here, next door to me.

As I listen to a few parents talk about their children's budding sports careers, my eyes catch on a framed picture sitting on a bookshelf. They're engrossed in their conver-sation, so I don't feel bad stepping away to get a closer look.

I would know this artist anywhere. When Lo made this and gave it to him, I don't know. It's a drawing of Jonah and all his animals—each one labeled with a name above its head.

Then I notice all the little painted rocks sitting next to the picture. Smooth stones no bigger than a Post-it, all painted like ladybugs and frogs. *The work of my girls.* I know this because my girls have scattered dozens of them in my backyard and home over the years.

He may not be right for me (no one is), but I can't deny

he's right for my children.

The crackling laughter of fourth graders leaping through a sixty-foot-long inflatable obstacle course greets me when I walk outside. Limbs peek over the side as kids tumble over each obstruction, racing each other to the end. Rugger sits next to King, the pair of them watching between the obstacle course and the pony rides.

Parents and kids stand along the fence watching kids take turns riding the sweet old mare. Jonah leads them around, encouraging the riders to take in the beauty.

"See?" he says, smiling up at Delta's friend Clementine. "You're a natural! And you know what? If you scratch right there next to her mane—yeah, right there!—she loves that."

Clementine giggles when Ginger huffs appreciatively and bobs her head. "Mom, look!" she hollers.

Her mother, Zoey, calls back. "I can see!" She smiles, and I don't miss the way she's watching *him* more than her daughter. My skin prickles when her gaze dips to his ass as he walks away from her. When she bites her bottom lip, I have to walk away and cool down before I embarrass myself.

Inside the barn I find one kid feeding Timothy apple chunks from her palm. Lo and three other kids are petting the goats and the Quack Pack under Amber's supervision. Thelma and Louise wear party necklaces around their necks—an addition by their father early this morning—and streamers and party decorations are hung all over the barn and fences.

It takes considerable effort to convince everyone to leave the inflatable obstacle course and animals and come to the porch for birthday cake and presents. But once the stragglers hear Jonah strum his guitar and play a few riffs, they're racing to join, their eyes wide and gap-toothed smiles bright.

He plays "Happy Birthday" while everyone sings, and I

capture the happiness of a ten-year-old on camera, including the blush spreading across her face as she tries to hide behind a party hat.

People devour cake and ice cream in minutes before Delta shreds her presents. Her friends ooh and ahh over everything. After all the presents are opened and fawned over and stacked in a heaping pile on the table, some kids race for the outdoor activities again.

"Hold up," Jonah shouts. "Everyone come back here! I got something for you!"

What did he do now?

He pops around the corner with a massive box before opening it with a flair. "Everyone gets a Nerf gun! Go go go!"

I can't hold back my laughter as all the kids grab a new, preloaded plastic gun and leap for the backyard.

"Come on," Jonah yells, grabbing one for himself, tossing one to me, and shoving some into the hands of parents. "Scatter!"

I'm too caught up in his rally cry and the thrill of a chase to guard my emotions. Foam bullets whiz past me as I aim at any kid in range. Everyone's running around like gas molecules when an idea strikes.

I jump inside the unoccupied inflatable and scale one obstacle shaped like a triangle. From up here, I have a perfect vantage point and pop one kid in the back. He doesn't feel it, but the tiny victory is sooo satisfying.

When I pull the trigger on Delta, nothing shoots out, and I curse.

"Looking for this?" a familiar voice asks. Jonah runs over the unstable floor and falls over with a laugh before throwing a magazine of pink bullets at me. "Reload, soldier!"

He hops up on the triangle behind me, mirroring my position on the west side, and unleashes his toy weapon with a maniacal laugh. "Happy birthday, ya filthy animal!"

We shoot off round after round until we exhaust our supply.

"We need more ammo," he says.

My heart is pounding as I look around for a solution. "There!" I shout. "On the floor!" Like scuba divers sitting on the edge of a boat, we fall backwards and land softly among stray bullets. Of course, the floor is made of air and plastic, and with each other's weight counteracting the other's stability, we're falling over at every attempt to stand. I'm laughing so hard I'm in danger of peeing my jumpsuit, and Jonah's in no better shape.

At the same moment, we realize there aren't enough bullets for both of us to reload. Kids giggle and shriek outside our walls as we tear through every nook and cranny for spare ammo. When I spot three lonely rounds in the far corner, I lunge—and so does he.

"Oh, no you don't," I cackle, sharper than I mean to. But the usual patient, sweet Jonah is gone; in his place is a chaotic, competitive gremlin, and he's ready to throw down.

We collide before either of us can claim victory, tumbling in a ridiculous tangle of elbows and determination. Our combined weight plummeting into the bouncy floor causes the three precious Nerf bullets to go flying, then reappear in Jonah's fist as if he manifested them by sheer competitiveness.

"Unfair!" I gasp, scrambling after him. He rolls, I roll after him, and we're a whirlwind of limbs, laughter, and way-too-serious grunting for a fake foam-dart apocalypse.

He clamps his hand tighter around the three bullets. "Mine," he declares, breathless and triumphant.

"Over my dead body," I snap back.

I lunge, trying to pry his fingers open. He's stronger. He's faster. He's smug. And I realize I'm officially out of moves.

On pure impulse, I do the most ridiculous, desperate

thing imaginable.

I kiss him.

It's quick—just a press of the lips—but the effect is nuclear. Jonah goes completely still, like someone yanked his batteries out. The tension in his hand releases and the foam bullets slip.

I'm frozen too, because I absolutely, definitely did not think this through.

Our eyes are wide and unblinking.

"Uhhh..." I manage to say.

Jonah opens his mouth to say something—or maybe to short-circuit like me—but before either of us can recover our brain cells, a volley of foam bullets patter against the walls.

We both jolt like we've been struck with real gunfire.

"Right. Battle. Birthday party," I huff, clambering upright because apparently I process emotional shock by not addressing it at all.

Jonah blinks hard, shakes his head as if someone's shoved his batteries back in, and then crawls toward the front flaps. "We should, um... secure ourselves." His voice cracks, and it's honestly adorable, which is a very inconvenient thought at the moment.

He reaches for the zipper, ready to seal us in, but before he can, the flaps are yanked open, and my daughters tumble in like tiny raiders in rainbow jumpsuits.

Seeing them is like a bucket of cold water has been poured over me, and I thank God they didn't come in here ten seconds earlier.

Jonah's eyes snap back into focus when he sees the spare magazines they each carry. "You're on our team!" he announces, instantly slipping into battle commander mode. "Quick, get in and zip the door shut."

Guess we're ignoring that kiss. I mean, who has time to unpack that emotional load in the middle of a war?!

The girls struggle to balance atop the triangles, so Jonah kneels and perches a squealing birthday girl on his shoulder so she can peer over the wall. Inspired, I attempt the same with Lo, but we collapse in a puddle. She's smiling ear-to-ear, racing to climb back on. I'm a little steadier this time, and she's able to fire off a round.

When we exhaust the ammunition and use all the spare bullets that land inside our fort, I'm ready with a new plan of attack, but a loud voice booms from outside the walls.

"Attack!"

Suddenly our entire inflatable bunker is shaking as kids and parents climb over the sides and fall in like paratroopers.

"Stand your ground," Jonah hollers. He takes a massive leap and bounces his full bodyweight a mere foot away from another dad, sending him flying back.

All three of us take his lead and slam into the ground to knock our attackers off their feet while Jonah collects their ammunition.

This chaos continues until every adult is dead tired and in need of a break. My legs feel like Jell-O, and it takes an alarming amount of time for the world to stop spinning once I'm on solid ground. The second before I fall into a bush, Jonah wraps his arms around me. I'm too delirious to hide my smile.

He leads me to the porch where I hold up a hand. "I'm okay, really."

"You sure?"

"Yes," I giggle. "Now leave me alone because I need to use your bathroom. Try and remember that I gave birth twice and was just jumping in a bouncy castle."

He laughs so hard, he leans against the wooden porch banister, clutching his sides. I can't wait for him to collect himself, so I sprint inside for the nearest bathroom. Even while I struggle to peel off this one-piece disco jumpsuit, my smile remains plastered to my face.

When I finish my business and wash up, I'm surprised by the woman staring back at me in the mirror. Fiery red hair down and crazed, some of it sticking to my face. My eyes are bright with joyous tears I have to wipe from the corners.

I chuckle when I discover lipstick stuck to my teeth. *How long has this been here?*

The adrenaline from our Nerf battle subsides and reality crashes into me. *Why did I kiss him?* I'm going to need a serious debrief with Amber later.

I spend a few extra minutes fixing my appearance so I look halfway normal—or as normal as I can look while wearing disco getup... on a farm.

A loud clanking sound alarms me before I step into the kitchen, only to find one of the goats has made her way into the house yet again. Judging by the plastic bowl of cheese puffs she's knocked on the floor, I'd say she was counter-surfing.

"Louise! Bad girl," I chide good naturedly as I attempt to shove her to the side so I can clean up, but she's intent on "helping" me. I do my best to corral the cheese balls on the tile floor, but it's a fight between us.

"Really, you old goat? Eating children's snacks? Have you no shame? Just wait until I tell your father."

My worry is temporarily abandoned as Louise and I pick up every apocalypse-surviving snack—but the cheesy crumbs on the floor drive me bananas, so I soak a towel under the faucet and wipe the floor.

"You certainly have a way with kids," I hear someone say, just outside the open door a few feet away. It's Zoey, Clementine's mom. I can't see, but I'd know that smooth, feminine voice anywhere.

"You think so?" Jonah asks. "I do take my role as Fun Uncle pretty seriously."

"Would you like to have some fun with me?" Zoey asks,

her tone flirty and seductive.

My heart stops while I'm on all fours and I stiffen. Louise sniffs around in search of crumbs to suck up, oblivious to my shock and rage. Eavesdropping on a cougar is not something this old goat seems to care about.

Why do I care for that matter?

"Sure! Where's your Nerf gun? I'll find some more bullets."

"No, Jonah," she says through a hint of laughter. "Would you like to have some *fun* with *only* me. Alone." She poses it like a question but it's not. There is no gentle, rising lilt at the end. She's deadly serious and her request brokers no other meaning. If Jonah doesn't pick up on it, I'm going to slam my head against this floor and if I'm lucky—*really lucky*—I'll concuss myself enough to forget about this stupid crush.

Fortunately (or unfortunately depending on how you look at it), he *does* catch her meaning and laughs nervously. "Oh! Oh. I'm flattered, but no. I'm—I'm actually taken."

The reminder of that hot young thing standing in this very kitchen with her wet hair and buttered toast haunts me. I shouldn't care that Zoey's making a move on Jonah and yet I'm blindly enraged in a storm of jealousy. And now he's literally confirming his relationship with someone else, but my validation feels like hydrogen peroxide bubbling over an open wound. I knew the truth, and yet...

I'm crushed. All... over... again.

"That's too bad," Zoey replies, casually. "If you and your *partner* are ever interested in a guest star, let me know."

Chapter 23

Taken

Jonah was none the wiser to my emotional turmoil when we left after the party, and I certainly did not want to acknowledge the stupid mistake I made by kissing him. I got up from his kitchen floor and schooled my features into a picture-perfect mom determined to give her daughter the best tenth birthday ever.

After her shower, Delta fell asleep as I braided her hair in the living room. Carrying her to bed, as large as she's grown, made me miss all those times I carried her as an infant and a toddler. When had I stopped carrying her? *Why* did I ever stop?

Amber and I sit on the couch and catch up on a show to decompress after the girls go down. The TV is on, but my mind is still back with Jonah. Surprisingly enough, I don't focus on the conversation between Jonah and Zoey that I overheard. Rather, I think about the joy on my girls' faces as they rode Ginger, their giggles while they fed the ducks and alpaca, their squeals as three different dogs licked them head to toe.

I think of Jonah's face turning up to carefully watch each of them as they rode his sweet, blind horse. The way he looked as we fell over each other in the bouncy house, the September sunshine kissing his golden hair, his laugh so big it pulled me into its orbit. I could replay that moment in slow motion for the rest of my life.

He didn't have to do any of this today, but he wanted to.

I shouldn't have kissed him, but I was so wrapped up in the moment that I forgot my inhibitions—I forgot he's in a relationship with someone else.

I need to apologize and thank him.

I stand up to leave. "I'll be right back," I tell Amber. "I forgot something at Jonah's." She's distracted by the TV but nods without looking at me.

I snag a flashlight and slip out of the house. The evening air has cooled and I've ditched the jumpsuit for matching lounge wear. Halfway there, I realize I'm not wearing shoes when I step on a twig.

When he opens his front door in only a pair of low-slung gym shorts, he's surprised to see me. "Hey."

"Hi," I say a little breathlessly, and I sort of... forget why I'm here.

In all his shirtless, muscled glory, he stands with his hands in his pockets just... watching me like he has nothing better to do. Like he'd be perfectly content standing here in silence all night.

"You changed your clothes," he says.

"Yeah," I say like a fool. I swallow. "It wasn't terribly comfortable."

A sad smile pulls at his full lips. "That's too bad. I liked it. It was fun."

Fun! I remind myself. *That's what I want to talk about!*

"Would you like to come in?" he asks, and gestures for me to do so.

I nod once and step past him, inhaling the scent of sage and citrus wafting off his body. "Thank you."

He indicates I should follow him to the living room just off the foyer. "Have a seat," he says, before taking his own in an arm chair.

I sit on the edge of the sofa directly across from him and hold my hands in my lap to keep them from fidgeting. "I just wanted to say thank you for today. Delta thinks of her birthday like the Super Bowl, or... what's the equivalent in rugby?"

He chuckles. "The Rugby World Cup."

"Yeah." I smile. "That. She had the best time today. I'm not quite sure how I'm supposed to match that same level next year, but... I'll try."

"We'll figure something out." He flashes a sweet and knowing sideways grin and gently stares at me, unblinking. Lord Almighty, his eyes are piercing; they're as deep as the sea and as bright as the sky.

"But there's no need to thank me, Renée. I had a great time today."

There's a pregnant pause as I struggle to blurt out why I came over. Finally, I release it. "And I'm sorry for kissing you. That wasn't okay." I stand, ready to leave. "I'll see myself out. I'm sure your girlfriend wouldn't love knowing another woman is alone with you in your home at night."

He stands. "My what?"

"Your girlfriend," I reiterate, calmly.

He screws up his face. "I don't have a girlfriend."

I level him with a look that says I *don't buy that for a second.* "I've seen her, Jonah."

"Have you?" He crosses his arms. "Care to tell me what she looks like? I'm curious."

I roll my eyes and sigh. "Tall, long blonde hair, a beauty mark on her cheek, a love for oversized T-shirts and buttered toast."

The man has the gall to still look confused. "Oddly specific. And where did you see her?"

"In your kitchen. The evening we started planning the birthday party, I actually came over a bit early," I admit. Embarrassment kicks up in my stomach. "She was standing at the counter eating. Looked like she had just taken a shower. She caught me off guard and I—I didn't want to intrude, so I went home."

"You told me you weren't feeling well."

"Not really the point, Jonah."

"Wow," he chuckles, which morphs into a full belly laugh. He struggles to breathe for a while, but I stand firm. He blows out a long breath and dabs his eyes. "That was my sister, Ivy. She's a midwife and was crashing here because she had a long delivery just a few miles away. She was too tired to drive all the way back home. This... is... *rich!*"

"But... your SUV was the only one in the driveway."

"She parked in the garage. She has the code."

"She wasn't wearing pants!"

"She never does. She probably had on her tiny spandex shorts."

My mind whirls back to what he admitted on the porch earlier. "But I heard what you said to Zoey today."

"Who's Zoey?"

"Clementine's mom."

"Oh, her! What did I say?"

"Th–that," I stammer. "That you were taken."

"I mean," he shrugs and doesn't look a bit sorry about it. "I am."

Now I'm plain mad and I can't hold back the frustration in my voice. "Care to explain?"

Jonah closes the distance between us until he's only a foot away. He might be significantly taller than me but I hold my head high. Those sea and sky eyes lock into mine and his voice is quieter now, lower. "I am taken. I'm taken by three ladies, actually."

He can't possibly mean...

"Do I need to spell it out for you, Professor Wilde? Thought I was supposed to be the dumb one."

"Me?" My voice is so small I'm not confident any sound came out.

But he watches my lips so intensely that he doesn't need to hear my question. He nods. "You."

My heart is racing and suddenly everything around him blurs. "We're not together," I drawl, unsure if I'm reminding myself or him.

"You're right. We're not officially together, but I've been yours for a long time."

"I..."

He grins, amused at my inability to speak. "You."

He smells so good and his skin looks so warm and firm and grabbable. *Maybe, just one touch wouldn't be so bad...*

He steps back, my hand frozen midair. I blink.

"You don't trust me," he says, matter-of-factly.

"I–I don't?"

He shakes his head, takes another step away, and folds his hands behind his back. "I don't want to be meaningless to you. The next time we kiss, I want to know that I've earned you."

The very air I breathe is suddenly sucked out of my lungs. Did he say *the next time* we kiss? As in he thinks it's inevitable—that *we* are inevitable. But he doesn't know my shadows, my traumas.

I narrow my eyes. "You seem sure of yourself."

"I might be, but you're not." He falls back onto the sofa and pats the cushion next to him. "Come. Tell me things. You're never gonna trust me until you do."

I can't argue with that; I *don't* fully trust him. Before he moved in next door, my fortress was secure, safe. Strong foundation, steady walls, locked gates. I never imagined I'd allow another man in like this. But the walls I built are cracking, and Jonah's sunlight is bursting through. For the first time since Greg, my heart aches to open the gates and discover what's on the other side.

"If I'm gonna sit here, you're gonna need to put on a shirt."

He chuckles and returns two minutes later donning a dark teal and white T-shirt that reads "Philly Fathers Sevens Rugby," and under that in a smaller font it says "Who's your daddy?" He's brought his shepherd along with him and King hops up on the couch to lay between us as if this is a totally normal thing we're doing. I've already covered my legs in a heavy knit blanket, ready to tell what lies beyond my walls.

"Where should we start?" I ask.

"Tell me about your family."

King's fur is thick and fluffy and fills in the spaces between my fingers. His breathing is even and I watch his relaxed face while I speak. "You already know my parents were famous in the bluegrass and country music scene."

"Mhm."

"I grew up on the road with them, touring all over the country. They were incredible songwriters and musicians. Voices that could pull you in hook, line, and sinker. If I wasn't on a tour bus, I was in a recording studio or playing in the closest brook looking for creatures."

"That's cute."

"It was. When I got a little bit older, they let me play on stage with them. Just a few shows in the beginning. I guess the crowd went bananas whenever I came on with my mandolin. And then, when I started singing, it was like the floodgates were opened."

"What do you mean?"

"The more I sang, the stronger I felt. It was like I was feeding the crowd my energy, and they somehow boomeranged it back to me tenfold. I was in love with performing. And it wasn't even the size of the crowd that mattered. I could be in a recording studio playing or singing something solo, and just watching the audio engineer or a producer's jaw drop could give me that same high."

A playful grin plays at the corner of his mouth. "I know that feeling well."

"You do?"

He nods. "I'm in an off-and-on garage band with my brothers. It's not even close to the scale you grew up with, but I felt that energy transfer every time we played a gig. Didn't matter if it was a cruddy bar, a college party, my friend's quinceañera... I felt invincible. I still do, even if it's for an audience of toddlers now."

"Your family?"

He hums his acknowledgment happily. "I'm one of five siblings. You know Dane, obviously. But there's also Angie, Isaiah, and Ivy. Oh, that's right! You know Ivy," he chuckles. "My younger sister who is also my girlfriend according to you."

I bury my face into the nearest pillow. "Stoooooooop," I groan. He yanks it away and immediately throws it at my face, and I giggle. "I'm sorry."

Jonah settles back against the couch and crosses his arms. The smirk he can't wipe off betrays his fake outrage. "There's also my dad, who you met already." I nod, remembering the day Jonah brought Ginger home and my girls went flying over there. There's a long pause before he breathes deep. "And, my mom died when I was three. Car accident."

"Oh. I'm so sorry," I reply in a whisper. The words are automatic, but when the meaning truly sinks in, it's nearly crushing. It's impossible not to think of myself leaving behind my children like that. "That's tragic, Jonah. I know you were only three, but do you remember her at all?"

"Not much, but she left these diaries about each of her babies. We didn't know about them until my dad gave them to us recently. When I read it though, I can see her so clearly. I can feel her warmth—which sounds so crazy to say."

"No. That's not crazy."

Even with a defined jawline and strong features, there's a softness to his face when he watches me. A moment or two pass in comfortable understanding before a thought etches itself between his eyebrows.

"I remember you saying your dad died, too?"

I nod. "He had a heart attack six years ago."

"I'm sorry. Were you close?"

A sense of self-loathing tightens around my heart. "Once upon a time. I hadn't spoken to him for at least four years before that. Haven't spoken to my mother since then either."

"Why not?"

My heart races, and for a brief moment, I consider changing the subject. I swallow the lump in my throat and force myself to tell him the truth. "My former husband, Greg, convinced me my parents used me for their success. That I was just a pawn in their game and the love they showed me was all an act."

"Was it?"

"No," I reply confidently. "But I really did believe him. I know now he was trying to separate me from them, from everyone except him. He wanted me to be totally reliant on him so he could manipulate me however he saw fit.

"When Delta was born, my parents flew in, but Greg refused to let them in the hospital room. After that he filed a restraining order against them and my sister."

Jonah gapes at me, utterly shocked and unable to speak. "So, the girls have never known their grandparents?"

It hurts to admit, but I shake my head. "He's been gone for two years, but the shame I feel for being manipulated and staying in that toxic hellscape for so long still eats me alive. I haven't reached out to my mom; I haven't tried to bridge the gap or make amends. I'm too scared."

Sorrow is evident on his face and the silence between us only compounds my hurt. "I'm so sorry," he says. "That must be a tough thing to navigate. What about Amber? Does she talk to her?"

"She's in a similar situation. She's a recovering drug addict, and my parents cut her off financially because she was burning through their money, lying to them, using them. Right before she moved in with me, she got clean, but she has a lot of shame around the way she treated our parents. I think she's been working up the courage to address it with our mom, but it's hard—for both of us."

"So how did you and Amber reconnect? I thought your ex had a restraining order against her too."

Chapter 24
The Funeral

Renée

Six Years Ago

As soon as we're in the lobby of the theatre, I can sense the weight of everyone's stare. Hundreds of people are already here to pay their respects to my father, and even with the low volume at which everyone speaks, when we enter, silence falls over the crowd. I swallow and hold Loretta a little closer to my chest while Delta clutches at my hip.

"I told you," Greg whispers in my ear.

Yes, he did. Many, many times since I first told him I wanted to fly to Nashville and attend his funeral. Even through his sharp, discouraging words and bruising hands, I had to try.

Sure, what my parents did to me as a kid wasn't right, but the pull—the need—to be here today outweighed keeping the peace with my husband. From the bottom of my heart, I knew I had to come today—everyone's judgmental stares and Greg's intense desire to shield me aside.

Consequences be damned.

Mercifully, many folks either don't remember the schism between me and my family, or don't care, and they approach us with their condolences regardless. Greg accepts their sorrowful smiles, never acknowledging he had anything to do with our removal from their lives.

"He was taken too soon," he agrees with everyone. "A huge

loss to bluegrass and country music," he affirms to the artists and music professionals.

"My goodness," a few of them say. "Your daughters look just like your father David. So do you, dear. You always have. A spitting image of him."

Greg is glued to my side the entire time, and when I inevitably find my mother, her eyes bloodshot and watery, my stomach lurches. She spots me at the same time and her chin quivers before she breaks out into a full cry. My mother, older than I've ever seen her, steps toward us, abandoning the person she was talking to. I panic, unsure what to do in this situation because she's legally not allowed to be anywhere near us, but today we had to make an exception. Do I accept this interaction? Can I?

Before my mother can make it five feet closer, Greg pushes me back and stares her down. "Don't," he growls. My mom stops, her longing gaze falling over my daughters. I don't get the chance to read into her expression any further before my husband directs me away.

We walk into the grand theatre, down the red carpeted aisle, and past the hushed murmurs of on-lookers, my extended family and friends. My heart races and a sense of wrongness nearly steals my breath as Greg leads us straight to the front row, as if we belong here.

My arms are tired as Loretta squirms, begging to be put down so she can crawl around. Delta won't stop tugging on my dress, trying her best to glue herself to me and keep safe from all these strangers.

I don't notice the casket on stage until Greg has me sit. Hot tears spring up fast as lightning. My jaw trembles. No, no, no, I tell myself. Stop crying. He's gonna be mad at you.

They used me, I remind myself. Cutting them out of my life was the right thing to do, and yet all I can remember was the good. The songs. The afternoons spent writing music as it flashed in my mind like a flood, followed by the over-the-top *joy my parents had when they read it for the first time.*

I know there were terrible things they did to me, but as hard as I try, I can't think of a single one sitting here now.

Greg stands in front of me watching over the crowd, for what, I'm not sure. I don't want him to see me cry because I can't let him think I miss them. To my surprise, he hands me a packet of tissues from his old suit jacket, but says nothing.

The rest of the seats fill in, and my mother takes the seat at the farthest end of the front row, while I sit at the other. My outpouring of emotion is put on the back burner as I wrangle the kids. Delta takes off her shoes in a huff of frustration and Loretta rips an enormous poop.

Ughh.

My husband looks at his watch. "Service is about to start."

I fling the diaper bag over my shoulder, pick up Delta's shoes, and take both girls out of the auditorium for the bathroom. Greg stays back, which both surprises me because he hasn't left my side since we got here, and doesn't because changing diapers is not his thing.

The smell makes him sick.

Barely anyone is in the lobby when I hurry to the women's room. There are several stalls, and the whole bathroom is empty. Before I can shimmy Loretta's tights off on the changing table, the door swings open.

My baby sister stands before me, eyes red-rimmed, and she stares at me so intensely that I'm instantly transported to our childhood. She looked just like this when she'd come into my room at night, scared of the dark or a shadow or monsters under her bed. And just like then, I open my arm for her.

Amber[1] crashes into me as I keep one hand steady on Loretta. "I miss you so much," she cries.

It's been years since I've seen her. Greg didn't want me

---

1. If You Go Down (I'm Goin' Down Too) by Kelsea Ballerini

around someone who thought my parents were good people. "You can't trust her," he would tell me. But this hug is telling me something different.

I want so badly to say I miss her too, but I don't. "It's been so long," I whisper instead.

She pulls back and tries to shake off her emotions before studying my daughters. "Hi," she says. She starts bawling. "Oh God, they're beautiful, Renée. Oh, I love them so much."

"Hi," my oldest child says, stepping away from me to get a better look. "My name is Delta."

My sister squats down, her bare knees hitting the floor. "Hi Delta. It's so nice to finally meet you. I'm your—" She cuts herself off and looks at me for an answer. I don't say anything and she turns back to her. "I'm Amber. I'm your momma's sister."

"I have a sister."

Amber wipes tears from her eyes. "I know. And I bet you're the best big sister."

Delta nods.

I nudge her. "Sweetheart, please put your shoes back on."

Amber stands and takes the package of wipes from my hands. "Let me," she says. "I could tell from watching you out there you don't get much help." For a second I'm stunned while she coos to Loretta on the changing table and swiftly pulls down her tights. "Such a stinky girl. That's okay, I can be stinky too. We Wilde girls are a tooty bunch, so you need to wear that badge with pride."

Memories of two gassy sisters trying their hardest to capture farts in an empty Pringles can and release it upon unsuspecting victims pulls an unexpected smile to my face. God, we were gross.

I fix the strap on Delta's shoes and when I'm done, so is Amber. She tosses the dirty diaper and holds Loretta in her arms. If my husband saw my sister holding her right now, all hell would break loose. I'd probably be marched out of here without giving so much as a goodbye or listening to the service we flew here for. Amber holds my daughter like she knows she's not supposed to but can't help herself, like she's afraid this might be the only time she'll ever hold her.

So I let her because there's still a soft spot inside my heart for her.

"We don't have much time, Renée." She checks to find Delta occupied at the sink before continuing. "I wouldn't be surprised if Greg came in here looking for you in five seconds, so I'm gonna make this quick. I see how he treats you. He doesn't leave your side. He's ostracized you from your family, and I'd bet my left tit you have bruises on your body right now and it is not the first time, nor is it the last. You deserve so much better, sister. When you can't take it anymore and come to your senses, I will be there for you. I'm not kidding, Renée. I will drop everything and help you. I will move across the country for you and your girls. I will find the lawyers. I will find the money. And you know what? I look pretty good in orange. So good in fact, I wouldn't mind wearing it for the rest of my life."

"I think you're being a little dramatic," I say, just on the edge of nervousness and refusing to acknowledge any of her assessment as true.

It's all true.

"I'm. Not. Kidding." She punctuates each word through clenched teeth and the tendons on the sides of her neck strain. She kisses the top of Loretta's head before handing her back to me. "Now go back to your seat and I'll join you in a few minutes so he's not suspicious."

I'd like to tell her it wouldn't matter because he's always suspicious, but she has a point, and it's better not to add fuel to the fire.

Music fills the air when I get back to my seat, and Greg is still standing at the front, watching for me. Delta settles in with a drawing pad, and I retrieve a cold bottle of milk from the bag to feed Loretta. Amber doesn't acknowledge either of us when she strides to the front row and takes the seat next to our mom.

With an iron-set jaw, Greg takes the seat between us.

Chapter 25
My Choice

Renée

My fingers comb through King's fur in gentle, measured strokes as I debate just how much to tell Jonah. "Amber and I reconnected at our father's funeral," I say. "And I paid dearly for it."

The beautiful blond man sitting beside me furrows his brow, and it's such an odd, unfamiliar look from him. "What do you mean you paid for it?"

With a deep inhale, I admit the thing I have kept hidden from almost everyone. Embarrassment and shame rear their ugly heads in an attempt to keep it locked inside, but I push through. "Greg mentally and physically abused me," I say. I don't sugar-coat the truth or tell a more palatable, vague version. In no uncertain terms, he beat me.

Jonah's eyes round. "Because you wanted to attend your dad's funeral?"

"Because of that. Because he didn't like the way I dressed. Because he didn't like the way people smiled at me. Because he didn't like how our babies would keep him up at night. Because he didn't like eating leftovers and I should know that. Because because because."

Staring at my freckled hand, frozen in fur, I'm lost in painful memories until Jonah's covering his over mine. Warm, big, and slightly calloused, his hand gently envelops mine and gives a tender squeeze.

"I'm so sorry." His words are genuine and he drags them out as if each one weighs a ton. "Tell me you're safe now.

And the girls."

I nod. "He died a couple years ago."

Jonah releases a breath and flings his head back on the couch. "Jesus. I hope it was painful." He turns his focus back to me, and a wicked gleam lights his eyes and a curl forms at the corner of his lips. "Did you kill him? Don't worry, I won't tell anyone. Sounds like he deserved it."

My eyes roll to the side and I sigh. "He died of botulism."

Jonah racks his brain for a moment. "What's botulism?"

"The botulinum toxin is known to many parents because we're warned about it with infants ingesting honey. That's why children under the age of one can't consume it. Their immune systems are not mature enough to handle the spores of the bacteria. But what a lot of people don't realize is that adults can die from it too.

"In the early fall, I would often can vegetables, eggs, soups, and sauces at home. I learned how to do it so we could save money by using what I had grown and buying in bulk. I always took proper care to can everything the right way. But... I guess something went wrong with one of my batches."

Jonah's mouth drops. "He *died* from eating food from a jar? Wait, why didn't you? Didn't you eat it too?"

I lift one shoulder. "I don't like chili."

"So, did he just collapse right there at the table?"

"No, and I didn't know it was from the chili until much later. He was fine the next day, but after that, he was lethargic. He had a fever and difficulty swallowing and speaking. Said his vision was blurry. But he was always such a big baby about being sick. He would be completely out of commission with only a runny nose sometimes, so I thought he was being dramatic.

"He died in our bathroom in the middle of the night."

"What the fudge," Jonah whispers. "D–did the girls see him?"

"No. Thankfully they were staying at a friend's house that night. I called the police when I found him early that morning. I was questioned and our home was searched. Later, when it was revealed he died of botulism, they seized all our canned food and it was tested. Sure enough, the only thing that contained the Clostridium botulinum bacteria were a few other jars of chili. Just that one batch."

·········

My mind reels back to that fateful day over two years ago. Not to the day my husband died, but the weeks just before.

There's a knock on my open office door, and I peer up from my work to find Professor Lewis holding a gift box in her arm. "Happy New Year, Renée."

I swallow the last bite of my homemade soup. "Hey," I smile. "Happy New Year, Tracy. Ready for your last semester?"

She steps into my office and sets the present on the floor. "I've been ready to retire for the last ten years," she says.

"I'm sure you have."

Without asking, she closes the door and sits on the other side of my desk. Okay... a little weird since we don't speak all that much, but maybe she has something hot she wants to discuss.

"What's going on?" I ask.

She leans back into the chair, crosses her legs, and folds her hands. "I just read the most fascinating story recently. Well, it's more tragic than anything, but, I guess it depends how you look at it." I watch her closely and push my empty bowl and glass mason jar to the side. "This man in Iowa almost died from eating tuna from a can. Apparently, there was a recall on those easy-open pull-tab cans, you know the ones?"

I nod, but wonder where she's going with this odd topic.

"They were recalled for a high risk of Clostridium botulinum." Tracy keeps going because she doesn't have to explain to me, a biologist, what that bacteria is. "I guess he didn't hear about the recall and ate one of those cans. He was out in the woods camping with his family, but after a few days he had blurred vision, trouble keeping his eyes open, and abdominal pain. On their last day of the trip, he had difficulty breathing, so his wife took him to the nearest hospital where they discovered the toxin. They had to give him mechanical ventilation and an IV of antitoxin."

"Jeez," I wince. "You don't hear about that a lot."

"You don't," she replies. "They said if he hadn't come in for treatment within another two days, he could have died. All from one can of tuna. And you know, if he hadn't gone in for treatment, if the level of bacteria was higher, he would have been much weaker. Unable to speak. His limbs and diaphragm would go into paralysis... eventually leading to respiratory failure."

All at once my body goes still as ice—complete with a shiver licking up my spine. Why is she telling me this?

"But without a recall, how can anyone know for certain their canned food is safe?" She shrugs, "We're at the mercy of the Food and Drug Administration and the quality checks from food manufacturers. But then that got me thinking... What about those who can their own food at home? I'm not so certain they're testing their food at home. And I mean"—she chuckles softly—"not everyone has access to a laboratory, do they?"

I shake my head almost imperceptibly, and my stomach tightens and twists until I'm actively fighting back a full-body tremor. She... she knows I process my own food. We don't talk much, but she's seen me eat lunch enough over the years to pick up on this.

Tracy trains her focus to my empty mason jar for a second and slowly drags her attention back to me. She waves a hand dismissively. "But home canners probably know all the proper methods like pressure canning—not just boiling the water. And I'm sure they're careful about acidifying the foods they're canning. Like, oh I don't know, tomatoes for instance. Or beef.

"You know, under the right circumstances, the level of Clostridium botulinum could be so high in just one jar of food, it could take a grown man down in a matter of a few days. Isn't that wild?"

Slowly, silently, I nod—not missing her choice to use the word 'wild' to describe this hypothetical situation. If she's telling me this for a reason, and it very much feels like she is, what else does she know about me? I've always kept my personal life hidden away for fear of judgment, for fear that others will see what I ignore, what I endure.

Tracy slaps her hands on her thighs and stands up—the picture of cool, calm, and collected. "Anyway," she sighs, before picking up the gift box and placing it on my desk. "I hope you had a fantastic holiday break with your family. I'm happy to see that bruise on your face is almost all gone."

I suddenly feel as though I could faint, and my heart jackhammers until sweat instantly forms under my arms. How did she know about that? I covered up that bruise with full-coverage foundation and concealer.

My knee-jerk reaction is to touch my face, search for the pain his hand left on me the day before classes were let out for the holiday break, and cover what I thought had disappeared. But I refrain—for what purpose, I'm not sure. I guess I worry that If I cover it, I'll only validate her suspicions. But what's the point in denying it now?

Tracy taps the box, poised and serious. "Sorry I didn't get this to you sooner. It's just a few jars of chili. Homemade gifts are always more special, aren't they?"

And with that, my colleague leaves me in a cold sweat, feeling like I've been handed a loaded gun.

. . . • • • . • • • . . .

I clear my throat and meet Jonah's eyes. "I don't can food at home anymore."

He runs a hand through his hair. "Obviously! Sugar, that's messed up."

I cock an eyebrow. "Sugar?"

"It's my replacement cuss word," he replies, but his mind is elsewhere. "I'm trying to stop swearing in front of kids."

Well that's adorable, I think to myself, despite the unnerving flashback.

"How are you doing after all of that? I mean, I know he hurt you in so many ways, but I would think something like finding your husband dead..." he trails off.

"And accidentally causing his death?" I finish for him, knowing it's a partial lie. I'd rather he think it was an accident, just like everyone else.

Between my sister's bathroom ambush at our father's funeral to tell me she would drop everything in her life to help me get rid of Greg, and Tracy's plan she literally gifted me, I knew the universe was sending me a message.

Yes, I killed the bastard. I prevented him from seeking medical attention, and I watched him die over the course of several days. It was far and away the most vile thing I've ever done and will ever do, and if hell is real then I'll gladly suffer for eternity knowing I saved my daughters so they could have a better life.

Only Amber and Tracy know what I did, and I vowed they would be the only ones to know. It doesn't matter that Jonah, a man I'm learning to trust, just smiled and told me it was okay if I killed him. It doesn't matter if I grow to trust him more than anyone else in this world, I will never admit it to him. I won't put that stress on someone else.

This is the kind of thing I take to my grave.

My eyes meet Jonah's and I breathe. "Being free of him," I say, "is the greatest gift, but it doesn't mean I'm not haunted. I don't trust easily, Jonah."

"I know."

"I swore off all relationships after him, and I especially don't allow men in. Not in my home. Not in my heart."

"I get it. You're protecting yourself."

"And my girls."

"Did he ever hurt them?"

"No. He was close many times, but I always intervened."

"But they saw how he treated you," he hedges. "How he spoke to you?" I nod just once. "Then good riddance to that fff—"

The way he cuts himself off his own rage in order to stop cussing brings a smile to my face. "Just say it. You know you wanna."

"That *fucker!*"

King pops his head up in concern in the aftermath of Jonah's outburst and trails after him as he paces the living room. Hands on his hips, he weaves between furniture as his breathing picks up. A pink flush grows on his neck and spreads to his face. "Were the police never involved before then? Did you have anyone in your corner?"

"I called the cops on him only once. He was let off with a warning, and said if I ever tried that again he would take the girls away from me." That's completely true. I'm finding the hard truth is easier to spill to him than I thought it would be, but it doesn't mean I'll reveal I killed my husband on purpose.

"You think he would have taken your daughters from you?"

I shrug. "He made me believe my parents and sister were the enemy. He took me away from them. Why wouldn't I believe he could do it again?"

Jonah finally sits back down. "Was he like this before you got married?"

"No. He knew me since I was a little girl. Greg was my parents' music producer."

"What?" he exclaims. "How much older was he than you?"

"Fifteen years. He never made a physical move on me until I was in college, but by then he had laid the groundwork. I was completely in love with him. We got married after I graduated from undergrad. He put me through my master's and doctoral programs... supported me the whole way.

"Things started going downhill when the record label fired him. He convinced me my family was to blame, and he filed a restraining order against them. And when I told him I'd like to perform again, he convinced me that I was never truly talented, but rather I was an embarrassment."

"There's no fucking way," Jonah growls, and he's up once again, this time charging out of the room. Just when I'm about to get off the couch to find him, he rushes back into the room with a mandolin and a guitar in hand. "There's no way you're not talented. I've watched the videos of your live performances with your parents."

"You have?"

He sets his guitar down and tunes the mandolin. "What do you wanna do first? Play or sing?"

Panic bubbles up in my chest. "No. I can't. I haven't done either in over a decade."

"So be terrible," he shrugs. "It's just me. No one has to know how rusty you are."

"I'm not just rusty, Jonah. I... I..."

"You said he convinced you your family was the enemy, and you know now they were not. Then you said he *convinced* you that you had no talent. That means deep down, you know that was a lie. You know he manipulated you. The Grand Ole Opry doesn't allow amateurs, Renée."

The wind is knocked right out of me when his words register. He's right. I know he is and yet the idea of trying again after so long—after being degraded the way I was—it's impossible.

"Music is in your blood." He draws out each word, his eyes locked on mine.

"Well if that were true, then Amber would have some musical ability, but she can't keep a beat."

I expect an eyeroll as a response, or maybe a quirk in his mouth, but there's nothing funny in the way he's watching me. There's an uncharacteristically serious man standing in front of me, and the gravity of what he's asking for settles heavy in my chest. Not because he wants something from me—but because he sees something for me.

"I'm not asking you to play for me," he says quietly, as if he can hear the old voices clawing their way back in. "Or for anyone else. I just hate the idea that you stopped because someone convinced you of a lie." His jaw tightens, then softens. "If you never touch it again, if you never sing again, that's your choice. I just want you to know *it is your choice.*"

My choice.

It's my choice.

Why have I never framed it like that for myself? Why have I let this wound that Greg created fester?

All at once, a dam opens and a flood of power surges through me. Instead of drowning in shame—exactly where Greg always wanted me—I'm swept into a current of encouragement and possibility.

Before[1] I lose my courage, the mandolin is in my hands, the strap flung over my shoulder. The weight and feel is both familiar and a sharp reminder that I haven't held one

---

1. Top of the World by The Chicks

in more than ten years. Jonah hands me a pick, grabs his guitar, and sits in the arm chair across from me.

The first strum of eight perfectly tuned open strings has me standing. It's my turn to pace the room now, reacquainting myself with the instrument that was once like another limb. Jonah gives me the space to find the first familiar tune, and when I realize what song it is, I close my eyes in anguish.

I think of my daughters as faint muscle memory guides my unpracticed, uncalloused fingers, and the notes to "Top of the World" by The Chicks flash behind my eyes.

My girls needed me.

I should have had them out of his chokehold, his aggression, his aloofness sooner. The cycle needed to be broken. But Lo's silence is a daily reminder that it wasn't broken soon enough.

All I can do now is be better for them and be the mother they need and depend on. I can show them a life of love and growth and hope—the kind of life that was impossible before.

But am I truly allowing them the space to spread their wings when I've been so closed off to music and song? I saw the way Delta bloomed when she sang "Blackbird" with Jonah in his studio the night of the storm. I saw the way Lo couldn't take her eyes off them. I saw the same wonder and yearning reflected in her eyes.

Sometimes I hear Delta sing softly to her sister in their bedroom late at night. They hide it from me.

They hide.

I can't let them hide anymore.

I cannot hide anymore.

The mellow strum of an acoustic guitar begins to fill in the gaps of my tune—though it's much more than a tune now. I'm surprised I remember most of it, but even more surprised at how natural it is. It's like the song has been living at my fingertips this whole time.

And how does he know this song? Or did he just listen to me fumble my way through it a few times and figure out where I needed support?

"Do you know this song?" I ask over the music.

He shakes his head, but he doesn't look away from me and doesn't stop playing.

"It's by The Chicks," I say.

A few more bars pass between us and again he doesn't look away. He's reading me, studying my hands, following my lead.

"Do you know the lyrics?" Hope shines in his eyes in the way he asks, but it's not hope that I know the words, it's hope that I'll take the bait.

Like the song itself, the words start out low and slow, each line like a memory unspooling the life I lived. Words of regret and distance told through the eyes of a careless and neglectful husband while shining light on the ones he hurts. Of love that never stood a chance.

I think of the years spent making excuses for Greg and the ache that settled in when the laughter left. When my voice cracks on a line about pride, Jonah just nods, his fingers steady and sure, like he understands that breaking is just another part of this song. There is no need to start over. We move forward.

By the second chorus, I give up trying to sound good. The lyrics are too real, the music too life-breathing. The mandolin hums beneath my fingertips and my heart pounds with every downstroke of his guitar. We're in an enormous living room of an eight-thousand-square-foot estate, yet the room feels small and warm, like we've stepped into the song itself. I told him about how Greg treated me, but here in this song together, it's like I've flayed myself open to show him what I could not say.

I close my eyes as the words of regret and loneliness pour

out of me. For a moment, it's not about being a mother or a woman reborn. It's only me, stripped down to my truth, singing beside someone who doesn't need me to be anything else.

When the last note fades, neither of us can move, and there's something almost holy in the silence and the way we lock in on each other. My hands are trembling, but I smile through the tears.

Why did I keep myself closed off for so long?

I blink and Jonah's up, wrapping me in his arms. I don't push him away. I welcome him. "Renée! I knew you still had it in you."

"I didn't know," I cry into his big, warm chest.

"It's okay," he soothes, his fingers pressing into my back like a massage. "Let it all out."

Neither one of us cares that I'm painting his T-shirt in my tears, or that we haphazardly discarded our instruments in a rush to hold each other.

I made no room for my own joy—no room for forgiveness. I pull my face away just enough to look at him. "I want music," I say in an exhale. The admission alone shakes the very foundation I thought I reinforced with rules of steel. "I want music in my life again. I don't want to be afraid of it anymore."

"Okay then." Mesmerizing pools of blue scan every inch of my face, like he's wondering how many freckles I have or what they could possibly taste like. He brushes away the hair from my face, curling it behind my ear, before a gentle finger traces my jaw. I melt like ice. "May I be a part of that?"

"It would mean so much to me if you were."

That boyish grin appears once again because he knows I'm doing the impossible and opening the door to my heart. He knows he means something to me.

I fist his shirt and marvel how his chest rises and falls under my hand. My eyes flutter from the bunched white cotton to the column of his throat, to his cerulean eyes, and finally land on his parted lips.

I need those lips. Because I need *him*.

Our kiss is like no other. It's long and languid, like neither of us have plans or lives outside this perfect moment. Like hunger for food is a thing of the past because we could sustain ourselves—*thrive*—on only this kiss.

Passion erupts when our mouths part. His curious tongue searches, but it's not too much. It dances with mine and against my lips. A great kiss is never about how much tongue there is, it's about how you use it—and this man knows how to use it.

Jonah is eager by nature and it manifests itself so deliciously in the way he grips me, breathes into me, and presses his full lips into mine in an effort to become one.

I'm unsure how long we stand there making out, but when my neck begins to hurt from craning it, I reluctantly pull away and lower to the heels of my feet. His eyes are still closed, and the way he tries to inch his lips closer—searching for mine once more—has me silently giggling. His eyes finally open, glazed and lovelier than I've ever seen.

"Thank you," I whisper.

"Ohhh, you sweet thing," he says with a little unhinged sparkle in his voice, before taking my mouth in a quick, desperate kiss. My toes curl. "I'm gonna want a lot more where that came from. Please, *please* tell me we'll do that some more."

I pat his chest. "We will... if you can be good for me."

"I'll be the best."

I take another kiss and relish in the way he relaxes. I'm so fucking high on this man. "I have to go now," I whisper against his lips.

"No," he whines. "Just move in here. Right now." He peppers me with more kisses and I laugh. "Bring the girls. Bring your sister."

Minutes later when my giggles fade away and our lips detach, he tells me to use his music studio whenever I want, and he gives me his door code before I can stop him. This man is too trusting, but I would be lying if I said his offer didn't give me butterflies and fill my head with hope.

Separating from Jonah proves to be too difficult after we move to his front porch to say goodnight. Our "last kiss" turns into several, and when my skin starts to pebble from the evening chill, Jonah decides it will be safest to wrap me in one of his blankets and walk me back to my house.

"There are dangerous coyotes in these parts," he tells me gravely on our walk. "Better stay close to me."

I hum and lean a little closer. Never mind that I haven't seen a coyote the entire time I've lived here.

All the lights are off inside the house except the one we keep on over the stove. I pop my head in and double check to make sure no one's around before giving him one last goodnight kiss.

When I float off to bed, his words replay. "I'll be the best."

Teetering on the edge of sleep, I suddenly jolt. *God-dammit! I didn't ask how he has so much money.*

Chapter 26
Man-to-Man

Jonah

The next day, I have three dozen roses delivered to Renée's university office. She deserves the entire flower shop, but I didn't want to freak her out. She giggled mid-kiss when I asked her to move in with me last night, so hopefully she thinks I'm joking.

Let me be so clear: I wasn't.

But my filter was gone and the words just spilled out and it wouldn't be the first time I was accused of love-bombing. The thing is, I've never purposefully done it. Heck, I'm always the one being dumped. I'm the one who attaches like velcro! Angie once said something about me having anxious attachment... something or other. Guess when your mom dies young and your dad is emotionally unavailable for most of your life, things like this can happen.

I need to keep an eye on that, because I cannot rush this and risk scaring her off. From what she told me last night, it doesn't seem like she's had the opportunity to make many decisions for herself—and I want her to choose me with confidence.

I laid in bed most of the night replaying every moment with her and reminding myself that the work isn't done. I haven't won anything—except maybe those sweet lips of hers. Then I remembered I still had her panties from Strip Tease, so I wrapped them in my hand—*again*—and jerked off to the temptation of her plush, wet mouth.

I'm deliriously rereading the one text she sent me earlier

thanking me for the flowers when my dad's voice cuts in. "Son!"

"Huh?"

"I said can you hand me the drill."

"Sorry."

Dad unscrews the outside metal grate to my air conditioner to reveal a disturbing amount of dirty... lint? "That's disgusting."

"Yeap," Dad sighs. "My bet is the last home owners didn't clean this out for the last few years. You gotta stay on top of it every year." He unscrews the rest of the grates as I begin scraping off sheets of fluffy matted dust.

"Heard you had a little birthday party yesterday." He waggles his eyebrows but focuses on his task.

"Yeah, it was pretty cool. Between the animals and the inflatable obstacle course and the Nerf guns and the cake. It was perfect. Delta had a blast. I watched her snipe a few dads right in their chests," I laugh. "Great aim. And she can sing too! Ugh, her cover of 'Blackbird?'" Incredible. The Beatles should give her the rights to that song because she owned it." I smile dreamily. "She's just like her mom."

"Sounds like you're pretty taken with them."

"I just want... all the good things for them. I used to think I wanted to be the one who could provide that. But now, I'd rather see Renée and her girls find the good for themselves and be able to trust it."

My father's eyebrows pinch together like he doesn't believe me. "You just bought your three-year-old niece and nephew a drum set and keyboard."

And when my sister's face dropped, it was worth every penny.

"What's your point?"

"Even without money, you're a generous person. I once watched you help a troop of Girl Scouts sell cookies because you felt bad that you didn't have any cash to give them."

I gasp. "That's right! Y'know they gave me a badge for that?"

"Can you honestly tell me you don't wanna spoil them?"

The thought of giving them everything they've ever wanted feels incredibly satisfying.

Dad seems to sense where my head is. "That's what I thought," he chuckles to himself. "If your mother was still here, I would do the same."

Holy moly, he's talking about Mom.

No one make any sudden movements!

I try to act casual in my reply. "Oh yeah?"

"I mean, we didn't have a lot of money to begin with, but I always did what I could to make her comfortable and happy. It would have been nice to finally spoil her properly."

Aww.

"She was..." He fondly pauses. "She was too good for me. By some miracle or poor judgement on her part, she loved me. When we started having kids though, I finally saw why we were meant to be together: no one else would have been able to love and care for her and you guys the way I could. And, before you think it, I *know* I fell short with you kids after she died. Really short. I was neglectful and that's completely on me and not taking care of my mental health.

"But when she was alive, so was I. I wanted to do *every-thing* for her. Nothing felt like a duty—it was all instinctual."

His words float around my head while we work in silence. So many thoughts and feelings and memories kick up.

I would have loved to know that version of my dad before Mom died. My whole childhood I tried to find that guy.

Weirdly enough though, I sort of understand what he means by being the only one who could care for someone the right way. Renée, obviously, is out of my league, but the more I learn about her and the more time I spend with her daughters, the deeper my confidence grows. I could happily be what they need—what they want—because providing for them *is* what I want.

"What would you have done with her?" I ask. "Y'know, now that you're retired and financially comfortable."

He pours some kind of cleaning solution into a spray bottle before attaching it to the hose. "Traveled with her. I would have liked to see what she looks like in Paris. Maybe we would have bought a boat."

"I don't know, Dad. I think Raf would shoot down that idea. He told me I couldn't buy one."

"Because you wanted to buy a yacht," he replies with snark. He sighs like he's imagining himself out on the water already. "We would have bought something like a wood runabout."

I snort. "You want the kind of boat yacht owners use to zip around with? Dad, I think we're missing an excellent opportunity to pair up our boating interests. I'll get the yacht, you get the runabout! Everyone's happy. Except maybe Raf. And Ang. And Isaiah. And Dane. And my financial advisors."

"Maybe sit on that idea for a while, son. That's a massive purchase."

"Fine," I mumble. "Doesn't mean you can't buy your runabout."

He doesn't reply right away, choosing instead to spray the soap and water mixture all over one side of the AC unit. I can tell he's not focusing on the task so much as he's contemplating my question.

"I don't know," he finally says. "It's not as appealing without her."

"Have you thought about dating again?" As soon as the words are out of my mouth I freeze. Where is my filter?

Dad looks frozen too. *Sugar.* I really stepped in it this time.

"That would imply I dated in the first place," he says. "Your mother and I just sort of fused to each other as soon as we met in college. But..."

But?!

"...It's something I've been discussing with my therapist."

"Are you allowed to date your therapist?"

He furrows his brow. "No. Dating is something my therapist thinks I'm ready for... with *other* people," he clarifies.

"Ohhh," I drawl. "Wow, dude. That's kinda huge."

"It's weird when you call me dude. But yeah, it's a big step. I'm not so sure though."

"Jonah!" screams the voice of a little girl in the distance. Dad and I both turn our attention to find Delta running toward us from where the school bus has dropped them off at the end of their driveway.

Her toothy smile brings one to my face as well. "Ladybug!" She launches herself into my arms and Lo joins in a few seconds later. "Hey Shortcake. How was school today?"

Lo doesn't reply with words, but she digs through her backpack to show me a collage she's made. I see cutouts of butterflies, dogs, horses, waterslide, sparkly shoes, cookies, baking equipment, a duck and a goat. "Shortcake, did you make this?"

She nods eagerly.

"It's so cool. Dad, look at this." I twist around and show him the thick paper with dozens of pictures glued to it.

He steps closer and leans in to look before he smiles. "That's very good. Are these all the things you like?"

She nods again, a little less eager and a little more wary. That's when I remember I should reintroduce them.

"Girls, do you remember my dad?"

"Yes," Delta says, and Lo nods once.

"Dad, this is Delta and Lo."

"It's nice to see you again, ladies."

All at once I notice Delta has clearly cut her bangs again. "Ladybug," I gasp. "What happened to your hair?"

If she had a tail it'd be tucked between her legs right now.

"I didn't mean to."

"What do you mean, you didn't mean to? Did you pick up the scissors?"

She frowns. "Yeah, but I didn't mean to cut this much."

I sigh, wanting to gently tug at the short remaining curls. "They had almost grown back," I say, more to myself than to her. I place my hands on my thighs as I kneel before her. "Hmm. Tell you what." I untie my hair and let it fall down. My hair is thick and a little wavy and can cover my entire chest. "I'll let you cut my hair whenever you want if you promise to never cut yours again."

Her eyes widen. "Really?"

"Sure, why not? I don't need all this hair."

"Can I cut it all off?"

"Well," I sigh. "If you do that, you'll have to wait a long time for it to grow out before you can cut it again. So maybe just a bit at a time?"

"I can definitely do that."

"Perfect! Whenever you feel the urge to cut your hair, you come find me. Deal?"

"Deal! Jonah... and Mr. Jonah's dad, do you wanna come over for a snack? Aunt Amber always makes us a snack when we get home."

"Oh man, I wish we could," I say. One, because I love snacks, but two, even though Renée and I are *something* now (I hope), she still hasn't invited me in her home yet. She's not home from work, and I will not be crossing that line until she says so. "Sorry, girls. My dad and I need to finish working on this project," I say with a thumb thrown over my shoulder. "And then I have a rugby meeting after this."

"Okay," Delta says. "But can we come over soon to play with your animals?"

"Of course! Just make sure your mom's cool with it. Oh, and before you go..." I stop them before they run off and pat my pockets. I find a receipt from earlier today and pluck a marker from Lo's backpack before writing a note and folding it up. "When your mom gets home, give her this. But no peeking!"

·· • • • • • • ··

Renée

Before I even reach my front door, it's swinging open and the girls come barreling out. "Hi," I laugh. "What a reception."

"We have a message for you," Delta hollers, waving around a small piece of white paper like she's signaling for an emergency crew to save her. "It's from Jonah. We did *not* read it." She says that last part as if she's on trial.

Two notes in one day? The last one he had attached to the roses, read: *Your hair is red, My eyes are blue. I'm not very good at poetry, but I will be for you.* I may have read it several... dozen times today. *May* have.

She hands me the note and I gape at her. "Did you cut your hair again?"

"Yeah," she says with a shrug, like she's been over this. "Jonah said if I stopped cutting my hair he'd let me cut his."

"He what?"

"Just read the note, Mom! What does it say?"

"Don't think we're done discussing your hair, young lady." I unfold what is clearly a receipt and find handwriting in purple marker on the back.

I have tix to the PA Bluegrass Festival next weekend for all of you. Be my dates?

And then there are two boxes, to check either "Yes" or "Yes" with a heart next to it.

I'm grinning like an idiot, and my heart is ready to punch

its way out of my chest.

"What does it say?"

"I need a pen." Lo runs inside and back out holding another marker, this one green. I make the mark and fold it back up. When I look over to his place from my spot on the porch, he's in the driveway getting into his SUV. "Go run this to him," I say in a rush. "Hurry!"

Both of them don't ask any questions and are sprinting over. He spots them before putting the vehicle in drive and hops out. They're too far away for me to hear, but I watch him unravel the note and jump up and down, pumping his fist in the air. He leans down and says something to them and then they're all jumping.

He sends them running back and spots me before holding up his hands to form a heart.

Chapter 27

Career Plans

Jonah

Despite horrendous traffic, my drive to the team training facility is spent in bliss. I am taking the Wilde girls to a bluegrass festival. She agreed, and like, pretty enthusiastically! She checked both boxes on my note. She could have created another box and declined me—though I purposefully didn't leave her much room on the receipt to do that—but she didn't!

"What's goin' on Joner Boner?" Joaquín asks as he enters the facility with his brother. "You look... manic."

I hug them both. "I'm taking her on a date!"

"Renée?" Raf asks.

"And her daughters. We're going to that bluegrass festival Christina told us about."

"Does she like bluegrass?" Raf asks. "Do *you* like bluegrass?"

"Of course I do. Just because I haven't listened to a lot it doesn't mean I don't appreciate it. And Renée..." I sigh. "She's so talented. She plays mandolin and sings and... God, you have to see for yourself one day. Amazing."

My best friend and brother-in-law take me through the renovations of our state-of-the-art rugby training facility. Though still under construction, it's nearly finished, and I gape at the transformation Joaquín and Raf have pulled off in such a short time. Granted, I did end up throwing more money at the project to speed things up, but it was worth it!

No one outside of my family knows I funded this. Not Coach, not even the team's executive board. As far as they know, it came from an anonymous donor.

Every week since this began, I've been meeting with the Jimenez brothers. Raf worked with the e-board and planning committee on all the details and financial reporting, while Joaquín was the project manager. To keep myself anonymous, I was never present for those meetings, but the guys still filled me in.

I haven't been here since they started renovation a couple months ago, and I'm floored with the results. No training equipment has been moved in yet, but the indoor field is done.

"Holy smokes." I huff and take in the magnificence. Bright LED lights illuminate everything—the faux grass, our enormous team logo painted on the far wall, benches, newly-painted field lines, and beckoning goalposts.

In the planning phase, we didn't know if we'd be able to squeeze in a whole practice field, but the owners of the vacant bowling alley behind our lot sold it to us for a song, and voila!

Raf produces a rugby ball seemingly from thin air. "Go long."

Before I can think, Joaquín and I are sprinting to the other end of the field, each of us turning to look back as we run. Raf's kick is long and flies over our heads before bouncing chaotically. I pick it, but as soon as I turn, Joaquín is there and I side-step. "Sugar," I grunt, and barely make it out of his grasp.

"When did you start playing rugby?" I yell.

My friend laughs as he tries to catch me. "I've picked up a few things over the years."

The three of us take turns kicking the ball, and thirty minutes later when we're breathing hard and sweating through our clothes that were not designed for exercise, we call it.

"I can't wait for the rest of the team to see this place." I smile. "That was fun."

Raf opens the door back into the main entry area. "Yeah, well," he says, "I did promise my wife I'd take you for a run tonight. You know, get all your energy out before bed."

I shove him and chuckle. "Thanks."

"Did she get the job?" Joaquín asks.

I look between them. "What job?"

"She has two offers actually," Raf smiles. "She's waiting to see if we make the Premier League. If we do," he explains, "then I'm going to step down from my role as CFO at Define."

My mouth drops. "What? But... you like your job."

"I do, but when am I ever going to get the opportunity to play semi-professional rugby? I'm not gonna move away to do it. My life is here. I'm also in my mid-thirties, so how much longer can I realistically play at this level?"

I suppose he has a point. I wouldn't want to move away either. Not like Isaiah did playing professional rugby in England all those years ago. I love the sport deep in my bones, but part of that love is being able to play alongside my brothers.

"So," Raf continues, "Ang is gonna take a job in the private mental health field. She'll make a lot more money than working in public schools."

"But I gave you guys two million each."

"Yeah," he smiles. "And we took a sick tropical vacation and invested the rest of it. Jonah, there's nothing to worry about. She's happy to make the change, I'm happy about playing rugby."

"And he's not leaving Jimenez Brothers Properties," Joaquín tacks on. "He's still the money guy for our company." He cocks his head and tsks. "Some people can't handle all that pressure."

Rafael laughs before pushing his brother. "You jackass.

Sorry I don't want to juggle *two* CFO positions, a semi-professional rugby career, marriage, and three kids."

"It's like I don't even know who you are anymore," his younger brother grimaces, trying to keep a serious tone but loses it once they start tussling like children.

I know Joaquín is only teasing him. The Jimenez brothers are a couple of the smartest, hardest working people I know. The pair of them always know what to do, and they're always two steps ahead. That's how I know Raf's decision to leave his executive position at the architecture firm wasn't made lightly. He and Angie both are rearranging their careers to make Raf's dream come true—and if I know my rugby super-fan sister the way I do—this is probably her dream too.

They're so... confident in their careers, and I'm... not. I mean, no one needs a career when you have the kind of money I have, but I can't help this disconnected feeling I have. It's like I'm standing on the outside watching real people live their lives, jealous over their shop talk.

Of course, I still want to play rugby and I'm doing everything in my power to level us up. But what Raf said about not knowing how much longer he can play has me thinking, what if I got injured and couldn't play anymore? What would I do to fill my time? That feeling of disconnection would grow.

But then something one of the parents said to me at Delta's birthday party pops in. "What if I opened an animal sanctuary?" I ask the guys.

Joaquín's dark eyebrows shoot up. "Like, at your house?"

I consider that. "Well, my barn might be better for most of the animals."

"Is that what you wanna do?" Rafael asks.

"I don't know. Maybe. One of the moms at the birthday party suggested it. I think it could be kinda cool. Now that Dane trusts me, he keeps sending me old or abandoned animals he can't rehome. And I loved seeing all those kids light up around them—the parents too. It felt good."

Raf smiles. "Then I think that's a great idea."

"Me too." Joaquín nods. "Do you think you could acquire a cow? Because I've always wanted to snuggle one."

I laugh. "I'll put in a request to Dr. Brother, DVM. I'm sure Delta and Lo would love for me to get a cow, too."

"Speaking of," Joaquín drawls, "have you told her about your lottery win?"

I raise an eyebrow. "No. I'm not allowed to tell anyone."

"Has she asked about how you can afford your house?" Raf asks. "Or where your money came from?"

"No."

The Jimenez brothers share a look.

"What?" I ask.

Raf winces. "It's a little suspicious, isn't it? She knows you play rugby, but she's smart enough to know rugby players at the club level aren't paid. Even if we make the Premier League, our salaries will be less than what teachers make. Hell Jonah, most of the Philadelphia Eagles wouldn't be able to afford your place."

"Go Birds," Joaquín and I add reflexively.

"Go Birds," Raf repeats. "All I'm saying is, I hope she doesn't have dollar signs in her eyes whenever she sees you."

"You think she's after my money?"

Rafael looks pained. "I hope not," he says. "But if she hasn't asked how you have all this money... she might be the kind of person who doesn't care how you made it, just that you have it."

I scratch my head. "She doesn't seem like that."

"But what if she's the one?" Joaquín asks his brother. "Jonah's gone for this woman."

"Yeah!"

Again, Raf is pained. "I know, and I'm happy you are. But,

aren't you like this in every relationship? Jonah, you have the biggest heart and love to see the best in people, but sometimes that's your downfall. You have a tendency to throw yourself into loving people and putting blinders on. You ignore the red flags."

I scoff. "Name one time that happened."

"When your college girlfriend Paris went on spring break and swore up and down she didn't have sex with that bartender even though everyone from her sorority confirmed it. You refused to believe it until you saw her cheating on you. Then there was Kendall who used you as a meal ticket because you had an unlimited plan on campus. Oh, and how about Jessi who was only dating you to get closer to your roommate, Devin?"

"Didn't they get married last month?" Joaquín adds, unhelpfully.

"Yeah," I sigh. "But it's different this time, I swear."

"So what is he supposed to do?" Joaquín asks. "Never tell the women he dates that he won the lottery?"

I'm never dating anyone else again, I think to myself, but then backtrack to the point Rafael just made. I do be love-bombing. I do ignore warning signs and maybe I trust too easily...

"I can't lie to her," I say. "Maybe I could if it was someone I just met and they asked me how I made my money, but I don't want that with Renée. She deserves to know."

Raf takes a moment to digest my words. "If she ever asks."

"Bro, come on," Joaquín says. "Have some faith. You know, *some people* think it's rude to discuss personal finances."

He sighs, "That's fair."

"Well I'm gonna tell her," I state. "She kissed me for the first time last night—"

Joaquín's eyes bug out and he grabs my shoulders before I can continue. "She did? Dude, lead with that kind of info!"

"That's huge," Raf beams.

"I know! It's taken her a long time to trust me so she deserves to know. And you know what? I don't care if she *is* a gold digger because I wanna spoil her. I want her to relax. Everyone tells me how I should and should not spend my money, and sure, maybe a yacht isn't a great idea, but giving Renée and her girls a comfortable life? That sounds like *the best* idea."

Chapter 28
The Festival

Jonah stands next to his Yukon, now parked in our driveway, with all four doors open as wide as his arms. He's wearing dark jeans with a white undershirt and lighter denim shirt over that. His sleeves are rolled up to his elbows, and he's pulled half of his hair back. He's delicious. His enormous smile and the way his eyes light up when we step off our front porch has me soaring.

"Ladies, your chariot awaits."

The girls bound for him, each giving him a hug and gushing about their excitement for the festival today. He hands each of them a four-leaf clover that he's pressed between two strips of clear tape, and I can't stop my laughter when they lose their marbles over it.

He's already installed their booster seats, but I double-check that they're installed correctly. He simply grins at me when I'm satisfied and leads me to the passenger seat. His large hand cradles mine before he assists me high up into his SUV, and I catch a whiff of his decidedly sexy sage and citrus cologne.

"You look beautiful," he whispers, so close he knows only I can hear it.

"Thank you." It's then I realize my thin denim dress is the same shade as his shirt... and I like that we match. I like it a lot. "You're very handsome yourself," I whisper back. To my great pleasure, the apples of his cheeks burst into a shade of pink, and he bites his bottom lip.

I straighten out my dress once he closes my door. It's shorter than any skirt I've worn as an adult, but Amber insisted I wear the dress. The hemline ends just below mid-thigh, and it's modest by most people's standards. I've paired it with tall suede boots and there's something about the combination that has me feeling myself. I like the way I look, and when Jonah hops in the driver's seat, I catch his gaze going straight to my exposed knees. The corners of his mouth only curl more devilishly when his eyes crawl up my body.

Oh yeah, I think smugly. *This boy likes the way I look, too.*

My oldest cuts through the tension. "Can we please go?"

The drive takes an hour, but it passes quickly with all the questions Jonah has for the girls. He asks about their favorite subjects and their favorite songs. I play passenger DJ with his phone, and he happily listens to all their suggestions.

When we arrive, he leads us past the long festival line, heading straight to the front.

"We're cutting," Delta says worriedly.

"No we're not. We're VIPs." He hands the tickets to the staff member who scans them and sends us through with wristbands.

The grounds are filled with music,[1] and people milling between vendor tents, food trucks, and a beer garden. On the far end of the festival grounds is the stage, set low into an amphitheater. All at once a memory hits me upside the head and I stop.

"I've been here."

Jonah flicks his eyes from me to the stage and back. "For a concert?"

"I've performed here with my parents. I remember this

---

1. Know It All by Billy Strings

stage."

"When you used to be a singer with Grandma and Grandpa?" Delta asks.

I nod. My girls knew a little bit about their famous grandparents before their father passed away. Amber helped me open up more to them in the years that have followed, but this last week I've been spilling my guts to them. I finally felt ready to teach them the significance of bluegrass in our family. Online, I showed them pictures and videos of our performances. What shook them the most out of everything wasn't that they had famous grandparents or that we toured across the country—it was that their mom could *really* sing. Not just a little tune hummed into their copper heads before bedtime.

"Yeah," I reply. "When I was a singer."

Jonah hooks a thumb over his shoulder toward the stage. "Want me to go backstage and see if they need a world-famous bombshell to headline?"

I giggle, "Don't you dare. I think I would die if I went up there right now."

He scoffs. "I was talking about me."

"You're famous?" Delta asks.

"Oh yeah!" He hoists Lo up in his arms as we make our way down an aisle. "Have you ever heard of a band called Agony Nectar? It's... pretty much the coolest band ever. But do you know what we don't have? A pretty mandolin player."

I roll my eyes and Lo points at me.

He feigns surprise. "Really? Y'think she'd do it?"

Loretta's smile is crooked and she's missing a tooth, but this moment, with her little arms wrapped around his neck as he carries her through a throng of people, she's never been more happy.

And neither have I.

"Here we are," Jonah says, stepping into an intimate, sectioned-off area with outdoor lounge seating and a coffee table.

"This is where we're sitting?" I ask.

He sets Lo down and the girls flop into cushioned arm-chairs. "We're so close to the stage," Delta cheers.

Jonah joins them and spreads his muscled arms over the back of the couch and crosses one foot over his knee. "Heck yeah, this is where we're sitting. VIP treatment, remember?" He winks. "It's reserved for us all day. We can come and go as we please."

A young man in a red polo and holding a note pad comes up to us and tells us he'll be our server. He explains that he'll fetch us any drinks we'd like and directs us to help ourselves at the VIP buffet at any time. He also offers to bring us blankets if it gets chilly later.

I grew up well-off. No, my parents weren't rockstars, but they did well enough that this kind of treatment was fairly standard for me. But it's been a long time since I've experienced this.

Our server takes our drink orders and the girls eagerly ask to see the buffet. We take them, and Jonah loads up a couple plates with hors d'oeuvres and the giant soft pretzel Lo *needed*.

A funky bluegrass band of women has taken the stage when we get back to our private patio, and our server delivers our drinks. The girls chow down like the dainty and refined women I've raised while bouncing around to the music. Jonah resumes his spot on the couch. He holds a beer in one hand while the other rests behind me.

"Cheers," he says, before our plastic cups clink.

"Cheers."

For more than the last decade, if I went out to eat, I was mindful of prices and only ordered water. But Jonah seems like the kind of man who orders pre-dinner cocktails and appetizers and dessert. It's mind-blowing that I've some-how found myself a part of this scene I didn't think I'd ever be a part of again.

As every second ticks by, I'm rudely aware that our bodies are not touching. I'm also tantalizingly aware of the heat pouring from his body and how it's amplifying his scent. I could easily lean a couple inches closer and I'd be cradled under his arm.

"I'm sorry Amber couldn't come," he says.

"She is too. But the country club was hosting a banquet today, so she had to work."

"I'm glad you have each other again," he says. "I'd be lost without my siblings."

I weigh his words. "I was lost for a long time. Amber can be chaotic, but she has my back... even when I didn't think I needed support. Even when she was pushed out of my life, she didn't blame me."

He juts his chin forward. "And she loves these two like they're her own."

I sigh, "That she does."

"But that's not hard," he grins, watching them inhale garlic shrimp and sway to the music. "They're amazing, Renée."

I have to take a few deep breaths to calm my racing heart. If he would have said that to me after he first moved in, I would have snarled at him because those are *my* babies. I know exactly how amazing they are and if another man told me that, I'd consider biting their head off. But now I'm sitting next to a man so pure and kind and wholly unbothered by our age difference, a man who has done nothing but respect my boundaries and push in where it was safe. Somehow, this himbo made me trust him.

With one more steady inhale, I lean into him. "They like you."

Without skipping a beat, his arm falls over my shoulder, like he was waiting for me to do exactly this. "I like you."

I can feel his heartbeat and the slight way his chest puffs out. From the outside (and from an antiquated heteronormative facade) it may look like he's the leader, the one in charge. But he knows as well as I do I'm the one captaining this ship. And the pride that's obviously swelling inside him right now? It's feeding me while a dull ache forms between my thighs.

"I like you too," I murmur.

For as smart as my girls are, they don't blink an eye when they finally catch us snuggled into one another. I was mentally preparing for a reasonable explanation, but they're more concerned with lemonade refills and visiting the vendor tents.

That's how we find ourselves hand-in-hand, strolling back through the festival thoroughfare, with my youngest on his shoulders while my oldest holds his other hand.

There must be over a hundred vendors selling everything from banjos and records to T-shirts and jewelry.

"Mom, look!" Delta gasps, and ducks into the next tent up. When we come into view of her find, my jaw drops.

"No way," Jonah breathes. A T-shirt hangs on the end of a rack with stylized portraits of me and my parents. All three of us are frozen in time with our mouths posed in song—our instruments hung around our shoulders. And arching at the top in familiar font, just below the neckline, it reads "The Band Wilde."

Jonah's excitement only skyrockets my daughters'. He gently lowers Lo down to the ground before searching for more sizes. "Can you believe this?" he asks, holding the garment against his body. "I mean look how cute you are!"

I touch the fabric like I'd caress the cheek of a sleeping baby. I stare at my father—his rich baritone vocals sing in my head while I remember what his shaggy chestnut hair felt like and how funny he could be. I stare at my mother's long, flame-colored hair and hear the twang in her mezzo-soprano. She used to dance her fingers across my freckles and claim *this one* was brand new and it was the best one yet.

And that's me—a face transposed on cotton—sharing the features of the two people next to me. As happy and alive as ever.

Jonah pays the vendor for five shirts (because we can't forget about Aunt Amber), and Lo doesn't seem bothered in the least that her adult-size shirt will be too big for years to come.

The next vendor we stop at is at the behest of Jonah. There are cases upon cases of handmade jewelry featuring every shade of stone and gem under the rainbow. Loretta points to one wedged between velvet rows intermixed with other inexpensive rings.

"That one?" I ask.

She cannot stop her body from wiggling as I pluck the ring. It's gold and adjustable, with four emerald-green stones that create a sparkling clover design. Jonah catches me slipping the ring on her index finger and tightening it to fit. He doesn't say anything. Lo fans out her hand and bends her wrist, admiring its splendor.

"That one is lovely," I say softly. "Do you think it will bring you good luck?"

Her eyes, the same color as the stones glinting on her finger, dazzle with magic.

"I think it will too," I whisper.

A portly white woman with gray hair leans over the counter to speak to Lo. "That one was *made* for you."

Delta pops her head between us to see for herself. "Can I get one too?"

"I'm afraid that's the last one." The vendor sighs, but doesn't appear to be that disappointed in Delta's frown. "But... I do have a matching necklace." She pulls a necklace from the rack on the next table, and dangles the fine gold chain in front of Delta, displaying the emerald green clover leaf pendant against the back of her hand.

Both Jonah and Delta whip their heads in my direction, and at the same time ask, "Can I?"

We leave the tent a minute later, the girls one piece of jewelry richer, and Jonah eighty dollars poorer.

"Should we head back to our seats?" he asks, and flings back a handful of warm candied almonds he snagged for us. My girls' mouths are full of said candied almonds, but they agree wordlessly. "Hold up," Jonah says, and stops us again. "One more thing."

We follow him into a tent where instrument straps cover every square inch.

"Everything you see here is handmade by me," the vendor boasts in a southern accent. "And I can customize anything you want."

Jonah casually points to me. "She's looking for a strap."

I have to close my eyes and bite my tongue because my mind immediately goes to an inappropriate place.

The young man behind the table doesn't look the least bit phased. "Alright, let me help you. What kind of instrument?"

I smile and wave him off. "I don't need one right now. I don't even know where my mandolin is."

"Mom, look how pretty this one is," my daughter says from the other side. She holds out a woven strap and as I step closer, the details come into focus. All different shades of blue and purple stitched into striking florals. "You should get this one."

"I have exactly that one in the size you need," the man adds. "And I can stamp the leather buckles with any design you like right here."

It is so pretty and reminds me of one my mom had, but I shouldn't be buying a new strap when I don't even know where my mandolin is or what shape it's in. "Maybe another time," I say.

Suddenly Jonah's hand is tugging mine and he herds me a couple steps away. "Come on. Let me get that for you."

"You've spent enough on us already today. I don't need this."

"First of all, no, I have not spent nearly enough on you three today, so strike that from your excuses. And B, you *do* need this. You've reignited your passion, Renée! Let's celebrate that with something new—something *you* choose."

I didn't have choice with my ex-husband. But I've been on my own for two years now. I've been the one to call the shots and design my life, and I've centered it around my daughters. It's a natural instinct for parents to center their lives around their kids.

I think about what happened between me and Jonah in his living room the night after Delta's party. This man pushed me out of my comfort zone and made me remember another love I once held. My music—and everything that touched it—was stripped away and weaponized by Greg.

Jonah saw it all and gave me the strength to play again.

I do need this strap. I need to start prioritizing the things that make me Renée and not just a mom.

"Okay," I tell him. "I'll get it."

He lights up in his signature Jonah way, and the vendor shows me the leather buckle options. On one piece of leather, he brands a four-leaf clover per my request. And on the other, in stunning calligraphy, it reads "The Band Wilde."

Familiar music grows louder as we walk back to our private patio in the amphitheater, hand in hand. Each of my children are distracted by their new pieces of jewelry, and before I can nudge them out of the way of a stranger who is also not paying attention, Jonah guides them out of the flight path without a second thought.

Fuck, that turns me on.

By the time we make it down the long aisle, I'm singing along to the lyrics. My body absorbs the rhythm and Jonah absorbs me under his arm once again. When the next song plays, he knows the lyrics and sings along with me. His voice is much lower and not as refined, but I like the way it accompanies mine.

He chuckles, "Can you tell I've only ever been backup vocals? Actually, I was more like the backup for the backup."

I take his hand in mine and he kisses it. "I like your singing voice. It might be the only mellow thing about you."

He preens before me with all his teeth on display.

Towards the end of the song, the big screen behind the band shows a closeup of the lead singer, Desiree McKnight. She's a few years older than me and blew up with her band when I was in high school. With long, dark, wavy hair, a girl-next-door face, and one of the most unique voices in bluegrass, I was enamored.

I'm tapping my toe way too fast and I force the shake away.

Greg was the kind of guy who appeared to be an ally, but his maddening opinion on bisexuality kept me in the closet because it was safer to not upset him.

I'm in charge of my own safety now. Fuck testing the waters. "I had a crush on her back in the day," I admit to Jonah.

Pleasantly curious, he raises his eyebrows. "Really?"

"The summer after I graduated high school, we were playing at the same venue in North Carolina, and we kissed behind her tour bus."

Mouth gaping, he looks between me and the big screen. Wheels are turning in his eyes like he's heard the juiciest bit of drama. "Did you date?"

"I would have liked to, but no. We were both on tour, but we'd call each other sometimes. Then she went and fell in love with some actor and we never spoke again."

"Ohhh," he frowns. "I'm sorry."

My heart expands and settles my nerves because he's

genuinely bummed for me. And I can tell he's not doing that thing where he's picturing two women kissing for his own personal satisfaction.

"It's okay. It was a long time ago. No hard feelings."

"Have you ever been with another woman?" he asks innocently enough.

I nod. "Not until Greg was gone. There were no feelings involved. Just…" I trail off and check to make sure the girls aren't paying attention. "Just sex," I mouth silently.

"I tried to date a man once," Jonah says. *That* does surprise me. He continues, "A bunch of my family and friends are queer and so I thought I'd try it out." He shrugs.

"Have you ever experienced attraction to men?"

He winces. "No, but I was determined to try. When we tried to kiss, I got scared. I may have…" He closes his eyes and sighs. "I may have ducked down to avoid it."

I have to cover my inappropriate giggle with my hand.

"But that's cool that you're bi. Is that the right label for you?"

"Mhm."

With a satisfied smile, Jonah tucks me in closer and rubs my arm. "Professor Renée Wilde," he hums. "The bisexual biologist bluegrass bombshell."

When the band on stage ends their set, the sky has turned a pinkish orange, bursting behind fat, sleepy clouds. Much of the audience leaves or stretches their legs and mill about while recorded music plays and stagehands change out equipment. Our server comes back around with an offering of blankets, and even though it's not *that* cold, I do like the idea of sharing a blanket with Jonah.

He spreads the blanket over our laps with a shit-eating grin, but before we can settle back into each other, both of my girls join us, dragging their own blankets with them.

"Can we sit with you?" Delta asks, but she's already settled her four-foot-six body in my lap.

I laugh. "Sure. Make yourself at home."

Lo crawls into Jonah's lap, which doesn't surprise me as it once did. But he still turns to me, asking with his eyes if this is okay. I nod, and my heart swells with gratitude for Jonah once more. Loretta is wary of men, and part of that was because of Greg, but part of that was me for keeping men as far away as possible.

Delta plays with her necklace in front of my face. "Mom you should go back and get one too so we can all match."

"They only had those two."

"Yeah, but maybe Jonah can buy you something differ-ent."

I chuckle at her audacity. "I can buy my own jewelry, thank you very much."

"What do you think I should buy her?" Jonah asks.

My daughters share a wide-eyed, conspiratorial look. "A *big* wedding ring."

I choke. "Whoa, whoa, whoa—no ma'am."

"Why not?" she whines. "You should marry Jonah. He's so much nicer than daddy was."

Jonah's face turns beet red and he clamps his mouth shut.

I'm now reevaluating their casual indifference to us hold-ing hands earlier. Are these two out of their minds? If I would have known going on one *group date* with this man would result in my kids getting their hopes up over some-thing that will never happen, I would have reconsidered.

I maybe also should have seen this coming. This is the first person they've ever seen me be affectionate with since their dad. I have to remind myself that to them, affection equates to a happily ever after.

"You don't need to worry about that," I tell the girls. "Things between me and Jonah are very new, and we don't know where it's going," I say, as gently as I can. "If anything changes, I will let you know. But for now, we're just holding hands. Okay?"

She shares another look with her sister and huffs. "Fine."

Chapter 29
Truth and Trauma
Jonah

Both girls fell asleep on the ride home. Renée and I twirled our fingers and spoke softly about safe topics like her job. I talked about my siblings and rugby. But when I pulled into her driveway, neither of us wanted the night to end. I had the most amazing date and I think she did too, judging by her near-constant smile that she doesn't easily give away.

I was floating on could nine when she leaned into me earlier. I felt like I could climb a mountain or bench-press the sun. I've never done hard drugs, but I'm sure this is what it feels like.

"Are we home?" Delta murmurs, and rubs her eyes.

"Yes, sweetie," Renée replies. "Wake your sister up and go inside. I'll be right there."

Both girls lazily hop out of the SUV and wave back before tapping the door code and entering their house.

"Come over in thirty minutes after the girls go down. We can talk in the back a little longer, if that's okay?"

I kiss her hand and play with her painted nails. "Of course. I gotta check on the animals anyway. I'll be right back."

After I let the dogs out and everyone's settled in their respective beds for the night and given a truckload of lovin', I cross the yard to Renée's and wait for her in a chair. Crickets are chirping when she slips out a couple minutes later wearing the same denim dress and suede boots as before, but she's thrown on a long cardigan that she pulls tight around herself.

I'm already taking off my barn jacket. "Are you warm enough?"

She declines me gracefully. "Yes, Jonah. But thank you." She takes the other chair right next to me. "I wanted to thank you. Today was quite possibly one of the best days I've ever had."

Cartoon hearts flutter from my eyes and circle my head. "You mean it?"

"I really do." Her smile is soft, and I have the overwhelming urge to expose as much of that softness as I can. All day she's let her guard down and it looks good on her—better than the evening gown I bought her for my brother's wedding. Better than the sparkly jumpsuit. She takes my hand in hers. "It's been a long time since someone made me feel that special, and I didn't think I'd ever feel that again. I didn't want to."

"I know you probably only told me the tip of the iceberg about your ex and how he treated you, and I hope some day you can tell me more, but I would never do that to you. I–I don't know how you'll ever believe me, but, if you'll allow it, every chance I get I'm gonna keep showing up and proving it to you."

She studies me for a long time. Probably longer than I ever studied for her class. "I do believe you're a wholly different man than my ex-husband. Outside of the rugby field, I don't think you have an aggressive bone in your body."

"I don't! I accidentally bumped my knee into King a little bit ago and I about died of guilt."

She nods and continues. "But that doesn't guarantee I will always think you're safe. Trauma's a bitch like that. I only say this because if we do this," she says, squeezing my hand a little tighter, "your sunshine and four-leaf clovers are not always gonna work on me. For a very long time, my body was trained to distrust. I want you to think about what that might look like down the line."

Renée is right—I do need to think about what it would mean to be with someone who might need more emotional support than most. The road that led me here has been long and eye-opening, and I've learned so much about her and myself. Like how crazy-good it can feel to be steady and reliable. I never fully understood the weight of everyone's disappointment in me until I started to change. Now the thought of slipping back into who I was before three freckle-faced ladies moved in next door makes unease tumble in my gut like a shoe in a dryer.

"I will think about that," I say. I gesture between us and rub my thumb over the back of her hand. "But if we can always speak like this, then I bet we can work through anything." She hums a contented sigh. "What else do you need to be certain of?"

"There… is something I've never been able to figure out about you and it's been eating me alive. I didn't want to ask at first because well, it's not something you should ask people you barely know."

Oh gosh, she's gonna ask me. I've been preparing for this and it's finally time!

She hesitates. "I need to know… Where does your money come from? There's no way in hell you made that from lap dances."

I bring a hand to my chest. "Rude. My lap dances are top-tier."

Renée rolls her eyes. "I know they are, but no one makes *that* kind of money"—she gestures to my house—"working at a strip club slash hair salon."

"I'm curious," I start, and the corner of my mouth curls. "If you had to guess, where do you think my money comes from?"

"So help me Jonah, if you're some social media influencer—"

I chuckle, "No, but my brother's husband and wife are."

"At one point I thought maybe it was family money," she says. "But the more time I spend with you, well... you don't exactly carry yourself like someone raised with a lot of money."

Fair.

She tilts her head like she's weighing options. "Pretty privilege, yes. Money, no."

"Alright," I grumble, but my tone is teasing. "Point taken. You're right, I don't come from money and I didn't earn all my money from stripping." I swallow, suddenly nervous. I want to tell her and have for a long time now. But the constant reminders from my family and lawyers to not tell anyone nips at me.

No, I trust her. She deserves to know.

"I won the Pennsylvania lottery earlier this year."

The hand holding mine goes limp and her shapely brows drop. "Be serious, Jonah."

"I am."

She rips her hand away and tucks both under her arms. "Y'know, I really didn't peg you for a liar."

Suddenly there's a swarm of invisible bees trapped beneath my skin. "I'm not! I really did win the lottery!" My hands fumble with my phone as I pull it out of my coat pocket. "I won $540 million dollars. Well, after taxes it was more like $397 million. I had to create an LLC to claim the winnings anonymously and hire a financial advisor and attorney who claimed the money on behalf of the LLC."

She still doesn't look like she believes me. "What's the name of the LLC?"

"LLAN Trust." I tap Raf's contact in my phone.

Her face screws up. "What does LLAN stand for?"

I smile. "Long Live Agony Nectar."

My brother-in-law finally answers the call. "Hey man."

"How much money did I win?"

He chuckles, "That's one way to start a conversation. After taxes... would have been something like $400 million. Maybe less." Renée's eyes go wide as reality strikes her like a bolt of lighting. "Did you forget?" he laughs.

"No, I just needed Renée to hear you say that."

His laughter dies. "Wait—"

I hang up and switch the phone to silent. "That was my brother-in-law," I explain to the frozen woman before me. "Only my immediate family and closest friends know about this."

"So you... bought this place," she says with a pointed finger, "because?"

I shrug. "I had the money and my dogs were pretty cramped in my west Philly townhouse."

Her humorless laugh is adorable. "You bought a farm for your dogs?"

"Kinda, yeah."

"Okay," she breathes. "This is going to sound blunt, and I'm sorry but, what are you doing with your life?"

A quiet curve tugs at my lips. "Trying to make you a part of it."

She bites back a smile and slowly shakes her head—the way you do when the punch line is you. "I mean, what are your career aspirations? Obviously you don't need to work, but..."

"Well, I'm going to play rugby as long as I can. I donated a bunch of money to the team for a new training facility and to maintain the neighborhood around it. Other than that, I haven't really decided what I want to do yet. I have to do something though. It feels weird keeping all this locked away. I'd like to do something meaningful with the money and my time. Like an animal sanctuary!"

"I think you have enough for several hundred animal sanctuaries."

"If you have any suggestions, I'm all ears."

"You really haven't told anyone about your money?"

I shake my head. "I was told I couldn't say anything because people might take advantage of me."

She looks away for a moment like she's agreeing people *would* take advantage of me. "This is blowing my mind," she says.

"Are you mad I didn't tell you?"

She exhales long and hard, no less setting me at ease. "Now that I know, I'm not mad. I understand why you couldn't."

Relief rolls through me like a warm tide, sweeping away my fear.

"Thank you for telling me," she says.

My heart takes the driver's seat and I hop out of my chair, kneel in front of her, and take both of her hands in mine. "Renée, what we have together is already more than I've ever had. I've never felt *this* connected to someone. And your girls, my God..." I groan. "I swear I'm not just saying this because I'm over-the-moon for you, but your girls are amazing. They're so smart and fun and creative! Like, legit, I wanna hang out with them all the time."

She laughs quietly.

"Whatever this is between us," I say, before kissing her fingers, "I'll take it at whatever pace you need. I know I'm not the brightest knife in the toolbox, but I have enough sense to know you need control."

She's eyeing me like she's torn between saying more and asking for a repeat of the night we reconnected. "I do Jonah." Her voice drops to a hushed seriousness. "He took so much from me."

"I know."

"I'm done having my voice taken away."

I dip my head in agreement. "I would never. I wanna know what you think day in and day out. I wanna hear you speak because your voice..." I trail off trying to collect the right description. "Your voice is like that hum you get in your chest when you hear a live orchestra. Like when the music starts low and the crescendo is long. It's gentle but... you've never felt so alive and hopeful."

Tears well in her eyes and she blinks them away like they've offended her.

"Renée," I murmur. "I'd very much like to take care of you, and that might be hard to accept given your past, I know. But I'll never tell you what to do. I just want you to be happy."

"Me too."

The air shifts between us, quiet and heavy, and it's weird and natural all at once. "Is there anything I can do to make you happy?"

The gravity of my question hits her eyes first, and they darken. Control moves like a current, unseen yet undeniable, and it comfortably settles between us.

"I like to be in control," she warns. "Not just in my life, but in the bedroom, too."

Desire moves through me like a storm front—charged air, a clash of warm and cold that makes the hair on the back of my neck stand up. "I'm so *good* with that."

She seems pleased and my balls tighten as I brace for her reply. "I had a feeling you would be." Renée removes both of her hands from mine and places one index finger under my chin and blood rushes to my groin. "I'm going to tell you to do something in a moment, and I want you to know you can say no. I want to control you Jonah, but the most important thing is your consent."

"Yes, Professor." She inhales sharply and shuts her eyes. "Was that okay?"

She nods quickly and mutters a curse I don't quite hear. "Yes. In fact, I quite like that," she says breathlessly. Her lusty gaze hones in on me once again. "You kneel so well for me. Such a good boy. Now get lower and kiss my feet."

Have I ever done this before? Nope. But it's suddenly the most erotic thing I've ever heard, and my body reacts accordingly. Knees scraping on the concrete, I shimmy back and lower my upper body. She's still wearing her tall suede boots and when I try to remove one, she stops me. "Boots stay on. You haven't earned my skin."

I lower myself once again and nuzzle the top of her shoe and ankle. "Sorry, Professor. I'll do better." I frantically kiss every inch. "Please don't fail me." My fingers trace the boots' curves, and the suede is soft and warm beneath my lips.

"You think you can just take me out and spend money on me?" she asks cooly, but there's heat in her meaning. "You think that's going to save your grade?"

"No, Professor Wilde," I say into the leather, but it comes out far too quick.

"Do you think I haven't noticed how desperate you are? You're like a puppy begging for attention."

The idea of her leashing me causes my dick to surge. "I'm sorry," I murmur again. "I really like you and I wanna do good. Please don't fail me. I'll do whatever you want."

"And what do you want?"

I don't stop kissing her feet when I speak, and I don't hide the truth. "I wanna take you out again and spend every last dime on you. I wanna be available for your every whim. I want you to use me."

"Get up and look at me," she commands, and I obey.

My God, it feels good to obey her.

"I do not want your money," she says, measured and deliberate. But when my brows furrow, her demeanor softens. "Oh no," she drawls. "Don't give me those sad boy eyes."

"But I *want* to spoil you," I whine, like a man.

A delicate smile touches her face. "You already do. The way you treat me and my daughters..." She sighs happily. "I feel rich."

"Please let me take you out again. *Please.*"

Once again her finger finds my chin and she pulls me into a long, drugging kiss. It's the kind of kiss your heart custom designs just so you can look back in your memories and die a sweet death.

"Okay," she whispers. "You can take me out again."

Chapter 30

Office Hours

Renée

The next day at work, it takes considerable effort to not think about Jonah kneeling before me—desperate and perfect.

I sent him home shortly after that, but not without a kiss and not without a whisper in his ear that he should think of me when he takes care of himself tonight. I marveled at his restraint, at the way his hands gripped my hips and slowly let go.

Such a good boy.

It's still early in the early afternoon, but this semester I don't have any classes after two o'clock. I'm packing up for the day when there's a knock at my office door that pulls me from going too far down the sexy rabbit hole I've fallen into.

"Delivery for Professor Wilde," comes the voice of a tall man standing in my doorway. He's hiding his face beneath a ball cap he's pulled low, but his familiar body and blond hair poking out the back are a dead giveaway.

I rush to him, unable to fight the smile splitting my face in two, and remove his hat. "What are you doing here?"

Jonah gestures to the vase of rich burgundy dahlias he's holding. "I came to ask if you were free October second." I furrow my brow. "Yes," he chuckles. "I know that's your birthday. Amber told me." He shakes his head. "I can't believe you weren't going to tell me it was coming up."

I sigh, "It's not that big a deal."

"It is now," he grins and shimmies the bouquet under my face. "You said last night I could take you out."

I take the flowers and admire them. "I did say that."

"So is that a yes?"

"Yes." I smile. "You can take me out for my birthday."

His reply is nothing more than the biggest Jonah Johanssen smile—so wide it creates deep ravines around his mouth.

God, how I want that mouth.

Arousal courses through my veins and charges my brain. I place the flowers on my desk, step away from him, and lock the door. His eyes round and my fingertips creep up his chest. "Last night you said you were good with me taking control. Is that still the case?"

He looks at me like I've just said something really stupid. "Oh yeah."

"You always have the choice to stop, at any time, with no repercussions. Is that understood?"

"Yes."

I already have a sense of what I'd like to do with him, so I'm not too worried about establishing safewords and digging into our sexual interests and limits just yet. But there isn't a shadow of a doubt this man likes the idea of a little naughty professor roleplay.

"Did you follow my orders when you got home last night?"

"Is this really happening?" he huffs.

I smooth my hands over his shoulders. "That depends, Mr. Johanssen... Did you do your assignment?"

He grins.[1] "Yes, Professor."

"You thought about me while you stroked yourself?"

He bites his pink bottom lip and nods.

---

1. Dirty Thoughts by Chloe Adams

"Did you record it?"

"Um... I..." his voice cracks. "I didn't know I was supposed to."

I step back, lean my ass against the desk, and cross my arms. "Then how am I supposed to grade you, Jonah?"

"Um..." He looks around my office like it's going to provide him with answers. "I don't know. But I'll do anything you want."

I arch an eyebrow. "Anything, hmm? Well I appreciate the offer, but I can't show favoritism amongst my students, Mr. Johanssen. Surely you know that."

My heart skips a beat when his knees hit the carpet. "Please," he begs, and it's like music to my ears. When he kisses my shoes, I can't help appreciate how very trainable he is. "Maybe just this once?" he murmurs. He presses his lips on my bare ankle and slowly trails them to my calf.

I hum. "Just this once."

"What can I do?"

I order him to stand, and I slide back on the desk until my feet are hanging. "You're going to touch between my thighs and you're going to show me how strong your hands are."

He shudders. "Of course, Professor." His breathless tone ratches up my need for him, and he's hiking my long skirt to my thighs. When his broad hands skim up my legs and try to yank my panties, I grab his wrists tight.

"Everything stays on." His gaze flicks from mine, down to where his hands are hidden under my skirt, and back up. He tilts his head and I smirk. "Get creative." From my hip to my aching center, he slides one finger under my panty line. "That's it," I encourage. I plant my hands on the desk to get a better view of my naughty little student.

When he finds my seam, I cant my hips ever so slightly, and he bites his lower lip. When he pushes in, he and I can both tell I'm not quite ready. Once again, I hold onto his wrist and guide that hand to my mouth before sucking his first two digits. He gasps, his chest heaving as he watches me swirl my tongue around, wetting his fingers. I pop them out with a messy squelch. "I don't get wet as fast as I used to," I tell him with absolutely no shame. "If you wanna be with an older woman, you better know that."

"Yes," he whispers, and I'm surprised he can even speak from the way he's still staring at me like I invented sex.

I spit on his fingers for good measure and his knees buckle.

I am going to ruin this man, I think with no small amount of glee.

With his dry hand, he pulls my panties to the side and smears his slick fingers through the slit—dipping in and dragging out slowly—grazing my clit with every pass. The chest-deep moan I let out is quiet, and my head falls back as he massages me.

"It's not just about my grade, Professor Wilde. I've wanted this for a long time."

"Yeah?" I ask, my voice growing shakier by the second. "When you were alone in your room with your hand on your cock, what did you think about?"

He circles my clit with both fingers and adds a little more pressure. "I thought about your gorgeous pussy," he admits, his voice thick and tinged with something feral. "I thought about how warm and perfect it would be, and how many times I could get you off, if only you gave me the chance. I thought about you in my bed riding me, my face, my fingers." He grunts and shoves them inside me with a powerful thrust. "I thought about bending you over this very desk so you'd know how crazy I am about you."

He adds his thumb to my clit while he strokes my G-spot, and I'm already seeing stars. "Yes," I moan. "Keep going. You're doing so good."

My head is still thrown back, but then he surprises me with an open-mouth kiss to my neck. My chest heaves with aching nipples that are pounding on the door to my bra for me to unleash them. *Ughh, his mouth would be so good there...* but I stay the course.

Kind of.

His other hand, the one holding my panties to the side, is removed, and he wraps it around my waist before pulling me close. Our chests are touching and through his ministrations to my cunt, neck, and ear lobe, he asks, "Is this okay?"

That's when I lose it.

Contractions erupt in my lower half and I grip his shoulders to ride out my orgasm for dear life. I can't speak, but he understands when I nod frantically against his warm chest.

Is this okay? All he did was ask me if it was okay for him to hold me close and kiss my neck—and I came.

Correction: am still coming.

Suddenly our mouths are a gnarled mess of lips and teeth and heavy breathing. I ride his hand for as long as I can, and he never relents, never pulls away. He keeps the exact same pressure and rhythm until I'm fairly certain the second I open my eyes, the sun will be down.

"You're so fucking wet," he rumbles into my mouth, and—*oh my God, did I just hear him swear?* I revel in his profanity and slowly make the trek down from my climax. His hand and our kissing slow into appreciation for the other. My mind is in the clouds and my fingers have found their way into his hair. I drag my nails gently across his scalp and he goes limp.

His fingers are still inside me when I whisper in his ear, "You did so well, Mr. Johanssen. Do you think you could do one more thing for me?"

I'm still scratching his head when he nods, eyelids closed. I remove one hand and palm the erection trying to escape his zipper. His eyes fly open.

"I want you to ride my thigh and make yourself come.

Could you do that for me?"

"Yes," he says, an octave too deep.

I slide off the desk but keep my ass planted against the edge. My hand glides down his rigid length and I cup his balls before squeezing—making it painfully obvious who calls the shots. "You're going to paint the inside of your pants and you're not going to get *a drop* on my clothes, is that understood?"

"Mhm," he whines.

I pull him into me and command him to hold my hips. Jonah has to bend his legs significantly to make everything line up, but I love making him work for it. I tug his head down and nestle it into my neck. His breath is hot and his tongue glides over my pulse.

"Such a needy little puppy, aren't you?"

"Yes, Professor," he says, and the way he says it is so damn pathetic I could combust.

Heat blooms between our bodies from the friction of our clothes, and his thrusts pick up speed—every hard inch of him pushing into my soft thighs. The aching muscles between my legs involuntarily tighten and release with every stroke—coaxing me to find more more more.

"Did you think about these?" I arch and lean back to push his head into my chest—nails digging into his head. "And just how much you could take in your mouth?"

His reply is muffled by my ample breasts and blouse, but the way he's nuzzling me sends his message loud and clear—and I want that. I haven't let anyone see my bare tits in all this time I've been attending parties and hooking up with submissives. It's been a soft limit I've held, but the idea of Jonah never seeing them, never touching them? I think I'd be doing myself a disservice. I want to watch him worship my breasts with tiny darts of his tongue and long, flat strokes. With maddening nips and suffocating mouthfuls.

When Jonah's breathing becomes erratic, I yank his face to mine and push my tongue into his mouth, and he groans.

"That's it," I murmur against his lips. "Come for me. Be a good boy and earn your grade, Mr. Johanssen."

He bites my lip as his body stills. "*Unghhhh. Fffffuuu—*" he grunts, tortured and lovely. A few more jerks follow before he slumps against me, panting like the puppy he is. "Whoa," he breathes.

Over every ridge and plane of muscles, I stroke my hands up and down his back. "Good boy," I praise, my tone as gentle and soothing as my hands.

He kisses my lips and draws in a deep inhale. "Thank you."

I smile. "Thank you for the flowers."

For a while longer, we stand there soaking up each other's pheromones and exchanging languorous kisses until our heart rates return to normal. The voices of people walking through the hallway just outside my office door have us both grinning like a couple of naughty kids.

"Sit down in my chair," I say, and nudge him until he does. I grab a bottle of water from my mini fridge and open a desk drawer to retrieve a Twix candy bar I have saved for the days I need a sweet fix. He watches me like I hung the moon as I stand between his spread legs and hand him the open water bottle. "Drink this please."

His brows raise. "What? No, that's for you."

"I won't take a sip until you do." I force him to take it.

"But... that's not how this works. I'm supposed to get you water."

I lean back against the desk and open the candy wrapper with a knowing smirk. "And why's that?"

I flick my eyes to him and watch the confusion stir. "Because... I'm the man?"

A snort escapes me. "And I'm the Domme. It's my job to take care of you after a scene like that. I need to make sure you're cared for and you feel safe. So please drink your water..." I trail off with a smile and wait for him to drink half of it before handing him a Twix. "And eat this."

"What if I don't like Twix?"

I level him with a glare. "You've eaten every cookie my kids have ever made you."

He chuckles and takes the chocolate-covered caramel cookie. "Guilty," he says, and bites off half.

"Are you okay with what happened here?"

With a full mouth, he looks at me like I'm bananas. "Uh, yeah!"

"Good." I hand him the second cookie. "Me too." Something less fun must cross his mind because his focus goes distant for a moment. "What's wrong?"

He takes his time finishing what's left in his mouth before speaking.

At least he has good manners.

"Have you ever..." he starts, and looks around the room.

It's my turn for my eyebrows to shoot up. "Done stuff in here?"

He lifts one shoulder, a picture of innocence despite that fact we defiled each other minutes ago. "Like with other students?"

"With no one, Jonah."

"Really?"

"Really," I confirm, praying he can feel my honesty. "I've never had feelings for a student, and I've certainly never withheld grades for sexual acts. Believe me, I'm all too familiar with students thinking they could *tempt me*," I teasingly accuse, and he blushes because he knows he did that to me when he was my student. "But that's never a line I would cross."

"I didn't think you would," he says. "I just... I don't know why I even asked."

I run my fingers across his cheek and cup the side of his face. "It's okay that you asked. This is why aftercare is so important." I kiss his forehead and hand him the water again.

"Did you enjoy it?" he asks. "Is there anything I can do better next time?"

"Next time?" I tease, and he flashes a smug smile because he knows as well as I do, there will most definitely be a next time.

Chapter 31

Harvest

Renée

The rest of the week passes much the same as previous ones, but every evening after the girls go down, I sneak out to find Jonah on my back patio, sweeping leaves and waiting for a goodnight kiss. Sometimes we talk for a bit, and sometimes nothing is more important than making out like horny teens. Can you blame me? There are nights he comes home wearing tiny rugby shorts and a cut-off shirt.

I'm only human.

On Saturday the girls and I attend another one of his games. I still don't know the rules of rugby, but my body knows it likes his. And his long, thick legs with that slutty team crest tattoo on his mid-thigh… *Mmm.* It's so trite, but his athleticism turns me on. The incredible speed at which he can run the ball and the way he can just get up from a tackle like it's no sweat off his back…

For completely unrelated reasons, it pleases me to know he has a high pain tolerance.

Amber leaves after breakfast to work the club's Sunday brunch service, and the girls and I make plans for the day. They promise to help me harvest the rest of my garden in exchange for play time with the animals. Fine by me, I didn't even have to propose that idea.

The early autumn morning is warm, but there's an undeniable crispness creeping in, a tender reminder that change can be sweet. Baskets in hand, I open the garden gate and let the girls in, giving them each a pair of sheers and gloves with instructions to cut all flowers.

"Uh-ohhh," Delta says a few rows back. "Mom?"

I pull a beet. "Yeah? Do you need a different pair of gloves?"

"No, look at the pumpkins!"

I just saw them two days ago and they were fine, but I stride back to check them out. My jaw drops when half a garden bed of pumpkin carcasses come into view. "What on earth?" The jarrahdales, pie pumpkins, heirlooms—all of them have been gnawed open. "How did this happen?" I ask myself aloud. I check on the rest of the beds but nothing else has been touched.

"Was it a squirrel?" Delta asks. "They've eaten our jack-o-lanters before."

"Sweetie, these teeth marks are not from a squirrel. And there's too much wreckage." That's when my eye catches on the back fence where it meets the ground. My steps are slow and careful when I step up to the massive dirt hole that's been dug under the fence. But it looks like whatever broke in didn't get that idea first and tried mawling the fence.

"Oh noooo," Delta gasps, and Lo joins us to stare at the hole, the size of which both of them could fit through.

"It's okay," I tell them, although I'm already thinking of how much it's going to cost to replace this part of the fence. "The good news is we're harvesting everything that's left today, so no more stuff can be eaten."

"But what are we gonna use for Halloween?"

I huff a laugh and redirect their shoulders. "Sweetie, it's late September. There are pumpkins at every store and farm stand across the country. Why don't you both pick up any pumpkin seeds you find and we'll save them for next year?"

Pleased with my idea, they use their little fingers to comb

through everything like little archeologists. For the next hour, I pull the rest of the beets, butternut squash, cabbage, and Brussels sprouts while wracking my brain with what could have possibly done this to my fence and pumpkins.

And seriously? Only the pumpkins?

The familiar sound of Jonah's returning SUV rumbles up the road, and I peer up to wave. I can hear his engine turn off and in minutes, he's knocking at the gate. "Good morning, ladies."

"Hi Jonah!" Delta cheers, and the girls race to let him in before I can.

That's when I see Yogi next to him, all one hundred and eighty pounds of slightly discolored white fluff, with bandages on his front paws. The puzzle piece clicks into place.

"What happened to Yogi?" Delta asks, and both boys step in.

"I'm not sure, but I found him this morning in the barn with all these cuts on his feet and a dew claw gone. We just got back from the vet."

Both girls wrap their arms around the dog and he wags his tail. "Poor buddy," Delta coos.

My heart does break for the big guy, far worse than any of the damage to the garden. I can't help rubbing his ears and pouting over him too.

But I sigh and catch Jonah's eye. "I think I know what happened. Follow me."

Jonah has to cover his mouth when I show him the damning evidence. "I'm so sorry, Renée. I'll get this fixed, I promise." He apologizes so sincerely—like this is my property, not his.

"It's okay. We'll figure it out." I look down at the dog who has followed us with his ears tucked and head low. "But I would like to know what the heck is so special about our pumpkins, Yogi."

"Hey I know I just left," Jonah says into the phone he's

now holding to his ear. "But it looks like he tore up Renée's garden. Yeah, he climbed under the fence and ate all their pumpkins. Is he going to be okay?" He scans the graveyard of gourds. "He ate... a lot of them."

We all stand by waiting for a sign of relief, but he chews on his bottom lip and inspects the bits and pieces left. "Doesn't look like it," he replies. "Okay. Thanks bro. Love you. I said I love you, Dane! Say it back," he says petulantly, and eventually smiles. "That's better. I'll see you later."

"Is he gonna be okay?" I ask.

He pockets his phone and sighs. "He should be fine. It doesn't look like he ate the stems or leaves, which is good. If he doesn't poop for a while I'll have to bring him in. But he should be fine once his paws heal." He claps his hands and turns his sunshine on the girls. "Okay, who wants to help me make a little recovery center in the barn for this goober?"

They both raise their hands as if there's an entire audience behind them hoping to be picked.

I chuckle and nod to Jonah. "Go ahead. I'm gonna finish up here and I'll be right over."

The girls race out of the garden and beeline for the barn, with the dog limping behind them.

I shake my head watching him walk off. "Poor guy."

"I'm sorry he ate your pumpkins," Jonah repeats. "I'll get the fence repaired before the snow falls."

I could argue with him. I could stand my ground and reject his offer. But I remember his words that night after the bluegrass festival, as he knelt before me with my hands in his. *I'd very much like to take care of you, and that might be hard for you to accept. I just want you to be happy.*

Greg promised me that same thing in a manner of speaking. As a twenty-two year old, what did I know? I questioned nothing. I had no reason to believe he'd lie to me, or that anything bad would ever happen.

Jonah on the other hand... he's nothing like my ex-hus-band. Generational differences aside, their personalities and demeanor are night and day. I don't think Jonah's even capable of saying harsh words. I mean what kind of man cares for old, sickly, and unwanted animals because he feels bad for them? Because he wants his dogs to have friends? That's a four hundred-level class in Good Boy Behavior.

So no, I'm not going to argue with him about who will pay for the fence repair. I'm going to brush my hands of the task and he's going to handle it.

"Okay," I say, and temporarily lose myself in his gaze. "Thank you for taking care of it."

He sneaks a glance over his shoulder toward the barn where the girls have run inside and when he turns back, a grin crawls over his face and he eyes me head to toe. "You look so pretty today," he says, before sectioning off a long length of my hair and combing his fingers down to the ends. "I like when your hair is kinda... half-up, half-down like this."

I'm wearing jeans and an embroidered short sleeve blouse that has seen better days—but I don't think I have. "Thank you. Now give me a kiss before they come out looking for you."

I'm caught off guard when he lays one on me so fast it takes a second for me to catch up. Then he peppers me with a dozen more in rapid succession all over my face. Giggling like a school girl, I'm left standing there in a cloud of his sage and citrus as he runs away to make a recovery bed for his dog.

Once everything's harvested, I take it all inside for a good scrub. Every vase, pitcher, and jar I own are suddenly filled with flowers, and the scent takes over our home. When I'm finished, I head back to Jonah's and place one of the arrangements on his outdoor table before checking on their progress in the barn.

Sure enough, they've essentially made Yogi a pillow fort

in the hay. The girls have made signs featuring a giant red cross and another that says *Shhh!* There's even a first aid kit nearby with all his medical supplies. Of course Yogi simply lays there, soaking up every ounce of affection he's given.

On his porch, the four of us have a late lunch of simple sandwiches and apple slices. Blind as she is, Ginger—with her super-horse powers—can smell the apples all the way from her paddock and neighs until the girls bring her a special delivery.

Jonah and I clean up, and he hands me a couple beers for the porch and directs me to relax. "I'll be right back," he says, before dashing back into the house and reappearing a minute later with his guitar and mandolin. He's already staring at me with a mischievous grin like he knows the outcome.

I don't argue.[1]

I take another sip and set my beer on the wooden porch next to a couple ducks and an adorable snoozing German Shepherd. Pleased as punch, Jonah hands over the instrument and pick, and I sit back. He takes the other chair, waiting patiently for me to tune. Mandolins are temperamental and require constant tuning, but Jonah looks like he could listen to me pluck the same open string a million times.

When I'm satisfied, it's his turn, and he's done in less than ten seconds. He tilts his head. "Lead the way, Renée."

I have no hesitation and I have no fear. I don't overanalyze the song choice or worry if my voice can handle it. The music finds me, and Jonah strums along trustingly the whole time.

My girls come and go, running between the barn and porch, listening to us play and putting in requests. I haven't the faintest idea how to play some of their songs, but

---

1. Wildflowers by Miley Cyrus

Jonah sets up his laptop with the sheet music—most likely because he can't say no to these girls.

For hours we play side-by-side and take turns listening to each other explain our lives, our histories, and hope through music. It's an easy Sunday—golden and sweet—the kind that inspires poets and dreamers.

The afternoon hums around us and time blurs. At some point, the kids set off down the main trail of Jonah's property with one of the goats running alongside them. Girls will be girls.

I set my mandolin aside, fingers buzzing from hours strumming. Jonah leans back, eyes half-closed, looking entirely too pleased with himself. That's when Delta barrels up the porch stairs, clutching a pair of kitchen scissors like a prize.

"Jonah, can I cut your hair?" she asks, breathless.

He's already untying his bun. "Sure."

"Whoa, whoa, hold your fire." I reach for the shears she clearly took from our kitchen as Lo joins us, also out of breath. They both look at me like I'm about to crush their plans and a sharp ache forms in my heart. I don't blame them. Only a couple months ago I would have pulled the emergency brake on a situation like this.

It's a good thing Cool Mom is here instead.

"These aren't the right kind of scissors," I whisper, like we're hatching a top-secret plan. "Come on!"

The three of us race for the house while Jonah fluffs his hair. "Good scissors are in the top drawer next to the fridge," he casually calls out.

We reappear with the good scissors and a hair brush I swiped from the bathroom. Judging by the hair woven into the bristles, he definitely shares it with King.

The girls take turns brushing his ridiculously long hair, and he teases them the whole time. Dramatically yelping and groaning, drag after drag. Then I watch as Delta grabs the shears in her hand and sticks out her tongue to better concentrate. She hesitates over the bottom three inches, then suddenly jerks her hand four inches higher and cuts.

My heart stops, and I'm too afraid to blink in case I miss something even worse.

Jonah can't see what's happening, but I know he can *feel* how high she's cutting. Yet he's completely unphased. Lo raptly watches her sister chop the rest off in an uneven layer and then taps Jonah on the shoulder.

"You wanna turn?" he asks her.

She bobs her head.

"Go for it, Shortcake."

I send Cool Mom on a smoke break and hold up one finger. "Okay," I wince. "But only a little bit, Lo. Just—" I point to a particularly uneven part. "How about this bit right... here?"

Thankfully Loretta has never been as much of a risk taker as her sister, and she snips off a satisfying section.

Jonah shakes his hair out. "Am I finally beautiful?" I hand him my phone with the front camera open and he gasps. "I love it," he exclaims, flipping his new shoulder-length hair.

The girls dissolve into a puddle of giggles and are snatched up in his arms. His hair cut is objectively awful, and the more I study it, the more it makes me laugh. Eventually I find myself wheezing and holding my sides in pain. Dogs and ducks and goats flock to the chaos, eager to protect my daughters from their father.

That last thought buzzes through my mind well into the evening. I meant *their father* as in *Jonah is the animals' father*. That's what I meant, but I can't stop myself from considering the other way that sentence could be considered.

Their father.

For dinner, Jonah orders pizza from Mike's Deli and Tractor Repair, the only place in town that will deliver to our street. The pizza is hot garbage, always has been, but somehow it's never tasted better.

We help Jonah feed and medicate all his feathered and fur babies before the pair of us head out on the trail. The girls are somewhere, doing their best to avoid going home for bath time, and I don't blame them. I don't want this day to end either. But when the sun begins her sleepy descent, we both know it's time.

The trailhead opens to his backyard and he places a hand on my shoulder for a gentle squeeze. "Let me go put everyone in their stalls for the night," he says. "And then I'll walk you home."

"I'll join you."

As we head for the barn, the sound of Delta's familiar soprano grows, and it's louder than I've ever heard. Wait, no—that's not only her voice. My feet and heart stop at the same time and I clutch Jonah's arm, my hands shaking like a leaf. "Listen," I whisper.

The timbre of the second voice is a bit sweeter, brighter, like a soubrette.

Realization dawns on his face, and he clasps a hand over his mouth. Tears spill down my cheeks as I fight to stay silent, praying this isn't a dream—that Lo is *singing*. Words from *her* beautiful little mouth. I can't believe it.

Jonah turns to me, and the tears streaking down his face are gasoline on my emotional fire. *He loves them.* It's so obvious how much he loves them and he hides it from no one. He parades us around like we're crown jewels: one little girl who had no voice, another with messy, self-cut micro bangs, and one who used her thorns to keep people away.

He catches me, pressing my head to his chest, our hearts beating erratically. My tears soak through his shirt and I cling to him, certain that if I let go, I'll fall.

I already have.

Chapter 32
Search and Rescue
Renée

I'm woken from a dead sleep by a small hand touching my arm. I know it's Delta without even looking. She's always been one to come into my room at all hours of the night with random bits of information, and the impulse to explain her dreams.

"Mom?" she murmurs. "Lo's not in her bed."

I respond, still half-asleep. "Mmm... she's probably in the bathroom. Go back to bed."

"No, she's not."

I glance at the glowing red numbers on my alarm clock: 5:02 a.m. I sigh and roll out of bed before wrapping myself in a robe and slippers. We walk into their shared bedroom and I do my best to reassure her. "She's probably under the covers somewhere." But she's right—Lo's bed is empty. Even her safety blanket is gone.

"She's around here somewhere," I say, this time trying to reassure myself and quell the tendril of worry in my blood. The house is too quiet. No cartoons or creaking floors or the rustling of a snack bag. I open Amber's door abruptly. "Is Lo in here?"

Amber groans, "No. Should she be?" I flick on her light and she covers her face. She's not here either. *Shit.*

"Lo?" I call through the house and hustle from room to room, closet to closet. "Lo where are you? Sweetheart, this isn't funny. Please come out." Amber and Delta check under beds and furniture and the pile of clothes in the laundry.

"The back door's unlocked," Amber says, and my fear skyrockets. I grab my cell phone and we bound for the chilly backyard with whatever jackets we can find.

"Loretta!" the three of us call. We split up, Delta staying close to her aunt and circling the house while I check the shed. When she's not there either, I don't waste any time and call the police.

I give them my address and explain my seven-year-old daughter is missing. I describe her features and that until yesterday she hadn't spoken in almost three years, so there's a possibility she won't verbally respond. Dispatch informs me a police officer will be here in fifteen minutes.

I hang up and immediately dial Jonah. I'm already running to his house when he picks up. "Hey," he says, voice cracking with sleep.

"Lo's missing! I just woke up five minutes ago and she's not in the house. The police are on their way. Please tell me she's with you?!"

"What?" He clears his throat. "No... I don't think so."

I run up his back porch and pull on the locked door. "Let me inside!"

"I'm coming down right now!"

My pulse is thundering as we search every room in his house with King, calling her name with no luck. We're jumping off the porch when the silhouette of the barn comes into my view against the faint pre-dawn light.

"The barn," I say, already running. But Jonah and King run faster, and the motion-detecting flood light turns on above the door. Jonah slides it open and King slips through first. I'm only three feet away when Jonah cries, "I found her!"

He ushers me in, and I immediately spot her outline in the glow of the outdoor light. She's curled up next to Yogi in his makeshift recovery suite. Both Rugger and Yogi have already popped their heads up to see what all the fuss is about, and Lo shifts under her safety blanket.

Jonah flicks on the interior barn lights as soon as my knees hit the hay, and I'm hauling her into my chest, sobbing with relief. Suddenly Jonah's arms are wrapping around both of us.

"Why on earth are you here?" I choke out.

"He's hurt and scared," she murmurs, half-asleep and trying her best to keep one hand on her fluffy patient.

"Oh my God, Lo." I cry, my whole body trembling. "Don't you ever leave the house without telling me, young lady."

Jonah rubs her head and kisses the top of it. "He's okay, Shortcake. He's a big boy." He lets out a ragged sigh and sniffles. "You scared us. We didn't know where you were."

"I'm sorry," she says.

"It's okay, sweetie. I'm just glad you're safe."

In the distance, I can hear Amber's voice calling for Lo. Jonah scrambles to his feet and runs outside. "She's in here!"

The police arrive five minutes later, even though I had already called dispatch back to update them on my daughter's desire to sleep like a barn animal. They question each adult and perform a quick mental and physical health screen with Lo. To my delight, she actually speaks to them. Not much, but it's the most amazing sight to see.

Dawn turns into bright beams of light casting through the trees by the time the police leave. We wave goodbye to Officer Ryan, and I can feel my adrenaline is fading fast, but I'm still shaken.

"I need to stay away from your barn," I tell Jonah. "Every time I'm here, I cry." His expression softens and he opens his arms to hold me.

"Girls, let's give them a minute," Amber coos, and nudges their shoulders to our home. "Let's get ready for school."

When I pull away from his embrace, I'm embarrassed and exhausted. He studies my face. "You're running on fumes. Don't even think about going into work today."

I'm about to protest, but Amber's voice rings out from several yards away. "He's right!"

Jonah smirks and I roll my eyes. "You're probably right. But I am going to drive them to school. I need that confirmation of where they are."

"I get it. But come right back here, okay? I wanna take care of you today."

I tell work I'm taking a personal day, but I leave out the part where my child decided she was feral and wanted to live in a barn. I call the school on our drive to inform them the Wilde sisters will be a bit late, and I drop them off with the strongest goodbye hug. I cry a little more alone in the car before collecting myself and driving home.

By the time I pull into my driveway, the whole world is illuminated and the morning chill is gone, and the worst of the adrenaline has drained from my veins. My hands are still shaking a little, but in the past-crisis way—like my body hasn't received the memo that everything's fine now. Lo is safe, and Delta's working on perfecting her dramatic retelling of her "barn sleepover rescue."

I take a quick shower, blow out my hair, and apply a little moisturizer. When I make it back to Jonah's place, he's already made coffee and breakfast for us. I don't tell him I stopped at the donut shop with the girls.

We sit on his porch with all three dogs and sip our coffee without talking about it. The silence is gentle, not awkward. Like the kind you get when you've run out of words but still want to bathe in the same air.

"Sorry you had to play search-and-rescue at five in the morning," I say finally, my voice hoarse from yelling earlier.

He tilts his head, a soft smile through a cloud of coffee steam. "I'm glad you called me. I hope you always do. For any reason."

The words hit somewhere behind my sternum, deeper than I'm ready to admit. I look out on the pasture instead of at him. "She scared me," I whisper. "One minute I was asleep, completely unaware, and the next..." I trail off. "It's like my brain went straight to every bad headline I've ever read." There's a long pause, and he lets me work through it. "It was like those first few months after each of them were born, I couldn't turn off my brain from imagining the most heinous situations where I would need to save my babies. I thought today was going to be one of those situations."

Jonah sets his mug down and puts an arm around me. "I can't say I've ever thought about that. But for what it's worth, you weren't alone in your fear. I think my heart nearly broke this morning."

I set my coffee down and lean into him, and our arms wrap around each other. "I know. I could tell."

The companionable silence eases back in, and every so often, he glances at me, like he's checking to make sure I'm okay. I sigh. "I'll be fine. Eventually. I'm just frayed. Motherhood is a delicate balance between panic and guilt sometimes."

"Seems like you're doing great to me."

"At 5:00 a.m. I was screaming in your backyard, wearing a robe and slippers with no bra, talking to the police, and crying into your shirt."

He tucks his chin to inspect said shirt and swipes his hand down his chest like he's dusting off invisible dirt. "*Ughh*, thanks a lot. It *was* a good shirt."

I chuckle and flick his nose. "You ass." The levity feels strange after everything, but good.

So good.

Chapter 33
God is a Woman

Renée

When Jonah suggests a walk to "burn off the nerves," it's an easy yes. He loads up a backpack with God knows what, and we follow the main trail between his pasture and woods. My right hand brushes along the wildflowers that are still hanging on to the last bit of their season. Jonah holds my left.

He points out all the plants he's investigated—to which I politely remind him the correct term is *researched*—and pride fills me with everything he's learned.

Somewhere along our walk, the humor fades into something softer. The breeze hums with it—the quiet kind of tension that feels like standing in the sun too long.

We stop when we reach the little creek that bends and snakes through the trees. "You okay now?" he asks.

I nod. "Yeah. I think so."

And just like that, we're kissing. I can taste his coffee and the remnants of his toothpaste. Every bit of relief flows between us like we share one body. When he pulls me closer, everything in me relaxes.

That is, until things turn indecent. I mean, is it *my* fault he's so much taller than me and his ass is easier to grab than his shoulders? Is it *his* fault that the rod between his legs keeps pushing into my stomach?

Okay, yes to both, but we're not on trial here.

What we are is hungry.

Jonah breaks the kiss to dig through his backpack. I'm

about to protest, but he retrieves a blanket and lays it out.

"What a good little boy scout."

Grinning and proud of himself, he sits and extends his hand for me to join. We both kick off our shoes and resume our makeout session. I pin him down and he makes no effort to fight his fate.

"You like it when I'm in charge. When I'm on top of you like this."

He palms my ass and groans, "I'm exactly where I want to be."

I pull gently at his bottom lip and release it before whispering in his ear, "Let me thank you for what you did today."

His neck is so close to my face that I can feel his Adam's apple bob. "I'll do whatever you say," he huffs.

I lift the bottom of his T-shirt, bunching it at the top, and kiss a trail down his torso. "I know you will."

"Is there anything I should know before I play with you, Jonah?"

"Um... I like to keep it bare down there?"

I don't even try to suppress my giggle. "No, puppy. When was the last time you were tested?"

Suddenly his bravado returns, and he stretches his arms behind his head. "Well, I got this hot professor neighbor who loves to grade me." He smirks. "Does that count?" That smirk dies when I grab hold of his balls. "Five months ago! Everything is ship-shape!"

I release him... a little bit. "That was pretty long ago."

"So?"

"Sooo, you may have contracted something by now."

"But I haven't been with anyone. That night at Strip Tease with you? That was the last time I was with someone. Well, until last week when we got freaky in your office with our clothes on."

My brows furrow. "But that was back in February."

"And I was tested after that." He points to his dick and

nods. "All good in the hood."

"Hang on, you haven't been with anyone since then? Like, no one?"

He wiggles beneath me and smiles. "I'm saving myself for youuuu," he coos, the picture of sarcastic innocence.

I shake my head at his antics, but another thought pops in. "Wait, are you a virgin?"

He looks to the sky and lets out an exasperated gasp. "No!" He looks back down at me hovering above his zipper. "Now please *please* touch me."

I chuckle and unbutton him. "I do love it when you beg."

His eyes round like saucers and he pumps his fist in the air. "Yes!"

This playful side of Jonah has my inner dominant thrown off-kilter. I've never been with someone so... youthful. But God help me, I like it. I like how effortlessly he falls from exuberance to *Oh shit, I'm in danger.*

I finally remove his jeans and boxers and hike his long, wildly muscular legs to the sky.

"Whoa," he whispers.

I settle his hairy legs over my shoulders and stare down at him. I trace a finger from his taint, up the seam of his sac, and follow the thick vein leading to his tip. "You're so beautiful."

Blush covers his face and he has a strange sort of look about him. "Really?"

With a featherlight touch, I push five fingers down his wide, ruddy crown, like I'm rolling on an invisible condom. "Very. And one day soon, I'm going to take my time investigating every inch, mark, and hair on your body."

He glows with a knowing smile and a waggle of his eyebrows. "I think you mean research."

I lean down and lick the bead of precum from his tip. "Shut up and let me thank you."

He exhales a shuddering breath. "Ohhhhkayyup."

My tongue teases all the way down his thick shaft. He smells like he took a shower when I was gone earlier, but there's also that addictive salted aroma of his natural body odor that could eat me alive if I stayed down here long enough.

God, I would love that. The idea of torturing him all day long with massages from my mouth... maybe nothing more than little puffs of air around his groin and temptation in my eyes.

I think I'd like that very much.

When I reach his base, I kiss and lick across the blond stubble before gently sucking. His sac tightens when I drag a flat tongue through the center and straight to his crown.

"Oh. Oh yeah. Yes, thank you," he whispers. I fully lower myself to the blanket and lift his balls to feast on his taint. "Holy fuck! What are you doing?"

Has he never been eaten like this? If that's true, what a fucking crime. I decide not to explain myself, instead settling for a hushing sound. When the area is sloppy and wet, I incorporate my nose, fingers, and chin—all of it massaging his taint until he's breathing so hard I have to back off before he blows.

I shift back to my knees and bend forward, swallowing his head and allowing the pool of saliva to fall down around him. I add one hand to his length, stroking in rhythm with my suctioning mouth, while the other hand plays between his balls and taint some more. Jonah's losing his mind—stuck somewhere between *what the fuck is happening* and pure adoration.

And it's that exact combination that unlocks my floodgates. Wetness pools between my labia and I feel it soak into my leggings. Feeling rather smug about that, I stroke harder, faster. I spit on his dick just because it's lewd and I'm the one in charge.

"*Unghh,*" he moans. "Renée, Renée—*oh God*—I'm gonna..."

Both hands stroke in tandem—one on his shaft and the other below—and a sinister feeling takes over my body when I smile at him. "Yeah, you are. Come in my mouth, puppy."

A bizarre string of vowel sounds echo off the trees as my big, muscly play thing erupts warm ropes of seed in my mouth. I linger, waiting for his waves of aftershock to end before lifting off and swallowing.

·········

Jonah

I think Renée just sucked the life out of my body, because I'm floating to the heavens. What a way to die, huh? Kinda sucks I'll never be able to experience it again.

"Jonah. Jonah..." God sounds like a woman. *Cool.*

"Yes, God. It's me."

"Jonah," God giggles, and then there's a warm press to my lips.

There's kissing in heaven? *Awesome. Maybe dying isn't so bad.*

Suddenly one of my eyelids is forced open and a gorgeous redhead is staring back at me with a smile. "Are you okay?"

Reality settles in—some of it at least. "What happened?"

"I gave you a blowjob."

I shake my head. "That was no blowjob. What's it called when someone clears your brain?"

"A lobotomy?"

"No, the other one. When you raise your hand and they bring you on stage and make you do silly things by controlling your mind."

She quietly laughs to herself. "Hypnosis."

I roll my head to the side with a sigh and snap my fingers.

"That's the one."

She lays next to me and strokes my hair. "You've had a blowjob before."

"Not like that. No one has ever touched underneath my balls." I wrap my arms around her. "I'm not letting you out of my sight. Congratulations, you now have a stage five clinger. Perks include: kneeling at your feet on command, personal chauffeur service, and bringing you coffee in bed. The list is actually much longer than that, but you get the picture."

"Would you believe me if I said I didn't even use my full skill set?"

"No. There is absolutely no way that can be improved upon."

She kisses me. "Guess you'll just have to see for yourself."

"I'll make the funeral arrangements."

"See that you do," she teases, and I think I might be enjoying this post-nut back-and-forth even more than my hypnosis blowie.

"I'd also like to mention, as part of my stage five clinger service, I offer oral with several sub-categories: general oral, face riding, and reciprocation. I should also clarify there's no orgasm limit."

"*Mmm*, there better not be."

A small shiver runs down my back because I'm obsessed with her sexual confidence. I don't think I've ever had half of what she does. What I do know is I *love* obeying her.

Renée stands, and my heart rate picks back up watching her leggings peel away. I help by tugging at the ankles, then bunching them in my face and inhaling. She smirks, unphased, and I wonder just how depraved I'm allowed to be with her.

She arches an eyebrow and peels off her panties. "A little amuse-bouche?"

My heated gaze lands between her freckled legs and I bite

my lip. "I love your bush."

She looks like she's about to say something but thinks better of it, and lowers herself to my chest. Coarse, wavy red curls are suddenly hovering above my neck and her heat seeps into me. She's still wearing her shirt, but she's rucked it up a bit, exposing her belly button and pale skin. Long, white stretchmarks cover her stomach and my previously spent cock stirs. *She used to be pregnant*, I gleefully remind myself. *Oh God*, I wish I could have seen her like that. I wish I could have been the one to make her like that.

Do I have a breeding kink?

I swallow—cock rising and body buzzing as I wait for her instructions.

She lifts my chin with one tiny finger. "I thought about you a lot after our first night together, Jonah. I think it's time you remind me how talented that mouth is."

I nod eagerly and she leans forward. I'm about to tell her not to hover, but she shuts me up and sits—like *really* sits on my face with all her weight—and I savor the way Renée takes what she wants without reservation.

She latches onto my hair and says, "Use your hands however you want, and tap me three times if you can't breathe."

Said hands are immediately squeezing her bare ass, and I'd rather die than tap out. I search for her clit right away as my chin is coated in her arousal. My head, neck, and shoulders are encased by her soft, plump body, and the sensation of digging my fingers into her fat ass is better than any stress relief ball.

"*Mmm*," she sighs, and I open my eyes to find hers closed, enjoying me. "I missed this."

I start slow, taking my time between her clit and dipping my tongue into her wet center and smearing it everywhere. *I thought she said she didn't get wet right away?*

My hands come around, and I spread her open so I can pay special attention to that little bundle of nerves. She groans and rocks—using me exactly the way I've always wanted to be. I don't like guessing what makes women feel good. But with Renée, she tells me exactly what she wants, and it's a damn turn-on that she *expects* it from me.

Me!

With one thumb lifting her mons, I use my other to rub her hardened clit. I'd love to insert some fingers but I don't have room. She doesn't seem to mind though, because she's riding my tongue and chin like I'm her rodeo bull.

"Yes," she screams, bringing me back to the more important and sexy task at hand. She writhes and pants and then her muscles are seizing. Contractions rip through her, and she clenches her thighs tight around my head.

Hair gently blowing in the warm fall breeze, she's completely blissed out, and I'm in awe. I'm in some kind of fantasy.

All at once I'm left laying there, lungs restored to full capacity, with a wet face. My mouth is already hanging wide open when she crawls on all fours and presents her ass to me. She looks back. "You're not done. Get back in there."

My body responds instantly and I'm on my knees behind her, squeezing her hips. "Are you serious?"

"Did I stutter?"

She didn't, but I do. "I–I get to eat your ass?"

"Do you know how?" Her tone is a little teasing, a little mean, and I like it.

"Y–yes. Of course. I just..." I trail off. I shake her butt until ripples form, causing a reaction to burst from the depth of my soul. I scream—and it's loud and high-pitched and it might cause the dogs to come find me. She looks back in concern. "Sorry," I huff. "I'm just really excited. I wrote about this in my dream journal."

Her concern morphs into hushed laughter. "Good to know."

I lean in and brush my nose over each cheek. There are

far less freckles on this part of her body, so I lick and kiss each one. Her natural scent is mixed with a little bit of fruity and floral body wash and I inhale.

Fuck, I'm hard.

I lay a wide tongue across her rim and drag, instantly causing her to sigh. "Ohhh... Yes, puppy, just like that."

No one ever called me puppy before her, and I never knew it could make my knees weak and blood rush to my dick, but it does. Or maybe that's just the effect she has on me. Everything she says makes me weak.

Between her cries of pleasure and my animalistic feasting, our bodies make a different kind of music—bold and reckless. Perfect.

Her hole clenches when I finally shove two fingers in her dripping pussy and she moans—dropping her head to her arms braced in front of her. "Harder. Harder, Jonah—Yes! More."

I add two more fingers without breaking the incredible force behind my thrusts. Her rim is licked and sucked and every so often I slip the tip of my tongue inside and she mewls. Then I reach under with my other hand and play with her clit again.

She detonates seconds later. Her entire body trembles and tightens. My tongue and fingers are swallowed and held hostage, but I can't stop. There's a flood of pleasure racing from my feet up my spine and before I can stop it, I'm coming again. "Fffffuck."

My vision goes white, and the next thing I know, I'm laying down with my head in her naked lap. *Nice.*

"You did so good, puppy," she says, softly sweeping hair out of my face.

I feel a vague wet spot underneath me. "Am I lying in my own jizz?"

"*Mhmm,*" she hums, and it's a lovely mix of amusement and pride. I'd lay in a pool of jizz anytime if it meant she would stroke my hair.

Chapter 34
The Training Facility
Jonah

R enée's mouth falls open when I pull into the parking lot of my team's newly-renovated training facility. I step out of my Yukon and open her door. Her hair is still down—a little wild from our outdoor activities. And if I lick my lips, I can still taste her cum.

"Jonah, I was picturing a shady little gym, not an indoor stadium."

I take her hand and scratch the back of my neck. "Technically it's a semi-professional rugby training center. Fingers crossed, that is. We still have to qualify."

I open the main doors, and the first thing we see is the club's massive team crest painted on the wall and large decals of current and former players in action shot photos.

"Is anyone here?" she asks as I lead her upstairs to the gym.

"I think Joaquín is boppin' around here somewhere doing a final inspection before the grand opening tonight."

"Are you excited to show it off?"

"I'm excited for everyone to see it. But I won't be the one showing it off."

"Why not?"

I smile. "Because no one knows who the money came from, remember?"

Renée takes in the brand new equipment—bikes, treadmills, weights, row machines. "Do you wish the team could know you paid for it all?"

"I didn't do it for attention."

I guide her toward the track that opens up over the field and she glances at me. "I know. You're very… quiet in your responsibilities. Which is not something I thought you were capable of back in the day."

I toe the track, suddenly feeling like I'm back in her college classroom again. I never thought she paid attention to me unless I got in her face and showed off. Turns out she could read me like a book. Still can.

I lean against the railing and look down on the illuminated indoor field. "You're right—I wasn't capable then. I used to show off a lot to get my dad's attention. Never really worked."

She leans against the railing and gives me a little shoulder shove. "Didn't work on me either."

I huff a laugh, "I know."

We stand together for a long time looking out over the field while I work through some things and decide if I want to show her everything. When she leans her head against my shoulder, gentle and reassuring, I give up holding back anything more.

"Do you wanna know why I like you so much?"

Someone please clap for my amazing restraint from using the word love.

Renée's already watching me when she nods. "I would."

"You tell me like it is. I've never had to guess how you feel about me." A curl forms at the corner of my mouth and I shrug. "I was perhaps delusional at times. Some might say obsessed…"

She chuckles and squeezes my bicep.

"I like that you take control. I'd be lying if I said I didn't. It's not just a… sex thing either. I like having directions, and knowing that I've pleased you. In my past relationships, I was always guessing and falling short." I sigh. "And then I'd look dumb. And it sucks when the person who has your heart thinks you're dumb."

"I don't think you're dumb."

"I know you don't. You've never made me feel that way. It's one thing when it's friendly teasing from my siblings or teammates. But with all my previous girlfriends, they'd find something I didn't know and make me feel bad about it. And because I couldn't let go of them, I'd do anything to prove I'm not stupid, which always lead to me looking like an even bigger idiot."

"I'm sorry, Jonah." She studies me for a beat, her eyebrows pulling together. "Do you know why I like you?"

"Because I'm an amazing dancer."

"One of the many reasons, yes," she laughs. "Because you're *fun*, which is something I wasn't having. I like that you wear your enormous heart on your sleeve. And you've shown me that you don't give up."

I lower my head. "Yeah, but I used to. I used to rely on everyone else to take care of me, and clean up my mistakes. I didn't take responsibility for anything. But once all the money came, and I bought the house... I don't know. I felt like I had to step up—like it was my time to prove I could be trusted."

"And that's what you've done, Jonah. I hope your family can see that, too. I trust you, and it has nothing to do with your money or your home. You've shown me you're a man of your word." Then she lightly tugs at my shorter hair. "You should feel proud of yourself."

I gaze into her eyes—speckled with every shade of green imaginable and fanned with long lashes. "I wanted to step up for a lot of reasons, but stepping up for you was my biggest motivator. When I first moved in, yeah, I just wanted to get in your pants again. I had a one-track mind."

"You don't say."

God, she's funny.

"Buuut, when everyone got sick and you couldn't go to

the wedding with me, it made me see the bigger picture. You had people who relied on you. You had responsibilities that outweighed our night. It made me realize I had to shape up if I was ever going to have a chance with you. I had to prove I could take care of myself, my home, my animals... all because I wanted you to know I was not another person *you* needed to take care of."

Renée tilts her head lightly and studies me. "You have a point, and your evaluation of me is... accurate. However, this is not a one-way street. If we really do this, I will be taking care of you."

"But that's what I'm afraid of. If I let someone take care of me again, I might fall into my old ways, and I don't want to put that responsibility on you."

"You're not going to fall back."

"But how can you know that?"

"Because I was young once. You're twenty-five, Jonah. That's about the time people start getting their shit together. It doesn't happen all at once, and some people may never get there. But you own and maintain a home, regularly spend time with your family, and are part of a team you're so confident in that you spent millions of dollars on a state-of-the-art training facility! You've invested in your life, Jonah."

She leans away from the railing and turns me until we're pressed together and she locks her arms behind my back. "I will be taking care of you," she repeats, her tone that of a professor who holds all the answers, "because I want to and it's natural. And you're going to take care of me for the same reason."

For some reason her words bring me back to her classroom—not a memory, more like a vision. Everyone's heads are down, concentrating on the test before them. I'm stuck on the last few questions when Professor Wilde pulls up next to me and hands me a note card with all the answers.

I bring myself back to that same woman standing before me, holding me tight to her. My hands rest on her petite shoulders and I can't help fluffing her long hair and smile. "I like that you're on my side."

"And I like that you're on mine."

"Are we doing this?"

Her eyes twinkle as she pauses, and by the sincere smile she gives me, I already know the answer. I already know it, yet my chest tightens.

"I don't see any other choice."

Chapter 35
Birthday Dinner

Jonah wouldn't tell me where he was taking us for my birthday dinner tonight, just that we needed to dress nice. Yes, we. He made it very clear Amber and my girls were to come. My heart softened at that.

But now I'm face-to-face with a valet who's opening my car door on the curb of a swanky restaurant, and I tense. Jonah's wearing a fitted sweater polo and slacks, and his hair has been professionally trimmed—thank God. He swings open the back door to assist the valet, then takes my hand.

My heel clicks on the pavement when I step out. "*This* is where we're having dinner?"

"Wow." Lo marvels at the building's facade, all glittering lights and crawling ivy. "So pretty."

It's been more than a week since she started talking again, but I'm no less amazed and proud of my little girl. Every word, no matter how small, is a gift.

Jonah places my hand in the crook of his elbow and leads us to the front door.

"Don't you think," I whisper, "this is a little too fancy for a seven and ten-year-old?"

"Don't worry. The girls and I have been practicing this week."

"Is that what all those tea parties were about?" I ask. I thought it was a little strange that the girls were suddenly interested in tea parties again, seeing as they haven't hauled out the plastic set in years.

He hums his confirmation as we walk through the massive door. Crystal chandeliers hang from a tray ceiling, and sleek wood panel accents and mossy green decor give the space a modern glow. There's a muffled cacophony of conversation, low instrumental music, and the clang of a busy kitchen. A bus boy changes a white table linen as another quickly sets it with dinnerware and a new candle.

Everything is warm, intimate, and lively all at once.

"Reservation for Wilde, party of five," Jonah says to the hostess—wait, no. She is most definitely a maître d'.

"Right this way," she says with a smile.

"Think they're hiring?" Amber mutters to me, taking in the beauty. "I bet the tips are amazing."

We're seated at a round table in the center of the dining room, and Amber stores a few gifts under the table. As soon as our water glasses are filled, Lo's spills. Jonah's up with his cloth napkin before me—already dabbing at her skirt.

Heat floods her face and her eyes start to well. "I'm sorry."

"Hey, it's okay," Jonah says with a shrug. "You got this. You did so good when we practiced."

My heart pitter-patters listening to them—at the genuine way he speaks to and cares for my kids.

Jonah sits back down next to me and takes my hand under the table before giving it a squeeze. He throws me a look, silently asking if we're still sticking to the plan we made yesterday. I swallow and prepare for what life holds on the other side.

"Do you think they have ribs?" Amber asks, scanning the menu. "Because I brought my own barbeque sauce just in case. Last time I had ribs I was under the heavy influence of the Devil's lettuce and thought I was eating my own ribs. Freaked me out so much I could never touch them again. But I think I'm ready for a little experiment tonight."

"Does the Devil eat salad?" Delta asks.

Amber looks up from her menu. "What? No—I mean yes!" She turns her attention back to the menu. "Oooh, they have table-side caesar salad. Let's get that."

"Ladies, get whatever you want tonight," Jonah says. "It's my treat."

Loretta beams. "Do they have shrimps?"

Delta opens her menu with gusto. "I hope so!"

The girls regale us of their buffet experience at the blue-grass festival as if we weren't there gawking at how much shrimp two girls could put away. Through the story and placing our order with the server, Jonah strokes his fingers between mine, waiting for the right moment.

After our drinks are delivered, I take the opening. "Girls, I have something important I want to talk to you about."

"Are we finally getting a hot tub?" Amber asks. "Cuz I got a guy."

"No," I reply incredulously, then mutter, "I'm trying to tell them *the thing* we talked about earlier..."

"That you and Jonah are boyfriend and girlfriend?" Delta asks, and sips her ten-cherry Shirley Temple. Lo doesn't blink an eye either.

I stiffen and Jonah chuckles. "How did you know about that?" I ask them.

"Because we're very smart."

"That you are," Jonah laughs.

"And he buys you flowers," Lo adds. "That's something boyfriends and girlfriends do."

"Guess we weren't as sneaky as we thought we were," Jonah says under his breath.

Throughout the entire evening, Jonah keeps at least one point of contact on me. A hand on my thigh, an arm around my shoulder, a fingertip grazing the back of my neck. And it's so, so hard to concentrate when he does. I want to be alone and have my way with him, but I'm not sure how to mix our sex life with real life. I mean, what am I supposed to say? *Sorry girls, Mommy can't have movie night with you, I'm sleeping over at Jonah's tonight.* Ughh, that feels hideous to even think about.

At the same time, I'm not sure if I'm ready to invite him into my home. He would be the first man in our house since Greg died. But you know what, I've taken a lot of big steps lately, I think I'm allowed to have a little grace with myself. Rome wasn't built in a day and all.

I need a night with him though. Several. Weeks. Months. Whatever I can get—I'm ravenous for this man. I mull over the logistics while eating some of the best pasta I've ever had.

When the last of the dinner plates are cleared away, Jonah and Amber pull out several gifts from under the table.

Happy tears free fall when I open the handmade jewelry from my daughters featuring clover charms. Jonah scoots his chair even closer—his arm around me—and smiles when I roll on the stretchy bracelet, necklace, and ring.

Amber gives me a bar of my favorite gourmet chocolate with a gift card secretly taped to the bottom—a gift card for a high-end sex toy shop we've been known to frequent. While the girls discuss their preferences for milk versus dark chocolate, Amber and I share a knowing look, and I slip the card into Jonah's pocket.

Then it's his turn to place a large box in front of me. He smiles adorably, knowingly—like whatever it is, he knows I'm going to love it. He can't fight the blush coloring his face. I pull the ribbon and open the lid to find a hard leather case. I instantly know what it is and my fingers are flying to unlock it.

"Jonah," I whisper, mesmerized by the glossy eight-string mahogany mandolin before me. I take it out and run my fingers over the mother of pearl trim and floral designs. "This is gorgeous."

Amber lets a surprised cuss slip out, and the girls are

rounding the table for me so they can get a better look.

"I know you said yours was somewhere, but you didn't know where," he explains, his fingers gently circling the back of my neck. "Thought maybe you'd like to start fresh."

I look at him—sincerity and a little sheepishness wrapped up in a man who only has eyes for me. A man who once pushed my buttons and now pushes me to let down my walls. "I do want a fresh start. Thank you."

Delta reaches forward and strums the instrument so loud everyone in the restaurant turns their head. Jonah winces and silences the sound before tucking it away in the case. "Okay, let's play with that later." He laughs nervously, and shoos them to their seats. "Now I have one more present, but I couldn't wrap it," he says to the table. "But for the whole weekend, starting tomorrow when you guys get home from school"—he pauses for dramatic effect—"we're all going to Pennsylvania's crown jewel: Paradise Jungle Indoor Waterpark!"

Both girls gasp and jump and squeal until I feel every eyeball staring at us. Amber whoops and leans over to high-five Jonah. "Told you," she says.

"You knew about this?" I giggle.

"Well yeah. I had to make sure we didn't have any plans. I got Marie to cover my shifts this weekend in exchange for me doing all her side work next week."

"Oh my God. Jonah, that's really sweet of you to book this. But... can I talk to you in private for a second?"

"Of course." He pulls out my chair before we make our way back to the entryway. "What's going on?" he asks.

Like magnets, my hands snake around his back and I pull him in. "I love my presents."

A proud smile splits his face and he flips my hair behind my shoulder. "Good."

"But I was kind of hoping... this weekend..." He raises his eyebrows and waits for me. "That we could have a sleepover at your place."

His grin drops like a lead balloon and his pupils blow. "You want to come over?"

I lean in as close as possible and whisper, my tone low and seductive, "I want to come over... and over, and over."

His fingers dig in to where they're placed on my shoulders and he closes his eyes. A deep breath. Then another. "Are you serious?"

"I am. Why don't we send the girls and Amber to the waterpark this weekend, and we can stay at your place where I can tie you up and have my way with you for thirty-six hours."

His features twist up in a mix of emotions I can't quite figure out.

"I want that so bad," he mutters. "But... Paradise Jungle," he whines.

I laugh. "Bet you never thought you'd have to choose between sex or waterslides, did you?"

Chapter 36
Restraint

Jonah

I choose sex with Renée over an indoor waterpark. I'm used to playing Would You Rather with two repulsive options, not two best-case scenarios.

I stand in Renée's driveway with an arm around her and wave to Amber and the girls as they drive off for Paradise Jungle—*without me.*

"Have a great time," she calls.

"Take pictures," I yell.

Once the car is out of sight, Renée steps inside her house to grab two small duffle bags. She bends over, and usually my eyes would train on that round backside, but they're more interested in what's behind her. I try not to peek inside, but curiosity bites—urging me to find out more about her. I want to know everything about Renée Wilde and her life. Doesn't she want me to? Am I not a part of her life now?

She's been protecting herself for so long, so I understand why she's still holding back, why she's not letting me inside her home yet, but I'm itching to know when she'll open the door for me.

I smile, carrying her bags to my place, and remind myself that doing the right thing takes time. Pressuring her isn't worth the risk.

"Two bags?" I ask.

She shrugs, and it's both adorable and saucy. "I wanted options."

"I didn't realize this weekend would require clothing."

She winks. "It doesn't."

I open my front door and narrow my eyes as she strides past me. "What do you have planned, you minx?"

All three dogs greet her with kisses, and it warms my heart watching her love on my babies.

"Did you know there are mallard drakes in your living room?" she asks, gesturing to where two of my male ducks lie, curled up in a blanket on the floor.

"Yeah," I chuckle. "Emilio recently bonded with Steve and they enjoy the soft life."

"Aww, queer ducks."

"You should see Peggy right now," I laugh. "She's pissed Steve left her this mating season." Renée's eyes twinkle when she turns them on me. "What?"

"Look at you, knowing about duck mating seasons and same-sex bonding."

My eyes bug out. "Have you seen ducks in mating season? They're the opposite of cute. They're criminals. Every last one of them could have their own episode of *Law and Order: SVU.*"

The dogs follow us to my bedroom where I set her bags down. I give them a kiss on their heads and guide their sad faces out of the room so we can have privacy—or some semblance of privacy. I can hear them all grunt their displeasure as they lay down in the hallway. They'll survive. Short of the world burning, not much is going to stop me from this valuable alone time with Renée.

She sets something on my nightstand and turns to me with a look that tells me she's as ready as I am. Our sexual hunger has reached an all-time high, and now that we have the space and time to explore—now that we have mutual trust—it's all about to erupt.

My heart thunders as I cross the spacious bedroom toward the woman I'm head over heels for.

She tilts her head and strokes her hands up my arms. "Are you ready to give up control?" she asks.

"It's funny you think I had any in the first place."

"You know what I mean."

I delicately play with one of her gold earrings. "You want to control me. You want to be in charge of what we do in the bedroom."

Her emerald-green eyes are fixed on mine and she nods almost imperceptibly.

"Yes, Professor. I want you to control me."

The corner of her mouth curls and her gaze darts away. "You have a king-size bed."

"I'm six three," I counter with a smirk. "I needed the California king. Why? How big is your bed?"

"I'm five two. I have a full."

I run my hand over my face and groan. "I can't wait for my feet to hang off."

I shouldn't have said that. She shouldn't feel pressure to let me inside her home, and I don't want her to think I'm expecting it, even though I am.

Thankfully, she chuckles at my response, and hope ignites in my chest. Maybe she's picturing us cuddled in her tiny bed, my bare feet poking out from the end.

I glance at the nightstand to find the pair of tortoise shell glasses she set down moments ago. "These are *hot*." I grin and place them on her face.

"They're for reading."

"Oh no no no no. They're naughty professor glasses and they're for *always*."

"You know," she starts, and traces a finger just above my belt along my bare skin and it prickles. "I'm not the only one with a sexy job. I do believe you have a special talent that makes you rather desirable with the ladies."

Oh... "Guys too."

"I'd like to see you dance for me, Jonah."

Heat rushes through my body at her first command, but I suddenly remember I haven't danced like that in over six months. "I might be a little rusty," I say, and pull at the back of my neck.

"That's okay," she smiles. "I've also been dusting off some old skills recently."

A flashback of that night in my living room when she sang and played the mandolin makes my insides all fuzzy and warm. Knowing that she shared that vulnerable moment with only me renews my cocksure attitude. But it's more than that—now there's a new feeling swirling beside it: the urge to submit to a powerful woman.

I've never wanted to dance for someone more.

"Can I have a moment alone to practice?"

"Of course," she says. "I'll wait in the den down the hall. Come out when you're ready."

When she shuts the bedroom door, I run through my old stripping playlist and am pleasantly surprised to see my muscle memory is alive and well.

I hook up to the bluetooth speaker[1] in the den, which is just a small, informal living room up here on the second floor. When I emerge, Renée has drawn the curtains and dimmed the sconces. The den is decorated like the rest of my house, with warm red and cream tones, sandstone work, wood elements, and cozy leather furniture.

The music I selected thrums low through the space, softer than the club speakers I danced under, but somehow it hits harder. Maybe that's because she's the only audience tonight. Just her. No lights, no crowd, no stage—just the woman who accidentally walked back into my life eight months ago.

It wasn't an accident, if you ask me. It was fate.

---

1. Toxic Pony by ALTÉGO, Britney Spears, and Ginuwine

I nearly choke when I round the couch and see she's no longer wearing the cute, long dress she was in fifteen minutes ago when she left me in my room to practice. Blood rushes to my dick and it's suddenly a struggle to remain in performance mode, because CHEESE AND RICE, SHE'S HOT. She's wearing a skin-tight, short-as-hell leather dress, with lace and mesh at the sides that showcase her wide, beautiful hips. The deep V neckline converges into a gold zipper that travels all the way to the hemline.

Holy smokes. Has she been wearing that the whole time?

I came out of my bedroom like a jaguar on the prowl, but she just threw the Uno reverse card and now I'm her willing prey—her boy toy she can do what she pleases with. I know I'm lucky, but I never thought I'd be *this* lucky.

She crosses her legs, and there's heat smoldering in her stare like coals. Her posture is so elegant in the way it always was when she lectured, except now she's relaxed. Watching me. Enjoying me. Not pretending not to.

I move with the beat, letting it sink into my soul the way it always has. I didn't know that night she came into the club would be my last time dancing. I hung up the fireman costume, packed away banana hammocks, and said goodbye to breakaway shirts.

But I'm dancing once again, and *only* for her. If I would have known she wanted this, I would have worn something a little sexier than jeans, an undershirt, and a button up.

My shoulders dip and I let my long sleeve drop. I roll my hips like I did onstage, but slower, sweeter—a little less performance, a little more devotion. She notices the difference. I can tell by the tiny tilt in her head, the subtle softening of her seductive mouth.

"Still got it," she purrs, barely loud enough to hear over the music. Her praise hits deeper than any applause or screaming crowd ever could. I push my palms against my groin and thrust in rhythm to the music.

I grin—probably too wide, too eager—and slide my hands down my chest in a practiced line that once got me ridiculous tips. But here? I don't care about tips. The greatest payment is the way her eyes follow every inch of my body, like she's studying or devising a plan. Renée looks at me like she owns the view. And I love that.

I bite the hem of my undershirt and expose my abs before leaning over her. I quickly rip open her crossed legs, and plant one hand on the couch back. I roll my hips and rub my jean-clad erection into her chest. And because she knows she owns me, her firm, little hands slide anywhere she pleases. Through the valleys of my hips, up my chest, until she's toying with my nipples.

"You're doing so well," she murmurs. "You're beautiful, baby."

Baby?!

I push my face into her neck and run my tongue along that column of creamy freckled skin. "I am your baby. I'm yours."

She stuffs a hand into my hair and tugs. She licks my cheek—branding me, sending another jolt of hot pleasure straight into my balls. Then she releases me as fast as she claimed, pushing me off her with a sadistic smile. "Keep going."

In the club, customers might playfully demand something from me, but it was always my choice to agree or decline. But with her, right here, it doesn't feel like I have choice—and that imaginary power imbalance consumes me in lust.

Why do I like this so much? Why does this make so much sense to me? It's like when I suddenly notice my breathing, and then I'm questioning if I ever knew how to breathe in the first place. But there's no question that my body wants and *was made* for her instructions.

Her eyes sharpen and her teeth dig into her bottom lip when I tear off my undershirt. I don't need words to feel her praise and appreciation—her energy flows into my veins like an IV drip. I skim one hand from my neck, down my stomach, and it slips under my belt for a quick grip before straddling her. I hold on to her bare shoulders, only thin leathers strap under each palm. I look down at myself, and on my way to her eyes, I take a brief and totally necessary pit stop at her tits that overflow from the floral leather cutouts of her Dommy Mommy armor. I can't help whimpering at the thought of burying my face in her chest.

I slide my hands down her soft arms and move her hands to my belt. She knows what I want in no uncertain terms. Renée doesn't even watch herself unfasten me—she chooses instead to bore her soul into mine. My heart punches through my chest and sweat starts to form.

Suddenly she blinks and looks down at her hands. "You weren't wearing any underwear?"

Heat rises in my face. "I want you to have easy access."

She laughs, but I can't hear it over the music. "So thoughtful." She glides her hand along my shaft and strokes. "So eager." The next steps of my choreography are forgotten as my eyes roll to the back of my head and I moan. Another hand slips to my ass and I'm pulled against her body as she massages my aching cock.

I groan, very nearly about to nut.

She laughs like a villain. "Already about to blow, puppy?" But she doesn't stop—enjoying every second of my torture as much as I am. "I love how pathetic you are."

"*Mhmm*," I whine. I'm humiliated in the best way, and the coil of pleasure winding in my lower body is about to release.

"Don't you dare."

But does she stop? No!

"RenéeI'mgonnacome," I warn, then instantly gasp for

air as she death grips the base of my shaft. "Ahhh! Ohhhffffffuuuuuuck!" I shudder above her as the weirdest climax-but-not-a-climax screams through me. My body jerks the way it would from any intense release, but gone—*gone*—is the blissful sensation of cum shooting through my urethra.

OhmygodI'mgonnadie.

I'm gonna die, I'm gonna die, I'm gonna die!

"I told you not to come," she says evenly, all poise and control.

I fall from my ruined climax, completely sexually frustrated, but thankful she's let me live—*for now.* "What the fuck just happened?" I ask, panting like the puppy I very clearly am.

She's not looking at me, though—she's watching, waiting, feeling my shaft soften as the song I chose for her is allowed to finish.

So unfair.

"I taught you a lesson, Jonah. From now on, you don't come unless I give you permission."

"But... but what if I'm alone and I miss you?"

"Then you call your Domme and you beg her *so* sweetly. And only then will I allow it—maybe." She finally tilts her chin up and the intention in her eyes makes me feel like her bad, bad student who didn't do his assignment—so the ultimate fantasy feeling.

"But you're not leaving my sight for another two days," she purrs. "And I have many, many plans for my good boy."

Her death grip eases from my soft cock and I gasp once again. The warm ejaculate that should have shot out of me like a canon now dribbles from the slit—slow and embarrassing. She collects it in her palm and pushes me with the other hand.

"Sit."

I don't know if she means on the couch or the ground,

but I choose the more degrading option. Shins flat and my hands planted on the floor, I wait for her next instruction. She doesn't give one with words, however. Palm full of my cum, she extends her hand. "Does my puppy want a treat?"

I don't think twice—hell, I don't even think once—before I'm licking the sticky white puddle out of her hand. It's not the first time I've tasted my own semen—I got curious, sue me—but it is the first time I've had *this* much. It's not the most pleasant flavor, but I tongue every last drop—the pleasure I receive from her appreciation is the real treat.

"Very good," she praises, and arches an eyebrow. "Now move back." I obey and she stands, straightens her short leather dress, and turns away. "Crawl to the bedroom, Jonah."

Okay!

She walks in front of me and without turning around says, "Don't look at my ass."

I turn my head down immediately. "Sorry, Professor."

I don't know what she did with the dogs, but they're not in the hallway when I crawl through. Once I cross into the bedroom, I sit on my heels and wait with my head down—and it feels so right. When we fooled around outside, I wondered how depraved I was allowed to be with her. Now I'm wondering if there's anything—anything at all—she'd turn her nose up at. She's incredible.

"Take off your pants and lay in the center of my bed."

"Of course," I reply, rushing to obey.

I lay back on my duvet. *I hope I don't ruin it...*

Smiling, she lowers to the bed and sits on her heels next to me. I lick my lips when her thick thighs spill wide. "I'd like to explore you," she says, and traces a finger up my hip bone. "Is that okay?"

"Absolutely. Have your way with me."

"I think it's time we establish a safe word, Jonah. Do you have one?"

My pulse picks up. "Um, no. This is all pretty new to me."

She continues delicately tracing through my abdominals—her simple touch making my heart expand—and a grin spreads across her face. "I know. It pleases me to teach you once again."

That nearly steals the breath from my lungs. I brush back my hair and groan, "Do you have any idea how often I pictured us like this?" She smiles. "Like from the second I walked in your classroom for the first time."

"Not that long ago, really. And I have a lot more experience than you baby, so I need you to pay attention. What we just did, and what we're about to do, are scenes. My role as a Dominant is to guide you, take from you, but I will always give you exactly what you need."

"And I'm your... submissive," I say, not really a question.

Her eyes twinkle. "That's right. And a very good one at that. You just need a bit of training. But right now, we're not in a scene. It's just me you—Renée and Jonah—and we're going to discuss some things."

"Okay."

"I'll have you fill out a form later to better understand your limits, kinks, and any fetishes you might have, but for now, we're just talking." I nod. "My safe word is cranberry. You should pick one that you'll remember and is weird enough that you'll never accidentally say it."

I chew on my inner lip for a second. "How about clover?"

She giggles. "Perfect. You're going to need all the luck you can get."

Uh-oh.

"So what do you like?" she asks.

I think for a moment, because I'm sure she won't appreciate it if I say *whatever you like*. If I learned anything from her failing me for plagiarizing as her student, I know she likes when I think for myself.

"I like the way I feel when I please you."

She nods like she already knew that. "You like praise."

"It's more than that. Just making you smile or come…" I take a deep breath and close my eyes, imagining that exact smile. "That turns me on so much."

"What else?"

"I like being told what to do. I really liked dancing for you, and I like it when you use me like an object." I chuckle. "You look like you already know this about me."

She bobs her head in confirmation. "I suspected a while ago that you were a service sub."

"When? When I kissed your feet after the bluegrass festival?"

She shakes her head. "That day you helped me plant seeds in the garden."

I gape at her. "You knew then?"

"Like I said, I have more experience than you," she laughs, and the sound is sweeter than honey. "I'm also a trained Dominant and it's very easy for me to spot submissives."

"What's a service sub exactly?"

And because she's Renée, my extraordinary professor girlfriend, she doesn't scoff or make me feel dumb for asking. "A service sub is someone who finds fulfillment in acts of service for their dominant partner. Those acts can look like a lot of things, both sexual and nonsexual. Often, this kind of submissive derives a lot of pleasure from focusing on their partner."

Well she's got me pegged.

I place a hand on her wide thigh. "You're my favorite thing to focus on, Renée."

"I can believe that," she hums.

Something she said flies back into my consciousness. "Wait. What do you mean you're a trained Dominant?"

"So, when Amber came back into my life, she opened me up to the lifestyle. I was educated and trained by other experienced Dominants and submissives. I'd go to these parties once a month and... let it all out," she shrugs.

"Do you still?"

Her face softens and she cups my cheek. "Last time I went was before we started anything. Before the festival. Before we kissed in your living room the night you helped me face my fears."

My heart swells with the enormous emotion we haven't admitted yet and I kiss her hand.

"Even that last party I went to... nothing happened. I couldn't stop thinking about you. I didn't want anyone else. I *don't* want anyone else." Before she says another word, I'm pulling her into a kiss.

Several minutes later, when I've thoroughly expressed my appreciation and devotion in makeout form, she brings me back to our discussion. Once we're both more familiar with each other's sexual appetites, she slips back into the Dommy Mommy Professor and I'm so *ready* to be her good little student.

She straddles my lap, and my cock is already hard from our discussion. "As punishment for failing your test today, Mr. Johanssen..." she starts, and I mentally squeal, "You're going to lay here while I inspect every rippling muscle, every strand of hair, every crevice—and you're not going to touch me. I might do this for five minutes. I might do this for the rest of our weekend."

Wait, what?

Gently, she presses her hands into my stomach and massages up to my chest. "I want to know every inch of this body, starting with these tattoos." True to her word, soft fingers travel over each piece, and I sink into her whisper-light touch.

I'm quiet while she explores, but occasionally she'll ask me what each one means. When she asks about the head of a cat sporting a mohawk, I explain that it's Razzle Dazzle—our family pet, who by some miracle is still alive—and what she's looking at is Agony Nectar's band logo.

She laughs at the tattoo on my ribs of Animal from *The Muppets*, banging on his drums. She tells me it's fitting and I preen. My whole body—from head to toes—is touched, tested, and gripped. The little patch of hair on my big toe is tugged, and I'm filled with pleasant confusion. Far be it from me to stop her, though—she looks to be having the time of her life.

When she begins paying special attention to my groin area, my dick twitches. If she notices, she doesn't care. She's laying between my long legs—playing with my sac before using both index fingers to open my slit? Then she licks my frenulum and I exhale a sharp breath. Yes! We're *doing this!*

"Flip over," she calmly instructs.

A complaint bounces at the end of my tongue like a diver, but I hold it back and obey. All over again she inspects the other half of my body, no more hurried. She pops a blackhead on my back and plucks a random hair from my shoulder. She asked me earlier if I was interested in spanking and pain, and I said I didn't know but I'd be interested in trying. That pleased her. Surely she was talking about more pain than plucking a hair, right?

She takes even longer to inspect this side of my body and when I'm certain she has to be done, she commands me again. "Put your ass in the air."

Uhhhhh...

"Do I need to remind you who's in charge, Mr. Johanssen?"

I throw my ass up. "No, Professor Wilde!"

Two hands rub in large circles, and then she's dragging a fingertip against my asshole. *Oh God.*

"You didn't think I'd forget about this, did you?" she croons, and applies more pressure. "You didn't honestly think I'd neglect this pretty little hole. Tell me no one has ever touched you here."

"No," I huff, and it's the truth. I told her I was open to the idea because she blew my fucking brains out with that blowie-taint job the other day, so I figured trying this might show me uncharted sexual pleasure, too. Real, true fear boils inside me at each pass of her finger over my back entrance. But then there's hot, slick pressure sliding between my cheeks and my balls climb into my body. "Holy mother of God," I bellow, and it's quite possibly the lowest my voice can go.

She hums around my rim and I shudder. This is officially the most out-there sexual thing that's ever happened to me. I'm scared, thrilled, and confused all at once—and I have the haunting realization that this may only be the tip of the iceberg for Renée.

Smack!

I yelp as a razor-sharp stinging sensation seeps into my ass cheek.

"Very good, Mr. Johanssen. Very good! I'm going to give you some extra credit for keeping it clean back there, too. Now flip over and spread your legs."

I turn over and stammer. "Uhh, okay."

I'm so in shock from that spanking I don't register her movements until she's binding my ankles together in re-straints. "What's your safe word, Jonah?"

"Clover?"

Another leather restraint is wrapped around my legs like a belt. "Do you wanna use it?" she asks.

"No, Professor."

"Good." She ties me up with two more around my chest and stomach, each one pressing my arms into my sides. Then she kisses me several times like you might kiss a cute animal. "You did so good keeping your hands to yourself."

"So why am I being restrained?" I ask, and flex my fingers.

She toys with the last one and shoots me a playful grin. "I

told myself I would only restrain you if you got handsy, but I changed my mind." She watches me in fascination, clearly proud of her work and I swell with pride. "Now I'm going to ride you—"

I clench my teeth. "Yes!"

"And you're going to *last*, Mr. Johanssen." I swallow her humiliating words, and by some sexy Domme magic, a silicone cock ring materializes and she slides it snugly down my half-hard shaft. "This is to make sure you don't *embarrass* yourself again."

"*Ohhh*, oh thank you. I won't, Professor. I promise."

"Have you ever used a cockring?"

I shake my head in reply.

"It's thought to make you last longer, but in reality, it's going to make you more sensitive."

Great...

She continues.[2] "It's supposed to trap your blood in your cock so it'll stay harder, longer, so I can keep using you after you come." Her sinful gaze hoods. "But you're not going to come until I tell you."

So she's making me more sensitive and expects me not to blow too soon? *Fuck me, I'm in the best kind of trouble.*

The restraints are double-checked and all I can do is wait in suspense. Renée pulls a wand from her bag and stands at the foot of the bed. She pushes her tortoise shell glasses up and it's probably on purpose because I told her exactly how feral they make me. I curse under my breath because all I want is to whimper, "Please Mommy," but I'm way too scared to say that out loud.

She gnaws on her lower lip and admires me. "You look perfect, Mr. Johanssen. You're absolutely perfect." My blood runs hot when she slips off her sheer black panties and

---

2. YES MOM by Tessa Violet

crawls over my legs, her leather backside shaped like a heart behind her. "You're getting all high marks so far," she says, her voice seductive and a little throaty. She crawls up the rest of my body until she perches on my chest. "Get me ready for your cock."

"Yes, Professor."

Then she leans forward just enough for me to eagerly lick and prepare her. She's not using her full weight, but I suppose with restraints I wouldn't be able to tap out in the event I did stop breathing.

Aww, she cares about me.

I feast on her plush pussy, inhaling her decadence and making her as wet as possible. But she pulls away sooner than I'd like, taps my nose, and shimmies down my body. "Don't be greedy. Do you trust me to take care of you?"

Suddenly that warm spot between her legs is rubbing against my dick and I groan, "Yes."

Her lips take mine and she whispers, "I'll give you *exactly* what you need."

This is a million times better than any dream I've ever had about her.

My Domme plants her hands on my chest, and like a heat-seeking missile, I nudge until my crown kisses her wet center. "That's it," she says, and rubs herself against my cock—my *bare* cock that's never gone on mission without his protective shield before. But I can't be blamed for wanting this—she told me earlier she has birth control covered, and I'm *just a man!*

Everything is slick and we can both hear how ready she is to take me. She tosses her head back and rides me without penetration, moaning my name as if I have anything to do with her pleasure right now. But, in a way she's giving me exactly what I want—she's using me to get herself off.

Dreams really do come true.

I can't stay quiet. "You're so pretty, Professor Wilde. Using me like you are—God, I've always wanted this."

"Did you fail your test on purpose just to be punished by me?"

"I did," I whine, fully embracing our roleplay. "I'm so sorry. I didn't know how else to get your attention."

"You could have asked me for private tutoring," she pants, pauses her movements, and in one fell swoop her pussy swallows me.

"*Unghhhh*," I moan, my brain completely lost and unable to form coherent thoughts.

A fresh zap of electricity pulses through me as she bounces on my cock and tweaks my nipples—pulling them taut against the thick leather strap on my chest. My hot Domme girlfriend was on to something tying me up like this, because I'm testing the limits of these restraints. The need to hold her hips and fuck fuck *fuck* into her is killing me, but watching her ride me like a queen is something I could write albums of music about.

Renée grabs the wand from beside my hip and turns it on before pressing it to her clit. Immediately her walls tighten around my buried cock. "Fuck yes," I breathe. "You're so fucking hot like that. Take everything from me."

She doesn't require my permission to come but she explodes right then. Her pussy flutters around my length, and I'm dangerously close to following in her footsteps. Fiery tresses of hair swing down from her pony tail as she hunches over me, riding every last convulsion to its end. Without opening her eyes, she switches off her wand and tosses it back on the bed.

"You did," she breathes, "so good."

Yay, I did it. "Thank you for using me."

Her soft body falls over me and she has to slide off my cock to reach my mouth for a kiss. My toes curl. It's always thrilling when we lock lips. From little pecks to ravenous makeout sessions against a wall, every single one is a dopamine rush. I will never tire of kissing this woman.

When we come up for air, her eyes are hooded in lust and she plays with the stubble at my chin. "I can't believe how perfect you are for me, Jonah."

The cartoon hearts are back and burst all around me. "Why do you think I never left you alone?"

"Because you have a thing for chesty little redhead professors."

"Hey." I furrow my brow. "Don't forget about the glasses."

Big, snorting laughter erupts between us, and there's something special about the way we're paired in this moment. When I dreamed of us, I never imagined moments as perfect as this. Me, naked as the day I was born, my limbs bound. And her, draped over my chest, head in my neck, our bodies shaking in laughter.

"How are you doing with all this, baby? This is probably more than you're used to."

I huff, "I'm having a great time."

Renée draws circles on my chest, her face serene. "And... you enjoyed it when I played with your ass?"

Heat flushes my face, and it takes me a second to form the right words. "It surprised me how much I enjoyed that."

"I'm glad," she says, and hops off to dig through her toy bag. "Because there's more where that came from."

"Oh, really?" I grin. "What's next, a butt plug?"

"Better," she replies with her back turned. She fiddles with something before spinning on her heel and holding a strappy harness with a pink dildo attached. "Pegging."

"You wanna put a dildo in my butt?!"

She smiles like a kid on Christmas. "I do. A cute one too. And look." She steps closer to give me a better view. "It's just a little one—perfect for beginners."

"Beginners? What's the biggest one you have?" She goes back to her bag of kink and rifles through—occasionally murmuring things to herself before turning. My mouth drops when she displays an enormous dildo like she's a showgirl on *The Price is Right*. It's three different shades of green, complete with balls and a suction cup at the base. "That's a tree trunk!"

"I call him The Troll," she says affectionately, and tucks the monster away in what I have gathered is her equipment bag. "Don't worry." She winks. "We'll work you up to that." My mouth is suddenly dry and I swallow. This amuses her, and she plants a kiss on my forehead. "You're so cute when you're nervous."

"Now back to this." She dangles the strap-on between us. "Personally, I think you'd look rather beautiful taking me, but we don't have to."

"But you want to?"

"Only if you do. Pegging isn't a deal-breaker, Jonah. It makes me feel powerful, but not at the expense of your limits."

I study the small dildo—about the size of my index finger, maybe a little longer. "I did try to date a man," I reason.

She rolls her eyes. "That doesn't necessarily mean you would have bottomed."

With my very recent experience having my asshole rimmed, I stare unblinking at the strap, and sigh. "No, I probably woulda." My mind set, I smile. "Okay, Professor. Let's do it. Show me what I've been missing."

Renée beams the entire time she releases me from my restraints and teaches me how she wears a harness. I pay close attention and ask questions because knowing her, she'll test me, and I'm a good student... *now*.

Before she asks me to, I'm on my hands and knees.

"What are you doing?" she asks.

"Um, getting in position for you? Or wait—" I spread my knees wider to accommodate our height difference. "Is that better?" A sudden sharp pain bursts from my ass cheek where she's bitten it!

"Wrong way, Mr. Johanssen. On your back. I want to see your face when you take my cock."

Not words I ever thought I'd hear, nonetheless I've been set on fire.

I apologize and flip over. My own cock (much larger and thicker than the dildo for the record) is like stone. In the lamp light, Renée's hair is warmer and more vibrant.

She adjusts her harness once more—every movement deliberate and precise. When she climbs between my legs, I expect her to insert something into me, but instead she lowers herself, pushes my knees up, spreads my ass, and licks.

"Holy shit," I huff, as a web of white hot pleasure spreads through my body. Incoherent words and incomplete sentences tumble from my lips as the hottest woman on earth eats my ass. Her tongue expertly flicks and prods at my entrance while her nose grazes my taint, and I'm baffled at how incredible it feels.

Precum drips and I'm panting when she resurfaces. Lube is applied generously to my hole and the longer she takes, the more comfortable I feel about this. She's so serious, so focused on making sure I'm taken care of that she's absorbing my fear and tossing it away with a reassuring smile.

When she pushes a finger in, I tense.

"It's okay, baby. You're going to feel a lot more pressure than this, but you just need to relax and accept me. There you go."

"It's so much," I wince.

"That's only half of my finger," she teases. "But look—*hah*," she gasps, and pushes in further. "You did it," she praises, before pumping in and out slowly.

Sweat beads on my skin and my heart hammers. "Oh my God."

For a few more minutes, Renée opens me up until she's

confident I can take the strap. She removes her finger and lines up the dildo. "You can stop any time," she reminds me, but I shake my head. "Okay then. Deep breath in, deep breath out." When I release it, she pushes inside me. The dildo is a little more than the width of the finger she opened me with, but it's... it's nice.

"*Ohhh*," I sigh.

"Mhm, there you go," she says, dragging in and out of me—easy and unhurried. "How do you feel?"

"So good," I moan. "More, please."

Her hands find my waist, and with a little more force, she thrusts. My fingers dig into the pillows behind my head for something, anything to hold onto. And then she's throwing her hips in earnest—her gaze flicking between my face and where she's fucking me, like she's never seen anything more miraculous.

"Hold your balls so I can fuck you harder."

Wordless, I obey and groan when she leans forward, hitting an even deeper spot that has me entering a whole new dimension. She kisses my chest because she can't reach my mouth, and she sucks on each nipple until I'm a squirming mess.

Renée sits back up and roughly strokes my painfully hard cock while pegging me, and I'm a goner in less than ten seconds. "I'm sorry!" I wince, erupting long white ropes of cum on my chest and all the way up to my neck. "I didn't mean to," I whimper, still jerking through my orgasm.

"Poor little puppy. It doesn't take much for you, does it?"

I shake my head, unable to open my eyes as the last of my climax finishes. But... she's not finishing.

"I'm not done," she says, a wicked gleam in her eye.

I throw a pillow over my face and scream into the void because the pressure, the pleasure, everything is too intense and I'm too sensitive, no thanks to the cockrings she put on me. She cups the back of my knees, holding me hostage.

I love being her hostage.

"Try and give me one more, baby."

I remove the pillow and screw up my face. "What do you mean? I'm a man. I already came. It's gonna be—*unghhh*—be a while before I'm ready again." She grabs a vibrator from the bed and presses it against my balls. "*Ahhh!*"

"Just try for me. Lean into the pleasure, Jonah."

I have no idea how, but I try. Renée's encouraging smile and heated stare help me focus. Then I take in her plump little body riding me—breasts spilling out from her leather top, and a sheen of sweat forming across her forehead.

All at once another orgasm, one I didn't think I was capable of, rockets through me and I stare in horror as nothing comes out—muscles contracting all the same. "What the *fffffuuuuuck.*"

Finally, her hips stop. "Yes," she shouts. "Oh yes, baby. That's so good."

Good? I feel like I've been hit by a Mack truck.

I'm clenching when she pulls out of me, then I'm only vaguely aware of my surroundings until she's sitting next to me, strap discarded, and stroking my hair.

"Have some water," she coos, handing me a glass and a mild pain killer. I down it in three gulps, and she lays next to me. "Talk to me. How do you feel?"

"Fuckin' awesome. And like I need a break."

Her lips touch mine. "We can do that. I'm going to run you a bath. I brought epsom salts to help with any soreness. Then I'll make us some food."

"You don't—"

She presses a finger to my mouth. "Shh. Aftercare, remember? Do not fight me."

I narrow my eyes. "And what happens if I fight you?"

"Then I'll have to reconsider your reward for being such a good boy."

"I'm sorry, there's a reward? More than mind-blowing

sex?"

She traces her fingertip down my stomach. "I was planning on taking you to Paradise Jungle on Sunday morning."

I scramble up, eyes nearly falling out of my head at the thought of gravity-defying waterslides. "Really?"

Chapter 37
Paradise Jungle
Renée

We called Amber ahead of time to let her know the change in plans, and she agreed to keep it a surprise for the girls. Which is why Jonah and I left the house early this morning so we could be the first ones in the waterpark when they opened.

The place is massive, with two-story waterslides, giant buckets of water that spill from above, a lazy river, and human-sized lily pads. Connected to the waterpark is a hotel with a couple restaurants, an arcade, and candy shop. Paradise Jungle is a literal dream for children—and Jonah, who is already cannon-balling into the water before I can even set my towel down on a lounge chair.

"It's so warm," he calls over once he surfaces. "Wait, what are you doing? Come in with me!"

I take my coverup off and fold it. "I'm fine, I'll watch from here."

Ignoring the ladder three feet away, he hoists himself out of the water and marches toward me. My eyes go wide and I scramble when I realize he's on a mission. "Oh, no you don't," he says before snatching me around the waist.

"Jonah," I squeal in laughter. "Put me down!"

"If you say so," he chuckles, and he flings both of us into the pool. Water engulfs me and bubbles float around my body until I break the surface. I'm about ready to smack him, but his gleeful face is the first thing I see, and I instantly forgive him.

"I don't wanna hear it," he chastises, but it's playful and adorable. He holds my hand as we swim for shallower waters. "I'm the fun police."

I raise one eyebrow. "The fun police stop fun from happening."

"Mmmm, no, they make sure everyone is having fun. I would know Renée," he says, sarcasm dripping like the droplets from our skin. "I went to Fun Police Officer School and I took an *oath* to serve and protect good vibes."

I run a finger over his bare deltoid. "In certain circumstances, I do love a man in uniform."

When he can reach the bottom, he hauls me into a bridal carry and I relish in the effortlessness of it all—floating in this handsome, laughing man's arms—letting him take care of me, which includes forcing me to have fun.

He sets me down as a high-pitch shriek rips across the pool.

"They're here!"

Before I can turn, a ten-year-old torpedo slams into Jonah's side, followed by a smaller, squealier one who belly-flops next to both of us. Delta and Lo surface like triumphant little otters, hair plastered to their cheeks.

"You didn't tell us you were coming," Delta yells, her wet ponytail smacking her in the face.

"That's because it was a surprise," he says, wiping his eyes. "And your aim is criminal."

Amber marches through hordes of children without a care for anyone else's path—like a woman who hasn't slept much in two days and is powered entirely by caffeine and fruit snacks. She pops a squat at the pool's edge and sighs dramatically. "Good surprise. Great surprise. The only surprise I got was waking up this morning to a seven-year-old hovering over my face, asking if sharks could live in fresh water."

"Let's play sharks," Delta cheers.

"Not until you show me every waterslide in Jungle Paradise," Jonah says, lifting each one of them out of the water. "Show me which ones are your favorites!" Jonah takes both of their hands and they weave through the crowd.

I drift closer to my sister and she leans in conspiratorially. "I'm guessing things went well for you two this weekend?"

I can't stop watching him walk away with my girls. "Very."

"How... *spicy* did you get?" she asks in code.

"I showed him The Troll," I smirk. "Amongst other things."

My sister erupts in giggles. "And he's not running for the hills? Okay, girl. Got yourself a keeper, I see."

"He is."

Amber gets up. "Come on. Let's go chase some waterfalls."

For the next few hours, Paradise Jungle lives up to its name. We shoot through waterslides, float down the lazy river until our fingers prune, and let the giant tipping bucket drench us at least four times. Amber somehow befriends a group of volleyball moms. Delta negotiates for three trips to the snack bar. Lo becomes queen of "the best lily pad" and splashes anyone who dares to siege. It's loud and chaotic and wonderful.

Somewhere between the last waterslide and a much-needed break, I realize I haven't seen Jonah or the girls for a little while. There are a million life guards here, so I'm not too worried.

"Do you know where they went?" I ask Amber, wringing out my hair.

She points vaguely toward the back of the waterpark. "Arcade, I think. Delta was ranting about needing to win enough tickets to buy a giant elephant plushie. Jonah said he had a strategy, which"—she snorts—"I cannot wait to hear."

I laugh and don my coverup. "I'll go find them."

The path from the indoor park to the arcade winds

through a humid tunnel of fake vines and plastic parrots that squawk every ten seconds. The moment I step inside the arcade, the air changes—cooler, loud with digital bleeps and music, neon lights flickering across the carpet. Kids swarming like nectar-drunk hummingbirds.

And then I spot them.

My oldest is aggressively whacking a crocodile in *Whack-A-Mole.* My youngest perches on Jonah's hip while he studies a towering stack of flashing machines like he's about to perform brain surgery. Their backs are turned toward me, and he's explaining something with serious hand gestures. Lo stares at him like he's unveiling the secrets of the universe.

Smiling, I start toward them, but stop.

Because Lo tilts her head, tapping his cheek. "Hey, Jonah?"

"Yeah, Shortcake?"

She tries to whisper, but her version of whispering is... not. "Do you love Mommy?"

My breath lodges in my chest and my vision tunnels on only them.

Delta, still holding her foam mallet, nods with sage authority. "Yeah, do you? Because you should tell her so you can be our dad."

And before I can even think to move, to interrupt, to pretend I wasn't listening, Jonah answers. "Of course I do," he says, soft and sure. "But the whole dad thing..." he trails off. "That's something your mom will have to decide."

Something inside me goes liquid, warm, and impossible to contain. And I stand there in the glow of blinking arcade lights, falling even harder than I thought possible.

Chapter 38
The Conservatory

Renée

Amber waves me off with the smug grin only a sister can pull off. "Have fun and don't even look at your phone tonight."

"But you'll call if there's an emergency, right?"

Amber shuts the door in my face, and I'm left standing on my front porch in the black gown Jonah bought me for his brother's wedding. Silky black material hugs my waist; the high slit makes my short legs appear long. This dress has absolutely no business being worn by a woman who spent the afternoon vacuuming kinetic sand out of the carpet.

But Jonah asked. Actually, Jonah *begged*, in the soft, earnest way that turns my brain to goo and makes my insides fizzle like champagne bubbles.

He's waiting beside his sparkling SUV, leaning against the door like he's posing for the Sexiest Man Alive. He's not wearing the same tuxedo he did the night of the wedding. Instead he sports a tailored, dark blue dinner coat with black lapels, a bowtie, and trousers. I could ogle him for hours.

His eyes widen, and he bounds toward me. "You look like you should step out of a limo in Monte Carlo." He leans in for a kiss, and I can't refrain from touching his chest. Red lipstick transfers to his lips, but I don't wipe it away. He's mine, and everyone will know it.

Rich blue eyes scan me from head to toe, and he grins. "You wore it. The dress."

"You asked."

He leads me to his SUV and opens my door—a perfect gentleman who instinctively knows how to please me. And it's those little unnecessary gestures—like the way he lifts me into the seat so I don't work too hard and disturb my elegance—that I find so meaningful. They're the kind of gestures my late husband only used around other people to make himself look good.

I shake the thought away before it steals our special night.

"Are you going to tell me what you have planned?" I ask once we're on the road.

"We're going to the Longwood Conservatory," he says, his voice vibrating with barely contained excitement.

"Jonah," I beam. "God, that's going to be so beautiful."

He takes my hand in his and brings it to his lips. "Nothing is as beautiful as you."

My chest flutters because I'm not immune to a genuine compliment from a genuine man—especially not from *this* genuine man.

When we arrive, the sun is setting, turning the glass conservatory gold. Twinkling lights wind up the walkways, and the air smells like jasmine and damp earth. It's beyond romantic, and I don't think I've ever been on a date as picturesque as this.

We wander through a greenhouse filled with towering palms, burbling fountains, and lush succulents. Jonah tucks my hand under his bicep—so easy and confident, like he knows he's allowed to.

"Are we the only ones here?"

"We are. I reserved it."

My face drops. "I didn't know they allowed that."

"They do if you make a sizable donation."

I have to collect myself for a moment before staring at him. "Jonah. How much did you donate?"

"Let me spoil you," he chuckles, like he's gotten away with some harmless crime, and tugs me along.

After a few minutes, we stop to admire wisteria hanging from an archway, and he clears his throat. "So, I've been thinking about the future."

Uh-oh. The memory bursts through my mind of Delta asking if Jonah and I could get married, and my body temperature plummets.

"The future?" I try to sound normal.

"Yeah." He kicks at a pebble. "I really want to do something with the animals. I enjoy rescuing them. Rehabilitation, maybe. Just... something that actually helps."

Warmth spreads in my chest, and I can breathe again. "You know, I was thinking about this last night," I say. "Lo hadn't spoken for over two years, and I know without a doubt it was because of trauma surrounding her father. But we saw how she bloomed around you and the animals. You offered this safe space to her, to all of us. She was so comfortable around the dogs—and we saw firsthand how they helped her do that. What if you opened an animal therapy farm?"

"Like a vet's office?"

"No. People use animal therapy, or animal-assisted therapy, for medical, social, and emotional issues. You know how special therapy dogs will go into hospitals to comfort patients? It's like that but more goal-oriented, and patients would come to your farm.

"You'd partner with a veterinarian—hello Dane"—I waggle my eyebrows—"and a therapist or a team of them."

"My sister Angie is a children's therapist," he says, wheels turning.

"Even better. And if this isn't in her repertoire, she can probably help find you someone who would be a good fit. This could be perfect for you."

His broad shoulders drop like he's been carrying that

hope quietly for too long. "You think?"

I squeeze his hand. "I know."

His expression softens in a way I've never seen. "Renée, that's... that's everything. We could do that. We could *make* something like that."

My heart stumbles. We. He said *we*.

I swallow. "You want me to do it with you?"

"Of course."

"Jonah, I don't know. I think it's a great idea, but I can't leave my job."

"I mean..." He shrugs. "I have more than enough to take care of you."

"I know, but I need my job as a safety net. You know I trust you, but I need the ability to support myself if need be."

He holds my hands—a flicker of doubt, perhaps, appearing then vanishing—before thumbing circles on them. He speaks with a gentle, pleading expression. "Renée, I'm planning my future around you. I need you to know that."

My chin trembles and I nod, deciding now—*now* is the time to bite the bullet. "I don't want to be married ever again." The words spill out fast, tangled with fear and honesty. "I can't. After everything with Greg, after what he—" I stop and recenter. "I will not rely on anyone like that again."

Jonah steps closer, anchoring me. There's a fierceness in his eyes, and his voice is quiet. "If that's not what you want, then I don't want that either. All I want is to love you and the girls for the rest of my life. That's it. Whatever it looks like, in whatever way you'll have me."

There's suddenly a lump in my throat like a boulder, making it difficult to swallow. Each breath I take constricts me, as if a vise is slowly tightening around my neck. The sting behind my eyelids intensifies, and I blink rapidly, trying to force back the tears that threaten to spill over. My vision blurs slightly, and the world around me seems to soften at the edges.

"And you know as well as I do I'm nothing like him," he says, so self-assured and intense, but he's right.

Compared to the older man I married when I was twenty-two, this ridiculous, soft-hearted rugby player, with a barn full of emotional-support livestock, is more mature, more responsible, and more loving. He may be young at heart, and fourteen years my junior, but Jonah Johanssen is more than the safety and security I've longed for.

He's gentle.

And gentle is what I need.

I stare into the calming sapphire eyes of the man who always waits for me. "Jonah?"

"Hm?"

The air hangs thick and heavy, saturated with the scent of wisteria and damp earth. My breath hitches, and there's a knot of anticipation tightening in my stomach. This is it—the culmination of months of unspoken feelings, the dismantling of plans, and a growing sense of exhilaration and dread. I take a deep breath, trying to imprint every detail of this moment before I change everything.

"I love you."

His inhale is sharp. Then, a grin spreads across his face, a blinding flash of white teeth that blaze with the intensity of the sun itself. His eyes change from a calm, steady blue, now sparkling with an unrestrained joy. He leans forward, voice laced with a breathless, infectious energy, the words tumbling out in a rush. "Yeah? Because I love you too! A lot, like... aggressively too much." He laughs, the sound vibrant and full as our declaration hangs in the air, weighted with our history and the overwhelming emotions that have finally found their voice.

I giggle and clutch my hands into his chest. "That sounds threatening."

"It is. I'm aggressively in love with you."

When he kisses me, it's not a playful, flirty kiss, like

we've shared in stolen moments. It's deeper and steadier—a promise without the claustrophobia of one.

He's not the boy I thought I was protecting us from—he's the man I didn't know we were waiting for.

· · · • · • · · · ·

After the private dinner he had booked, where I let him feed me dessert and stare into my eyes like the disgusting lovers we are, he drove home the long way with my hand in his lap and delivered kisses to every finger.

"Keep going," I say, before he turns into my driveway. "I want to stay at your place tonight."

"You don't have to tell me twice." He smiles because he knows exactly what I want, but there's a hint of an emotion I can't place.

"Is everything okay?"

"Of course," he says, turning into his driveway before flicking his gaze toward me. "My gorgeous girlfriend told me she loved me tonight. I'm not sure I could feel any better."

King greets us at the door, and we promptly give him the love he wants, but his heart nearly breaks when Jonah tries to close him out of the bedroom. "Bro, don't give me those eyes." He sighs and squats down to press their faces together. "I'll see what she says after she's had her way with me," he stage-whispers.

I giggle and scratch behind the old shepherd's ears. "Sorry, buddy. This is for my eyes only."

By some miracle we convince the dog to hang out in the den. When Jonah's bedroom door shuts, he removes his dinner coat and kneels before me with his hands on my shoes and his forehead on the rug.

Desire courses through my veins, and I stare at the white dress shirt pulled taut over his back muscles. "You spoiled me tonight, puppy. I'd like to reward you for making me so happy."

"Thank you, Professor."

I order him to take off my heels, and I sit in his armchair while he rubs and kisses my pinched feet. When the ache abates and a new one has formed between my thighs, I order him to remove my dress. Sweeping my hair to one side, he takes his time unfastening me, stealing long whiffs from the crook of my neck. "You always smell like vanilla and lavender."

When the dress falls away, I'm left in high-cut lace panties and a matching strapless bra. Delicate and feminine, it's the kind of set that can transform a person.

Jonah plays with the strap, his finger sliding over and under. "You're so pretty it hurts," he murmurs.

I relax against his chest, and a stiff length presses into my lower back. I move his hands to my breasts, and his warm mouth latches onto the column of my neck. Large hands roam from my chest to belly, and I revel in his touch. There's no doubt in my mind that this man loves every inch of my body—every stretch mark, every freckle, every dimple of cellulite is beautiful to him, just as they are to me.

He licks my jaw and I order him to undress for me. I sit in the middle of his made bed—dark and masculine colors like the rest of his room. A comforting sense washes over me, like I belong perched on his covers.

Jonah loosens his bow tie, and realization dawns that he probably tied it himself. That thought doesn't sit right with me—I should be the one tying his ties and telling him how good he looks.

He slowly unbuttons his shirt, the fabric whispering against the silence of the room. Each unfastened button builds a bit of tension, a subtle ratcheting of desire. The first one at his collar is a bit stubborn, and requires a good tug. The second, a little easier, reveals a flushed Adam's apple. As he works his way down, the shirt falls open, exposing the landscape of his chest, the faint tracery of veins and muscles, the soft indentation of his ribs. He pauses, his fingers lingering on the last button, a moment of hesitation before the final release.

"You're so handsome, Jonah." Even in the low-lit room, I can see color spread into his cheeks. When he's standing in nothing but his black boxer briefs, he waits for the dip of my chin before he slides them off. His cock stands like him—proud and eager.

"Take my panties off and kiss your way from my toes to my cunt."

His knee propped on the bed, he slides off my panties with a bottom lip tucked beneath his teeth. "Thank you," he whispers. He presses open-mouth kisses to every toe, and pleasure electrifies my blood as he slowly works his way up to my inner knees.

I'm already on edge when his breath ghosts over my labia, and he pushes the bridge of his nose through my seam. A warm tongue is next, followed by his gaze flicking up to meet mine.

I fist a hand in his hair. "Just like that. Yes. Get it wet for me."

Thumbs part my sex, and he darts for my clit—licking, sucking, humming until my climax explodes, and I'm forcefully humping his face. "Fuck, that's so good. *Unghhhh.* Don't stop." Like a leech, his mouth remains latched, and then he adds fingers—pumping into my pussy fast and rough. I moan profanity and prayers, and I give praise with abandon, as my sustained orgasm plows through.

When I can't take it anymore, I push him off and stare at the way his face glistens like icing. I pull him down until all that hard muscle is on top of me and I can taste myself on his lips. "Fuck me," I breathe, then wrap my legs around his narrow waist. "Fuck me right here—just like this."

The wide crown of his cock has already found its target, and I buck my hips to make the point abundantly clear.

"I'm allowed to?" he pants.

"I'm telling you. I need to feel you like this."

Broad arms bracket my head, and he suddenly stops kissing me to read my face. It's only for a couple of seconds, then his expression softens. "Thank you for trusting me."

They're not the words I thought he'd say; they're the words I didn't know I needed to hear. Validation that he understands the significance of allowing him on top of me—a man, someone bigger and stronger, who could easily overpower me. I'm not in the safety of my own home, and I'm completely vulnerable.

And Jonah understands.

"I'll do anything you want, Renée."

I cup underneath his jaw with both hands and kiss him deeply while urging him into my body. "Who's in charge?"

He sinks a couple of inches and his forehead falls against mine. "You are."

I moan when he slides all the way in. This man has a perfect dick—not too big, not too small—it's that thick Goldilocks cock—and it's all mine.

He moves inside me with a deep, slow rhythm until everything feels slick and our lips throb from kissing. His forearms stay planted next to my head until I give him the green light to touch my breasts. He gropes them, and kisses the flesh spilling over my bra.

"Gorgeous," he growls, feasting on them the way he feasts between my legs, and sending fresh waves of lust crashing over me.

"I love you, Jonah."

Then, his mouth is back on mine. "I love you too."

"Then fuck me hard. Show me how aggressive your love

really is."

He groans like giving him this permission is more erotic than the penetrative sex we're currently having.

Jonah sits on his heels and grips my hips—his thumbs sliding in that cozy little spot where my hips and tummy crease. But there's nothing cozy about the way he slams into me, or the fire burning in his eyes as he watches himself fuck my swollen pussy. He's thrusting so hard, I have to reach for the headboard and lock my arms to keep from sliding up the bed.

Jesus, this man can fuck.

When he adds a thumb to rub my hard little bundle of nerves, my eyes roll back. "Yesss," I moan.

"You like that?" he asks, voice shaking, but he knows the answer.

"Yes," I swallow. "Talk to me."

"Should I tell you how sexy you are? Writhing here... taking me," he grunts. "Squeezing my cock with that tight pussy, and your fuckin' tits bouncing every time I slam into you."

My breathing is hard, and I nod.

"I *love* how hard you make me work for it," he says. "Never stop."

"Jonah! Jonah, I'm almost there. Put your hand here," I instruct, and with his other hand, he presses his palm to my mons. With the added pressure, his cock easily rubs against my G-spot, and I shatter seconds later.

Pleasure rockets through my body, every nerve ending is alight with my orgasm. The soles of my feet are scorching hot—something I haven't felt from an orgasm in years—and there's a mind-numbing fullness inside my ears.

He curses at the vise grip my cunt has on him. "Yes baby," he groans. "All over me. God, you're making such a beautiful mess. Use me, use me, use me. Yeeees, yes that's it, thank you."

All at once, he maneuvers my legs until my feet are above his shoulders. He holds onto my thighs and lets himself have free rein with wet, slapping cracks echoing through his room. Sweat beads on his skin, and loose hair falls into his face. And I love seeing him like this—mindless and animalistic—all because I said he could be.

Jonah leans forward, bending me in half. His palms slide under my shoulders, and he holds me in place so he can fuck harder, and—*oh my God*—the pounding this man can give is next level. His core strength is out of this world.

"Can I come? P-please," he whimpers, and his change in tone makes me smile.

"You've been such a good boy for Mommy."

His eyes round and slam shut and his thrusting stalls, like he's no longer in control of his body. "F*ffffuuuuuuuck*," he shouts, releasing himself inside me.

Note to self: he likes when I call myself that.

"Yes, Jonah! Fill my pussy until it's dripping with you."

I love how wounded he looks when he comes.

After a couple more thrusts, he finally inhales, and everything relaxes between us. My legs fall and bend at his sides. But when he comes in for a post-O kiss, I wrap my arms around him and gator-roll him to his back.

"Whoa—"

"I'm not done with you."

Jonah's losing his faculties, though. "But I already... Oh, oh my—*shit*."

"I know it's intense, puppy, but you can do it. Just lie here and let me breed you."

The mix of confusion and overstimulating pleasure battles on his face, and it's so, so satisfying to watch—almost as satisfying as the moment I take off my bra.

His eyes round as he gets his first view of my bare chest—the chest I've never shown another submissive. What I did with those people was nothing like what I have with Jonah.

He gets all of me.

"My God, Renée," he huffs in disbelief. "They're beautiful."

"Touch them." I plant a hand on his chest and rock my hips against him. I let him grope and fondle and pinch to his heart's content. His spent cock is still hard and buried inside me, and I only have little time before it goes soft. I grind against his pelvis, seeking that perfect spot, and—

"There!" I cry. "Right there, don't move."

And because he's such a good boy, he listens and accepts his fate with my tits in his hands. I add my fingers to my clit and a minute later I'm seeing stars. My third orgasm wipes my vision, and the entire lower half of my body contracts.

I can't see him, but the sound of Jonah's labored breathing brings a smile to my face. Sated and delirious, I fall into him and roll to the side, where giggles turn into delicate petting and tender kisses.

I push back his fly-aways. "How do you feel, baby?"

"Rode hard and put away wet." High off the endorphins, we laugh until we cry, and then we're catching our breath again. "No, I feel amazing. I didn't know what to expect without your toy bag."

I narrow my eyes and whisper, "I hope you never know what to expect from me."

He chuckles, and I kiss that happy mouth once more before climbing off his bed and padding to the bathroom.

"Did you notice how my whole body can fit on this bed?" he calls. "Sometimes bigger is better," he teases.

I step into his bathroom and look back at the gorgeous naked man. "The Troll will be thrilled to hear that." The muscles in his face go slack, and I cackle before closing the door.

I quickly do my business and wash my hands before searching for a cup so I can give him some water. I open the medicine cabinet and no dice—but my focus snags on the one orange bottle. Nestled right on the middle shelf, between a few over-the-counter pain relievers, is a prescription for Adderall extended release.

Bottle in hand, I read the label. *Take one capsule by mouth in the morning for increasing attention and decreasing impulsivity.*

It was filled four weeks ago.

Has he always taken this? I mean, it makes sense that he would. I could tell he had ADHD back when he was my student.

I open the door. "Jonah," I say, and show him the bottle. "How long have you been taking this?"

He tosses an arm behind his head. "I just started back up. I've had a script for that since I was kid, but I was so bad at remembering to take it."

I sit next to him. "And how are you doing now?"

"Really good. It helps that I have a fairly routine morning, thanks to the animals. That's why I keep it in my bathroom so I remember to take it when I get up. Also, Angie hooked me up with an ADHD coach and they're in total support of the habits I've created."

My heart swells with love for this man because he just... took care of it. He once again found an area of his life he wanted to improve, and he made it happen. "That's amazing, baby. I'm proud of you for sticking to it. Now that I think about it... you have seemed more focused these last few weeks."

He smiles. "Yeah?"

I nod and kiss his forehead and the wonderful brain behind it. "Good job."

Relaxed and swimming in his endorphins, he waits for me to return from the kitchen with water and snacks. King has seized his opportunity and landed himself a spot at Jonah's feet.

He declines my offer to fetch him clothes, but shows me

to his walk-in closet where I can find something warm. He pulls a pair of old rugby sweats from a low shelf and reveals a large, elegant black gift box.

"What's in here?" I ask, but I'm already opening it.

"Oh, *sh*– um... well..." Dark green lingerie lays neatly folded under crisp tissue paper. I look up at him with a furrowed brow and he pulls at the back of his neck. "So I bought that for you a while ago."

I'm relieved it's for me, but still confused.

"I bought that for you after we went dress shopping. I got your measurements from that boutique."

"It's beautiful. Why are you acting weird?"

"Because when I bought it, it was with the intention that you'd wear it for me"—he lowers his head—"after my brother's wedding."

Ohhh. "You... thought I was going to sleep with you."

He nods but doesn't look at me. "I'm sorry. It was before I knew I wanted... so *much more* with you. Before I realized what kind of man I needed to be for you."

Be still my beating heart.

Under certain circumstances, I would consider sexually punishing him for such a thing, but that's not what my heart wants.

"Baby," I coo, pulling all six feet three inches into me and petting his tousled, golden hair. "It's okay. You don't need to feel sorry about that. Not anymore."

"But I am. It wasn't fair, and I lied to you when I said I wasn't expecting anything in return for being my date. I–I mean, I wasn't expecting—"

"Come on," I interrupt, and guide him out of the closet. "Let's lie down."

Once we're under the covers and face-to-face, he continues. "I wasn't expecting you to have sex with me. I was just really hoping and very confident that I... could change your mind."

"I was kind of expecting you to try."

He raises an eyebrow. "You were?"

I snort. "Wasn't gonna work, but I was ready for it."

"It was dumb," he sighs.

I place my hand on his neck and glide my thumb across his warm skin. "It was, but you're not. What matters now is the journey we took to get here," I say, with a kiss to his pout. "I love you very much, Jonah. And I love that lingerie. And someday soon, I'll happily wear it for you."

"I love you too." There's a hint of a smile, but his downturn mouth persists, causing a pang of heartache to spread in my chest.

I lift his chin and force him to meet my eyes. "What's going on?"

Long blond lashes fan over his cheeks and he swallows.

"Tell me the truth, Jonah." I wait for his answer, and my stomach churns as a feeling of detachment claws its way up my throat.

"I don't want to pressure you."

"You never have."

"I know, and look where it's gotten me—in your arms and in your heart. I don't wanna risk this."

"Baby, you're scaring me. Please, just tell me what's wrong? I promise, we can work through it together."

"You trust me, right?"

"Of course I do."

When his haunting eyes finally meet mine, I stop breathing. "Then why haven't you invited me inside your home yet?"

My pulse won't slow, even though his body is warm against mine. The question hangs between us, heavier than it should be, sharp in a way I thought it might be.

Why haven't I invited him in? Almost a month together, six months of circling each other like something fragile and precious, and I've still kept that door shut. I tell myself it was caution, habit, survival—but lying here now, with distance pressing into my chest, I know it's fear wearing a better name. Letting him cross that threshold means trusting him with the one place my past still owns. But I'm tired of shutting myself in.

Moreover, I'm tired of shutting him out.

If I want him to stay, then I have to do the thing that scares me most and open the door I've been guarding for years.

"I do trust you. I trust you with my heart, and I trust you with my daughters. There's no reason I should keep you out of my home any longer." I press my forehead to his. "I'm so sorry I made you wait this long. I'm sorry I hurt you and made you doubt just how much I trust you. First thing tomorrow, we're having breakfast at my place."

He rears back, eyes blown wide with pure delight. "Really?"

"The girls pre-made cinnamon rolls for tomorrow."

He bites his bottom lip and groans as his eyes roll back. And it's such a quintessential Jonah expression, it's impossible not to find joy in it. My heart flutters when his sunshine returns, and with faith renewed, I seal my promise on his lips.

"Thank you, Renée."

The muscles in his neck work beneath my palm, and a lovely idea comes to mind—one that I think would show him beyond the shadow of a doubt how serious I am about us.

"How would you feel about a collar?"

"It's a little formal for bedtime, don't you think?"

I smile. "No, like a submissive's collar."

"Oh, like a kink thing. Sure, why not? I am your dog afterall," he says with a smirk.

"Well, there's more to it than that. When a dominant collars their submissive, it's a symbol of commitment, ownership, and trust. It signifies they're in a serious relationship."

Jonah's O-shaped mouth morphs into a wide smile, like the idea has been drilled in and there's no way to pull it out now.

Good—because he's mine.

"You wanna collar me, Professor?"

"I do."

Chapter 39

Inside

Jonah

I wake up with Renée in my arms and giddy with anticipation. Today is the day. Today, after all the time I've spent lingering on her doorstep giving goodnight kisses under moonlit skies, Renée Wilde is finally letting me inside her home. The thought sends a fresh shiver of excitement down my spine.

This is more than just a home tour; this is a symbol of her trust in me, of her ultimate vulnerability, of the deeper connection I crave.

Because she *does* trust me, and that's no small achievement for either of us.

She stands with her back against the front door, and the way she looks at me speaks volumes. Hope, excitement, and a sliver of nervous energy hums between us before she wordlessly steps inside, my hand firmly in hers.

"This is it," she says.

I knew her house was small, but it doesn't feel that way. The house is quiet. "Everyone's sleeping in today. There's not much to see," she says, before taking my coat and hanging it in the bifold closet.

Backwards, she leads me through the tight galley kitchen, and from the window above her kitchen sink I can see my place just beyond the garden. Countertops and floors are both laminate, both clean. A four-person dining table sits just off the kitchen next to the back sliding door I've become very familiar with these last few weeks.

The laminate floor gives way to the shag carpet of the living room. Children's artwork hangs on every wall, and framed pictures top every available flat surface—bookshelf, TV stand, end table. I can't stop myself from picking up a frame holding side-by-side newborn photos of her daughters.

"Oh my God," I say with a pout. "They were so tiny and cute."

Renée sighs, and it's a beautiful sound. "So bald. So perfect."

"Was it scary?"

"Oh, terrifying. Especially with Delta. But when Lo came, I had more experience so I wasn't as scared. I had worse things to be afraid of than taking care of babies."

I know she's referring to Greg, and my heart hurts all over again. Here she was, raising babies while living in fear of her husband. What kind of life is that? No one deserves that. Her predator husband, however, deserved his early death—that, I'm sure of. I've never wanted to kill somebody the way I wish I could've killed that man.

Disinterested in discussing her past, Renée shows me to the front bedroom where her two redheads lie sleeping in two twin beds, both loaded with stuffed animals. A rainbow of bright colors blare from every wall, craft, and blanket.

"I like what they've done with the place," I whisper.

She chuckles. "They have an eye for detail, don't they?"

She gestures to Amber's room, but we don't disturb her. Finally, the last door. Hers.

"Are you ready?" she asks, placing both hands on my chest.

I used to think I was. Until a couple months ago, if Renée Wilde would have asked me if I was ready for her, I would have said yes without considering there could be more beyond my sexual attraction to her. Now that I've seen what's inside, I know the kind of partner she needs, and I'm ready to be exactly that.

I lean down and kiss her. "I'm ready."

Much like the rest of the house, her bedroom is small. Everything is a shade of earthy brown, tan, and white. Her bed is low to the ground, perfectly made with a fluffy duvet and extra nonsense pillows.

The mandolin I gave her for her birthday lays atop her dresser with nothing else. I open the case to find she's attached the custom strap, and run a thumb against the clover she had imprinted in the leather. My heart swells.

"I've been playing it for the girls," she says, and wraps her body against mine. "It may just be the best gift I've ever received."

"Do you mean that?"

"Absolutely. I feel like my daughters are seeing the real me for the first time. Our lives are so much richer because of you."

My throat works as love bubbles up inside of me. She doesn't mean the size of my bank account or the amount of money I spend on them—she thinks her life is better with me in it. *Me.* The guy most people don't take seriously; the guy who couldn't be relied on.

I make her life richer.

I turn around and we hold each other there in her modest bedroom, and I hope she can feel the weight of my gratitude.

"I like your room. It suits you. Including this tiny bed." I gesture to the double bed and laugh. "I don't know how I'm going to relax with my feet hanging off the end, but I'll make it work."

She arches an eyebrow and whispers, "Who said you would be relaxing in my bed?"

The image of me restrained to this very mattress, being tortured with pleasure at the hands of this woman sends a shiver down my spine.

"So where do you keep it all?" I ask with a flash of teeth.

She picks up on the question left unspoken, and wordlessly opens her closet—the whole time keeping a close eye on me. A small key is produced and she unlocks a wooden chest on the floor.

I blink and gape at her, unable to hold back my grin.

Chapter 40
Premier League or Bust

Renée

The stadium for Jonah's final season game isn't huge, but compared to the scruffy community park they're used to playing at, this place looks like the Super Bowl. The artificial turf glows under the early November sun, and the stands are nearly packed with actual fans. There's even a massive banner the hangs across the railing that reads:

GO PHILLY! PREMIER LEAGUE OR BUST!

We finally spot Jonah's family waving us over. We met them last Sunday when Jonah hosted a family dinner at his place. Everyone was so nice, and I could tell right off the bat that this family was tight-knit.

That same morning, I welcomed him into my home for the first time, and made sure he understood just how important he is to me. The sun seemed to shine a little brighter that day.

But even if we hadn't met his family before today, I think we would have spotted them. Every single one of them is wearing matching T-shirts with the faces of Jonah, Dane, and Rafael plastered to the cotton. Angie is standing on the bench, already screaming her husband's name, even though warm-ups aren't over yet.

As we walk up, Joaquín turns and grins. "There's the real MVP," he says. "Saved you ladies some seats."

I scoot in and take a seat beside Neal, rigid in his team hat. Part of me thinks he's going to shake my hand, but he surprises me and comes in for a hug. "Good to see you again, Renée. Hi girls."

"Hi, Grandpa Neal," Lo chirps, throwing all of us for a loop.

I catch the faintest hint of blush across his cheeks, and he chuckles. "Hey kiddo."

"Everyone cheer," Ivy (his sister, not his girlfriend like I wrongly accused him of having) says. She holds her phone. "I'm documenting everything, so look alive!"

We cheer and wave and say encouraging words into the camera before she moves on to film something else.

"There's a lot more people here than I thought there'd be," I say.

"That might be my doing," Robyn says. I turn around to find her sitting between her husbands. She winces, but I know she's not at all sorry. "I may have sent out the bat signal across social media."

Jonah showed me her profiles with millions of followers last week, and my jaw dropped. She's a professional rugby player with brand deals and modeling contracts. Her husband Dell has a similarly sized following for gym thirst traps. Jonah's family is something else.

"What do you have there?" Joaquín asks Delta.

"We made signs!" she announces, handing him a glitter-coated posterboard. One has Jonah's name, and the other reads TRY HARDER with absolutely no irony.

Joaquín beams. "The guys are gonna love this."

On the field, Jonah jogs across the turf with the rest of his team. Half of his hair is pulled into a topknot, and he looks damn good in that uniform—tight little shorts, thick hamstrings out for my viewing pleasure. I wanna bite into them.

When he spots us, his face lights up. He lifts a hand, and Delta jumps up to wave both signs at once. Lo blows a kiss like she's greeting the Pope.

And it's that signature Jonah grin of his that has my heart fluttering.

"Ladies and gentlemen," the announcer's voice booms through the stadium. "Welcome to the final match of the Division One East Coast Rugby Playoffs between Philadelphia and Richmond. Today's winning team will be crowned this year's champions. But win or lose, Philadelphia only needs to score seven more points to qualify for Premier League."

The crowd erupts, and Delta screams, "Let's get eight!"

Isaiah laughs behind us. "I like her."

Jonah takes his starting position, bouncing on his toes. He looks focused and ready. His team claps him on the back, trusting him, depending on him. I squeeze the railing, equal parts proud and nervous.

"Go Philly!" Angie yells right before the whistle blows. The ball arcs through the air, and the game erupts immediately into a flurry of body slams and scrums.

"Go rugby!" Lo screams. Wrong sport phrasing, but she gets points for enthusiasm.

Jonah takes the first tackle beautifully. Really beautifully. Like, I might need to fan myself a little despite the cool fall air.

Joaquín hollers, "Yes, JoJo!"

Angie echoes, "Hit him harder next time!"

After several rucks, Philly wins possession and moves the ball up field. Jonah gets it and passes cleanly to a teammate on a breakaway. I lose my mind and scream along with the roaring crowd as Philly gets dangerously close to scoring.

"Mom, he throws the ball really fast," Lo says.

"Yes, he does."

My heart clenches when it hits me just how in control he is—of his game, and of his life. He's worked so hard to get to where he is. Rays of sunshine cast over him, and he wipes sweat from his brow as he strategizes. He navigates the pressures, the expectations, the teasing with grace. This was built brick by brick, sacrifice by sacrifice. He's poured his heart and soul into this, and I can't help but admire the dedication, the sheer force of will that brought him here.

Whether he walks away victorious, clutching the trophy, or shoulders the weight of defeat, I'll be there. Win or lose, I'll make sure he knows that. I'll make sure he knows I see the effort, the grit, the man he is beyond the game.

Richmond closes in and things get messy. Dane and Rafael scrum down with the other forwards, but it collapses in a snarling pile of humans.

"Come on, Philly," Isaiah grumbles, his hands flying out in rage. "What was that?"

The scrum resets, and the ball finds its way through several pairs of feet until it's picked and thrown out to Jonah. He tears down the field, dodges a tackle, and the entire Johanssen fan section stands. Jonah looks like he might go for the try himself, but it's going to be a tight fit.

But he doesn't.

He passes.

Perfectly. Selflessly. The teammate he sends it to barrels through a gap in Richmond's line, and over the try line!

The crowd blows up and the whistle screams. I'm scooping the girls up in a hug and shaking them. Joaquín joins our circle and cheers with us.

"That's my boy," Neal says, so quietly I almost don't hear it.

"How many points was that?" Delta asks Robyn.

"Five. If they make this conversion kick, they'll have the other two points they need." She points to Dane who's lining up for the kick. "Looklooklook!"

Joaquín hauls Lo into his chest and holds tight. Delta squeezes my arm, and my vision zeroes-in on the ball. My heart pounds.

Dane runs forward in measured steps and *kick*—the ball soars through the uprights.

Everyone. Loses. Their. Shit.

The stadium explodes, and the team bounds from the try zone to where Dane's standing in shock—like he can't believe he really did that. Jonah and Raf are the first to pummel him, followed by whoops and hollers. One of the bigger guys lifts him in the air and carries him to his position.

Robyn and Dell are hugging. Isaiah shakes his fathers shoulders, both of them laughing and near tears.

Now that the pressure is off, the team starts playing loose, and I've never seen so many rugged men with grins. They steal a turnover. They score again. Jonah makes a huge defensive stop that sends half the crowd to their feet.

When the final whistle blows, the stadium erupts in a deafening roar. Philadelphia wins—by a lot more than seven.

Teammates from the sidelines rush the field as everyone hugs and slaps each other around. The teams shake hands, and Jonah laughs, red-faced, sweaty, and undoubtedly in his element—all of it turning me on and causing my chest to expand.

He turns and makes a beeline for me. The moment he reaches the railing, he hoists himself up, cups my face and kisses me—hard, euphoric, and breathless—and the whole world fades away.

When we finally pull apart, my daughters are shrieking, as is Angie, and Ivy's saying something about viral content.

Jonah brushes his sweaty thumb along my cheek, and I'm lightheaded from adrenaline and *him*.

"Go get your trophy," I murmur, nudging him back toward the field where his team is gathering for photos.

He gives me that grin—that wonderful, powerful grin. "I already have it."

Epilogue

Renée

Four Months Later

For the first time in more than ten years, I stand on the porch of my childhood home, with Jonah and the girls behind me.

"I'm ready if you are," Amber says, taking my hand in hers in gentle reassurance.

"It's time."

"You got this," Jonah whispers.

We[1] decided it was time we make amends with our mother. Amber has been holding onto her pain, even though she knew it was right to ask for forgiveness—part of her drug rehab and all. I had to make the leap too, not only for me, but for Amber and my daughters. I've faced so many fears since my husband died, all of them hard, but all of them worth it. It was time to face this one.

We called our mom last week and spoke briefly, letting her know we'd like to visit and try to work things out. I wanted to go into detail right then, but doing it face to face felt like the right thing to do.

That's how I find myself awkwardly ringing the doorbell to the place I once snuck in and out of as a teenager.

---

1. Landslide by The Chicks

Mom's anxious face appears through the glass door—the corner of her mouth curling into a hesitant smile before the door opens. "Hi."

I thought I would be stronger, but hot tears spring forth and my voice cracks. "Hi Mom. I missed you."

"I missed you too," Amber says.

In an instant, our mom wraps her arms around both of us in a fierce hug—and somehow, without words, she erases the shame I've been carrying around for no reason. The three of us stand there in the cool spring breeze, holding each other in the kind of love that could never be broken, no matter how much pain we may have caused.

I release them, wipe my tears with the back of my hand, and gesture behind us. "Mom, these are your granddaughters, Delta and Loretta, and this is my boyfriend, Jonah Johanssen."

All three of them wave and say hello at the same time, and I laugh.

"Well, it's about time," Mom cheers. "Everyone come inside."

Her grin is a mile wide as we follow her to the back of the house to the kitchen and living room. We pass by family photos, and my heart breaks all over again seeing myself and Amber—still proudly displayed amongst my parents' framed records—like we were never forgotten or disposed of the way I did to them.

The kitchen and living room have been updated, now with muted earthy greens, cream, and hickory, and it's so much the kind of home I could see myself in.

Mom has snacks and refreshments already laid out, and when the girls dig in, she leans against the counter with her hands propped under her chin, watching them in fascination. She asks them everything—favorite colors and subjects in school, what kind of music they like, who their friends are and what they're like.

"Jonah is our friend too," Loretta smiles. "He lives next door, and he's a rugby player, and he has a farm."

Mom beams. "Is that why you like him?"

"A hundred percent," Jonah teases. "They're all just using me for my animals."

She laughs. "And how long have you two been together?"

I take his hand in mine and stare at him affectionately. "Since November."

"She wanted nothing to do with me for a long time," he smirks. "But I never gave up."

I turn back to Mom and sigh. "After Greg, I was so closed off. It was just me and Amber against the world. I'm really sorry for closing you and Dad out. As you probably know, Greg was very controlling, and he made me believe I was just your pawn on stage."

Mom furrows her brow and frowns.

"I know," I say. "The truth is, I never felt like that, but he had me so twisted up that..."

She places her hand on my shoulder. "It's okay, honey."

"It's not, and I'm sorry. I want to reset everything. I want you to have a relationship with your granddaughters. I want us to visit each other all the time."

"Me too," Amber says. "And I promise, I'll never ask you for money again. I've been clean since I moved away."

Mom's eyes are round. "You have? Oh, Amber." She sniffles and throws her arms around her once again. "I'm so proud of you."

"Me too, Mom." She releases her. "And I have a steady job and good friends that are nothing like the ones I used to hang out with. No more unsavory characters."

"Thank God," she guffaws.

We spend the rest of the afternoon—and well into the evening—catching up on lost time, laughing like it was never lost in the first place. The girls discover her closet full of stage clothes and take turns parading around the house like they've found literal treasure, and Mom plays along, crowning them with the kind of ease I remember from childhood.

And Jonah—because he can't help being the bright soul that he is—wins her over in a heartbeat. When she learns of his musical abilities, she glows with quiet joy, as if she's instantly claimed him as one of her own. Before long, we're slipping into their home studio, playing The Band Wilde's greatest hits—because of course Jonah has learned them all. Mom hands him every instrument she has to test him, and he indulges her with a smile.

But when he finally sits behind the drum set and lets it rip, she's rendered speechless. He takes her classic blue-grass tune and turns it into something new and angsty and wild. Jonah is an incredible musician, but when he's on the drums, he's incandescent and unstoppable. He could give Travis Barker a run for his money.

Later, when the girls have dozed off on the couch in a tangle of small limbs and borrowed blankets, Mom pulls me into a quiet hug. It's brief, a little awkward—two people relearning the shape of each other—but it's honest. "You found yourself again," she whispers, and her prideful words hit with the force of all the years we didn't say the things we needed to say. She eases back from the hug, arching an eyebrow at Jonah. "And I would keep him if I were you."

We set our plans for the next visit after school lets out. Outside, the cool night night air wraps around us as Jonah carries a drowsy seven-year-old and reaches for my hand, our fingers lacing together. "How are you feeling?"

I think about my daughters chattering their grandmother's ears off. About the way Mom looked at Jonah, and the mistakes that brought us here. And somehow, instead of my pained truth—instead of the fear I've harbored for my parents—there's a warm, steady fullness in my chest.

"I don't know," I say, laughing a little. "Lucky, maybe?

Ridiculously lucky."

Jonah presses a kiss to my head. "You deserve all of this, Renée. Every good thing."

Maybe I do.

There's some saying that life is a series of beginnings and ends. For a long period of my life, I felt like I had no way out—that all life could offer me was bitter and charred.

Nothing feels like that anymore.

I believe good things are on my horizon—and every chance I get for a new beginning, is a chance worth taking.

Epilogue

Jonah

Ten Months Later

T he sound of the shower turning on from the ensuite wakes me. The house is still dark, but there's a hint of daylight starting to break its way through the curtains.

How'd she manage to get out of bed without waking me?

My morning wood begs for attention, so after a good stretch and a kiss to King's fuzzy muzzle, I pad over to the bathroom and watch that beautiful woman—hair long and untamed from sleep—strip out of her pajamas. Eyelids closed, she putters around the familiar room, unaware of me. My heart dances knowing she's this comfortable. This is now her home, after all. Renée, Delta, and Lo moved in six months ago, and my only complaint is wishing they would have sooner. But Renée wanted to be sure, and I wanted her to be sure.

I also wanted her to have the largest safety net possible. That's why I bought her rental house, renovated everything, and put her name on the deed. Amber lives there still, though she's over here more often than not. I keep telling her she should just move in with us, but she likes having her own space. It's also nice when the girls spend the night at their aunt's so Renée and I can be as loud as we want.

But there's moments like this—admiring the sexy redhead stepping into a warm shower—and knowing the plans I have for her will require us to be quiet.

I toss my sleep shorts in the hamper. Wearing nothing more than a lazy smirk and the silver day collar she gave me, I step in behind her.

"May I join you?"

She pouts. "But I smeared all that cum on your stomach last night. You're just gonna wash it off?" she teases.

I lather body wash onto a loofah and chuckle. "You know how weird the goats get when they smell cum. I don't need them eating my shirt during the photoshoot today."

We're having a professional photographer come to the house for family Christmas pictures—and I mean everyone in the family is coming over. Ever since Renée and I have made it official, I've been obsessed with having pictures. Every season we have a little photoshoot, and I'm perpetually taking pictures of my ladies.

I'm just so proud of them. And I'm proud of me. This whole family man thing is frickin' sweet—like, I *get* why Rafael loves it. Seeing joy on the faces of my little Ladybug and Shortcake... it makes all the hard stuff worth it.

Renée hums a laugh and angles her head to kiss me. Lips locked in a lazy adoration, I begin to soap up her curves. Slippery, sweeping strokes up and down until every inch has been polished. I lather her hair in coconut shampoo, and it makes me smile because she has no idea I'm taking them to Tulum over Christmas break.

I kiss her neck while rinsing her hair, and apply a liberal amount of conditioner and let it soak in. When she thinks she's finished, I push her against the tile wall dick-first.

"Don't you want me to wash you?" she asks breathlessly.

"Not yet," I murmur, then bite her earlobe. "I'm gonna get a little dirtier first."

"Oh," she gasps when I slide my fingers through her sex. She's already canting her hips and standing on her toes in offering.

"Such a needy thing," I growl.

"Mhmm."

Me initiating and being in control was not something Renée wanted until recently. Don't get me wrong, I wasn't complaining, but it is so very delightful when I am. Being in control of her body like this is a massive turn on. But knowing what it has taken for her to relinquish control—to trust me like this—it's something money can't buy.

I am so proud of her.

I dip two fingers deep inside her channel and collect that warm, delicious heat. "Baby, look how wet you are. I bet anything you're still carrying my cum inside you from last night. Such a little slut, aren't you?"

She shudders. "Yes."

"It would be so easy," I drawl, notching the head of my hard-on against her opening. "So easy for me to slip right in and claim you again."

Technically she claimed me last night. Shoved a plug in my ass, rode me like a cowgirl, bred me within an inch of my life, and rubbed her semen-filled pussy against my stomach when she was done.

But y'know... new day, new scene.

She moans and holds tight to my shoulders, but one hand slides to my necklace—my day collar engraved with her name—and she fists it. "Please fuck me."

I lift her leg to place one foot on the shower bench. "I woke up so hard for you," I say, my voice dangerously low. I push the wide tip inside her. "I watched you undress in here, and I *needed* this perfect pussy immediately." I inch further inside and lift her breasts, pressing them against my body. "I wanted these tits soapy and slippery."

She mewls. "You feel so good, baby."

I pump into her, deep and slow, adding an extra hit of pressure each time I bottom out. Renée's doing her best to stay quiet, but her face speaks volumes. Jaw slack and eyes hooded, she matches my rhythm until we're a frenzy of hips and lips. I grab her delicious fat ass, forcing her to take an impossible amount more. I get lost in the sensation of her hot cunt and the way her entire body jiggles when I slam into her—so, so soft.

I cannot get enough of this woman.

Her grip on my collar tightens and we're panting in each other's mouths, inhaling and muffling the sounds the other cannot.

I add a thumb to her clit and slam my groin against it. Between each thrust, I rub fast and within minutes, her head falls to my chest and she's coming around my dick.

"Yeeessss," I purr. "Oh, that's it. Come all over me. Come all over your man's cock. Yes yes, show me how long you can hold it." One of the many things I love about her is how long she can sustain an orgasm. It's truly incredible.

"Please don't stop," she silently cries.

Couldn't if I wanted to.

For several more minutes her pussy contracts until her body starts to sag. About to bust myself, I grab her thighs and she sucks in a sharp breath when I lift her off the ground and press all my weight into her.

"Oh my God!" she gasps.

"Oh my God," I groan, giving everything I have. Then I maneuver her again—throwing her legs over my shoulders so she's completely pinned and bent in half against the shower wall.

"Jesus Christ, you're strong."

Her praise creates a small curl on my lips, but it fades just as fast because the coil of pleasure in my pelvis breaks free. I grunt and groan, spilling every drop inside her until I'm drained.

We share our labored breathing and kiss until my muscles demand I release her so they can relax. I collapse on the bench and she stands in front of me—holding my head against her chest.

Mmmm. Boobs.

As soon as I'm clean, I leave Renée to finish getting ready, and I go downstairs. I brew a pot of coffee, and then King and I head to the barn for our morning chores.

Because of Renée's idea for an animal therapy center, I invested completely in it, right here on our property. Our charity, The Barn Wilde, opened in June, right after the spring rugby season ended. I was worried about how I was going to handle playing premiership rugby while managing a charity, but I've found a rhythm, and sticking to a routine has helped me stay on top of things. I still fall short sometimes, but Renée's right there to remind me that I don't have to carry everything all the time. I can ask for help, and that's not a weakness.

Dane has become our charity's head veterinarian, and Angie helped me find the right therapists to hire. She introduced me to the world of animal therapy, and the more I learned, the more I knew it was the right fit for me.

The barn has changed a bit in the last year. I renovated it with new stalls and a fresh coat of paint. I even had a little cottage built for the charity so the therapists and patients could work inside.

In the last couple of months though, The Barn Wilde has turned into more. Our doctors discovered our musical talents, so we've added in music therapy. Teaching and performing for kids and adults in this sort of setting wasn't something I ever saw for myself when I was playing in my basement band and bars in college, but I've never been happier. I get to play music and semi-professional rugby for a living—like, how is this my life?! I also get to work alongside my talented girlfriend.

Talk about rich.

Of course, Renée still holds her position at the university, but she's working part-time starting next semester, and she can still keep her tenure.

I'll do whatever it takes to reinforce her safety net. I'll also do whatever it takes to ensure she never needs one.

"Good morning, everybody," I sing, swinging the barn door open. The dogs roll out of their hay beds and stretch. "Such good boys," I say affectionately. "Looks like everyone's here and accounted for." I salute them. "Job well done, gentlemen."

Ginger huffs and snorts her indignation about the alpaca who pesters her every second of the day. I give Timothy some fresh hay and a hearty pet. "Buddy, you gotta trust me on this—it's never gonna happen with Ginger if you don't listen to her."

I feed everyone and sweet-talk them about the family photoshoot, reminding them they need to look their best today. "I'm looking at *you*, Rugger! I swear to God if you roll in poop again—"

"Hi Dad," a little voice coos, and my heart lurches. I turn to find Lo and Delta standing in the open barn doorway, cute as buttons and sporting muck boots with pajamas.

"Which one of you just called me Dad?" I breathe.

Lo raises her hand.

Delta runs up and wraps her arms around me. "Mom said it was okay when we were ready."

I knew that. Renée and I have talked about it at length and agreed if they wanted to, they could. But... but I didn't think it would be so soon. Tears form, and I can't stop them from falling when I blink.

Lo runs over to me, and I sit on the dirty barn floor clutching my girls—*my daughters*—so tight they think I'm playing. With every giggle and squirm, my lungs constrict and my heart expands to the size of the universe.

I sniffle. "I love you girls so much."

Pure and sweet enough to give anyone diabetes, Delta

kisses me on the cheek. "We love you too, Dad."

I'm still crying when we finish our chores and walk back into the house. Renée's made breakfast, but I grab her hand in a drive-by and haul her into the closest room with a door, and hold her.

"They called me Dad," I cry into her shoulder.

She smooths gentle hands up and down my back while it shakes uncontrollably. "Oh, baby... That's wonderful. I'm so happy."

"Me too," I try to say, but choke on my own tears. "I've never been this happy before." I sniffle. "No offense."

She laughs quietly, but she's crying too. "None taken. I know what you mean. Welcome to being a parent, Jonah."

THE END[1]

---

1. Put Your Money on Me by The Struts

Author's Note

If you think for one second Renée should have told Jonah the truth about killing Greg then please see yourself out. Are you kidding me? Who in their right mind would tell their new partner something THAT hard-hitting? She's a full-on criminal, y'all. I don't care if they were *fated mates*, that's not something you tell your new boyfriend. And I don't blame her for never telling him (I say that as if I didn't write her, lol). Renée is protecting Jonah by never telling him the truth, and I'll die on that hill.

Want to see some spicy (not safe for work) art from chapter 36? The sign up for my newsletter and recieve a free download by scanning the QR code below.

Acknowledgements

I dedicated this book to Zoloft because without it, I don't know if I ever would have finished. But really, the dedication should be to my best friend Sam (who is also one of my editors). She's been my best friend since we were 3 and 4 years old, and last spring she told me I seemed blue, that I wasn't myself. The first words out of my mouth were a lie, and the more I tried to excuse myself, the more I realized she was right. I found help, I found medication, and I found myself again.

Thank you, Sam. I love you.

Thank you to my alpha and beta readers: Ryan, Brittni, Melly, Taylor, and Sara.

To my editors Dani and Sam—thank you for polishing my turd of a manuscript.

To my ARC readers and street team members—y'all fucking rock. Thank you for believing in me.

To Jono, Adora, Tex, Shannon, Ryan, and Siân—thank you for helping me work through everything from plot to kink. It means the world to have people I can trust.

And as always, thank you to my husband, my real life book boyfriend. I love you more every day.

Also by Sloan

<u>The Structural Duet</u>
(Structural Damage + Structural Support)

<u>The Rugby Lovers Series</u>
Every Version of You
Every Move You Make
Every Chance You Get

Sloan Spencer also writes monster romance under the name Sloan Ambrose. Stay tuned for:

Rucked by the Minotaurs

About the Author

Sloan Spencer lives in metro Detroit with her husband, two kiddos, and dogs. She loves nature, scandalous stories, and thick thighs. You can follow her on her social media accounts or visit her website (and sign up for her newsletter!):

Instagram & Threads: @sloan_spencer_author
TikTok: @sloanspencerauthor
Facebook: Sloan Spencer's Reader Group
Official website: sloanspencerbooks.com
Be sure to follow her on Goodreads and Amazon!